The Little Doctor

Georges Simenon

The Little Doctor

Translated by

JEAN STEWART

A Helen and Kurt Wolff Book

Harcourt Brace Jovanovich

New York and London

HBJ

Library of Congress Cataloging in Publication Data

Simenon, Georges, 1903–
The little doctor.

Translation of Le petit docteur.
"A Helen and Kurt Wolff book."
I. Title.
PQ2637.I53P4513 1981 843'.912 80–7942
ISBN 0–15–152768–7

Printed in the United States of America

First American edition 1981

BCDE

Contents

The Little Doctor

The Doctor's Hunch

I. A Consultation without a Patient

'Hello! Am I speaking to the doctor? . . . Hello! Don't cut me off, please!'

The voice on the line was anxious. But the Little Doctor, as everyone called him, had just got in from his rounds and was sniffing the savoury smell of casseroled lamb that pervaded his house. Outside, the heat was torrid; indoors, behind closed shutters, the coolness was like a refreshing bath.

'Listen, doctor . . . I'm calling from the Maison-Basse . . . You've got to come over at once . . .'

'The young woman?' the doctor asked.

'Come quickly . . . I can count on you, can't I? . . . It's absolutely essential that you should come immediately . . .'

'Shall I need . . .'

He meant to ask if he should bring his instruments, or any particular medicaments, but the caller had already hung up. The doctor, at this point, was staring at the dining-room clock, rather vaguely, as one often does while telephoning.

Well! . . . He lit a cigarette. He called into the kitchen, through the half-open door, that he would not be back for a good half-hour . . . Outside, his two-seater car was standing in the hot sun, and the seats were scorching.

It was then, just as he was leaving the village and making towards the marshland, along a shadeless road with ditches on either side, that the doctor knit his brows and became so absorbed in thought that he nearly ran into a haycart.

And yet he did not suspect that he was living through the most important moment of his life and that serious events were going to result from the thought that had just crossed his mind; still less that from these events he was going to acquire a new passion, and that one day he was to become famous in a very different field from medicine.

'It's impossible . . . The clock hadn't stopped . . .'

He recalled the grey-green clock face in the dining-room, its hands standing wide apart at twenty-five minutes past twelve. He looked at his watch; it said half-past twelve.

Now the Maison-Basse, down there among the marshes, not far

from the coast, was connected by telephone with the village of Esnandes, which the doctor was shortly going to reach. And the Esnandes exchange always closed down between twelve and two, which was a source of much local discontent.

He almost made an about-turn, concluding that the phone call had probably been a hoax. But he had driven a long way already, and the road was not wide enough to turn. With a shrug, he drove on through Esnandes and turned left down a rough road.

What had that fellow said his name was? Drouin? Jean or Jules Drouin? And it must be just over six months ago that he had rented the Maison-Basse, a house which had stood empty for years because it was too far from the village, down in the marshes, and in winter one had to put down foot-bridges to get out of it. A long low one-storey house, whitewashed, with a roof of pinkish tiles like all the houses in the Charente region.

The shutters had first been seen open at the end of winter. Then a somewhat unusual couple had appeared: first a tall, rather lanky young man, invariably dressed in grey flannel trousers, espadrilles and a short-sleeved yellow pullover; then a very pretty young woman who sun-bathed in the garden.

'Artists,' the local people said.

They did no work. They had no servant. The man came in to do his shopping at the village store. He had brown hair and was always bare-headed, while the whole lower half of his face was covered with a short thick beard.

One evening, some three or four months ago, the doctor had been surprised to find this man sitting in his waiting-room. The stranger had introduced himself.

'I'm Drouin, the new tenant of the Maison-Basse . . . Oh, I'm not a very interesting patient, nor is my girl-friend . . . Only I sleep badly. I'd be grateful if you could prescribe something very effective but not dangerous . . .'

The doctor had suggested tablets.

'I'd rather have something that can be dissolved in water . . . I've a rather sensitive throat and I don't find it easy to swallow tablets.'

He seemed a likable fellow, the doctor thought; there was something attractive about him. You wanted to find out more about him. In particular he had a rather sad, remote smile, like that of certain T.B. patients who know they're done for.

'Thank you, doctor . . . What do I owe you?'

'We'll see about that another time . . .'

'I'm afraid there won't be many other times . . .'

The doctor was thirty years old. He had only been practising in the district for the past two years, and on account of both his small stature and his kindliness and simplicity, and perhaps, as well, because of the noisy little car that rattled along the roads all day long, he was affectionately known as the Little Doctor.

How often had he seen the woman? He had occasionally caught sight of her when driving past the Maison-Basse on his way to the Ferme du Renard. She seemed to be a cheerful, uninhibited sort of person. One's general impression was of two people passionately in love, enjoying their wonderful adventure in utter isolation.

On one occasion, though . . . The doctor's car had broken down in the marshes. She had come past . . .

'Is your friend sleeping better? Has the medicine worked?' he had asked her.

She had looked surprised. 'What are you talking about?'

'Nothing . . . I just wondered . . .'

The car drew up at the edge of a ditch crossed by a rickety wooden bridge. Geraniums made a splash of vivid colour and hydrangeas a milder, blander patch against the dazzlingly white walls of the little house.

The shutters were open but the windows closed. Nobody came out to meet the doctor. He knocked at the glass-fronted door behind which hung a red check curtain.

Perhaps the Little Doctor once more felt half inclined to make an about-turn, but his hand stretched out automatically to grasp the iron door-handle. The door opened, and a gust of cool air came from the shady kitchen which served as dining-room.

'Anyone there?' he shouted.

It was an awkward situation; he felt like an intruder.

'Anyone there? Hey, Monsieur Drouin!'

He thought he heard someone move in the next room; it was only a grey cat which brushed past his legs and went out. The second room was the bedroom, furnished in unconventional fashion; Drouin must have made some of the pieces himself.

There was a large divan by way of bed; it was unmade and still showed the hollow imprint of a sleeper's body. As for the telephone . . .

He seized the instrument, turned the handle two or three times, with no result, thus confirming his belief that the call he had received at twelve twenty-five had not come from this house.

Hitherto the Little Doctor, whose real name was Jean Dollent, had been concerned exclusively with medicine. He had never, in his wildest dreams, imagined himself becoming involved with anything else. He did not fancy himself endowed with exceptional gifts of observation, still less of reasoning power.

Meanwhile he felt ill at ease, and, absurdly enough, he was thirsty. So thirsty that . . .

He was taking a liberty, but never mind! Some of the shelves held books, the latest novels, but on others, within reach of the divan, there were bottles of apéritif. He picked out one of the mildest, looked for a glass, and drank a mouthful.

Then came the third surprise of the day. Whatever was that taste? . . . It was ridiculous; nobody would ever think of . . . And yet there was no doubt about it. He drank again, and rinsed out his mouth. There was no need to analyse the liquid. *Somebody had actually dissolved bicarbonate of soda in a bottle of vermouth!*

What had there been in the glass standing on the little shelf beside the divan? He smelt it; it was in fact vermouth.

Wasn't it crazy? Fancy dissolving bicarbonate of soda, that mildest of medicines, serving only to allay slight stomach-ache, in an apéritif!

'Is there anyone there? Really, it's impossible there should be nobody there!' shouted the Little Doctor angrily.

Only the cat, in the garden, was watching him through the window. Then Jean Dollent just sat down on the edge of the divan.

Firstly: if someone had bothered to ring him up, to send for him urgently, it meant that his presence there was needed.

But there was nobody to be attended to.

Secondly: at that time of day the call could only have come from La Rochelle, ten kilometres away. Drouin had no car and no bicycle. And the last bus had gone by at eight that morning. Had Drouin done the ten kilometres on foot? Had his girl-friend been with him?

Thirdly: only one person had slept on the divan that night, and that was certainly the young woman, for there was a long fair hair on the pillow.

Fourthly: no trace of breakfast. It was difficult to believe that she had begun the day by drinking vermouth laced with bicarbonate of soda, which would have been the height of eccentricity.

The Little Doctor did not realize that he was actually embarking on an investigation which looked terribly like a police inquiry.

Why had he been sent for? Who needed medical attention?

Unless . . . He frowned, for the thought had opened up fresh vistas. Suppose it was essential that somebody, anybody, should come to the Maison-Basse? Village people aren't on the telephone . . . Moreover at midday the telephone doesn't work . . . And what could they be told? Why should they take the trouble to come? Whereas the doctor is the one person who always takes the trouble to come, who is *morally obliged to do so* . . .

But why?

The coolness was delicious, utter peace prevailed . . . The nearest house, the Ferme du Renard, where the doctor had a patient, was over six hundred metres away. The buzzing of flies was the only sign of life in the atmosphere.

Suddenly . . . He stood up. He walked over to an old chest of drawers under which he had noticed something. He bent down and drew out a pair of espadrilles with fresh mud on the soles.

And that was the most surprising thing of all. There had been no rain for weeks, and the ditches had long been dried up. Where could Drouin have been to get his espadrilles so muddy? Not to the coast, for the ground there, amongst the shingle, was white and extremely chalky, whereas this was good brown earth from meadows or fields.

Wasn't Dollent making a fool of himself? Would he not do better to go back to his own house, where Anna, his cook, had prepared a savoury-smelling ragout for him?

The vermouth-and-bicarbonate had not quenched his thirst, and he selected another bottle, which contained an aniseed-flavoured apéritif. He tasted it first: no drug, no bicarbonate there. He poured himself a full glass, then went to stand in the doorway.

The house consisted of five or six rooms, all on one level. It had once been a peasant's cottage, and the Drouin couple, if one might call them that, had confined themselves to making a few improvements to the place, or rather to brightening it up with multicoloured materials, whitewood furniture, shelving, giving it somewhat the air of a Montparnasse studio. There was even a rather handsome Hawaiian guitar hanging from a nail, and it must have been in use, for it had all its strings and was properly tuned.

Wherever had Drouin . . .?

And now the Little Doctor, instead of getting back into his car, wandered round the house, followed by the cat which from time to time rubbed up against his legs, arching its back. The tiny garden behind the dwelling was as dry as the surrounding countryside. He peered down into the well; there was barely half a metre of clear water, at the bottom of which one could see the pebbles.

The village seemed very far away and the space boundless. Cows were lying in the marshy meadows, sunk in heavy sleep.

Heavy sleep . . . He remembered . . . But what was the connection? The connection between the sleeping draught that Drouin had asked him for and . . .

There was a little hedge, withered by the drought. He nearly walked past it. He leaned over, however. On the other side the clods over a small area had an unusual appearance. They looked as if they had been disturbed and then relaid. He stepped over the hedge and lifted a loose lump of earth; he found damp, crumbly soil like that which clung to the espadrilles left in the house.

It was none of his business. If something seemed suspicious to him he merely had to report it to the municipal authorities and they would inform the police. He was a doctor and nothing else.

But why the deuce had he been sent for? To discover what?

He was convinced that he had recognized Drouin's voice over the phone. So, if Drouin had rung him up at twelve twenty-five . . .

He looked at his watch. It said one o'clock, and Anna would be getting impatient. Nevertheless he went back into the house, opened doors at random, finally discovered a tool shed and picked up a spade there.

He kept thinking about that blonde hair on the pillow, about that young woman who never left the house, who seemed to shed around her an atmosphere of romantic passion.

He took off his jacket. The soil was loose. He threw up a few spadefuls, then . . .

He had dissected plenty of corpses in medical school. And yet! . . . when he saw that finger suddenly emerging from the ground . . .

He was dumbfounded; it was a man's finger. He dug, and uncovered the whole hand, a great coarse hand. Could it be Drouin's? No, that was not possible, since Drouin had telephoned. Suppose somebody had imitated his voice?

In any case Drouin, whose natural elegance had impressed the Little Doctor, hadn't got hands like that . . .

Well, it couldn't be helped. He drove off the mewing cat with a kick, threw up some more earth and eventually disclosed a face spattered with earth and blood.

Later, when he was asked what his chief impressions had been, he was to reply: 'I had no impressions . . . Or rather, a single feeling: stupefaction . . .'

For really he was stupefied at being there, alone between the earth and the sky, alone in a boundless expanse in front of a hole from which, little by little, he was extracting a man. His stupefaction was all the greater since the man was unknown to him, and almost certainly a stranger in the neighbourhood.

Later on, when he was feeling stronger, he was to assert: 'He had an ugly mug!'

And that was true. A thick puffy face, the mouth distorted by a hare-lip . . .

The heat . . . Yes, of course, it was the heat and not just disgust . . . He went back into the house; he poured himself a second, then a third glass of pernod . . .

'Why the dickens was I rung up?'

That question obsessed him. He wouldn't have thought himself so keen on logical argument. Had it been in order to discover the corpse? But what could be the sense of that? If Drouin was the murderer, why should he want his victim's body to be discovered? If he was not, could he have been unaware that there was a corpse in his garden?

And what part was played in all this by the young woman whose name the Little Doctor did not know? Where was she? With her lover? If they had committed a murder for one reason or another, why had they not gone quietly away? Days, perhaps weeks, would have elapsed without the people of Esnandes worrying about them. By then the grass would have grown again. There was a ninety per cent chance that the body would not even be found.

So . . . So then there must have been a reason. And the Little Doctor suddenly realized that he would not be satisfied until he had found it . . .

He could not decently dig up the whole body. He was not entitled to do so. He merely covered the head and hand with a curtain torn down from the kitchen window. Then he started up his car and it went buzzing along the road like a great angry fly.

He found the Mayor at table, in the farm he owned at the far end of Esnandes, towards Marsilly. He picked up a grilled sardine and ate it without thinking about what his hands had been touching.

'There's a dead body at the Maison-Basse . . .'

'What sort of a body?'

'A man's . . . Buried . . . I think the *gendarmerie* should be informed . . . And even perhaps the Central Police station.'

Another sardine. Excitement was whetting his appetite.

'It's none of my business, but what I'd advise you to do is to come back with me to my house, and from there you can telephone to La Rochelle . . . Meanwhile you could send the constable to the Maison-Basse to prevent anyone going in . . .'

The wretched constable was probably tipsy already!

'Won't you have a bite with us?'

'No, thanks . . .'

But while the Mayor was getting ready he grabbed half a dozen sardines and poured himself two whole glasses of white wine.

'Do you think there's been a crime?'

'Well, when it comes to burying a body in the garden without informing the authorities, nor the priest, nor the undertaker . . .'

'Let's be off!'

First the *gendarmerie*. Then the special squad. It all took time. Anna was furious. The stew was spoilt.

'They're going to pick us up on their way,' the Mayor announced. 'I've had the D.P.P. informed. I knew we'd have trouble with these foreigners . . .'

For in his view that title was automatically conferred on anyone who was not a native of the village.

'Will you excuse me? I've one or two phone calls to make myself . . .'

The first call was to the post office at La Rochelle. Ten minutes later, he learnt that the call he had received at 12.25 came from the Café des Navigateurs, on the harbour, three hundred metres from the railway station. And that no train would be leaving before 3.08 p.m.

'What about buses?'

'Ask at Brivin's, the bus company . . .'

That was the second call.

Brivin informed him that a bus left for Surgères at 12.40, and another for Rochefort at 1.10.

In answer to his third question, Brivin was positive that nobody answering to the description given had got on the 8.0 a.m. bus at Esnandes, nor had any young woman.

As for taxis, Drouin could have sent for one from La Rochelle, but that would not have gone unobserved at Esnandes.

So, that morning, Drouin and presumably his girl-friend had travelled the ten kilometres from the Maison-Basse to La Rochelle on foot.

At 12.25 Drouin had telephoned to send the doctor to his house . . . where there was a corpse . . . and where he himself had not slept that night.

The Mayor of Esnandes waited, while the Little Doctor strode up and down and then suddenly announced:

'There's been a mistake!'

'What d'you mean? You're not sure it's a corpse?'

'I tell you somebody's made a mistake . . . It's impossible otherwise . . . You'll see . . .'

Before he had finished speaking the telephone bell rang. He picked up the receiver.

'Hello . . .'

'Is that you, doctor?'

The doctor did not bat an eyelid. He had recognized the voice. It was Drouin's. The man sounded more anxious than that morning. He scarcely dared speak. Did he suspect that his call was being intercepted?

'Hello . . . You recognize me, don't you?'

'Yes . . .'

A glance at the Mayor, who was listening without understanding.

'Did you go there?'

'Yes.'

'And . . . how can I put it? . . . You . . . Didn't you . . .?'

'Where are you phoning from?'

An uneasy silence.

'I understand. All right.'

'You understand? So then . . .'

'You saw it? . . .'

'Yes!'

'I might have guessed as much. And you . . . Well, you . . . Tell me frankly . . . I can imagine what you're thinking of me . . . Perhaps I can tell you about it later . . . Have the police been . . .'

'Informed, yes!'

'Hello, doctor. Please hold the line . . . Do you . . .?'

Just then there was a crackling sound, and the telephone operators could be heard calling one another.

'Have you finished, Rochefort?'

'Don't cut me off!' Drouin cried in a desperate voice. 'Hello, doctor!'

'Yes . . .'

'You're still on the phone? How long do you think it'll . . .'

The Little Doctor glanced round at the Mayor of Esnandes, who was still listening with increasing bewilderment.

'In an hour's time,' he declared at last, 'they'll be watching all railway stations and buses . . .'

'Thank you . . . Shall I ring you again?'

'The telephone will be watched too . . .'

'Then . . . Wait a minute! Don't ring off . . . One question . . . Suppose an injured person should come to your house during the night . . . Can you hear me?'

'Yes . . .'

'Should turn up alone . . . in real need of your help . . .'

There was a silence. Anna, from time to time, came to listen at the door, visibly impatient.

'Go on!'

'Would professional secrecy? . . .'

'There's no formal rule on that point . . . I might speak, or I might keep silent . . . It's a matter for my conscience to decide . . . If I consider that the person concerned . . .'

'What will you decide?'

'I can't promise anything . . . It'll depend . . .'

A car drove up into the courtyard: people from La Rochelle, police officers and representatives of the Department of Public Prosecution.

'Suppose the life of this person, who is innocent . . .'

Anna had opened the door. The visitors were wiping their feet on the mat. The Little Doctor hung up the receiver.

'Good afternoon, *monsieur le substitut* . . .'

'Good afternoon, doctor . . . I understand . . . But you were telephoning?'

'Just some bore . . . Please come in! Anna, give these gentlemen a glass of armagnac.'

He was well aware that the Mayor of Esnandes was looking at him suspiciously.

II. The Superintendent Objects to Irony

'My opinion, *monsieur le substitut*, if I may venture to express it, is that when . . .'

The Superintendent broke off, his gaze suspended as though watching a fly, but what he was staring at in that sultry room was not a fly but the face of the Little Doctor, in particular the gleaming eyes that expressed intense delight.

'Go on, I'm listening, Superintendent.'

'Excuse me, but I wonder if certain ears . . .'

The Deputy Public Prosecutor had understood. This was not the first time since they had been on the scene of the crime that the Superintendent, who was undoubtedly a worthy fellow but something of a solemn bore, had displayed his resentment at the doctor's presence.

Although the magistrate was well acquainted with Dr Dollent, who was a young man like himself and whom he had met at bridge parties, he, too, was somewhat surprised at the doctor's attitude.

There were some ten people there in the Maison-Basse and in the garden. The village policeman of Esnandes stood beside the green-painted gate, keeping out inquisitive people, which was not difficult since these were no more numerous than the investigators. The heat was intense, and there was no shade. By and large, everyone kept rather quiet, except for the Little Doctor who was displaying unprecedented liveliness.

'So as I was saying, *monsieur le substitut*, when we know the identity of the victim we shall . . .'

Dollent kept a grip on himself, with difficulty. He was aching to burst out: 'Stuff and nonsense!'

They were all going about it the wrong way! They didn't understand and they never would!

It was the first time he had been present at such an investigation. He was no lover of detective stories, and he never read the crime reports in the papers. And now suddenly it came to him in a flash. They were all floundering about round him and he wanted to laugh in their faces, to say, for instance, to the fat sergeant who was hunting for prints underneath the divan:

'Don't be ridiculous, sergeant! A family man of your age shouldn't go about on all fours . . .'

True, he had not discovered anything himself yet, but he was convinced he would find the key to the mystery. He stuck to his line of argument; his mind never stopped working.

'If the man Drouin rang me up the first time . . . If he rang me up again from Rochefort . . .'

Meanwhile, it amused him to be surrounded by investigators and to say to himself: 'I'm the only one who knows where to find the man they're so anxious to lay hands on!'

For he had made clear to Drouin that his description had been widely circulated. So the man would not move. He was not such a fool as to let himself get caught at the station or at a bus stop. He was hardly likely to enter a hotel, and the Little Doctor pictured him wandering about the streets of Rochefort in the scorching heat, and taking refuge in the cool darkness of various little bistrots while waiting for night to fall.

'My personal opinion,' the magistrate pontificated, 'is that this must be considered as a crime of passion. Two men and a woman! The eternal triangle! No doubt the three of them were living here together, but where had the victim been hiding? Have you sent his photo to Paris by telephotograph, Superintendent?'

'We shall have the answer by the end of the day.'

Fortunately the Little Doctor had not been required to make a thorough autopsy, for that would hardly have been pleasant in such heat. The body had been undressed; it was that of an exceptionally brawny fellow, who had a bare-breasted woman tattooed on his left forearm.

The most interesting observation was that death must have occurred the previous evening between ten o'clock and midnight. The man had been stabbed in the heart with a knife, but before this final blow he had been struck several others, including some given with a man's fist.

This implied that the attack had not come as a surprise. As far as one could judge, there had been a quarrel. The adversaries had come to blows, first fighting with their bare fists. Then one of them had seized a knife.

The scene must have taken place in the kitchen, since there were no traces of a struggle in the bedroom. Moreover, tiny fragments of glass had been found between the little red tiles on the kitchen floor.

So Drouin, before leaving, had not only buried the body but furthermore had carefully tidied up the place. Then . . . that telephone call! One always came back to that!

It's surely rather odd, when one has killed a man and buried him properly, to send for a doctor for him!

'In short, *monsieur le maire*, you know absolutely nothing about the inhabitants of this house? Aren't you acquainted with the people under your administration?'

'What can I tell you? The schoolmaster looks after all the red tape for me and gives me the forms to sign. The man had registered under the name of Drouin and the woman wasn't registered at all. I thought they were just a pair of lovers and I didn't insist. That sort of thing doesn't concern us . . .'

The Little Doctor's eyes were still gleaming. *He* knew that things were not so simple! And as stubbornly as when he was playing bridge, he pursued his argument step by step, going back to the beginning as soon as he came to a dead end.

He pictured Drouin, in his grey trousers and his yellow pullover, with his short beard like a surrealist painter's. Right! In the house, and with his pipe, for he was a pipe smoker . . . And as he was tall he must have to bend down to go in at the low doorway . . .

The young woman, always half unclad, her tanned skin glowing like a ripe fruit . . .

He caught himself talking half aloud, muttering: 'Right! . . . Right! . . .'

He was trying to bring them to life, to imagine them in their setting, and he felt sure that when he had succeeded in doing that he would understand everything.

'There were only the two of them . . . That's for sure . . . in spite of the Deputy Public Prosecutor's nasty theory of a three-cornered ménage . . . The atmosphere of the house was that of a honeymoon couple concerned only with making love . . .'

As for the young woman, she was not the sort to submit to the embraces of the tattooed brute whose body lay there on the table, under a sheet.

Dollent gave a start. One of the policemen was speaking:

'I've just found this, sir.'

The doctor almost tore it from the man's hands. It was a folded scrap of paper containing some white powder. Dollent licked his finger, dipped it in the powder and tasted a little.

The Superintendent watched him, scowling more resentfully than ever.

'There's another thing we must discover,' Dollent declared authoritatively, as though he had been put in charge of operations. 'First of all, where did you find this packet?'

'That's what's so strange . . . It was hidden right at the bottom of the cupboard, among the lady's underclothes . . .'

'In that case, it's probably among the man's personal belongings that you'll find a small cardboard box with a pharmaceutical brand-mark . . .'

The detective looked at his chief to inquire whether he should obey. The Superintendent gave a shrug, as though to say:

'What can I do about it? He's giving the orders and nobody protests . . . Go and have a look if you like!'

People who take part in this kind of investigation experience something of that unwholesome pleasure that impels people, in auction rooms, to finger heirlooms and open the drawers of desks. For indeed the investigator is suddenly entitled to force his way into the life of a home, to try to discover its secrets. The clumsiest policeman can start handling a woman's delicate lingerie, and it becomes his duty to poke his nose into private correspondence.

Thus it was duly noted that although the young woman (of whom nothing was known, not even her name!) was most frequently scantily dressed, she none the less possessed a good many garments which, although by no means luxurious, were of good quality and above all showed excellent taste.

Drouin, on the other hand, unless he had taken a suitcase with him, which was unlikely since he must have gone to La Rochelle on foot, owned practically nothing. His grey trousers must have been his only pair, for there was no other in the cupboard. However, his yellow sweater, badly washed, was lying in a cupboard with some dirty linen. His espadrilles had been found too, which implied that he had gone off wearing his only pair of shoes.

He was an educated fellow, as was evidenced by the books on his shelves.

'I bet . . .' the Little Doctor suddenly exclaimed.

For the past ten minutes, while the policemen were turning everything topsy turvy as they hunted for the little box, he had been thinking, and his gaze had settled on an earthenware pot containing about a pound of tobacco.

'Look underneath the tobacco . . . I'll be surprised if . . .'

From that moment onward they viewed him not merely with curiosity but with respect. And in fact the detective who thrust his hand into the tobacco did not withdraw it empty. He was holding a cardboard box. Without looking, Dollent told him the brand name.

'It must be half full,' he added.

He was discovering a new sort of delight. Not for anything would he have missed that morning's telephone call. He was jubilant. He looked out of the corner of his eye at the sullen Superintendent and the smooth, sophisticated magistrate, and said emphatically:

'You can be quite sure that what's in that box is bicarbonate of soda!'

To tell the truth, it must be added that a few minutes later, as the magistrate was expressing his astonishment, the Superintendent ventured to mutter:

'Don't forget that he came here before us . . . that by his own admission he was alone in the house for almost an hour . . .'

'You're not insinuating? . . .'

'Oh, of course not! Nevertheless . . . H'm! . . .'

The telephone bell rang. Paris was on the line.

It must have been five in the afternoon. Little by little, everyone had begun to relax, and all the men, except the magistrate and his clerk, had taken off their jackets. They had quite forgotten that what was lying on the kitchen table was a corpse.

One policeman had cast longing glances at the bottles of apéritif, for he was extremely thirsty, but his courage had failed him; and then the Mayor of Esnandes had proposed:

'I'll send home for a few bottles of white wine.'

The village constable had gone for them. They now stood, uncorked, on the table of the studio-bedroom. The perspiring clerk stopped writing from time to time to drink a mouthful.

The Superintendent, who had just had a long telephone conversation with Paris and had been making notes, reported to the magistrate:

'They identified the man immediately, as I expected. I could even have sworn I knew him myself. It's Boxer Joe.'

The name meant nothing to the rest of them.

'A bad character who chiefly hung around the bars in the Place des Ternes. He's had half a dozen sentences . . . He was last let out of Poissy three months ago.'

'Three months!' the doctor repeated, as though to fix the figure in his mind.

'What business is it of yours?' the Superintendent's stern glance seemed to say. And he went on:

'As you heard, I asked if Joe had been seen in Paris recently. As an ex-convict, he should not have been there . . . None the less he had been observed several times, and indeed only last week, in the neighbourhood of the Etoile . . .'

'So he wasn't hidden here!' the Little Doctor said with satisfaction.

'I never said he was hidden here!'

'But you thought so!'

'It doesn't matter what . . .'

'Gentlemen, gentlemen! Don't let's argue,' intervened the Deputy Public Prosecutor, for it looked as though the Superintendent and the doctor were about to come to blows.

'If this gentleman persists in taunting me . . .'

'I swear I'm not taunting you!'

'Please go on, Superintendent . . . So Boxer Joe was in Paris recently . . . He probably came here by train . . . What had he come for?'

And the incorrigible doctor broke in: 'That's the question! He certainly didn't come intending to get himself stabbed and buried behind a hedge . . .'

'We may assume he came to see the woman,' ventured the magistrate, who still clung to his theory.

No, it wasn't like that. The Little Doctor felt sure of it. The thing was simpler and at the same time more complicated. He'd get there. He might take some time about it, but he was sure he'd get there.

'What was his latest sentence for?' he asked.

'If I hadn't been constantly interrupted I'd have told you already. A night-club owner was killed in the Rue Fontaine . . .'

'How long ago?'

'Two years . . . A shocking crime, with robbery as a motive . . . Several men, it was never known exactly how many, but at least two, stayed on in the place after it was closed, intending to rob the till. When the proprietor was left alone they attacked him . . . He defended himself; shots were fired. Boxer Joe was the only one to be caught. He was sentenced as an accessory to the crime, since the finger-prints found on the gun that had been dropped in the room were not his . . .'

At that point something unexpected happened. The Little Doctor put on his jacket again. He looked very cheerful and good-tempered, as if there had never been any mention of a crime or a murderer, and he had just been visiting some favourite patients or some friends.

He shook hands all round and remarked with a disarming smile:

'Well, gentlemen, if you don't need me any longer I'll go and see my sick people . . .'

But he did not stop his rattling little car in front of his home, although he could see from the street that the waiting-room was full of drowsy patients.

III. A Perfectly Useless Stabbing

Everything went well as far as Rochefort. The road was fine, birds were singing in the trees and the Little Doctor repeatedly caught himself whistling.

He was pleased with himself. More than pleased! For he had just discovered that he possessed exceptional talents which, into the bargain, would offer him a vast field of hitherto unsuspected delights.

A phone call . . . Previously he had taken no interest in the Maison-Basse and its inhabitants . . . He had gone past without thinking about them. He had once spoken to Drouin, half-heartedly prescribing a commonplace drug which could have been bought over the counter . . . On one single occasion he had spoken to the young woman . . .

And nevertheless in the space of a few hours he had discovered everything, he was convinced of it. He knew it. The others, the Deputy Public Prosecutor, the Superintendent, and of course the worthy Mayor, had floundered, and the doctor said to himself that this must always be so, that this was bound to happen, almost inevitably, in a criminal case.

Because they set about it in the wrong way!

Whereas he . . . Actually, how did he set about it? He could not have said precisely, but he felt he knew. He put himself in the place of . . . Or rather . . .

It didn't matter! The chief thing was that he was going to get the answer, that the Maison-Basse held no more secrets for him.

His job was simply to get hold of Drouin, and that wouldn't be hard. Rochefort is not a big place. Since the arsenal was abolished it has been almost a dead town, with lifeless streets.

He started with the Café de la Paix, on the square, because he was anxious not to neglect anything, but, as he expected, Drouin was neither on the terrace nor inside.

Café du Commerce . . . Café Joffre . . . Café de la Marine . . .

The sun was lower in the sky, but the heat was still oppressive and the Little Doctor was beginning to feel he had drunk enough beer.

At one bar he had a glass of white wine. Then, at another, a second glass of wine, and he felt something of the frenzied excitement of the gambler who is convinced his hunch is right, and who waits for the little white ball to stop on the number he has chosen.

'Provided he doesn't do something idiotic!' he muttered. Such as trying to run away, by train or by bus, which would be the surest way to get caught.

What could Drouin be doing now? Since early afternoon he had been there, in a confined area where there were maybe a hundred streets and a hundred cafés, including the smallest bars.

'Damn! I nearly forgot . . .'

He struck his forehead. He got back into his tiny car. Shamelessly, he drew up in a street where all the houses had closed shutters and bore large numbers on the doors.

He went into each of them. He would sit down, order a small drink as a formality, and ward off the advances of the ladies of the house.

'I'm looking for a friend, a man with a beard, who told me . . . Does he happen to have been in this afternoon?'

'A man with a beard, no . . . Anyhow, we don't get many people here in the afternoons . . . Just regulars . . .'

'An absolute fool!' he decided. 'I'm an absolute fool! Why didn't I think of it earlier?'

And so after cafés, bars and brothels he started visiting barbers' shops. He had to act fast, for it was nearly closing time.

'Tell me . . . I'm looking for a friend I was to have met at the station . . . A tall young chap in grey trousers . . . I know he wanted to have his beard shaved off . . .'

'Ernest! Have you done a beard today?'

'No, *patron* . . .'

One barber, two, five, ten barbers and never a beard! At any rate he didn't have to go on drinking, which was just as well, for his head had begun to reel.

'A beard? Let's see . . . Yes, round about three o'clock . . . But I didn't notice the colour of his trousers.'

'That doesn't matter . . . Was he by himself?'

'Yes . . . Unless he came with a lady, in which case she'd have gone into the ladies' department . . . Auguste! About three o'clock, did you have a lady who . . .'

No, but it hardly mattered. Things were good enough as it was, and pretty exciting! He had managed to pick up Drouin's trail, all on his own.

'You don't know where he went on leaving here?'

No, they didn't know. And so a quarter of an hour later, as the sun was sinking behind the houses on the main square, the Little Doctor was feeling disheartened again. He was back on the terrace of the Café de la Paix, where he had started his round, and he was wondering what to drink Some students were playing cards. A woman sitting alone in front of a glass of beer was ogling him.

'Well, it can't be helped! A pernod . . .'

He had never drunk so much in his life. He had never thought so hard either. And now time was running short. It was agonizing. An hour had been wasted and perhaps . . .

Let's see; where could he have gone wrong? Why, after picking up Drouin's trail at the barber's, had he failed to make any progress? There was a flaw somewhere in his reasoning. That was the only explanation.

'The second time he rang me up he asked whether, if an injured person turned up at my house, I'd be bound by professional secrecy . . . So . . .'

He sat there, hesitating, clutching his glass of pernod, with such a fixed stare that the young woman towards whom it was unconsciously directed believed she'd caught her man.

'So . . . He's got to go to Marsilly . . . Whew! The most obvious facts are those one thinks of last . . . It's forty-five kilometres from here to Marsilly . . . He can't take the train or the bus . . .'

A bicycle! That was what he'd forgotten! Five minutes later, having forgotten to pay his bill, much to the waiter's amazement, he was at the police station.

'I'd like to ask for some information . . . Has a bicycle been stolen this afternoon at Rochefort?'

The police clerk was even more surprised than the café waiter.

'A bicycle stolen? Why?'

'No reason . . . Just an idea . . .'

'No, Monsieur . . . We've had no theft reported.'

Drouin must be less daring than he had thought, since there's nothing simpler than to steal a bicycle or even a car.

'Are there many cycle shops in Rochefort?'

'I've no idea, Monsieur. I'm not interested in sports.'

There were eight of them, but he did not have to visit them all. By the third, his excitement revived. The owner, a somewhat mistrustful fellow in down-at-heel shoes, told him:

'No, I've not sold any cycles, but I hired out two . . .'

'A man's and a woman's?'

'That's right.'

'About four o'clock?'

'No, at six o'clock.'

To think that at that time he was actually in Rochefort and that with luck he might have . . .

'A man in grey trousers, wasn't it?'

'Might have been . . .'

The important thing now was not to lose the trail. He was under pressure, and he must make the most of it. The down-at-heel fellow was trying to get rid of him, but he persisted.

'Excuse me . . . One more question . . . He must have left his watch with you?'

A wonderful, unhoped-for stroke of luck! The Little Doctor's heart leapt in his bosom. Provided this clot of a salesman . . .

'Will you let me have a look at it? You needn't worry; I'm Dr Dollent from Marsilly . . . see, here's my driving licence . . .'

With such an idiot, one had to show one's credentials.

'I'm looking for a friend I was to meet at Rochefort . . . It must have been in order to visit me that he hired those bikes . . .'

'He could have gone by bus!'

'He can't have thought of that . . . If you'd let me see the watch I could make sure that . . .'

'Suppose you were a friend of the little lady's and it was out of jealousy that . . .'

All the same he produced the watch, cautiously, never taking his eyes off it. It was a splendid gold chronometer.

'Won't you open the watch-case? Maybe his name . . .'

And in fact it was so! The gods were kind. The watch-case bore a name, Jean Larcher, with an address, 67 Boulevard Raspail, Paris.

'Thank you; yes, that's him.'

He had to say something. He had, above all, to rush off, to catch up the two cyclists who must be riding towards Marsilly. Were they riding fast or slowly? It was important, frightfully important. Would they take the main road? As they were probably unfamiliar with the region, they were unlikely to venture into the by-ways of the marshland.

It was a crazy journey. Night was falling. The darkness was denser under the trees. Unfortunately there were a great many cyclists, some of them riding two abreast. The doctor had switched on his headlights. He tried to make out the cyclists' figures, then once he had passed them he would have second thoughts and stop to look at them from the front, so that his behaviour must have seemed extremely odd.

Twenty kilometres, thirty kilometres, and no signs of Drouin (otherwise Jean Larcher) nor of a young woman, at least not of the one he was looking for. It was quite dark when he saw the lights of La Rochelle and then panic seized him.

He was practically sure, now, that he'd get there too late. Drouin must be in a hurry. He could not act in broad daylight, but he was unlikely to wait until the middle of the night. Darkness had fallen half an hour ago. Therefore . . .

The little car sped on, its engine roaring, unable to exceed sixty-five kilometres an hour. Its frantic driver reared up in his seat, which did not help to increase the speed of the car.

Nieul . . . Marsilly . . . Here was his house, on the left, with its gate, its courtyard, lights on in the dining-room but also lights on in the consulting-room.

Too late! If the light was on in the consulting-room that meant . . .

He left the car outside the gate, forgetting to switch off the engine. He ran up the steps. The door opened; Anna, panic-stricken, greeted him:

'Here you are at last! I've been phoning all over the place . . . There's a poor lady here who . . .'

'I know!'

Seeing Anna's astonishment, he corrected himself: 'That's to say I guessed, when I saw the light . . .'

'She was knocked down by a car a hundred metres from the house, just at the corner . . . I always said that corner . . .'

He was not listening. He knew he had a job to do. Taking off his jacket, he opened the surgery door and closed it without even looking at his patient. And he growled: 'You've not been very clever! Couldn't you have waited half an hour longer?'

IV. The Little Doctor's Guess Was Right

'A bullet?' he asked, after making sure the curtains were drawn close so that nothing could be seen from outside.

She shook her head. She was pale, probably more from emotion than from pain . . . She was holding a bloodstained handkerchief to her shoulder.

'He used a knife? . . . He must make a habit of it!'

She answered, with a feeble smile: 'He hadn't got a gun . . . If he had, I don't think he could have used it . . . He was afraid of shooting . . .'

'Take off your blouse . . .'

Wasting no time, deliberately averting his eyes, he lit the gas to boil some water, prepared lint, gauze and dressings.

'Are you going to need stitches?'

'I don't know . . . He didn't strike hard . . .'

'Where is he? He didn't take the train, I hope?'

He turned round and with some slight embarrassment saw her splendid bosom bare, its beauty unspoilt by a wound two centimetres wide on the shoulder.

'He wants to reach Bordeaux by cycle before morning . . .'

'Is a boat leaving?'

'He read of one in the newspaper this afternoon, at Rochefort. The *Veuzit*, bound for Chile . . . If they don't let him on board he'll go as a stowaway . . . Once at sea . . . Anyhow, the *Veuzit* isn't a French boat.'

'Am I hurting you?'

'Not very much . . .'

'Hold the lint against the wound while I get my instruments.'

But that was not what was worrying him. He went into the kitchen, where Anna was eating soup that had gone cold.

'Listen, Anna . . . Nobody has been here tonight . . . You hear? . . . You haven't seen this lady . . . However, I'd like you to get ready the second floor bedroom; one never knows.'

When he came back he saw the look of alarm on his patient's face and he understood, quickly reassuring her: 'Don't be afraid, I haven't been telephoning . . . If our friend Larcher is able to do those hundred and eighty kilometres on his bicycle . . .'

'So you know his real name?'

'Sure!'

He was quite proud of that. He got ready his sutures. 'Don't be afraid . . . There won't even be a scar.'

'How did you find out his name?'

'I could even find out his whole story in a few moments . . . Without contacting the police, I'd merely have to ring up no. 67, Boulevard Raspail . . . I imagine I'd speak to a father and mother who want nothing more to do with their son . . .'

'They don't know . . . They believe Jean is taking a course in Algiers; he's an engineer.'

'And what about you?' he suddenly asked. He was hurting her at that point and yet she gave a wan smile.

'You don't know?'

'Absolutely nothing about you. Not even your name . . .'

'And you really want to know? . . . My name, for one thing, is Laure . . . Laure Delille, if you insist . . . I was a model in the Rue de la Paix . . .'

He went on hurting her. He was annoyed at not having discovered that for himself.

'What else do you know?'

He was frowning with concentration as he set his sutures.

'Everything . . . Everything and yet nothing . . . That you were Jean Larcher's girl-friend, of course . . .'

'We've been lovers for a year and a half.'

'That's right . . . Now when you became acquainted he had already killed a man.'

'I didn't know that. When I met him he was living it up and drinking a lot, probably in order to forget . . . To begin with I didn't like him much, because I thought he was just a playboy . . . Then I realized that there was more to him, that he was more serious, gentler . . . Very gentle, if you only knew!'

'Keep still a few moments . . . That needn't prevent you from talking.'

'We spent almost all our time together in Paris, but he was living in his parents' house . . . His father is an important civil servant, a very strict sort of person . . . One day Jean asked me if I loved him enough to live in the country with him in relative poverty . . . I said yes, rapturously!'

'Six months ago!'

'Yes . . .'

'That's to say a few weeks before Boxer Joe was let out of jail. I suppose he'd already written blackmailing letters to Jean?'

'I knew nothing about all that . . . We came to live at the Maison-Basse, just the two of us together . . . I was happy . . .'

'For three months . . .'

'How do you know?'

'Because it was I who involuntarily put an end to your peace of mind. You remember that day when I asked you if your friend was sleeping better? Well then! . . . Now just lie down on this couch and rest . . . It was that sleeping-draught business that enabled me to understand it all . . . Drouin, or rather Jean Larcher, since that's his name, had no need of drugs to help him sleep. Only, Joe must have got on to his trail, and probably written to say he was coming? . . . Or else Larcher may have seen him prowling about the neighbourhood, and dreaded a visit from Joe, above all because it might mean your discovering the whole story . . . He came to see me and asked me for a prescription for a sleeping drug that could be dissolved in some liquid – in other words, that could be given to somebody without their knowing . . .'

'I thought the vermouth tasted bitter,' she said. 'He told me he'd added a tonic to it. Some evenings he insisted on my drinking quite a lot of it, and next morning I could hardly wake up . . .'

'The evenings when Joe came to see him! You realize that for that bastard his secret knowledge was a godsend and he was determined to take advantage of it . . . Their meetings must have been stormy . . . He must have demanded sums of money that your lover could not provide . . .'

'That's right . . . Later on I heard it all . . .'

'Owing to me! My remark about Jean's sleep must have aroused your suspicions . . .'

'I had noticed a change in him!'

'So you searched his belongings. You found the sleeping drug. You realized why the vermouth had tasted so odd, and why you had slept so soundly after drinking it . . . Then you substituted bicarbonate of soda for the powder in the box and you hid the real drug among your underclothes . . .'

'Did they find it?' she queried innocently.

'So you witnessed meetings between Joe and your friend . . .'

'Two meetings, not to mention the final one . . . They thought I was asleep . . . I felt sure things would turn out badly . . . I didn't want to tell Jean that I knew his secret . . . I tried to persuade him to go right away with me somewhere, but he was so fond of the little house where we had been so happy . . . He hoped the man would give up eventually . . . Yesterday! for it was only yesterday – it feels like a century ago – Joe came . . . They had a quarrel . . . Jean declared that he wouldn't give a penny more, that what money he'd got had melted away . . . The man just sneered and advised him to tell his parents everything, and "they'd cough up", as he said . . .

'They came to blows . . . Joe pulled a knife out of his pocket . . . Jean, who's stronger than he looks, managed to seize hold of it and struck the man . . .

'I heard it all . . . A ghastly night . . . Comings and goings in the garden . . . He thought I was asleep . . . He left the house at dawn . . .'

'And he telephoned me,' the Little Doctor broke in, 'to get me to go and wake you up. He thought he'd given you too strong a dose. He was worried about you. Furthermore, if the body was discovered you wouldn't have been implicated, because I'd have found you in a drugged sleep.'

He went to open the door suddenly and found Anna listening behind it.

He said nothing, merely frowned, came back and automatically lit a cigarette.

'Do you mind?'

'Could I have one too?'

'As a doctor . . . Oh, well! You know what the starting-point of my argument was. If he rang me up, it was because I was supposed to find somebody at the Maison-Basse. And since there was nobody there . . .'

'I'd gone after him . . . I wanted to protect him, to help him . . . He saw me at Rochefort . . .'

'And he went nearly mad with worry! He'd done everything he could to keep you out of it! And since you hadn't been asleep, you had become his accomplice!'

'That's what he said to me . . . He confessed everything, the whole story . . . Two years ago he'd got mixed up with bad company . . . They'd persuaded him to take part in a robbery, the one in the Rue Fontaine; there was to be no bloodshed. It's a fact that he fired the shot, by accident, when the fighting broke out . . . Boxer Joe, when he was jailed, started blackmailing him . . . Jean had to pay the man's lawyer, send him comforts in prison, even support his mistress . . .

'Then he met me . . . He wanted to escape from the nightmare . . . He guessed that Joe would become even more rapacious when he was released . . . He scraped a little money together and we came to bury ourselves here . . .'

'Aren't you hungry?' the Little Doctor asked suddenly; he himself was feeling queasy after all the drinks he'd had.

'I can't think of food . . . I'm thinking of Jean who's out on the road, counting the miles . . .'

'You offered to go with him, naturally?'

'He wouldn't let me . . . He insists that a man on his own can stay hidden but that it's difficult for a couple to pass unnoticed . . . So in order that I should be safe, he thought of . . .'

'Of protecting you by means of professional secrecy . . . of giving you a slight wound so that I should be forced to take you in and hide you for a while . . .'

'That was his idea . . . Immediately after telephoning you he had his beard shaved off . . .'

'In the Rue de la Mésange . . .'

'You knew that too?'

He could not repress a smile of naïve pride. He was surely entitled to be pleased with himself! Right now the Department of Public Prosecution, the Superintendent, the whole lot of them were completely in the dark about the whole business. And he, the Little Doctor, was closeted alone with the girl they were all looking for. By reckoning the distance and the average speed of a cyclist he could have worked out the exact position on the road to Bordeaux of the man whose description had been circulated to every railway station.

He could even – what a joke! – he could have sent the solemn Superintendent the trimmings from the man's beard. Or his watch!

He was so absorbed in wonder that he forgot all about his patient. Then he noticed that she was looking for somewhere to put her cigarette ash, and he hastily offered her an ashtray.

'Thank you . . . If . . . touch wood! . . . if he reaches Chile he'll surely manage to earn his living there . . . As soon as he's made enough for my journey . . . even if I have to travel steerage . . .'

She had been too brave up till now. It could not go on; her lips began to tremble and she broke into sobs.

She hid her face. Her thoughts were only of Jean, and she kept repeating brokenly: 'He's a good lad . . . If you only knew! . . . If you knew him as I do . . . He was led astray . . . He didn't want to seem a coward . . . Then, once he'd got involved . . . I wish you'd heard that brute Joe talking to him about the guillotine, saying: "You're for it, my lad! You'll lay that handsome head of yours in the lunette . . . And who'll be in the front row of the crowd? Pal Joey! Pal Joey who'll have a good laugh!" '

Then she broke down hysterically, and the Little Doctor had to open the medicine cupboard to fetch smelling salts.

'Calm down, calm down, please! I promise you nothing'll happen to him . . . This time tomorrow he'll be out at sea . . . As the boat is a South American one, there'll be no question of extradition . . .'

'That's what he promised me . . . But I wonder if it's true?'

Incidentally, what had come over the Little Doctor to be clasping the moist hand of a bare-shouldered young woman, and speaking to her in such emotional tones? and worrying about the fate of a man he scarcely knew?

And what could Anna be thinking about it all, in her kitchen?

None the less he declared with the utmost solemnity: 'You'll see him again, you can depend on it!'

And he all but rocked her asleep in his arms!

The Girl in Pale Blue

I. In Which the Little Doctor Rescues a Young Lady from a Strange Situation and Receives an Even Stranger Reward

Later on, indeed, the Little Doctor was to display the fierce passion of a collector in seeking out every opportunity to solve puzzles, or rather to exercise the strange gift he had discovered he possessed: the gift of disentangling the simple human truth in the most apparently complicated stories.

But he had not yet got to that point. It was barely a month since his own talents had been revealed to him, on the occasion of the Maison-Basse affair, and since then he had prudently confined himself to giving medical attention to his rural patients.

The summer weather was still warm and radiant. This Sunday was even more radiant than the previous week-days, with a threat of thunder somewhere in the air, and the Little Doctor had driven over to Royan in his noisy, juddering little car.

Before he had been there a quarter of an hour he had fallen in love!

It should be admitted that this happened to him at least once a month, often several times a month, and that most frequently the object of his passion knew nothing about it.

Was he still, at thirty, as sentimental as a schoolboy? Was he unconsciously diffident, and was that why he was still a bachelor?

Today, as usual, he had fallen for a young girl. The most girlish of girls were capable of disturbing him deeply, making him blush and want to write poetry!

The beach, at four o'clock that afternoon, was covered with suntanned bodies in shorts, in swim-suits, in multicoloured bathing wraps. On the bandstand, down in the casino gardens, an orchestra was playing light music, and family groups sat round small wicker tables drinking orangeade.

In search of shade, Jean Dollent – universally known as the Little Doctor – had automatically gone into the gaming-room, where some thirty people were milling round the *boule* table.

'*Messieurs, faites vos jeux . . . Rien ne va plus!* . . . Number seven!'

The croupier was overdoing it when he called out solemnly:

'Gentlemen, put down your stakes . . .' For the gentlemen were elsewhere, playing roulette or *chemin de fer*. Round the *boule* table there were only girls whose parents were having a drink outside, some youths, and a sprinkling of elderly people.

'Put down your stakes . . . Seven again . . .'

It was while the Little Doctor was hunting for coins in his pocket that he caught sight of the young girl in pale blue, and from then on he never took his eyes off her. She wasn't just a girl; she was the quintessential young girl, with all her freshness, her immature grace, her clear downy skin, and the large soft eyes of a gazelle. She really reminded the doctor of a gazelle!

He forgot to play while he watched her admiringly, and the seven turned up yet again; with careless fingers she picked up the chips that the croupier's rake pushed towards her.

What could she be thinking of, playing like that, with so little keenness that she seemed absent-minded? Had she, too, got parents, sitting somewhere near the bandstand? None of the young men present spoke a word to her.

She stood there alone amidst the crowd; she picked up one or two chips and pushed them forward on the table. Then she would look away, and Dollent repeatedly glimpsed a look of anguish in her eyes, like the flashes of summer lightning in the depths of the sky.

He would probably never see her again. That couldn't be helped; it would not prevent him from being in love with her, from thinking of nothing else. For days to come he would dream of her as he visited his patients in the farms round Marsilly.

'Five . . .'

She touched the five. She had luck on her side, too. Then she touched the four. And now, among the white five-franc counters she held in her hand there were visible some red twenty-franc counters, and even a big hundred-franc one.

It was exciting to wonder who she was! The daughter of some rich bourgeois, probably; from the provinces or from Paris? If she were making a long stay in Royan perhaps he could come back and . . .

She was bored, there was no doubt of that. You don't play with such a nonchalant air unless you're bored. A stout elderly lady opposite gave her an angry look every time she won, as if to say: Is that little minx having all the luck?

For the old lady was losing; she was playing desperately, counting and recounting the hundred-franc notes lying in front of her, watching the throws like an habituée of Monte Carlo working out a cunning martingale.

A sudden clap of thunder broke out, apparently just above the casino. At the same moment there was a downpour of rain, a regular waterspout. The band, being under cover, went on playing. But the crowd scattered in all directions. A moment later the *boule* room was full of hurrying, jostling people, while the croupiers had the utmost difficulty in maintaining order round the two tables.

'*Faites vos jeux* . . . Nine . . .'

And the Little Doctor stood on tiptoe so as not to lose sight of his new idol, who remained quite imperturbable.

Somebody bumped into him. He turned round sharply to make a caustic remark, but refrained and, on the contrary, apologized when he saw that it was a white-haired old lady, one of those ageing coquettes who prettify their faces with make-up in a touching last attempt at self-deception.

'I beg your pardon,' he said.

She did not reply, but nodded and smiled. This trivial incident was the more ridiculous in that just at that moment the young lady in pale blue was looking in his direction, so that but for this old creature he might have met her eyes at last.

'*Faites vos jeux* . . . *Rien ne va plus* . . .'

The rain stopped as suddenly as it had begun, and a great hush fell outside. The trees were dripping; the crowd rushed back into the gardens just as they had rushed in, and only about twenty players were left around the *boule* table.

It was then that the incredible incident occurred, exactly a quarter of an hour after the rain had stopped. The Little Doctor blamed himself, later, for not paying closer attention to the girl's play. Was she winning or losing? It didn't matter, since only trifling sums were involved. In any case, she touched the four twice in succession, and then . . .

She had shifted her position. For one moment he was afraid he'd lost her. He was prepared to follow her wherever she went, just for the pleasure of looking at her. He dreaded only one thing – seeing her go up to some young man and lay her hand on his arm, greeting him with a spontaneous 'Darling!'

But this did not happen; she remained in the room, moving around the table; now she was behind the stout woman, who was playing with furious concentration and had pulled a fresh bundle of notes from her bead bag.

Jean Dollent frowned. Had he really some abnormal instinct? He *felt* that something was going to happen. The girl cast her eyes around with exaggerated indifference and then . . .

He nearly exploded with rage. No, the thing was unpardonable! And done so naïvely, so clumsily, so stupidly in a word! The disagreeable stout lady was sitting on the croupier's left. She was watching the little ball rolling. But she could not fail to feel the girl's hand slip close to her and seize some of her notes!

He could have beaten the girl! You can't be a thief when you're so pretty and fresh-looking, with such an artless gaze! 'And if you go in for stealing, mademoiselle, you ought at least to do it skilfully!' That was what he wanted to tell her bluntly.

Of course there was a sensation. The old lady stared at the hand that was clutching the hundred-franc notes, and gave a scream. The croupier, without moving from his place, was able to seize that guilty hand, to catch it literally in the act. Shocked exclamations sounded all round the table.

The croupier, firmly grasping the hand, ordered his colleague to call the police.

But the most surprising factor was the expression on the face of the girl in blue. Was she aware of what she had done? Did she realize her position? Was she capable of reflecting that she had just disgraced herself to no purpose?

She was all but smiling! She had not even blushed. She merely said with a sigh, indicating her wrist with a jerk of her chin:

'You're hurting me . . .'

And then . . . and then . . . The Little Doctor, scarcely conscious of what he was doing, oblivious of the possible consequences of his action, stepped forward, pushed past his neighbours and hurried towards the croupier and the detective who had now appeared.

'Excuse me, gentlemen . . .'

Everyone stared at him in surprise, and he flushed as he felt himself the centre of interest.

'It's all my fault . . . It was a joke . . . a very bad joke, I must admit . . .'

He only had a few seconds in which to think up a plausible story, but then he often had his happiest inspirations in such circumstances. People were listening to him, and that was something; their attention was diverted from the girl and focussed on himself

'Just now . . . I was talking to Mademoiselle . . . We were speaking of this lady . . . I suggested that she was scatter-brained – forgive me, madame! Mademoiselle, on the contrary, maintained that she was very careful and self-possessed . . . I said: "I bet you can take half the money that's in front of her without her noticing . . ."'

People were surprised and puzzled, not knowing whether to believe him or not. And he, his nerves on edge, took his card from his wallet and handed it to the inspector, introducing himself:

'Dr Jean Dollent of Marsilly . . . If you'll kindly take me to the manager, he knows me . . . This young lady was only playing a stupid game, and it was even stupider of me to suggest it . . .'

'Come this way . . .'

The croupiers were glad to have the incident closed so that play could be resumed. Somehow or other, the girl was forgotten; when Dollent and the policeman reached the door of the manager's office, they noticed that she had remained behind among the gamblers, as though the business had nothing to do with her.

'You needn't worry about her . . . You'll see that the manager . . .'

Dollent was in fact acquainted with the manager, whose youngest son had been a patient of his. He went through his act again, apologized humbly, and when the stout lady came in, still fuming, he put on his most charming manner, begging her pardon – how could he have behaved so, particularly towards a lady like herself . . .

He was eager to get out of the place. He was afraid of not finding the girl again; she might take this opportunity to disappear.

'I hope you'll allow me, madame, to send you a box of chocolates by way of reparation . . .'

The manager, glad to have avoided a scandal, supported him:

'I can assure you that Dr Dollent is a perfect gentleman and that he is sincerely sorry for his silly joke.'

She had gone!

Of course! he muttered between his teeth.

How could he find her among the thousands of people enjoying themselves on the beach and in the casino?

He behaved exactly like a schoolboy who has lost his girl cousin. He wandered about in all directions, rushing forward whenever he caught sight of a patch of pale blue in the crowd.

No luck in the casino! No luck in the gardens! Almost an hour had elapsed. He was very hot and his collar was becoming excessively limp when, on the promenade, he caught sight of the girl in blue quietly sitting on a bench.

You'd have thought she had nothing on her mind but the beauty of the sunset! She sat there, calm and motionless, her eyes fixed on the sea which was turning violet. On another bench the old lady with the elaborate make-up, who had jostled Dollent in the casino, was watching the passing crowd with interest.

He'd get a snub, but it couldn't be helped! He rushed up to the girl's bench and sat down beside her. He blurted out, awkwardly:

'I apologize for having butted in, but I was shocked at seeing a young lady like yourself . . .'

She looked the other way and he flushed, partly from anger.

'I know you didn't ask for my help, and you'll probably take me for a sort of Don Quixote. All the same if I hadn't intervened you'd be in the police station now, and your parents . . .'

She went on looking the other way, like a respectable woman turning a deaf ear to some lout's advances. She did not condescend to answer! He might have been speaking to the empty air!

'Please note, mademoiselle, that I haven't asked you for your name and that I only acted out of . . .'

He observed that she was impatiently moving her right foot. But he was gazing at the back of her neck, a lovely curved neck with little soft curls that he wanted to kiss.

'You must admit that I might have expected if not gratitude, at least a little consideration. I made a fool of myself deliberately, and if my patients at Marsilly were to hear of it . . .'

He thought he noticed a smile on her lips, but he couldn't be sure because her face was averted.

He was really losing his temper. He had never felt such a fool in all his life. And he was about to become even more ridiculous; the painted old harridan on the other bench had got up and was coming towards them.

'An old Englishwoman!' thought Dollent, scrutinizing her lean wiry figure.

She stopped in front of the girl and said: 'You know very well, Lina, that I have always forbidden you to speak to young men . . . Go indoors!'

With a scornful glance at the Little Doctor, the girl – so her name was Lina! – rose and walked away, shrugging her shoulders, escorted by her painted dragon.

Mother or aunt? he wondered. More likely a companion, the sort of chaperon provided for young girls on holiday without their parents.

Where had this chaperon been during the incident in the casino? Dollent had not noticed the little old lady at that point, being too preoccupied with the girl and with the other old lady, the fat one who had been robbed.

'Well, my boy, there's a lesson for you!'

A lesson it certainly was. Never again would he meddle with anything that did not concern him . . .

The girl and her duenna were walking away down the promenade. He would follow them. He couldn't help it; the thing had upset him too much.

But just as he rose to his feet he looked down automatically. The bench stood on fine sand, and in this sand, while he was talking to her, the girl had traced, with the tip of her shoe, a single word:

'*Idiot!*'

'Hello! Marsilly? . . . Hello, is that you, Anna? . . . It's the doctor speaking . . . I'm ringing to tell you I shan't be back for dinner . . . No . . . I may not be back tonight . . . Hello? What's that you said? . . . Yes, you did say something . . . I've understood, and you'll just have to put up with it . . . I'm talking quite seriously, do you hear, and I hate your insinuations . . . Hello! If I shouldn't come back tomorrow . . . yes, it's quite possible I may not come back tomorrow . . . you must ring up Dr Magné . . . tell him something has prevented me and ask him, if there are any urgent cases among my patients, to be kind enough to deal with them . . . I'll do the same for him another time . . . If he questions you, tell him family business is keeping me . . . No, you needn't mention that I'm at Royan . . .'

It was eight o'clock when he made this call from the telephone box at the Hôtel Métropole.

This was one of those comfortable, though not palatial, hotels which are patronized chiefly by well-to-do families. From the lounge he could see the huge dining-room with all its little tables, on each of which stood an electric lamp with salmon-pink shade.

At one of these Lina was sitting with her chaperon.

'Can you reserve me a room?'

'Not overlooking the sea, monsieur. We're full up on that side. But we can fit you in somewhere . . . Will you be taking dinner?'

He most certainly would, and as close as possible to the two ladies!

And it was no longer just because he was in love. He might still have been, but now he had other motives. Something had clicked in his mind, just as in the Maison-Basse affair. What had enabled him to discover the secrets of the Esnandes drama which had baffled the police and the magistrates? A simple, undeniable fact: *the telephone call could not have come from the house at half-past twelve, since, at that time, the Esnandes exchange was not working*.

Everything else had followed from that quite straightforwardly.

And in the present case, it was almost as obvious. *There had been the thunderstorm and the downpour!*

'Suppose a girl wanted to commit a theft in a gaming-room . . .'

Just as he had done in the earlier case, he tried to put himself in the shoes of the people concerned. There had been only about thirty players in the room, so the thief had little opportunity of acting unobserved. But then a providential thunderstorm had broken out, and a sudden downpour had obliged the holiday-makers outside to take shelter in the gaming-room. They were not gamblers, their eyes were turned towards the door as they waited for the end of the shower. And they were crowded so close together as to form a confused mass.

'That's the moment I should have chosen to steal!' decided the Little Doctor.

Lina, however, had waited for the calmest, quietest moment, five minutes later, for her senseless action.

Why?

What had prevented her from stealing when she could have done so successfully? What had impelled her to do so when it was practically impossible?

Lina, her eyes averted, was picking at her food, as girls often do. Opposite her, on the contrary, the duenna with the wiry frame and pointed chin was devouring red meat with a hearty appetite.

It was difficult to make out anything clearly amid the cheerful tumult of the dining-room, and yet, a few minutes later, the Little Doctor's attention was caught by a table set exactly opposite that of the girl. Unlike most of the tables, this one was occupied by a solitary man.

'Twenty-five to thirty years old,' Dollent guessed, looking at him somewhat enviously. For he had always regretted being small and slight; the stranger, on the contrary, was tall and of athletic build. His face was tanned, and he was presumably one of those swimmers who go so far out to sea that from the beach you can only make out their caps as red or white dots.

'I bet . . .'

Yes, indeed . . . there was no mistaking it . . . Watching patiently, he observed that Lina, when she thought nobody was noticing, cast a lingering glance at the unknown man, and that he returned it rapturously, with far greater warmth, before looking down at his plate again. In that case, what business had Dollent himself there? He must seem like a spoil-sport, all the more ridiculous in that he was uninvited.

When dinner was finished Lina and her companion disappeared into the lift. As for the young man, he smoked a cigarette in the lounge and then went off towards the hotel bar.

'Who's that?' Dollent asked the porter.

'Don't you know him? That's Bernard Villetan, son of the Villetan ball-bearings firm, and a speedboat champion . . . He won another race this afternoon . . . He comes here every year.'

Obviously, when one's the son of a rich industrialist and a speedboat champion . . . Why didn't the Little Doctor just clear out and make room for him?

'I'd like to ask you one more question . . . The young lady . . . h'm! . . . the young lady in pale blue . . . you know the one I mean . . .'

'Mademoiselle Lina?'

The porter gave a wink and queried slyly: 'So you noticed?'

'Well, of course . . .'

'So did I . . . Only there's the companion . . . The duenna, they call her . . . Mademoiselle Esther . . . She's a regular dragon and if she were to spot anything . . .'

'Who is Mademoiselle Lina?'

'I know nothing about her . . . It's the first time she's come here . . . She's been here a month already. Her surname . . . wait a minute . . .'

He consulted his register.

'Grégoire . . . Lina Grégoire, from Paris. Her people must be in big business or industry, to afford an English companion . . .'

'Do you know how old she is?'

'I'll look at her form . . . half a sec . . . Nineteen.'

'Thank you . . .'

A five-franc tip. Not very generous, but the Little Doctor was not rich, since his family were not in ball-bearings and he had never been able to spend his holidays in one of the best hotels in Royan with an English companion.

The Little Doctor was feeling sad. He'd have liked to go home to Marsilly, but he was reluctant to because Anna, his housekeeper, would make fun of him and would probably say triumphantly:

'Well, monsieur, so things didn't go according to plan?'

He returned to the casino, where he saw neither Lina nor young Mr Ball-bearings. He staked fifty francs at *boule* and lost them, while the croupier looked askance at him and kept careful watch on ladies' handbags.

He went back to bed in the hotel. They had put him into an attic which must normally be a servant's room. He locked the door, opened the window, put out the light and tried to go to sleep.

'In view of the fact,' he kept saying to himself, 'that a theft could only have been successful in the confusion due to the thunderstorm . . .'

He stuck to his idea. Since he had succeeded once by doggedly following through a hunch, there was no reason why . . .

Unfortunately he had made one mistake. During the Maison-Basse affair he had drunk a good deal involuntarily. This time he had done so deliberately, hoping for inspiration. And before going up to his room he had drunk another whisky in the bar, although he normally never touched whisky. It had made him strangely drowsy. He was at the same time clear-headed and yet sluggish. He was not asleep, but neither was he completely awake. For a long time a mosquito bothered him. Then there came a slight sound that he could not define, as though a mouse were scratching somewhere in a corner of the room.

Why had that girl Lina . . .

Suddenly he started up. He felt sure the mouse was there, close to his bedside table. He searched for the electric light switch, and spent a few seconds groping for it. At last he grasped the pear-shaped switch and pressed the ivory knob; light flooded the room.

Nothing! No mouse. The window was still open on to a pale sky.

His watch showed 2.0 a.m. He was sure he hadn't slept, or perhaps had just dozed off. He felt like a drink of water. Before going to bed he had put his jacket over the back of a chair – carefully, for he only had two suits.

And then he noticed a white patch on the jacket, a piece of paper pinned to the lapel.

So someone had come into the room while he was lying in bed, and it was this person who had made the scarcely perceptible noise, like a scurrying mouse.

Nobody could have come in through the door, which was locked and bolted. As for the window . . .

He leaned out. He was on the fifth floor. To reach his room would have meant climbing up the drain pipe and hoisting oneself up with extraordinary agility . . .

Still in his shirt, for he had not brought pyjamas with him, he went back to his jacket and finally read the note, which was written in capital letters:

'*If you keep on meddling with what doesn't concern you, you'll meet with a misfortune. If you go quietly home you shall have a nice present.*'

No signature, of course! The most astonishing thing was that the unknown writer of the note had managed to enter his room a few minutes earlier, without making a sound, without betraying his presence except by a mouse-like rustle, while he lay there, not asleep!

He suddenly noticed a telephone at the head of the bed. He remembered that there was a telephone in every room.

'Hello! Will you give me Mademoiselle Lina Grégoire, please . . .'

The bell rang three times. Finally a sleepy voice said plaintively:

'Hello! Who is it?'

He hung up, and rang the governess. A harder voice replied in a strong English accent: 'Hello?'

He hung up again.

'Will you give me M. Bernard Villetan's room, please . . .'

No reply. He called the switchboard and asked for the porter.

'Hello! Is Monsieur Villetan not in the hotel?'

'Sorry, monsieur. He's still in the bar. I'll call him if you like. But I must warn you that he's been celebrating his victory with the gentlemen of the Motor Yacht Club and that just now . . .'

'Thank you!'

A misfortune or a nice present?

There could be no hesitation: he stayed! And all night long he dreamed that he had been commissioned to steal the notes lying in front of an old lady gambler and that he was trying to work out the best method of doing so.

How could he have guessed that meanwhile a crime was being

committed a few yards away from him?

II. Some People Deliberately Come in through the Window; Others Involuntarily Go Out the Same Way

At six in the morning, when he had been awake for a good hour, the Little Doctor, seeing with what maddening slowness his watch marked the passage of time, jumped out of bed and decided to go for a swim.

He had no swimsuit, in fact no luggage at all. He simply wrapped himself in a huge hotel bath-towel, feeling sure that he would be able to hire bathing trunks on the beach. And since he would be practically alone at this early hour, it mattered little whether they were the right size.

He went down the stairs whistling to himself, for he was always cheerful in the morning, particularly when, as today, the sunlight was like champagne. He practically jumped over a cleaning woman who was scrubbing the lowest steps, and just as he was about to cross the lounge a voice called him: 'Hey, Dollent!'

It was Ricou, a fellow-student of his who had a practice in Royan. With the gravity befitting a respectable provincial doctor, he was already, at this early hour, clad in black jacket and striped trousers and wearing a wing collar.

'Where are you going?' he asked.

'For a swim . . . And you?'

'I was sent for half an hour ago by the management of the hotel. There's been a stupid accident . . .'

Jean Dollent's little eyes gleamed; his gaze became suddenly more piercing, like a newly-sharpened pencil.

'Tell me . . .'

'A fellow who stayed too long in the bar last night and mistook the edge of his balcony for his bed. It's a miracle that he wasn't killed. He fell from the third floor and first he bounced off the pergola. He landed on the terrace and must have been knocked out, for the cleaning women found him there when they turned up at five o'clock this morning.'

'Fractured skull?'

'Not even that! I sent him to the Chevrel nursing-home. He'll be there for a few weeks and he'll be in poor shape for a little while.'

'Do you know his name?'

'Bernard Villetan, son and heir of the ball-bearings firm . . . He'd won some race or other yesterday afternoon . . .'

It may as well be confessed: thinking of the splendid specimen he had seen the night before, the Little Doctor could not help murmuring thoughtfully:

'And you say he'll be in poor shape for some time?'

'Do you know him?'

'Oh, hardly . . . By the way, what was your patient wearing?'

'Evening trousers and white shirt . . . He'd taken off his collar and tie . . . his shoes too . . . He was barefoot . . .'

Ricou was astonished to see the Little Doctor turn round without a word and go back to his room. The manager of the hotel ran after him.

'One minute, Monsieur Dollent . . . I'd like to ask you to be very discreet . . . There's no need for our guests to learn what happened last night . . . We are not responsible, of course, but accidents of this sort are always bad for a hotel's reputation . . .'

'Are you sure his feet were bare?'

'Absolutely sure.'

'What's the floor of the balcony made of?'

'Concrete, like all our balconies.'

'Thanks!'

If Bernard Villetan had been barefoot . . . if the floor of the balcony was made of concrete . . . Come, now; *always put yourself in the other person's skin* . . . You go into your bedroom . . . if you've had too much to drink and want a breath of air, you may perhaps take off your collar and your dinner jacket before going to lean out over the balcony. But not your shoes! Not your socks!

Back in his room, the Little Doctor promptly picked up the telephone receiver, for there was one question he had forgotten to ask.

'Excuse me, monsieur. It's me again. Had his bed been slept in?'

The bed had not been touched. So this fellow Bernard, who was too handsome, too well-built and too rich to be really likable, had been getting undressed in his room.

'He heard a noise on the balcony and went to look,' the Little Doctor concluded.

Unless . . . Hadn't somebody been climbing about the house-front that night, somebody who had got into Dollent's own bedroom? Suppose that somebody could have been Bernard . . . and that Bernard, during the course of his acrobatic exercises, had slipped . . .

The Little Doctor dressed, but didn't shave, since he had no razor. With his two-days' beard he looked like some sort of political refugee, particularly as his clothes were never very neatly pressed.

Quietly, he pursued his train of thought; he went on pursuing it while he ate his breakfast in the lounge, at a wicker table. But he found it harder to do so because the girl in blue and her English companion were sitting opposite him. The girl was dipping croissants in a cup of chocolate; her sharp-featured companion, already painted all the colours of the rainbow, was tackling a sizeable portion of bacon and eggs.

The weather was splendid, the hotel was bright and airy. Already most of the guests were preparing to enjoy themselves on the beach and on the tennis courts.

The Little Doctor was once again savouring the delight of following a trail, of seeing people and things not as everybody else saw them, but from the wings.

The girl in blue did not cast a single glance at him; he, on the other hand, stared at her for a good quarter of an hour, consumed by an unaccountable impatience.

What was wrong? What was there about her that worried him? He felt vaguely uneasy . . . Let's see! She was pretty, more than pretty; he almost felt that she was *too* pretty, too much the *perfect young lady* . . .

That was the point! Perfection is seldom, if ever, met with; real children are never like beautiful dolls; in actual life, there's always some detail amiss . . .

Now with Lina there was nothing amiss; not a crease in her dress, no irregularity in her features, not a hair out of place on her dark head . . . Not a thing! Her lashes fluttered; she opened her huge, magnificent, innocent eyes, exactly like those sumptuous dolls he had just been thinking of . . . Even when she was eating, a prosaic enough occupation, she retained the same ethereal air.

'*She stole at the precise moment when she was most likely to be caught* . . .'

The old Englishwoman was watching him. From time to time he had a feeling that she was just about to smile at him.

He asked the porter: 'Do you know how those ladies spend the morning?'

'Well, doctor, they usually spend it like everybody else, sitting under one of the umbrellas on the beach. They read the picture papers . . .'

'Do they bathe?'

'The companion never does . . . The young lady goes in about eleven.'

He felt reassured; he now knew where to find them. Meanwhile he went into the bar, which was deserted and where Jef, the barman, was cleaning up.

'I'd like a port, please.'

Was it his fault if one has to keep on drinking when one's on a trail?

'Tell me . . . Bernard Villetan, last night, was a bit merry, wasn't he?'

'A bit tight, sure . . . He wouldn't go to bed . . . His friends went off, at one o'clock, I wanted to close the bar but he stayed on . . . He kept asking for just one more whisky, swearing it was really the last . . . You've got to hand it to him, he holds his liquor better than most people!'

'What time was it when they brought him a letter?'

'Why d'you ask that?'

'Just an idea . . .'

And the Little Doctor sensed that the barman was looking at him with a certain admiration.

'No, he got no letter . . . But he wrote one . . . I wonder how you guessed?'

'Have a drink with me . . . You say he wrote a letter; at what time?'

'It was two in the morning at least . . . I could see from the way he was drinking that something was wrong . . . I asked him: "You got worries, Monsieur Bernard?" Because, you know, he was an old customer, a decent guy, not in the least stuck up.

' "Something worse than worries," he tells me.

' "Then," I says to him, "you must be in love!"

' "That's it, and it's no joke!"

' "And yet you're not the sort of man that finds girls hard to get . . ."

'I could see from his expression that it was a more serious matter than I'd thought.

' "One last whisky!" he ordered. "And let's not talk any more about it." Then he picked up a paper that was lying on the bar. He read it as though he wanted to take his mind off things . . . rather like you read at the hairdresser's or in a dentist's waiting-room, you know, everything from beginning to end including the advertisements.'

The Little Doctor's eyes had narrowed.

'Wait, Jef . . . He was reading . . . he was drinking . . . and suddenly . . . Give me another port . . .'

And the barman remarked wonderingly: 'Just like him!'

'What d'you mean?'

'I mean that he looked up suddenly. He was quite different, as if something had suddenly struck him. He was looking at me without seeing me. He called out: "A whisky", and he didn't say it was going to be the last; he'd stopped thinking about that. He was hunting for something on the tables and finally, all excited like, he asked for some writing-paper.'

'At two in the morning?'

'It was quite that . . . Well, he didn't make too good a job of it. He wasn't what you might call blind drunk, but he was pretty sozzled . . . He might have been able to walk fairly straight, but as for writing! I could see he was having difficulties . . . Some letters he made too big and some tiny . . . He kept sticking out his tongue like a schoolboy doing his homework . . .'

'And he gave you the letter to post?'

'No . . . He took it off with him.'

'Did he go out of the hotel?'

'No, he didn't do that either. He went upstairs, telling me to put everything down on his bill.'

'Did he take the lift?'

'No, he walked up the stairs . . . His room's on the third floor.'

And the girl's was on the second!

'Do you remember what paper he was reading?'

'That's the worst of it . . . If you'd come half an hour ago, before I started cleaning up . . . Now all the papers I've collected are in the rubbish bin.'

'Can you let me see them?'

There was an amused twinkle in the barman's eyes. 'You know, they're not very clean. I picked them up all anyhow, mixed with olive stones, peanut shells and cigarette ends . . . However, if you really want them . . .'

They were a mixed lot of French and English dailies, weeklies and illustrated magazines.

'Try to remember, Jef . . . Was it a big paper? Were the pictures coloured?'

'Wait a sec . . . Monsieur Bernard was sitting on this stool . . . I remember the cocktail shaker was in front of him and I had to lift the paper to get at it . . . It was an English paper, I'm sure of that, with a great many pages . . .'

There were three English papers in the bundle, all of them as bulky as magazines, and the Little Doctor heaved a sigh as he carried them off.

Put yourself in the other person's shoes . . . Bernard is drinking with his friends . . . They're celebrating his victory, but he refuses to go to bed when they do . . . He's gloomy and depressed . . . He's on the point of unburdening himself to the barman, for lack of a better confidant. But at that point *it hasn't yet occurred to him to write a letter!*

He must have had some motive for writing that letter. But *at 2.0 a.m. that motive doesn't yet exist!*

So it must have been the newspaper that gave him the idea of writing, and of writing immediately.

'Excuse me, *monsieur le directeur* . . . It's me again.'

This time the hotel manager scowled, presumably reflecting that the Little Doctor was becoming a nuisance.

'When the injured man was discovered, I assume someone undressed him before lifting him into the ambulance . . . You were present. If he'd had a letter on him . . . a letter on hotel note-paper, I suppose you'd have seen it?'

'There was no letter!' declared the manager. He hoped that was the end of it, but Dollent hung on.

'One word more . . . I suppose you've searched his room?'

'I've just been through it with the police superintendent, whom I was obliged to inform of the accident.'

'That's fine!'

The manager did not share the Little Doctor's enthusiasm.

'You think that's fine, do you?' he retorted, almost peevishly.

'I mean that if there had been such a letter in the room you'd have noticed it . . .'

'There was none.'

'I was sure of it!'

'Why?'

'Oh, nothing . . . Everything's going nicely, *monsieur le directeur* . . . Can I keep my room another night?'

The hotel manager was by no means delighted.

. . . Bernard writes a letter at the bar some time after 2.0 a.m. He goes upstairs to his room. He is found lying on the terrace at five in the morning and the letter has disappeared.

So, presumably, it has been delivered!

So it must have been that letter that . . .

At a pinch, it all held together. But what was to prove that the letter in question was not the very one that some person unknown had deposited in Dollent's room?

Bernard had become aware of the doctor's attitude during the afternoon. He noticed him in the evening, not far from the young lady in blue . . . He was jealous . . . He threatened the doctor, and moreover promised him a reward if he'd go away and leave the coast clear.

'H'm, h'm . . .' the Little Doctor coughed gently as he walked along the promenade, his newspapers under his arm, staring at all the girls and old ladies under the many-coloured beach umbrellas. But what about the newspaper?

What role, in fact, did the paper play? Why was it while reading an English daily, thirty-two pages thick, that the young man had thought of threatening his supposed rival?

Moreover, for all his athleticism, who had taught him to scramble up house-fronts, an accomplishment generally confined to a few specialists aptly known as cat-burglars?

Jean Dollent was wearing his usual grey suit, the one in which he did his rounds in the countryside, and he felt ill at ease amid the half-naked crowd that thronged the beach. He thought he could feel his beard growing, and it always grew terribly thick.

Well, it couldn't be helped. He was no longer the admirer of the girl in pale blue. He was a man obsessed by a passion for deciphering human enigmas.

There were the two women! He was so preoccupied that he almost stumbled over the girl's body, for she was stretched out on her stomach on the golden sand, in a swimsuit of the same pale blue as her dress, getting her legs and shoulders tanned in the sun.

Two metres away, in the shade of a red-and-yellow striped umbrella, the companion was sitting in a deck-chair and reading – reading *an English newspaper*, identical in fact with one of the three that the doctor was carrying under his arm.

She did not see him coming. It would have been more proper to go and sit elsewhere, for there was room enough on the beach. Calmly, brazenly, he sat down on the ground barely three metres from the old Englishwoman and less than two from the girl.

He looked like one of those people who come between trains to spend a few hours on the beach, and who are conspicuous because they are dressed unlike the rest. Worst of all, he was wearing black shoes, whereas all about him people were bare-footed or wearing extravagantly fanciful sandals.

'What page has she got to?' he wondered.

And he leaned forward, as shamelessly as those theatre-goers who press on your shoulders in order to read your programme.

Page 4 . . . Good! He opened his own paper at the same page. It would have taken him hours, with a dictionary, to translate an English article correctly. But what chiefly interested him, since Lina's face was hidden in the sand, was the expression on that of her companion.

She raised her eyes. Are people really conscious of being looked at? She stared back at him, and her immediate reaction was to scowl. It looked as though she was going to take offence and tell him angrily that he was an unmannerly lout to come and plant himself so close to a young lady in a state of undress.

Her face clearly expressed these feelings, and he looked down at his paper again, so as to give himself time to think.

She raised her head . . . She was looking somewhat less cantankerous . . .

She lowered her head again.

Finally she gave a slight smile, the sort one gives to people to whom one has not been introduced but whom one has met repeatedly.

The Little Doctor, sweet as honey, smiled back.

III. Which Proves that Reading the Advertisements can Sometimes Lead to Violent Death

The strangest part of it, in the Little Doctor's opinion, was not so much the drama being surreptitiously enacted between three characters – the old duenna, the young girl and himself – as the atmosphere in which this drama was taking place.

How many people could there have been on the beach? A thousand, maybe? Two thousand? more, perhaps. And all these people were in holiday mood, enjoying the sunshine, concerned only with tanning their skins, performing gymnastic exercises or splashing about in the beautiful turquoise-blue water.

The groups were barely a few metres apart, and children, practically naked, raced about in the spaces between them, tripping over supine bodies as they ran to fetch beach-balls from tents.

Meanwhile what was at stake between the three protagonists . . .

Who could say what it would lead to? Wasn't Bernard Villetan, who the previous day had deafened the crowd with the proud roar of his speed-boat, now lying, swathed in bandages like a mummy, on a hospital bed?

The old duenna had smiled and then resumed her reading of the newspaper. As for the girl in pale blue, presumably considering that she was baked enough on one side, she had made a movement as though to turn over. In so doing she caught sight of the Little Doctor, so close to her that she could have put out her hand and touched him, and she had given a start, but without the trace of a smile.

From where the three of them were, the front of the hotel could be seen, with a balcony outside every room, including the one from which young Bernard . . .

What was the girl doing now? Really, she seemed to make a habit of writing in the sand. She was tracing letters with her finger, watching her companion out of the corner of her eye. Could it be another insult, like yesterday's?

The Little Doctor waited, with a smile . . . F . . . I . . . L . . .

She paused for a moment, because the English woman had moved. Then, patiently, she began again: . . . F . . . I . . . L . . .

'*Filez*!' Clear out! An odd expression, incidentally, for such a perfect young lady to use! It's true that girls nowadays go in for slang . . .

Yesterday he'd been an 'idiot', today he was unceremoniously ordered to clear out!

And he smiled. He sat unmoving, with his English paper spread out on his knees. He wished the man who sold sunglasses would come by, for the glare of the light on the sand hurt his eyes.

Well, it couldn't be helped! What page had the old lady got to? Page 8 . . . He looked at page 8 of his own paper. More articles, in tiny print, with politicians' names in the headlines . . .

'Clear out! *Filez*!'

But then a much more unexpected incident took place. He heard a voice, actually the voice of the old lady, the typical sugary tones of an elderly Englishwoman, asking him:

'Do you speak English?'

He was so surprised that at first he could not find an answer.

'Yes . . . No . . . I learnt some at school once . . .'

'It's very difficult, isn't it? But I'm sure you can read our language very well. Mademoiselle Grégoire can read English too, but she speaks it with a shocking accent.'

A very odd woman, decidedly! A caricature of a woman! At this stage in her life, why couldn't she admit her age once and for all? Why that old-fashioned get-up, that ridiculous dress worn over an obvious corset, those mauve stockings and above all that blatantly painted face which couldn't deceive anyone?

And as for her smile! A honeyed smile which allowed a glimpse of long teeth all ready to bite, half of them filled with gold!

'Are you staying long in Royan?'

'I haven't decided yet.'

'I'm ashamed of not having thanked you earlier . . . I have been told of the tactful and ingenious way in which you put things right after Mademoiselle Grégoire's mischievous prank. For that was what it was, of course, wasn't it, Lina?'

The girl had turned round and was glaring at the two speakers.

'You see how these things happen . . . I had left the room for a moment . . .'

He suddenly saw the light, and almost declared: 'It's not true!'

He did not say it, but he thought it. Now he recalled last night's scene. Forgotten details came back to him. And he was convinced that when the commotion occurred he had noticed the old spinster making her way towards the exit.

'These modern girls . . . Well, it will have taught me not to slacken my vigilance . . . I was just embarrassed at not having thanked you on behalf of Mademoiselle Grégoire's parents . . .'

'They live in Paris, I suppose?'

'For the moment they're in South America. They travel abroad a good deal . . . that's why they needed someone reliable to . . .'

'You've suddenly become excessively talkative, old thing,' the Little Doctor commented inwardly.

The funniest part of it was that a couple, not far off, seeing him in the clutches of this grotesque creature, were winking slyly at him as if to say, 'Isn't the old thing a scream? You're not going to be able to shake her off.'

She was, indeed, becoming tiresomely persistent.

'Aren't you too much in the sun? Wouldn't you like to come under the shade of our umbrella?'

'No, thank you, really . . .'

'Royan is a delightful resort. In England we only have . . .'

The hardest part was having to think fast and frantically, so as not to be taken unawares, and at the same time to display an innocent smiling face. Particularly as Lina was watching him, her brow stern, her eyes even sterner, giving the impression of having aged some five or six years in the space of a few minutes.

Where was the ideal, doll-like creature that she had been a short while ago, the image of rosy-cheeked innocence such as you only find on picture postcards?

'You're a doctor, I understand?' crooned the old lady.

'A country doctor, yes . . .'

'It must be fascinating . . .'

Why fascinating? And why this sudden impulse to speak to him? Why did she seem so determined not to let go of him, even if it meant keeping up an interminable pretence of conversation?

That was what he was wondering. He felt he must solve the problem very fast, that everything depended on that. He felt, moreover, that Lina was losing patience, longing to get rid of him, and trying to make it clear to him that the sooner he went off the better.

'I expect Monsieur would like a swim,' she said. 'The tide's high now.'

The old woman glared fiercely. 'If you want to swim, Lina, go and do so, but leave the grown-ups alone.'

It was highly comic, provided one avoided glancing back at the hotel and seeing the particular balcony from which, the previous night, a young man full of life and vigour . . .

'I suppose you're not here in a professional capacity but on holiday?'

'That's to say . . . You know, with my job . . . For instance last night they nearly got me out of bed to attend to an accident that took place in the hotel . . .'

He looked at each of them in turn. The old lady never batted an eyelid. Lina was waiting tensely.

'They didn't think of me and so they sent for a colleague of mine from Royan. Anyhow, the man isn't dead, which is a miracle . . . He'd fallen from the third floor!'

Two children who ran up and almost tumbled on top of him prevented him from observing the effect of his words. However, he heard the Englishwoman saying:

'What a shocking number of accidents there are these days . . . Are you staying in the hotel for a few days longer?'

'One night more, at any rate . . .'

'In that case I feel it's my duty to thank you, on behalf of Lina's parents, by inviting you to have dinner with us . . . I don't know if it would amuse you . . .'

It was really quite impossible to carry on a conversation on this beach. A red and blue ball, come from heaven knows where, nearly hit the old lady in the face, and she involuntarily brought her knees together to catch it in her lap.

'Quite informally, of course,' she went on. 'We never go out in the evenings and we don't dress . . .'

This time the girl used her foot to write in the sand: '*Filez!*'

She was very persistent, but Dollent had no wish to go away. He had suddenly flushed deeply. He watched the boy go off with his red and blue ball. Then he looked up at the dreadful balcony. Then . . .

The sea-breeze had turned the page of his newspaper. He looked down mechanically.

Then he looked up again. He had grown pale. He strove to put on a cheerful air.

'I accept your invitation,' he said, 'but on one condition: that you'll both have a drink with me first at the hotel bar. Jef makes admirable cocktails.'

'I never drink cocktails!' broke in Lina.

'Be quiet!' ordered her duenna. 'It's only too kind of Monsieur to invite you, particularly after what he did for you, and considering you haven't shown him any sign of gratitude. If your parents were here . . .'

He thought he saw a shadow pass over the girl's eyes.

'We accept your invitation, monsieur,' the old woman went on. 'What time do you suggest?'

'Why not now? Provided that suits you . . .'

'Lina! Put on your beach dress . . . I've always told you that swimsuit is dreadfully indecent . . .'

As he rose to his feet, the Little Doctor felt his hands damp and his throat dry. He wasn't used to this! Of course, practically every day he had to take risks with other people's lives, but this was the first time he had gambled with his own. And looking at the cheerful crowd around him, he braced himself by reflecting:

'It surely won't happen here, at any rate! . . . Among so many people, there's no danger. On the other hand, if . . .'

And he folded the paper to conceal the advertisement which had caught his attention so sharply.

IV. In Which the Little Doctor would Rather Have Been Working for His Own Benefit

It was all a question of choosing the right moment! Meanwhile a crowd of imbeciles were watching him with kindly irony, as he solemnly escorted an ageing spinster with a crudely and absurdly painted face. Some of them, maybe, were thinking:

'Cunning fellow! He's making up to the old girl so that he can get the young one . . .'

Nobody could guess that he had never in all his life felt so close to violent death. Had Bernard had any such suspicions the previous night, when he was quietly undressing in his room?

He must choose the right moment! And choose it so as to . . .

It was dreadfully complicated. The lay-out of the bar was fairly favourable; its chief advantage was that there was only one door, not very wide, apart from the small service door behind the counter.

It was a slack time of day. Most people were still bathing, and the crowd would not arrive for their pre-lunch drinks until about one o'clock. The only people there were the few regulars who, at Royan as at Deauville or Biarritz, kept up their Parisian habits and, no sooner risen, sought to remedy a hangover with a strong cocktail.

'Three pink gins, Jef . . . Please sit down, Miss . . . it *is* Miss, isn't it?'

His eyes were sparkling. He remembered the red and blue beach ball. He was so pleased with himself and his discovery, and the subtle train of thought that had led him to it, that he forgot to be anxious.

'Shut the window, will you, Jef . . . There's a draught . . .'

That wasn't true, but the window provided too easy an exit, for now they were not on the third floor but on the ground floor.

He still had his newspaper tucked under his arm; he could easily put his finger on page 8.

Now, how many people were there in the bar? Jef and the waiter . . . A pageboy at a loose end, looking on in a bored fashion . . . Two young men perched on high stools . . . A group of three businessmen at a small table, spending their holidays worrying how to make more money . . .

'I hope that cocktail isn't too dry for you, Miss . . . Excuse me, I'd like to ask Mademoiselle Lina . . . that *is* her name, isn't it? . . . I'd like to ask her, as a token of remembrance, to sign a postcard for me . . . I'd like her to choose one herself . . . She'll find some at the porter's desk . . . I know I'm taking a liberty, but it's a fad of mine.'

It wasn't a particularly bright idea, but he had no choice. At all costs, she must be got out of the way.

She went off resignedly, or rather resentfully. The pageboy was still standing by the door. Jef was a tough fellow. He must have had quite a few encounters with drunks in his time.

'I was saying, Miss, that when one is reading English newspapers . . . I say reading them, but my English is so rusty . . . Luckily there are pictures . . .'

She was holding her glass in one hand, slowly sipping its contents, and suddenly, while he opened the paper at page 8, the Little Doctor behaved like a lunatic – at any rate that was how it seemed to Jef and everyone else present.

Without warning, he seized hold of the old Englishwoman's left hand and with his other hand grabbed her hair and . . . pulled it off at one go.

A minute later they were both rolling about on the floor. Ten seconds had not elapsed when a shot rang out, and a bullet embedded itself in the mahogany panelling of the bar.

The Little Doctor was well aware that he could never get the best of it on his own. He knew, too, that Jef and the others would intervene. He knew that there was only one exit, and that this was to his advantage.

Miss Esther's wig was lying somewhere on the carpet, and the figure now to be seen wrestling with Dollent was an extraordinarily wiry and muscular one, bearing no resemblance to an elderly duenna.

'Call the police!' shouted the Little Doctor, hitting his opponent in the face with all his might.

For Miss Esther was a man, there was no doubt about that.

He was still panting. His jacket was torn over the shoulder. His face was bathed in sweat, which emphasized the darkness of his unshaven chin.

The hotel manager, who had put his office at the disposal of *ces messieurs* the police, glared at him fiercely, while the Superintendent did not conceal his bewilderment.

'You maintain that this old lady . . . I mean this man . . . well, this person . . .'

'It's not easy for me, Superintendent, to sum up in a few minutes, when I'm out of breath like this, things that I've spent hours and hours working out, bit by bit, linking up one idea to another . . . It all started from the theft at the casino . . . If *you* wanted to commit a theft . . .'

'No personal remarks, please, doctor!'

These policemen were all the same! And there was nobody to understand his own special methods! Well, it couldn't be helped.

'To sum it all up, I maintain that the person who committed that theft did so in order to get herself arrested, that's to say to remain for a certain length of time under police protection, to be safe from some danger . . . The proof of that is that after my quixotic gesture the girl called me an idiot, if you'll excuse me, Superintendent. Do you follow?'

They didn't, but he went on talking to himself.

'Bernard Villetan is in love with the girl . . . He can never get near her because of the terrible duenna . . . He's depressed about it, and he starts drinking . . . Then he happens on a newspaper . . . He sees an advertisement and the advertisement gives him an idea . . .

'Just think, gentlemen . . . There's something unnatural about the way the companion keeps guard over Lina. And the woman herself seems more like a caricature out of *Punch* than a real person.

'As for the advertisement, here it is . . . I'll translate it for you: '*She was getting bald . . . She looked ten years older each month . . . Then she tried Sanders' wigs . . .*' And see the two pictures: before and after. Before, the hard-featured, mannish face . . . After, the absurd, pathetic simper of an ageing coquette . . .

'I'm sure, gentlemen, that Bernard realised at that moment why he was being kept away from the girl he loved . . . He must have understood, too, why she avoided him . . .

'Miss Esther was really a man . . . Her lover? I don't know yet . . . The fact remains that Bernard asked for some writing-paper . . . He wrote a letter proclaiming his discovery, and slipped it under Lina's door. And this letter, of course, fell into the hands of the bogus companion who shared Lina's suite.

'That same night Bernard was thrown out of the window of his room and only survived by a miracle . . . And the same night I, too, received a note, ordering me to clear out.

'Now do you understand, gentlemen?'

No, they did not understand! The pseudo-duenna, however, stared at the Little Doctor grimly, but not without a certain admiration.

'I know I'm meddling in something that doesn't concern me. I apologize.'

The manager was nodding, as though in confirmation. Things had been quiet enough before the arrival of this tiresome little doctor, always as tense as an electric wire and ready to emit sparks!

'Just think! A girl who's so frightened that she'd rather go to prison . . . A bogus companion who has no hesitation in trying to kill the man who has discovered part of her secret, and to drive away with threats another man – myself – who seems to be following the same trail.

'This morning, when I sat down on the beach, the man whom I still can't help calling Esther – laugh if you like! – realised that I knew something and invited me to dinner this evening . . . And no doubt I'd have suffered the same fate as Bernard Villetan.

'I'll just add that when a ball was thrown at Miss Esther she drew her knees together to catch it, *instead of parting them* as a woman would instinctively have done.

'Do you follow me now?'

They were still puzzled. But it didn't matter. The Little Doctor knew! He knew that he could not have been mistaken, that there was no flaw in his argument.

'I got the girl out of the way for a moment . . . You'll notice that she hasn't come back, that she's disappeared . . .'

'That still doesn't tell us, doctor, why you became involved in . . .'

Could he say to them, 'Because, ever since the Maison-Basse affair, I've loved criminal cases as a collector loves old china or antique snuff-boxes!'

He merely replied: 'I'm thirsty.'

Three days later Scotland Yard, having received the finger-prints of the bogus 'Miss Esther', sent back a report which can be summarised as follows:

'Prints of John O'Patrick . . . Formerly a circus acrobat and conjuror. Met Lina Powel, whose mother was French, and who from the age of twelve performed the *danse des poupées*, dressed as a doll . . . After her parents' death in a railway accident she set up with John O'Patrick at the age of sixteen . . .'

So that was why the Little Doctor had invariably been reminded of a doll when he looked at her! She was ageless! She remained what she had always been, on the dance floor and on the music-hall stage . . .

'They both gave up the circus, following the death of a trapeze artist, the German Von Hoest, who had been an admirer of Lina. O'Patrick is strongly suspected of responsibility for the man's death.'

The couple had come to France. They were now debarred from working in circuses or music-halls. O'Patrick was a highly jealous man, particularly since he was twenty years older than his mistress and by no means good-looking.

Since he could not put on an act on stage, he devised the girl-and-governess partnership in order to plunder seaside resorts and spas.

Until the day when Lina met Bernard Villetan at Royan. She was tired of the life she'd been leading; she wanted to break free. But her lover threatened to kill her if she attempted to do so.

He was quite capable of that. He had already killed a man on her account.

Then one day, when she'd had enough of it, wanting to escape at all costs from his power, she took advantage of being in the casino to steal in the clumsiest possible way.

In prison, after all, she would be *free* . . .

The Little Doctor had gone back to his rounds, visiting the cottages and farms of his country practice.

It was six days since his adventure in Royan. He was clutching the telephone somewhat nervously.

'Hello, is that you, Ricou? . . . Yes, Dollent speaking . . . How's your patient? . . . You say he's making good progress . . . Yes . . . What? . . . Where's he planning to go? . . . Spain? . . . Why?'

And when he heard the answer he put back the receiver slowly.

Dr Ricou had said: 'Because he'd received a mysterious message from Spain . . . Somebody's expecting him there as soon as he's fit to travel . . . Some young man . . .'

Of course! The girl in blue!

As for his own role in the story . . .

A Woman Screamed

I. How what was Found among the Rushes at Bois-Bezard was not what the Little Doctor Expected to Find There

Strictly speaking, the candidates for death, in the three or four villages where the Little Doctor practised his medical expertise would not really have prevented him from sleeping. Those who got him up at two in the morning and kept him on his feet all night were the candidates for life. In the past month of October alone he had presided over twenty-three births.

On this particular day he was preparing to go to bed when other people were getting up, since at seven in the morning he was making a rapid breakfast before retiring for three or four hours into the quiet warmth of his bedclothes. On such occasions he liked to eat in the kitchen, chatting with Anna. But the housekeeper had just received the morning paper and was eager to look through it.

He noticed, at one point, that she was longing to talk and finding it hard to hold her tongue. Although his eyelids were heavy with weariness he immediately realized what it was all about.

For the past three weeks, in fact, ever since he had read the statement of the garage-owner from Ecoin, he had been liable to mutter at meal-times, for the benefit of nobody in particular:

'You'll see that those idiots won't discover anything!'

Anna knew what he meant. He was desperately anxious to go over there and exercise his gifts as a solver of problems. But 'over there' was in the neighbourhood of Nevers, some two hundred kilometres from Marsilly, and the Little Doctor could not afford to be constantly roaming the countryside.

'Have they found the body, Anna?' he asked, as he peeled off the skin from a substantial piece of sausage.

She nodded.

'How old was the woman?'

Anna was triumphant. 'For one thing, Monsieur, it wasn't a woman at all! You see you're not as clever as you think you are. It was a man, and no mistake about it, a man over six foot tall and weighing over a hundred kilos . . . I suppose you're going to set off right away instead of going to bed?'

She made the remark ironically, as though to challenge him, but he replied in all seriousness, with his mouth full:

'Quite right, Anna . . . Will you pack my suitcase with a change of underwear . . . While you're about it, put in a pair of stout shoes.'

Half an hour later his tiny car, which had been prone to back-firing all its life, was speeding along a road swept by a cold autumn wind.

About a month previously, on October 2nd, Jérôme Espardon, owner of a garage in the hamlet of Ecoin, five kilometres from Nevers on the main road to Paris, had appeared at the nearest *gendarmerie* at five in the morning and had made the following report, which all the newspapers had reproduced and which was to give plenty of people plenty to worry about:

'Last night, October 1st, I stayed up later than usual because I hadn't finished my monthly accounts. At 11.0 p.m. I was in the little office with the glazed door at the far end of the garage. The outside shutter was down and the light by the petrol pump was out; but some light must have been showing under the shutter.

'Suddenly I heard a car draw up and somebody knocked at the door. Usually I don't like serving customers at night, for that's how some people in my line of business have been beaten up by thugs.

'However, since I hadn't undressed yet I opened the little door in the shutter. It was very dark, for there was no moon and it had been raining a short while before.

'A big stout man whose features I couldn't make out asked me to give him thirty litres of petrol. The headlights of the car were off so that I could not distinguish as much as I'd have liked to.

'I worked the pump. The number-plate was just in front of me and though I didn't pay attention to the letters I automatically noted the figures: 87.75.

'Through the rear window I noticed, too, that there were two people on the back seat, a man and a woman.

'My customer handed me 100 francs, and I owed him 2.25 francs change, but he said: "That's all right."

'Just as he was getting back into his seat and starting up the engine, somebody lowered the rear window. I caught sight of a woman's hand, and a voice called out: "Help! Help!"

'The voice was a woman's, too, but it was immediately drowned by the noise of the car which drove off and disappeared at top speed in the direction of Paris.

'Since my phone's not connected at night I couldn't call the *gendarmerie*. Besides, I was all alone in the garage, for my wife's still on holiday in Savoy with her people.

'However, I didn't worry too much about the matter, thinking it was most likely a joke.'

The *gendarmerie*, it must be admitted, did not at first take it very seriously either. They merely rang up the District Office to inquire whether anything unusual had taken place in the region that night.

No accident had been reported, no alarm raised. Moreover, a *gendarme* had been stationed all night on the road just outside the small town of Pouilly, twenty kilometres away, on the look-out for a rabbit poacher. He had automatically noted the numbers of all the cars that passed, and he had seen no number-plate ending 87.75.

So the car reported by the garage-owner had not travelled very far. Indeed, it had been recovered, and Jérôme Espardon had been put through an uncomfortable quarter of an hour; since he was known to be fond of liquor the authorities had unhesitatingly accused him of having been drunk that night and making fools of them.

One single car, in fact, corresponded to the particulars given: that of Monsieur Humbert, a lawyer from Nevers.

And this is what Humbert, a highly respectable person and the son of a magistrate into the bargain, had declared under oath:

'On Friday October 1st, my wife and I took the car, as we do every Friday, to visit our friends the Lajarrigues in the Place Gambetta. We dine there every week, together with the Dormois and the Vercels, and afterwards we play bridge until midnight.

'Everything went as planned. It was raining when we reached the Place Gambetta. I parked my car behind that of the Dormois, who had got there before us. As for the Vercels, who live four houses away, they had of course come on foot.

'The bridge party went on rather late, as sometimes happens, and it was nearly 1.0 a.m. when we broke up. The cars were still standing at the door. My wife and I went home to bed, and we noticed nothing unusual.'

And yet the wretched garage-owner, whose word nobody would believe, maintained his assertions, 'I put thirty litres of petrol into that car on Friday October 1st at 11.0 p.m.'

He was vindicated two days later, thanks to Madame Humbert. She often used the car in the afternoons, and she remembered that on October 1st she had intended to fill it up with petrol. Two days later, although the car had not been used on the Saturday, she noticed that there was a considerable amount in the tank.

'Did you fill up?' she asked her husband.

'Me? No . . .'

That was how it had to be admitted that Jérôme Espardon had been neither lying nor dreaming. Somebody had borrowed that car during the bridge party, had driven it out along the Paris road, had been surprised to find that the tank was practically empty and had stopped at the Ecoin filling-station.

He could not have gone very far, since the *gendarme* on duty at Pouilly had not seen him. And he had returned to Nevers, where the car was back in its place just before one in the morning.

Meanwhile a woman had called for help!

For the past month the Little Doctor had been fuming.

'I shall have to make a trip there one of these days!' he kept saying to Anna, almost daily.

The inquiry could be described, without exaggeration, as slack. For one thing, nobody had lodged a complaint. Moreover, what facts were known? Had there been a murder? Had there been a robbery? And finally, whom did it concern? the Nevers police or the *gendarmerie*? and if the latter, which district, which squad was responsible?

Who was the woman who had waited until the last minute to call for help? Why had she not done so earlier, when her companion, unable to start the car since he was outside it, could not have interfered?

Who was the stout man? And the other man, inside the car, of whose figure the garage-owner had only caught a vague glimpse?

'Some sportsmen shooting in the marshes of Bois-Bezard, ten kilometres from Nevers,' the newspaper stated, 'discovered among the rushes the body of a stoutly built man of about fifty.

'The body has not yet been identified. The authorities are on the spot. Can there be any connection with the statement of the garage-owner of Ecoin, which our readers will recall?

'This puzzling story may have some surprises in store for us.'

The Little Doctor stepped on the gas, but his small eight-year-old car was already going as fast as it could, and an occasional gust of wind shook it so hard that it seemed about to topple into the ditch.

After all, none of his patients was seriously ill at the moment. There were no births due either; the series seemed to have come to an end. Dollent could afford to breathe easily for a day or two. As for minor ailments, sore throats and boils, they could just wait . . .

A woman's scream . . .

A stoutly-built man . . .

'I wonder if they've found the gun!' he suddenly said out loud, as though it were obvious that the man had been shot.

'What's that? what name did you say?'

'Dr Dollent . . .'

'Are you a friend or a relative of the victim? Did you know him? Are you acting for the D.P.P.?'

In a sector of fifty to a hundred kilometres around Marsilly and La

Rochelle, he was known and accepted by most officials. Here, he was confronted by a stubborn *gendarme* who knew only his orders.

'Nobody's allowed into the marshes of Bois-Bezard, at any rate without a note from the Public Prosecutor.'

'Where is the Public Prosecutor?'

'On the spot, three hundred metres from here . . .'

'How do you expect me to get a note from him if you won't allow me . . .'

'That's none of my business! Apart from the Press . . .'

At the side of the road a number of cars were parked and two of them bore the crest of leading Parisian dailies. Another car, as big as a truck, drove up, and the man who climbed out of it was loaded with cine cameras.

'Can I give you a hand?' offered the Little Doctor.

'Thanks a lot . . . Where do we go?'

'This way . . .'

He seized one of the cameras. He went through with his unknown companion, while the *gendarme* scowled but dared not interfere.

The wind went on blowing. Great clouds scudded past, almost as low as the tree-tops and as swift as aeroplanes. The fenland air was cold and dank; there was a row of poplars above which rooks were wheeling . . . Some men in dark clothes were walking to and fro, trying to avoid getting muddy . . . Nobody paid attention to Jean Dollent. The photographers took their pictures, the journalists bustled about. A policeman was taking measurements, and there in the rushes a body was lying, covered with a tarpaulin.

'Is she coming?'

'Inspector Leroy has gone to break the news to her, with the usual circumspection . . . She'll be here in a few minutes.'

'You're sure there's no mistake about the identity of the victim?'

'A man like that couldn't go unrecognized, *monsieur le procureur*.'

'What exactly was his occupation in life?'

The Little Doctor was standing quite close to the two speakers, with such an air of quiet self-assurance that each of them must have assumed he was in the company of the other.

'Isidore Borchain has been living at Nevers for some years,' the Chief Superintendent said. 'He owns a small private house in the Avenue de la République. I wondered at first why he had settled in our town, whereas he's from the North of France, from Roubaix I believe, and so is his wife. I was given a satisfactory explanation. Borchain is – was, rather – the French representative of one of the largest American firms selling dentists' equipment. He travelled a lot himself, for it seems his job was a fairly responsible one . . . So he chose a town roughly in the centre of France, which would enable him to go home at frequent intervals . . .'

And the Superintendent, who had just finished filling his pipe, asked the Little Doctor, whom he did not know: 'Have you a light?'

The principle never varies! The difficulty is to get over the first hurdle; after that, nobody bothers about you. Journalists take you for a policeman and policemen take you for a journalist; the D.P.P. assume that if you're there it's because you've a right to be there, and they ask you for a light; they practically ask you for your advice!

On the strength of this reflection, the Little Doctor brazened it out and inquired, as he held out a match: 'Have they found the gun?'

'Lying beside him, just one metre away . . . A revolver with a large-bore cylinder . . .'

There was a stir and a clamour of voices, then the noise of a car, and the rush of photographers and journalists to the roadside.

'I can't understand . . . I tell you it's not possible,' a woman was exclaiming.

Dollent guessed that she was Madame Borchain, and he had plenty of time to study her as she defended herself limply against the inquisitive professionals around her.

How could she have done anything otherwise than limply? He had never seen a woman so completely feminine; there was something positively old-fashioned about her. She made one think of boudoirs hung with faded silk, flower-patterned easy-chairs, embroidery frames, all sorts of cosy fragrant feminine things such as one seldom meets with today.

She was probably in her thirties: a pretty face with soft features and a very pale skin, that lilies-and-roses complexion that was once so prized. Tiny feet in elegant shoes, a black silk dress under a fur coat which she clutched around her.

'I tell you it's not possible . . .'

The sort of woman the Little Doctor used to dream of when he was fifteen, the typical heroine of nineteenth-century novels. He recalled a print in his parents' home: an exactly similar young woman in a sledge pushed by a gentleman . . . Her hat and cloak were of ermine and she kept her hands warm in a muff while the sledge glided over the ice . . .

Cameras clicked. The young woman was trying to make her way through the undergrowth, repeating with a forced smile: 'I swear that . . .'

'This way, Madame . . . I'm sorry to have to insist . . . Unfortunately it's essential.'

She drew near to the dreadful tarpaulin. Only the photographers remained unmoved and bombarded her relentlessly.

Now the Deputy Public Prosecutor, who had never been personally involved in such a situation before, was saying unctuously:

'You must be brave . . . That's life . . .'

'You mean that's death!' the Little Doctor longed to correct him.

'Take my arm . . . Don't be afraid of leaning on me if . . .'

The Superintendent bent down. The tarpaulin was lifted. Nothing more was heard, no more noise than when a small bird opens its beak in a final attempt to breathe. She had fainted. The Deputy Public Prosecutor was unable to hold her up unaided, and the Little Doctor came to the rescue, pulling a phial from his pocket.

'Leave it to me . . . It's my job . . . Lay her down on the grass.'

While he tried to revive her, his mind was detached enough to wonder, 'What can a woman like that call her husband in private, when his name is Isidore and he's six foot tall and weighs over a hundred kilos?' For downright comical ideas occur to us sometimes in the most dramatic situations.

Moreover, he got the answer almost immediately: 'Isi . . .' she murmured.

Then, reacting violently again: 'It's not true, is it? He should have been at Montauban . . . I want to see him once again to make sure . . .'

They almost had to carry her up to the body, and this time, although she did not faint, she burst into tears.

What happened next? As usual, there was a certain confusion. Ceremonies of this sort cannot be organized without making considerable allowance for chance, if not for emotion.

At all events the Little Doctor, who stuck close by his patient – for by now he considered her his patient – found himself in a strange car in the company of the Chief Superintendent.

'To Madame Borchain's, Avenue de la République.'

Others cars followed. It was almost a procession. And in a small hamlet straggling along the roadside they passed a garage on which Dollent read without surprise the name:

JÉRÔME ESPARDON
Motor mechanic

The said Jérôme was standing in his doorway, staring with some stupefaction at the fleet of cars which, but for him . . .

'Will you come in for a moment?' she asked, her hands shaking, her lips dry and bloodless.

'If I may,' the Superintendent replied.

As for the Little Doctor, he went in without being invited. The Borchains' home was a pretty eighteenth-century house which had been completely modernized, to an extent unusual in a small provincial town; it combined up-to-date comfort with sound taste. A manservant in a white coat had opened the door, and showed the visitors into the large ground-floor drawing-room, panelled in pale wood with a touch of gilding.

'I can't help it, gentlemen, I can't believe it yet . . . It's so unexpected, so remote from everything that . . . that . . . Joseph! Bring me something to drink . . . Serve these gentlemen . . . I apologize, *messieurs,* but I'm so upset . . . I'd better ask my sister to look after you . . . Joseph!'

She was speaking volubly, as though to distract herself, and her gaze flitted about restlessly.

'Ask Mademoiselle Nicole to come down . . . Don't tell her . . .'

'Mademoiselle Nicole knows, madame.'

'How? Who told her?'

'She came downstairs just as the newspaper had been put through the letter-box . . . She glanced at it . . .'

'What did she do then?'

'She went up into her bedroom and locked the door.'

'Tell her . . . Ask her . . . Do you mind, gentlemen, if I go and take off my hat and coat?'

'Ouch!' thought the Little Doctor. He was going to be left alone with the Superintendent, who would perhaps ask him questions and find out that he had absolutely no business to be there.

On the contrary, the Superintendent asked him: 'What's your opinion?'

'About what?'

'About that woman.'

'My opinion . . . h'm!'

'Do you think she could have killed her husband?'

Dollent dared not reply. He did not want to compromise himself. None the less the question had startled him.

'I'm not impressed by her fainting-fit,' the policeman went on. 'That was too obvious! On the other hand, I noticed . . .'

The Little Doctor never discovered what he had noticed, for the door now opened and the young woman came in, dressed in black – and her splendid dark hair made a striking contrast with her pale skin.

'Come in,' she said to someone behind her. 'These gentlemen are here to . . .'

It was her sister Nicole, who now came in after her and who was also dressed all in black. She was what they call a Titian blonde, with hair of a reddish gold. She was taller and slenderer than her sister, with sharper features, a piercing gaze and something tense about her whole appearance, joined to the wariness of a wild animal.

'Come in, Nicole . . . I told them that at this moment Isi should have been at Montauban, shouldn't he?'

'I think so too . . .'

'That was what he told us when he left . . .'

Joseph brought in drinks. The Superintendent was clearly less at ease in this drawing-room than in his own office, with its reek of tobacco-smoke.

'Pardon me, ladies. You spoke of Monsieur Borchain's departure. Would you tell me when he left?'

'Let me see . . . Joseph, wait a minute . . . You might be able to help us.'

Madame Borchain sniffed, dabbing her eyes and nose with her handkerchief of fine lawn.

'He had just got back from the dental congress at Casablanca . . . His profession took him abroad a good deal . . . That day he got back about . . . when was it, Joseph? We weren't expecting him . . . Instead of crossing by boat as usual he took the plane . . . It was about three o'clock . . .'

'Ten minutes past three, Madame . . . I opened the door to Monsieur myself . . . I'd thought it might be the postman with the registered letters, for he usually calls at that time . . .'

'And he left again?'

'The same evening, about . . . Let's see . . . We had dinner together, the three of us . . . Or rather, no, . . . Nicole didn't come down because she had a headache . . . I must explain that Nicole has been living with us since our parents' death five years ago . . . She has her own flat on the second floor. She's young, she's only twenty-three . . . Heavens, how hard it is to remember things . . . We had dinner in the next room. Then my husband went upstairs with me, and I went to bed . . . He left again almost immediately . . .'

'In his car?'

'He always took the car when he travelled in France.'

'And where was it kept?'

'Behind the house. We have a private garage; you get to it through the Rue des Minimes . . . That's right, isn't it, Nicole? I wonder, my memory is so confused, whether he went up to say goodbye to you . . .'

'He came up to kiss me goodbye, Marthe. He was in a hurry . . . He wanted to be in Marseilles by next morning and from there, to start his visits round the southern region . . .'

Marthe Borchain gave a weak smile. 'That's all I know, gentlemen.'

'Had he any enemies that you know of?'

'Why should he have had enemies? Rivals maybe, because he had done very well for himself; but not enemies . . .'

'Forgive me for asking you an extremely tactless question. Do you know if he had another woman in his life?'

'What, Isi?' came Marthe Borchain's heartfelt reply. With a sad smile, she added: 'He adored me . . . He lived only for me . . . He was longing to have finished with all the travelling that kept him away from home . . .'

'I must trouble you further. Can you tell me precisely the date on which he came back from Casablanca and went off again?'

She obviously did not know. She glanced at her sister and then at Joseph.

'It was on October the first, Madame. I remember because I was paid my wages that day and so was Cook, and we went together in the morning to pay the money into the Savings Bank.'

'And you never saw your husband's car again?'

'Never! Since he went off in it . . .'

She bit her lip, remembering what she had seen in the marshes of Bois-Bezard.

'I mean I thought . . .'

'I've understood . . . Was it a large car?'

'A powerful American car, very comfortable . . . My husband was a stout man and he liked his comfort; moreover he was full-blooded and . . .'

'May I ask you, Mademoiselle, if you have any information which might put us on the right track?'

The girl, who had not sat down but was leaning against the tall mantelpiece of white marble, replied curtly: 'None.'

'Did your brother-in-law seem particularly preoccupied that evening?'

'Not more than usual . . .'

The Little Doctor wriggled his legs under his gilded chair.

'He said nothing which might suggest that he was leaving reluctantly?'

'He always left reluctantly!'

And the girl stared resentfully at her sister.

'You mean that he disliked having to . . .'

'My brother-in-law was terribly jealous . . .'

'Nicole!' sighed Madame Borchain.

'Isn't it true that Isi was jealous?'

'Yes, it's true . . . Like all men! Like all men who have to be away from home a great deal . . . Nicole, you know that . . .'

'That was just what I said!' the girl retorted coldly.

The Superintendent did not know what else to ask. He got up, hesitating.

'I think, ladies, that at the present stage of our investigation . . . Excuse me, one word more . . . This is the revolver which . . .'

Once again it was Nicole who replied, with the decisiveness which was obviously part of her character.

'It's his.'

'You recognize it?'

'He always carried it with him. Like most people who travel a good deal . . . Once he was nearly attacked on the road, and ever since then . . .'

'You recognize it too, Madame Borchain?'

'I believe so . . . I think I've seen him with it . . . He knew that I'm afraid of firearms . . . He never used to show it me . . .'

'I shall probably have to question you again. You must forgive me if . . . Coming, doctor?'

They were back on the pavement together. The Superintendent growled: 'H'm, it's a queer story . . . Well, we shall see . . . As for you, doctor, I shall expect your report tomorrow morning and . . .'

'Excuse me, what report?'

'Aren't you the pathologist? Didn't you come with the D.P.P.?'

'I'm a doctor, indeed, but not a pathologist . . .'

'Why then, what? . . .'

'Nothing to say!' sighed the Little Doctor, who expected an outburst. 'The pathologist, as far as I understood, was the man with the beard who went off in the car with the journalists . . .'

To which the Chief Superintendent replied only with a curt:

'Good evening, Monsieur!'

'Good evening, Monsieur!' echoed Dollent.

He had been prepared for something worse! Now he was all alone in the streets of Nevers, and remembering his housekeeper's doubts of his efficiency, he made up his mind:

'Anna, my girl, I swear that you won't see me again until I've solved the puzzle of Isidore Borchain. And my word, if any women are rash enough to have their babies in the meantime . . .'

He turned about and, crossing to the opposite pavement, stared up at the Borchain residence like a sightseer gazing at a cathedral.

II. In Which Two Gendarmes Guard the 'Corpus Delicti' after their Own Fashion, while the Little Doctor goes in search of Fancy Stationery

'Doesn't it remind you of something?'

'Well, of quite a lot . . . The sky that's about as cheerful as a funeral announcement, the trees, the wind . . .'

'It reminds me of when I was little and we all went to the cemetery for All Saints' Day . . .'

'All Saints' Day is the day after tomorrow,' the first *gendarme* growled gloomily.

For this conversation was taking place between two *gendarmes* sitting on a heap of stones among the marshes of Bois-Bezard.

'Actually, what are we doing here? There's nothing more to keep an eye on, since they've taken the stiff away . . .'

'We're guarding the scene of the crime, I suppose,' the other *gendarme* said philosophically.

The truth was that they were guarding nothing at all, and if they were still there at 6.0 p.m. on a cold autumn evening, it was because the investigators had forgotten all about them.

'Talking of stiffs, I'm glad they've taken it away.'

'Were you scared?'

'Not scared, but he stank . . .'

And the gendarme with the sensitive nose began rolling himself a cigarette, sniffed his fingers, and frowned.

'The funny thing is that I've still got that damn smell in my nose . . . Can't you smell anything yourself?'

'I've got a cold . . .'

'I don't want to start fancying things, but I could swear that even my fag . . .'

Suddenly his eyes widened. He started up, stammering in a toneless voice: 'Ernest!'

'What?'

'Look . . . Beside your foot . . .'

Ernest leapt up too, and started back.

'Another stiff!'

Two fingers, at any rate, were protruding from between the stones.

'Shall we have a look at him?'

'I guess we'd do better to inform them at headquarters . . . You stay here, I'll go and phone them.'

'Why don't we both go? . . . He's not going to run away, after all!'

Consequently, at eight o'clock that evening, in the presence of the captain of the *gendarmerie*, a second corpse was extracted from the heap of stones: that of a man of about thirty, dressed in a sports jacket and trousers.

It was less than fifty metres from the place where Isidore Borchain's body had been found. But whereas Borchain's had been flung carelessly into the rushes, that of the unknown man had been deliberately covered with loose stones.

Night had fallen, and the *gendarme* who did not care for stiffs whispered to his mate:

'Let's hope they don't make us stop with him all night . . . Not to mention we're likely to get a wetting . . .'

The Little Doctor could not be simultaneously at Nevers and at Bois-Bezard, so he knew nothing as yet of this fresh discovery.

He was conducting his inquiry in his own way, independently of the authorities, and he was all the more pleased with himself in that this had obliged him to drink a couple more pernods. In order to telephone, obviously, he had had to go into a café. And in a café one's obliged to drink. Furthermore, he was kept waiting quite a while for his call to Montauban.

He had consulted the telephone directory and picked out the leading dentist in the town. At last he had him on the line.

'Hello! Monsieur Geroul? . . . I apologize for bothering you . . . I wanted to ask you whether you've recently had a visit from Monsieur Borchain, Isidore Borchain, the traveller for . . .'

'I know him, of course! I've been expecting him for the past three weeks, for this is the season when he usually visits our part of the world. Have you news of him?'

'What do you mean?'

'I mean I'm anxious to see him. I'm out of certain products. When he failed to turn up I wrote to him twice at Nevers, and I've had no reply . . .'

'Hello! . . . Hold on, please . . . You did write to him at his home in Nevers, Avenue de la République, didn't you?'

'Yes, as usual . . .'

'During the past three weeks?'

'My last letter was sent last Saturday.'

'You use headed notepaper?'

'With my name and address . . .'

'Many thanks!'

And he rewarded himself by ordering a second pernod as he left the telephone box. Then, in high spirits, a mischievous gleam in his eyes, he set off down the streets of Nevers, studying shop windows.

The display in a first stationer's shop caught his attention, but after contemplating the coloured inks, rulers and compasses laid out in the window he shrugged his shoulders and went further on.

He left the town centre and came to an outlying district where, at last, he felt he had found what he wanted: a narrow shop, part haberdasher's and part stationer's, cluttered with newspapers and novelettes, knitting patterns and sentimental picture postcards.

'I'd like some fancy writing-paper, please, Madame . . . The nicest you've got. Coloured paper if possible, pink for instance . . .'

His luck was in. The lady showed him a packet of six sheets and six envelopes, each of a different colour, from the finest pink to the finest green, and moiré into the bargain.

'This is our nicest line,' she declared with the utmost seriousness. 'It looks very tasteful . . .'

He bought the packet and fifty five-centime stamps.

'You insist on having five-centime stamps?'

'Absolutely!'

And then he had his third apéritif. Where could one write in a strange town, except in a café? The waiter watched him with some surprise, from a distance. On an envelope of a sugary pink he wrote in violet ink the following address:

Mademoiselle Nicole
c/o M. Isidore Borchain
25 Avenue de la République, Nevers

Into this envelope he simply slipped a sheet of blank paper. On the other hand, instead of one ninety-centime stamp, he surrounded the envelope with eighteen five-centime stamps, which gave the letter a most peculiar look.

Then came the turn of the green envelope, similarly framed with stamps but addressed, in this case, to Marthe Borchain.

'We shall see what comes of it!'

He had by no means finished his day's work, and his brain was as active as his wiry little legs. And whereas the Superintendent had already been informed by telephone of the latest discovery in the Bois-Bezard, Dollent was following out his own idea and had one last task to perform before nightfall.

It was close to the bridge, on the Moulins road, that he accosted a policeman.

'Excuse me, officer, can you tell me if there's a water-bailiff at Nevers?'

'A water-bailiff? You want to know if there's a water-bailiff? Let's see, young man . . . You'll find him somewhere near the lock. It's nothing to do with the municipal authorities.'

So it turned out; he found the water-bailiff's cottage close to a lock, and a tall strapping fellow in a uniform cap who was busy milking a goat.

'My good man, can you tell me what the river was like on October 1st?'

'What the river was like?'

'Yes . . . was the water high or low?'

'Low, of course, because it hadn't rained since summer . . . So low that in some parts the kids caught fish with their hands . . .'

'All the same – I'm sorry if my question sounds ridiculous, I must admit I don't know the first thing about hydrography – Are there any holes in the river-bed on its way through Nevers? . . . you've probably got another name for them . . . places where the water is deeper?'

'Sure! Near the third pier of the bridge there's a hole at least eight metres deep . . .'

'Third pier of the bridge? No, that won't do . . . I need another hole, near the bank . . .'

The water-bailiff was staring at him, round-eyed, wondering what this fellow was thinking of doing with a hole of that sort.

'How deep has your hole got to be?'

'How far can you see down into the water?'

'Depends on whether it's clear or muddy . . . Just now, you can see the stones or the sand to a depth of one metre, in spite of its having rained . . .'

'Let me work it out . . . Three . . . Three and two . . . Right! Is there anywhere along the bank, at a point accessible by car, a hole of at least five metres?'

The man reflected, shook his head, spat, grew suspicious.

'Depends what you want to do with it.'

'I don't want to do anything with it . . . I'm looking for a car.'

'A car? Then there's only one hole big enough and deep enough . . . It's at Tanners' Wharf, just next to a big pile of bricks . . .'

'If I were to make it worth your while, would you come along there with me? Bring a pole and a boat-hook . . . Perhaps a grapnel too?'

A heavy shower soaked them while the water-bailiff was unenthusiastically probing the bottom of the hole with his grapnel. The rain did not bother him, since he wore an oilskin jacket, but the Little Doctor had not brought a change of clothes.

'Well?'

'I couldn't swear to its being a car, because I can't see it. But there's something there other than the bottom of the hole . . .'

'Could you try and feel the shape of it with the pole?'

The man did so, and it became practically certain that a car was lying in the depths of the water.

'How did you guess?' asked the water-bailiff in astonishment, somewhat suspicious of this peculiar little fellow.

'I didn't guess! *I worked it out!*'

It was quite simple. Since Isidore Borchain had not gone off in his own car . . . Since it was he who had been driving the car borrowed from the Place Gambetta . . .

You've got to put yourself in the other man's shoes! Borchain was going somewhere for a special purpose and he did not want to go in his own car. He intended to return, obviously! For he was hardly likely to have gone to Bois-Bezard in order to commit suicide . . .

But he had not come back. On the other hand, *the Humberts' car had been put back in its place!*

So why had Isidore Borchain's car not been found anywhere in the neighbourhood?

And what's the quickest way to get rid of an unwanted car, in a town through which a river runs?

The secretary at the police station looked at him askance. Perhaps the Superintendent had mentioned his encounter with the Little Doctor.

'I must speak to your chief immediately. I've made an important discovery.'

'Unfortunately the Chief isn't here. And if you mean the second corpse, you're too late!'

Jean Dollent frowned.

'The second corpse?'

'Forget what I've said . . . If you want to see the Chief you must come back tomorrow . . . We'll find out then whether he wants to see you.'

A second corpse . . . a second corpse . . . a second . . .

Two minutes later, the Little Doctor was at the wheel of his car, back on the road to Bois-Bezard. He was annoyed. Of course he'd done pretty well to discover Isidore Borchain's car, but now that seemed relatively unimportant.

Why had he not followed his earlier hunch? For – nobody would believe him now! – he had almost exclaimed, that afternoon, while they were all floundering about in the little wood:

'Now we've got to find the other man!'

It was not merely a hunch. It was the next step in an argument which, though perhaps not very close, was none the less coherent.

If a second body had been found, it was bound to be in the neighbourhood of the first.

The garage-owner Espardon had declared: 'Two men and a woman . . .'

The first man, the heavy-weight, was Isidore Borchain. Right: well, he'd been dealt with.

The woman . . . They'd know about that next day, at least if the envelope trick worked . . .

'It must be the other man they've found!' he decided with an appreciative little whistle.

Dark forms were visible in the wood. Night had fallen. The little

rings of pale light cast by electric torches were flitting to and fro, and voices could be heard calling one another.
The Little Doctor passed close by a policeman who did not recognize him in the darkness. He almost collided with the Deputy Public Prosecutor, who was already on the scene.
'You here!' an angry voice began. 'Really, I must ask you . . . if need be I must order you . . .'
It was the voice of the Chief Superintendent, who next turned to address the Deputy Public Prosecutor.
'*Monsieur le procureur,* this man, who claims to be a doctor and whom I don't know from Adam, had the cheek this afternoon to pass himself off as the forensic pathologist . . .'
'Excuse me! You took me for the pathologist, but since you hadn't asked me who I was I didn't feel bound to tell you. And now I've come here on purpose with Tin Lizzie . . .'
'Who's Tin Lizzie?'
'That's a pet name I give my car. I took the trouble to come here with Tin Lizzie to give you news of the missing motor-car.'
He wasn't always in such a joking mood, but then he'd already drunk four apéritifs!
'What missing motor-car?'
'Isidore Borchain's.'
'You've found it?' asked the astonished Prosecutor.
'An hour ago . . . It's at the bottom of the Loire, in a hole by Tanners' Wharf.'
'Have you seen it?'
'I couldn't have seen it, for it's six metres deep under the water . . .'
'Then however. . . ?'
Moments like this made up for all his tribulations.
'Just an idea . . . I said to myself . . . By the way, what's the name of this second body?'

There had been no difficulty about identifying it. In the dead man's pockets had been found a wallet containing identity papers in the name of René Juillet, a business man from Roubaix.
The Superintendent no longer dared to try and get rid of the Little Doctor, whose achievement aroused the admiration of the Deputy Public Prosecutor. In fact, the magistrate had been heard to say:
'If he's not a practical joker, he's a remarkable fellow! Let's see what he's capable of . . .'
This was why, at ten o'clock that evening, Dollent was at the police station, where the investigation was being carried on despite the lateness of the hour.
The first words spoken over the telephone brought a gasp of

amazement from the Roubaix police.

'You said Juillet? . . . You've found René Juillet?'

Information about him they had in plenty, but none of it was of much interest.

Juillet senior owned a small spinning mill. His son René, aged thirty, unmarried, worked there with him. The son was chiefly concerned with the business side, and travelled a great deal. He had a season ticket for railway journeys all over France.

Having had no news of him for over three weeks, Juillet senior had informed the police, but their search had been fruitless.

'Was he known to have a liaison?'

'No, none . . .'

'Could his business have taken him to Nevers?'

'It's hardly likely . . .'

'Where had he last been seen?'

'He left Roubaix on September 29th to go first to Paris, then to Eastern France, where he was only going to stay three or four days. It was when he failed to return, and when his connections at Colmar and Mulhouse reported that he had not been to either place, that his father informed the police . . .'

'What do you think about it, Superintendent?' The Little Doctor assumed a deeply respectful tone which was not without a touch of irony.

'I think,' retorted the police officer curtly, 'that we shall soon know the answer to this puzzle.'

'So do I!'

The way he said this brought a suspicious glance from the Superintendent, who was convinced that he was hiding something.

'Could you tell me how it happens that you, a doctor practising at Marsilly, so you tell us, are here at Nevers, far from your patients, who must be in need of your expert care?'

'I came on purpose for this case . . .'

'So you knew about it?'

'Only through the newspapers, like everyone else.'

'And your curiosity was so great that you dropped everything in order to . . .'

The Little Doctor could not restrain a smile, for he felt that he was becoming suspect, and he could see himself being arrested by the Superintendent.

'. . . to solve the problem, yes, *monsieur le commissaire*. It's become a fad of mine these last few months. Other people play chess or collect stamps . . . But I don't want to detain you any longer . . . Goodnight, Superintendent . . . By the way . . .'

He had reached the door and was holding it ajar. He pretended to have forgotten something.

'One further question . . . If tomorrow morning, say about nine o'clock, I should have discovered the murderer of Isidore Borchain, should I inform you or go straight to the D.P.P.?'

'I shall be in my office all morning. But I very much doubt whether . . . H'm! . . . In any case, if you find the murderer of Isidore Borchain and René Juillet . . .'

'I shan't find René Juillet's murderer . . .'

'Why?'

'Because!'

Undoubtedly, if this went on, he'd have all the police Superintendents of the country against him.

'It's true,' he admitted frankly to himself, as he fell asleep in a little room in the Hôtel de la Paix, 'that if amateurs took it into their heads to interfere with my patients . . .'

III. In Which the Pink Letter and the Green Letter Play their Part, and the Little Doctor Draws Certain Conclusions while the Superintendent Glares at Him Fiercely

Six a.m. It's the early bird, so they say, that gets the worm. The Little Doctor shaved in front of a bad mirror, went downstairs, found nobody but a night porter who offered him some nasty warmed-up coffee; he drank a glass of calvados instead to set himself up.

The sky was brighter. All the clouds from the west had drifted eastward, leaving only a pale blue background behind the rooftops.

On Tanners' Wharf there was an unaccustomed din: iron clanking, an engine puffing, shouts, the blowing of whistles, enough to make any residents in the wharf who were still asleep jump out of their beds in a fright.

The Deputy Public Prosecutor and the Superintendent had lost no time. They seemed as eager as the Little Doctor to beat the record. There was a crane working, a flat-bottomed boat from the civil engineer's department and another with a diver's pump.

And the brass helmet of a diver had already emerged, while cameras clicked all round.

The Little Doctor had thought he was early, and he was almost late, since the authorities and the Press were there already.

For now René Juillet had come into the picture, a man of considerable wealth and political importance in northern France, and the Parisian papers had taken the matter up. They headlined: '*Mysterious*

Happenings at Nevers', as they used to headline sensations in Chicago. Orders had therefore been given to clear up the case as fast as possible.

The diver had fastened chains to the submerged car. The crane got going, and one chain broke and had to be replaced. The Little Doctor was surrounded by journalists, his first contact with the Press in his role as detective.

'It seems it was you who discovered . . .'

He feigned modesty, but actually he was very pleased. They took him along to a nearby bistrot so that he should tell them how he had worked things out.

Calvados again; was it his fault if the coffee was so bad? He knew it was a mistake, that it was rather early to begin drinking, but they encouraged him and made much of him.

'So really your methods are scientific?'

'Oh, not quite . . . I start from a given point, I say to myself . . . Goodness, it's difficult to explain!'

'Keep still . . . Thank you!'

Now he'd been photographed, as though he were a murderer or a film star.

'What's your idea about this case?'

'I'll tell you everything between nine and ten o'clock . . . I've promised the Chief Superintendent.'

'You claim that within three hours from now you'll have solved the mystery?'

He lowered his eyes with mock modesty. After all, these people were pressing him; he'd have been very happy to go on working alone in his own way, but they persisted in making him talk.

'In short, there were three people in the car, two men and a woman, and you started from there to . . .'

'Precisely! Put yourself in the place of . . .'

'Of the two men, no, thanks!'

'Of the woman, I was going to say . . . Excuse me, one question: at what time is the first postal delivery in Nevers?'

'Half past eight.'

'Many thanks . . .'

So he would know the answer by nine o'clock. Meanwhile, the car, full of mud, had at last been hoisted up on the jib of the crane. The number-plate had been checked; it was, as foreseen, Isidore Borchain's big American car, and as soon as it landed on the quayside a mechanic, fetched by the police Superintendent, climbed hurriedly into the dripping vehicle.

'Just as you thought, Superintendent . . . The engine had been started – the contact hasn't been switched off. The clutch pedal was kept down from outside by means of some object or other. Then the car was given a push and it started off and tumbled into the river . . .'

'Excuse me, Superintendent . . .'

'So you're here again, are you?'

It was the Little Doctor.

'I would like to ask you to accompany me at nine o'clock on a rather tricky mission . . . Perhaps the Deputy Public Prosecutor will be kind enough to come too?'

The other two exchanged glances. Obviously the magistrate was more tempted than the professional policeman.

'Should we have to go far?'

'Oh no . . . Avenue de la République . . . I fancy there'll be no further mystery after that . . .'

As they went on their way, followed by journalists and photographers, he could not resist saying: 'It's awful what a play-actor I'm becoming!' But perhaps it was really his line? On two occasions, in the Maison-Basse case and again at Royan, he had succeeded so brilliantly that he could no longer have any doubts as to his capability. And now again, with that car . . .

'What we are doing is not very regular, Monsieur Dollent,' sighed the Deputy Public Prosecutor. 'I hope you are not going too far, and that you won't involve the Law in anything that might make it appear ridiculous . . .'

He was frightened, so frightened that if he could he'd have gone into the nearest bistrot for a very strong drink to give himself Dutch courage.

'As soon as we're in that house, *monsieur le Procureur,* I shall tell you for certain whether we have succeeded or not.'

The Borchain residence . . . the steps up to the heavy front door, which was opened by the white-coated manservant . . .

Dollent glanced at his watch. It was nine o'clock exactly. The other two, the magistrate and the policeman, were looking at him.

'Tell me, my good man . . .'

He had adopted this expression since his conversation the previous night with the water-bailiff, but the butler did not seem to appreciate such familiarity.

'Who takes the mail out of the letter-box?'

'I do.'

'Have you already taken this morning's mail up to the ladies?'

'About ten minutes ago.'

'Good . . . Good . . . So it's always you who take up the letters?'

'That's to say I take them out of the box, I sort them and then hand them over to the ladies' maids . . .'

'I see the letter-box is locked. Has anyone a key besides yourself?'

'I believe Monsieur had one, but he never used it . . .'

'I suppose you would automatically glance at the envelopes . . . Note that I'm not accusing you of any improper curiosity . . . But when one sorts the mail it would be natural . . .'

'What do you mean?'

'This morning, for instance, did nothing strike you about the appearance of certain letters?'

The magistrate and the Superintendent were completely bewildered, and saw to their astonishment that the butler was himself staring wide-eyed at the doctor.

'How can you have known?'

'That doesn't matter! Tell us what struck you. Don't be afraid . . .'

'I was surprised to see an envelope of a funny green colour, with five-centime stamps stuck all round the edge . . . It was for Madame . . .'

'And that was all?'

'I can't think of anything else . . . Some advertisements, some bills . . .'

'You're quite sure that was all?'

'I give you my word, monsieur!'

'Can you take us into the drawing-room and ask Madame and Mademoiselle to come down for a moment?'

They kept their voices hushed as though in a vestry, and meanwhile they heard footsteps overhead. The magistrate urged:

'Before we go any farther, would you be kind enough to explain, doctor?'

'It's quite simple. Yesterday a dentist in Montauban told me categorically that he had twice written to Isidore Borchain to find out the reason for his silence, for he had been expecting Borchain since the beginning of the month . . . Now, nobody mentioned these letters to us . . . You'll admit that is rather odd, particularly as I inquired yesterday and was told that the mail was not forwarded, but that Madame Borchain usually dealt with it . . . If she read the two letters from the dentist she must have known that her husband . . .'

'Quite true!'

'Wait a minute! I sent to this house one letter on pink paper and one on green, and I chose these unusual colours to make sure they would not escape the notice of the person responsible for opening the letter-box each morning and distributing the mail . . . Suppose someone was in the habit of coming down to open the box before the manservant, and taking out some of the letters? *This person would inevitably have known that Borchain was not at Montauban . . .*'

The Superintendent was beginning to be irritated, particularly as the magistrate kept looking pointedly at him as if to say:

'He's a very bright fellow this! Did *you* think of that?'

Madame Borchain was the first to come down, wearing a negligée, pale and listless, and explaining apologetically:

'I didn't expect such an early visit, gentlemen . . . I didn't sleep at all last night . . . I was resting and . . .'

'It's we who must apologize to you, Madame, for our intrusion, but it was necessary for the sake of the inquiry and our concern to avenge your husband . . .'

Nicole came in next, more weary-eyed than her sister, with an anxious look and tight lips.

'What do they want with us now?' she asked. 'Are they going on tormenting us much longer?'

Then the Little Doctor, after seeking permission by a glance at his companions, launched his attack.

'Suppose that when Isidore Borchain came home unexpectedly – don't forget that he travelled by air instead of by boat as usual – suppose, I say, that Borchain found a man, a stranger, in the room of the woman he loved . . .

'You have only seen his dead body, but you can imagine the man as he was when alive: powerful, violent, full-blooded . . .'

'Oh, please!' sighed Madame Borchain imploringly.

'Forgive me, Madame, but I think it is necessary for me to go through with this . . . Borchain strangles his rival (for I understand, Superintendent, that marks of strangulation were found on the second body, that of René Juillet) . . . Furthermore, Borchain recognized the man, who had once been introduced to him at Roubaix as a friend – no more than a friend – of the woman he loved . . .

'I apologize once more, Madame, and I beg you to allow me to carry on to the end . . .

'When you married Borchain, your sister was no more than a little girl . . . She's grown up since then . . . And as she grew your husband's attitude towards her changed . . . When she came to live with you after your parents' death, the result was inevitable; she became your husband's mistress. *She* was the only important person in his life . . .'

Madame Borchain was staring at them wild-eyed, while Nicole's lips twitched in a sarcastic smile.

'To move on to the climax . . . Borchain comes home unexpectedly early from a journey; he finds a man, René Juillet, in his sister-in-law's room, realises that they have been lovers for a long time, ever since Roubaix, and he strangles him in a fury.

'That evening, when his wife has gone to bed, he forces Nicole to accompany him . . . He leaves his car on the square or in a nearby street. In order to avoid recognition he borrows the first car he sees, and packs the corpse into it beside his terrified sister-in-law.

'He had not foreseen one detail: the car he borrowed was almost empty of petrol . . . When he notices this he has just time to draw up in front of Espardon's garage.

'What are Nicole's reactions at this point? Knowing her brother-in-law's violent nature, she may be afraid of being killed herself. When the car starts off (possibly the jolt may have brought her into contact with the dead body) she cannot restrain a cry for help . . .

'And so we come to Bois-Bezard . . .

'René Juillet has been buried under a heap of stones. What kind of scene takes place next, between the two lovers? Nicole may have been threatened by her brother-in-law; at all events she manages to seize hold of his revolver, shoots him and leaves his body among the rushes by the pond.

'She has to take back the Humberts' car, to do away with Borchain's so that his absence will not be noticed too soon – the river is handy . . .

'After that, time passes. She only has to open the letter-box in the mornings and remove any mail that might reveal the fact that Borchain was not in the South of France as everyone imagined . . .

'And this morning, *to take out a pink envelope addressed to Mademoiselle Nicole,* so odd-looking as to be ominous . . .'

Nicole's lips still wore a sneering smile. Madame Borchain clasped her head in her hands and murmured brokenly:

'It's dreadful! It's dreadful! Who would have believed . . .'

The Deputy Public Prosecutor was ill at ease. Suddenly the Superintendent sprang to his feet; someone had rung the front door bell.

'Will you allow me?' he said. 'It must be for me . . . I am expecting an urgent message and I took the liberty . . .'

Seldom had any gathering of people in one room felt so uncomfortable. The Little Doctor himself, having finished his story, was anxiously examining the others in turn, wondering if he had perhaps overstepped the mark.

And yet he had followed his method. He had been consistently logical. He had put himself in the shoes of each individual concerned.

Why, then, was Nicole staring at him not with rage, but with withering irony?

'Gentlemen . . .'

The Superintendent was back, after spending a few brief moments in the entrance hall.

'*Monsieur le Procureur*, I am obliged to ask you for a warrant for the arrest of . . .'

A peculiar glance at the Little Doctor, who assumed that he had been wrong from beginning to end and wished the earth would swallow him.

'. . . of Madame Isidore Borchain, formerly Marthe Tillet, charged with murdering her husband with his own revolver in the marshes of Bois-Bezard . . .'

The young woman looked up in surprise. She tried to protest, 'But the doctor has just proved . . .'

'The doctor may be an excellent psychologist and an excellent logician, Madame . . .'

Dollent felt like bowing!

'. . . but he has not at his disposal the same resources as the police. This affair will show him that we are better equipped than he imagines. Yesterday evening, when I learned the identity of the second body, that of René Juillet, I immediately asked the Roubaix police to forward me by telephotography all the pictures of women to be found in the young man's room.

'Here they are; they've just come . . . You'll find there only your own likeness, sometimes with an inscription . . .

'You were Juillet's mistress . . . It was you who entertained him regularly during your husband's absence . . . And that is why poor Juillet never married . . . It was with you that Borchain surprised him . . . it was in your presence that he strangled him . . . It was you whom he forced to accompany him to Bois-Bezard to bury the corpse . . .

'It was you, Madame, who called for help at the filling-station, fearing an equally dramatic fate for yourself . . .

'Finally, it was you who fired on Borchain and who, on your return to Nevers, pushed his car into the Loire at a spot with which you were familiar . . .

'And it was you who got rid, every day, of such letters as provided official information of your husband's absence from the South of France . . .

'It was you who this morning found the pink envelope addressed to your sister, and who, to divert suspicion from yourself, removed that envelope . . .'

Somebody sprang up like a jack-in-the-box. It was the Little Doctor, crying out: 'Magnificent, Superintendent!'

The Superintendent, however, showed magnanimity: 'You made only one mistake, doctor, but you'll admit it was an important one. You believed that it was the person to whom the letter was addressed who had abstracted it. Now that person . . .'

The addressee in question, namely Nicole, now stood up and said with a sigh: 'That's enough! It's horrible, the way you flatter one another . . .'

'You knew all about it?'

'I suspected . . . Since yesterday I've been sure . . . But that's not a reason to embark on an academic argument.'

She was staring sternly at her sister. The Little Doctor noticed her look, and felt suddenly convinced that, in her heart of hearts, Nicole was jealous of Marthe Borchain, not on account of her husband but on account of René Juillet.

'It is my painful duty, Madame, to take you into custody and hand you over to the Department of Public Prosecution at Nevers . . .'

'Do you understand now, doctor?'

'What do you mean?'

They were lunching together in a small riverside restaurant, and the sky was now quite cloudless.

'You had ideas, undoubtedly . . . You discovered almost the whole truth by your own methods . . . But note that *almost*! We may not be as subtle as you are . . . We don't try to split hairs . . . On the other hand we have at our disposal an organization which . . . Thus, it never struck you that a young man who was so much in love that he came regularly to Nevers to see his mistress without telling a soul about it must have in his room some photograph of the woman . . . Even if you had thought of that, you could not, as a private individual, have obtained permission . . .'

Then the Little Doctor sought to redeem his petty sins of pride and admitted, as he savoured delectable fish *quenelles*, 'I never thought of it . . .'

All the same, he had discovered the whole truth – except that *it was the wrong sister*!

It would be a lesson for him in future.

For now he was well and truly bitten. And if Anna's stews were all too often spoiled, she would just have to put up with it . . .

The Haunting of Monsieur Marbe

I. In Which we Meet a Queer Old Fellow who Firmly Denies Believing in Ghosts, while the Little Doctor Comes Close to Considering Himself a Professional Detective

It happened sometimes, though all too seldom: a night free from calls, no urgent cases among his patients. So that at eight o'clock the Little Doctor was sitting up peacefully in his bed, his breakfast tray on his knees, and a few letters just brought by the postman lying within his reach.

It was too good to last. He had not even finished his coffee when the doorbell clanged – he had always intended to replace it by one less noisy, but he was forgetful – and muffled voices were heard in the passage, followed by the unwelcome sound of the waiting-room door opening and closing.

There could be no possible doubt: it was a patient! And a fairly urgent case, since Anna had not told him to come back for the nine o'clock surgery.

The Little Doctor hurriedly tore open the last of the envelopes lying on the blanket, and read its contents. Then Anna appeared.

'Who is it?'

'Old Canut . . .'

'Who's been drunk again and fallen off his bike?'

'His nose is all swollen . . .'

'Let him put iodine on it . . . I'm fed up with him, falling off his bike at least once a week and coming to bother me about his scratches . . . I say, Anna!'

'What?'

'What am I holding in my hand?'

'How do I know? A bit of paper . . .'

'Look closer . . .'

'*Pay Dr Jean Dollent* . . .' Anna spelt out laboriously.

'Haven't you seen yet that it's a cheque? Now read the sum: five thousand . . . five thousand francs, of course. And then, if you'd like to know what people think of certain talents of mine which you despise, read this letter while I take a quick shower . . .'

'But what about old Canut?'

'Let him stay where he is . . . When you've read the letter, you're to pack my case with my spare suit and enough underclothes for a few days.'

'And I'm to ring up Dr Magné and ask him to look after your patients . . . At this rate he'd better come and settle down here.'

'Read it, Anna!' he insisted, through the open door of the bathroom. And he began to sing while the water streamed over his naked body.

Monsieur,

Please forgive this letter from a total stranger. I must apologize for bothering you, particularly on a matter unconnected with your professional activities. But you will understand my boldness when you have read what follows.

I have lived for some years past at Golfe-Juan, between Cannes and Juan-les-Pins. Last week I had the pleasure of meeting a man I formerly knew as a colonial magistrate, Monsieur Verdelier, now Deputy Public Prosecutor at Nevers.

Since we had always been on friendly terms I spoke to him about my worries and the inadequate assistance I had received from the local police, and it was then that he mentioned your name.

According to his account, he watched you at work recently at Nevers, where you took part in a police investigation with astonishing results.

My friend the magistrate added, indeed, that you were not a professional detective, that you only took up a small number of cases for your own pleasure, and that you practised medicine regularly at Marsilly, near La Rochelle.

But I believe that my case will interest you, and that is why I venture to ask you to come here as soon as possible.

Don't think that I am out of my mind. It's true that the local people consider me an eccentric, but this is due, I fancy, to the fact that I have spent my life in remote parts of the world, which has inevitably affected my character.

For the past few weeks incredible things have been happening in the villa I have built myself here.

The police have been here, but they failed to make anything of it. I think they assume me to be mentally deranged.

This is not the case. My friend Verdelier, the Deputy Public Prosecutor, who is a calm and level-headed man, will bear me out if need be.

Twice a week my villa is visited by an unknown person, who turns the house topsy-turvy and of whom I have never succeeded in catching sight.

I have no idea what the cause of it can be. I don't believe in ghosts. And yet . . .

When you are on the spot, you will understand my anxiety better, and that is why I am taking the liberty of enclosing a modest cheque to cover your immediate expenses.

I am counting on you. I understand you have a passion for puzzles. Believe me, this is one of the most baffling you could hope to meet.

Send me a wire to say when you are arriving. I will be at the station. Fast trains

do not stop at Golfe-Juan, but I will pick you up at Cannes with my car.
Thanking you warmly in anticipation,
I am, yours very truly,
Evariste Marbe, former colonial administrator.

'Well, Anna?'

'Nothing, Monsieur . . .'

'When I went off to Nevers, you blamed me for wasting my time. It looks as if this time my gifts were being recognized!'

'If you're going to get letters from lunatics!' cut in Anna contemptuously. 'What am I to tell old Canut?'

'Tell him to put iodine on his nose and water in his wine!'

He considered deserting his little car, his old Tin Lizzie, but he discovered that there was no convenient train from La Rochelle to the Côte d'Azur and decided, after all, to go buzzing like a hornet along the main road.

Next day – it was a Saturday – after sleeping four or five hours at Marseilles he reached Cannes about ten in the morning, drove along beside the sea which was as calm and blue as a bowl of laundry detergent, and reached the tiny harbour of Golfe-Juan.

It was November. There was nobody about. The sun was still fairly warm.

'Where is Monsieur Marbe's villa, please?'

'Just next to the restaurant *La Rascasse*, at the end of a garden.'

But before the Little Doctor's car had reached the gate of the villa, a peculiar figure emerged from the bistrot-restaurant. It was that of a thin little old gentleman, whose thinness was enhanced by the loose pyjamas he was wearing. The jacket was open on a tanned chest abundantly covered with grey hair.

He wore slippers on his bare feet and a soiled and shapeless topee on his head.

'Pstt! Pstt!' he whistled after the car. And he began to run. 'Excuse me if I'm mistaken . . . Are you by any chance Dr Jean Dollent? My friend Verdelier told me you had a funny little car . . . I was just having my breakfast when . . .'

'Monsieur Marbe?' asked the Little Doctor, who did not appreciate such references to Tin Lizzie.

'That's me . . . I'm so glad you've come . . . But as you didn't telegraph you've caught me in a state of undress.'

He was fearfully nervous. While he spoke his features twitched constantly, he screwed up his eyes, his fingers shook . . .

'Usually when I get up I come to the *Rascasse* next door for a snack . . . Titin, the proprietor, is a friend of mine . . . What would you say to a few anchovies and a glass of Cassis wine? Then we'll go back to my place and I'll tell you about . . .'

Frankly, it must be admitted that the Little Doctor did not feel too confident. True, he had found out that he had a certain gift for nosing things out in criminal cases. On two occasions he had solved problems which had baffled the official police. And at Nevers, apart from one mistake, he had reconstructed a particularly complicated affair entirely off his own bat.

But this time he had actually received money. And as the cheque for five thousand francs was particularly welcome just now, he had no desire to return it.

What was he to do, though, if Anna had been right and this Monsieur Marbe was a lunatic, or at any rate a crank?

'Titin! Let me introduce an old friend of mine' (a wink to Dollent) 'an old friend whom I've met up with again and who's coming to spend a few days with me . . . For a chat, because we're good pals . . .'

Another wink which implied: 'You see! I'm respecting your incognito! There's no point in letting the whole neighbourhood know why you've come here . . .'

'Some anchovies, Titin! And some olives . . . And a bottle of Cassis, nice and cold . . .'

It seemed like an act of fate: every time the Little Doctor embarked on an investigation he was, for one reason or another, obliged to drink. And this time the wine in question seemed innocent enough while one was drinking it, but sent a glow to one's head a few minutes later.

'Come on . . . My sister's sure not to be up yet, but that doesn't matter. We'll have a chat while we're waiting for lunch . . . You mustn't mind my get-up . . . I've felt so hot all my life in various colonies that I'm only comfortable in pyjamas . . .'

The house was exactly like the man! An hour later, the Little Doctor had been all round it. It was the sort of villa of which there are plenty on the Riviera, containing samples of every conceivable style, including a sort of sketchy minaret and an inner court with a fountain, North African style.

Comfort was non-existent! There was a bathroom, but the bath was full of hat-boxes and objects of all sorts, while the geyser had obviously not functioned for a long time.

The dining-room was damp. The wallpaper was coming unstuck. The furniture was so heterogeneous that one felt one was entering an auction room rather than a private dwelling.

'One day,' old Marbe declared, 'I'm going to classify it all. Just think, there's a regular museum here! Things I've brought back from all over the place . . . I was at Madagascar first . . . You must have recognized weapons from that part of the world, in the lounge on the first floor . . . Then in Indo-China . . . Did you notice my engraved daggers? Some of them are very rare specimens . . . Bits from North Africa, like everyone else . . . And from the New Hebrides and Tahiti . . .'

After seeing all this bric-à-brac, through which one could hardly thread one's way, one could understand why he preferred to go to the bistrot next door for his meals.

'They're all souvenirs that I value . . . When I die I shall leave them to the colonial museum . . .'

In an attic, amidst various ethnic objects, the Little Doctor had noticed some children's toys.

'Have you been married?' he asked, lighting a cigarette to counteract the smell of all these musty things.

'Sh! . . . In Tahiti – to the daughter of a local chief . . . She died, and I brought my son back . . . He's a swimming instructor at Nice . . . I haven't yet told you about the real purpose of your visit . . . Come this way so that nobody should hear you, for I don't even trust Héloïse . . .'

'Héloïse?'

'My sister . . . She lives with me . . . She's a widow, with no children . . . While I was abroad, she married a station-master in central France. Now she lives here . . . She's a *very tired woman* . . . Now come into my study.'

The study was even more cluttered than the rest of the house.

'Just imagine, four years ago . . .'

It may have been because he was being paid for the first time that the Little Doctor decided to brazen it out and act like a real detective. With a self-possession that Cassis wine helped him to assume, he interrupted:

'Excuse me! If you don't mind, it's my turn to ask a few questions.'

He had never carried a notebook in his pocket, apart from his prescription pad. This he now produced, with the assurance of a veteran policeman.

'Let's see now, how long ago did you retire?'

'Six years . . . Let me explain . . .'

'Allow me! Later on you shall give me all the details you like. So you retired six years ago' (he wrote *six years* on the prescription pad) 'and you came to settle here immediately?'

'Excuse me, I didn't say that . . . When I left Tahiti six years ago I hadn't decided where to settle. I first went to live with my sister, who had a tiny house at Sancerre . . .'

'How long did you stay there?'

'Two years . . . I didn't know what climate would suit me best. I was unused to Europe . . .'

A note was inscribed on the prescription pad: *Sancerre, two years*.

'And then?'

'I bought this piece of land quite cheap . . .'

'For how much?'

'Twenty-two thousand francs . . . It was cheaper then than it would be now . . . It was quite a bargain.'

'And you built yourself a house?'

'A modest villa for my sister and myself.'

'Was your sister well-off?'

'She gets a pension of eighteen hundred francs a month.'

'And you yourself?'

'Three thousand five hundred . . . I was in the top grade of the administration . . . Now I'm coming to the facts . . .'

'Come on, then!'

'For the past three months . . .'

'But before that time?'

'Nothing . . . We lived here quietly, my sister and I . . . A woman comes in to clean every morning . . . We have most of our meals sent in from Titin's next door . . . I play *belote* with the local people . . . I go for walks . . .'

'And your sister?'

'She sleeps . . . She sews . . . She embroiders . . . She sits in the garden . . .'

'Right! Now, for the past three months . . .'

'*There have been footsteps in the house at night, twice a week!*'

'And you've never seen anyone?'

'I've tried to. I've got up and rushed out with a torch, but I've always been too late . . . If nobody else had heard those footsteps . . .'

'Your sister . . . remind me of her Christian name?'

'Héloïse . . . It's a bit old-fashioned, but . . .'

'Did she hear them?'

'Just as I did . . . Particularly in the attic . . . Besides, we generally find everything topsy-turvy afterwards, things put back in the wrong places . . .'

'Does nobody besides yourself and your sister live in the villa?'

'Absolutely nobody!'

'Are the doors shut every night?'

'Yes, and the shutters too . . . That's what I told my friend the Deputy Public Prosecutor . . . Listen, Dr Dollent . . . I'm not a credulous man, but I'm beginning to be terrified . . . I've lived in every quarter of the globe, and in each of them I've become familiar with the natives and with their beliefs . . . I've had to deal with cases of witchcraft in various places, including Gabon . . . So you see I'm not easily scared . . .

'A little glass of something? No, really? . . . I'll go on, then . . . I'm not easily scared . . . And I've always laughed at the English with their ghost stories . . .

'Yet there's one detail that I must confide to you, since you're here to discover the truth . . .'

'Don't be too sure, brother!' thought the Little Doctor.

'When I was in charge of a district in Tahiti, I had a wooden house built on a piece of land the natives considered sacred; in fact, you could still see there the stone that had been used for human sacrifices . . .

'I didn't take their superstitions seriously, any more than I did those of the negroes of Africa or the Solomon Islands.

'"You'll see," they told me, "the Tou-Papaou will have their revenge." Tou-Papaou is their name for their demons, doctor.'

'Did they bring you bad luck?' inquired the Little Doctor calmly.

'Not out there . . . But during these last three months . . . Don't laugh at me . . . I'm not making any assertion . . . I tell you again, I'm not credulous . . . I'm prepared to admit that the events which impelled me to send for you may have purely natural causes . . . Yet I can't help remembering those natives' threats when I hear those noises at night . . .

'Who could have anything to gain from prowling about in a house like this at three o'clock in the morning? Nothing has ever been taken, so it can't be a burglar! Nor can it have been a murderer, for he could easily have killed me or my sister . . . What could he have been doing, week after week, in the home of a poor old pensioner?'

'Excuse me!' Dollent interrupted. 'You mentioned the local police. Did they come?'

'For one week. Some men kept watch . . .'

'With what result?'

'None at all! The night visitor never came. So they took me for a madman . . . But I see my sister has come down and is waiting for us . . . She knows why you're here . . . Try not to alarm her, though . . . She's convinced it's the Tou-Papaou who are haunting me and . . .'

A woman in her early fifties, stout and placid, over-placid, as though drowsy from the warm Provençal sun.

'I'm sorry to have been such a bad hostess, doctor, but it's so hot in this part of the world! You'll take a little drink, won't you? . . . Yes, do! I've taken them out on to the terrace, in the shade of the fig tree.'

He realised why she was so sluggish; she set back her apéritif like a hardened drinker and poured herself another as she served the two men.

'Yes, do! It never did anyone any harm . . . So long as you haven't any work to do . . .'

The Little Doctor's thoughts had made him tense and edgy, and he had to fight against the drowsiness induced by the southern sunshine.

'About your son, Monsieur Marbe . . . Do you see much of him?'

'He comes from time to time, when he needs money . . . You mustn't get any wrong ideas about him . . . The people of Tahiti are much like ourselves . . . His mother's skin was as light as my sister's . . . As for him, you can't distinguish him from other inhabitants of the Riviera, except that he's better-looking.'

'While you were at Sancerre at your sister's . . .'

'He was at school at Cannes.'

'One more question . . . Does the ghost, if I may call him so, come on any special days?'

'Well . . . At first I didn't notice . . . You know, when one's retired one lives without bothering about dates or the days of the week. However, I eventually noticed that his visits occurred on Wednesdays and Saturdays . . .'

'Always?'

'I believe so . . . Isn't that right, Héloïse?'

'I believe so too . . . I wonder if ghosts are aware of dates?'

'What day is it today?'

'Saturday . . .'

'So there's some likelihood of his turning up tonight? I hope, Monsieur Marbe, that you've not mentioned my visit to anyone?'

'Not a soul!'

'Not even to your son?'

'It's ten or twelve days since I saw him! You heard what I told Titin . . . I made out that you were an old pal . . . You must forgive me . . . But I can't help thinking that if the ghost, as you call him, didn't come when the police were here, he must have been given some sort of warning . . . Provençal policemen are particularly prone to gossip.'

Thereupon Monsieur Marbe broke off to say: 'What about going to Titin's for a nice bouillabaisse?'

'I wouldn't say no . . .'

'Are you armed?'

'To go to Titin's?' the Little Doctor queried ingenuously.

'No! For tonight . . . For I presume we're going to keep watch tonight so as to catch my . . . our . . . well, whoever it is that . . .'

'You swear you've never had anything stolen?'

'On my honour!'

'You'd have noticed, in spite of the confusion in your house?'

'I'd have noticed if a single native arrow-head was stolen. You speak of confusion, but you don't realise that it is only apparent, that I know where to find every single object.'

'You've never had any threatening letters?'

'Never . . .'

Had there been a slight hesitation? The Little Doctor could not have sworn to it.

'In a word, to sum up all you have told me, you and your sister Héloïse were living happily here . . . You'd been in this villa for four years . . . You had no enemies . . . You played *belote* . . . Your son, who was born in Tahiti, gave swimming lessons at Nice . . .'

'Only since last year!' interrupted Monsieur Marbe.

'All right . . . And for the past three months, an unknown individual or some evil spirits come twice a week to disturb your house at night . . .'

'That's absolutely correct.'

'This individual – let's assume it's some individual – has never taken anything away. And he has never made any attempt on your life or your sister's . . . Have you any idea how he gets in?'

'Through the door!'

'What?'

'Yes, through the door . . . That's the only possible way . . . Either he's got a key or he's capable of getting through the walls . . . In any case, for the past three months we've been sleeping with the windows shut . . .'

'Suppose we went to eat our bouillabaisse?' sighed the Little Doctor. Why had he got himself mixed up in all this? Just to impress Anna? And what if his Monsieur Marbe was really crazy? And what if . . .

A suspicion struck him. Might not the Deputy Public Prosecutor of Nevers, resentful of his interference there, have given his name to Monsieur Marbe purely so that he should make a fool of himself?

And yet there were a few factors, not many but significant none the less, which Jean Dollent filed mentally while their bouillabaisse was being served on the terrace of *La Rascasse*.

Monsieur Marbe retired six years ago.

He lived for two years with his sister.

He had bought land and had a villa built on it . . .

'I say!' Dollent suddenly addressed Titin, who was serving them himself. 'What's the value of a villa like that?'

And Titin replied without hesitation: 'Four hundred and fifty thousand . . . Isn't that so, Monsieur Marbe? . . . If he'd listened to me he'd have paid thirty thousand less . . . But what's done is done . . . A little more broth, *monsieur le docteur?* A piece of *rascasse?* A potato? Oh, you should; it's the potato that absorbs all the flavour of the saffron . . . What will you take after this, Monsieur Marbe? Some nice grilled sea-perch with fennel?'

The Little Doctor, having already deposited his five-thousand-franc cheque at the bank on his way, was really worried. And meanwhile the sun was shining, and his glass was being constantly refilled with wine, and the savoury bouillabaisse made him so thirsty!

II. In Which we Learn of a Cellar Used as a Shooting Gallery, and Young Marbe, the Boy from Tahiti, Displays an Unexpected Fondness for Children

'Now what about a little siesta, doctor? In the Midi it's almost an official institution, particularly after Titin's bouillabaisse and the old armagnac he's going to give us. You probably spent part of last night travelling? And tonight' (a wink) 'I don't suppose' (another wink) 'that you'll feel like sleeping a great deal . . . Will you go and get a room ready, Héloïse?'

'I've already done so!' replied his sister, who was not at all anxious to miss the armagnac.

And the Little Doctor, drowsy though he was, sensed that Monsieur Marbe was annoyed. Perhaps he wanted to talk about his sister in her absence?

Ten minutes later, Jean Dollent was in possession of a room where a clutter of objects had presumably been removed from the bed and stacked in corners. The Venetian blinds outside were drawn against the full sunlight, but between the slats the Little Doctor could see his host settling down in the garden for his own siesta, under the big fig tree.

Monsieur Marbe was now wearing a suit of white tussore, fastened up to the neck with a single row of buttons, presumably an old uniform from his days in the colonial service. He unbuttoned it, covered his topee with a handkerchief and lay down in his deck-chair, while flies began circling round his head.

Dollent had barely had time to remove his jacket and shoes when there was a knock at the door and Héloïse came in, holding a finger to her lips.

'Hush! He's asleep . . . I wanted to talk to you for a few minutes without him . . . What d'you think of him, doctor?'

'What do you mean?'

She tapped her forehead, a universally recognized way of implying that someone is more or less crazy.

'Don't you think so? As you're a doctor . . .'

'What makes you think that of him?'

'You know, like most people who've lived in the colonies, my brother has always been a bit eccentric . . . Indeed, when he came back to France for good, I hesitated about setting up house with him, in spite of the fact that I was a widow . . . Well, the first two years he was quiet enough, and he spent his time, in our house at Sancerre, sorting and classifying all the junk he's brought back from every quarter of the globe . . . I ask you, what's the sense of loading oneself up with such filthy objects, when you can't even be sure they haven't been handled by lepers . . .'

Dollent glanced through the blinds at the apparently sleeping Marbe.

'Suddenly he suggested coming to live in the south and building a villa there . . . I didn't know he was well off . . . I asked him: "What about the money?" He said: "Don't you bother about that."'

'"Have you got savings?" I said. "That's nobody's business but mine", he told me. And since then, I've got to admit, things have gone from bad to worse. He's as close as an old woman . . . When he travels I'm not allowed to know where he's going . . . When he opens the letter box he always seems to be afraid of something.

'For he's nervous, doctor. He daren't admit it to you . . . For instance, he told you that when he hears a noise at night he gets up and goes round the house. Well, it's not true. It's possible he may have heard noises, although I myself have never heard anything definite . . . It's true that I sleep very sound.

'As for leaving his room, that's quite untrue, and I'm sure he stays behind the door listening and quaking. It's not until the next morning, in broad daylight, that he goes all round the house to make sure nothing is missing . . .

'What frightens me most . . . Just imagine, nowadays he always has two or three loaded revolvers in his room . . .

'And do you know how he spends his afternoons? He goes down into the cellar by himself. He flashes a torch on a row of empty bottles standing against the wall and then he shoots at them . . .

'Is that a way for a man of his age to amuse himself? Surely I'm right to conclude that he's . . .'

She could not understand why the Little Doctor was quietly smiling. The fact was that he had just seen through the blinds that Monsieur Marbe's deck-chair was empty. He guessed that its occupant had crept up the stairs noiselessly and had just been listening behind the door, and then . . .

And then, in fact, the door opened. Héloïse gave a guilty start.

'What are you doing here?'

'I came to make sure the doctor had everything he wanted . . . Isn't that so, doctor?'

'You can go now . . .'

It was a pity the Little Doctor was so sleepy after that méridional lunch and all the wine that had gone with it. Otherwise he would have been more keenly appreciative of the oddity of all these scenes and the picturesque character of the villa's inhabitants.

'What did she tell you? I dared not warn you, or rather I only dropped hints . . . Since her husband's death my sister has become somewhat addicted to the bottle . . . I don't mean that she's an alcoholic, but you'll notice that at certain moments her eyes glitter unnaturally and her speech is thicker than it should be.'

'Suppose we had a little rest, as you so kindly suggested, Monsieur Marbe?'

'I'll go down again . . . You must forgive me . . . When I realised that my sister had gone upstairs . . . My hearing is very acute, I'm used to being among natives who never make a noise . . .'

He went off reluctantly, and the Little Doctor did not even try to sleep. Indeed, fearful of succumbing to the torpor that was creeping over him, he resisted the wish to lie down on the bed, and stayed uncomfortably upright on a chair.

'Suppose Monsieur Marbe is not mad, but is speaking the truth?'

He did not want to give up the method which had succeeded so well in those earlier cases. He needed first of all to find some solid basis, some indisputable truth.

The truth, as he saw it, could be summed up as follows:

An unknown person was looking for something in the villa at Golfe-Juan.

The thing must be hard to find since during three months of twice-weekly visits he had failed to lay hands on it.

Finally, there had been no attempt by this unknown person to secure the object, prior to the last three months.

There were three alternative explanations:

1 Either the object was not there earlier;
2 Or the unknown person was not aware of its being there;
3 Or he was unable, at that time, to come and look for it.

And why did he only come twice a week? Always on Wednesdays and Saturdays?

The villa was not kept under closer watch on other days. The search would have been neither easier nor more difficult.

Presumably, therefore, the unknown person was only free on Wednesdays and Saturdays each week.

And in conclusion, he had been warned by some means or other of the presence of the police in the villa for a whole week, since he had not appeared during that time.

As for saying whether Monsieur Marbe was mad or sane . . . Although no psychiatrist, the Little Doctor in his days as intern had studied mental illness.

'He's undoubtedly in a state of nervous tension. He gives the impression of a man haunted by an obsession, or more precisely by fear. And it's not an indeterminate fear. It's the fear of a specific happening.'

So much so that if Héloïse was to be believed (and she had no reason for lying) he dared not leave his room at night when he heard noises about the house.

Did he know who was so stubbornly hunting through his vast pile of bric-à-brac?

And if he knew, did he also know what the man was looking for?

Why should he practise shooting in the cellar – and in the dark, too – if not because he was determined to take action some night?

Finally, the vital question: why, if Monsieur Marbe knew all these things, had he appealed to the Little Doctor, of whose skill he was aware only by hearsay, and why had he sent him a quite considerable sum of money before being sure of his acceptance?

'Tonight I mustn't drink!' Jean Dollent promised himself. 'For it's tonight that something is going to happen. Tonight, if ever, I shall find out . . .'

At that very moment something made him start. He had expected to be left in peace until nightfall, but things were happening faster than he had anticipated.

Voices sounded in the garden, then under the pergola, and they were the voices of two men quarrelling.

He tried opening the window a little to listen, but he could make out nothing but a confused murmur.

Well, it couldn't be helped. He put on his shoes and jacket again. He was not an ordinary guest and he had the right, if not the duty, to take liberties.

He went down, trying to look as though he were still drowsy after a good nap. In the dining-room he found Héloïse endeavouring to tidy up, if such a word could be used in connection with that house, and she said to him as though confidentially:

'His son's just come.'

The Little Doctor lit a cigarette, assumed as casual an air as possible and appeared in the pergola. He received a definite impression that Monsieur Marbe, who had been the first to notice him, was making signs to his son to keep quiet.

'I'm sorry if I'm disturbing you, but . . .'

'Not at all, doctor . . . Let me introduce my son Claude; I've told you about him, haven't I? . . . You see what a fine big fellow he is . . .'

H'm! . . . Claude was not quite the sort of son the Little Doctor would have liked himself . . . A big fellow, indeed, of strong and yet flexible build, with rather plump features due no doubt to his Tahitian origin. Dark hair, a smooth tanned skin; huge eyes and fleshy lips.

What was disturbing, however, was a certain showy elegance, and something in his whole attitude, the look in his eyes and the poise of his body, which suggested the underworld of the Riviera.

A swimming instructor he no doubt was. But in all probability he also frequented certain little bars and from time to time dabbled in shady business on a small scale.

'Good afternoon, Monsieur,' he said rather curtly.

'The doctor is a friend of mine . . . An old friend who has come to spend a few days with us . . .'

Monsieur Marbe's glance informed the doctor that his son was ignorant of the situation.

'Were you in the colonial service?' Claude queried mistrustfully.

His father answered for Dollent, for fear the latter might make a blunder:

'No . . . The doctor and I knew each other at Sancerre. When I learned that he was spending a few days in this part of the world . . .'

'Look here, doctor!'

A vulgar fellow, this young Claude. Dollent disliked him; he disliked above all the aggressive sarcasm with which he addressed one.

'I don't know if you're an old acquaintance of my father's, but I can tell you this about him: he's a blasted crank . . .'

'Claude!' interrupted Monsieur Marbe uneasily.

'What? I don't see the need to hush things up. What I came to ask you for is natural enough for anyone to hear about it, particularly an old friend, if that's what he is . . .'

'Monsieur Dollent, my son is . . .'

'Let me speak. In the first place you must admit that I don't often bother you . . . For one thing I'm earning my living, which is pretty creditable, since it's not my fault if I have Tahitian blood in my veins nor if Tahitians aren't particularly keen on work . . .'

'Claude!'

'You get my meaning, doctor . . . I plan my own life . . . It's only very occasionally, when I'm in low water, that I come to ask my father for a thousand or two . . . All young men of my age do the same and it wouldn't be fair for him to enjoy his fortune all by himself . . . I came today because . . .'

'If it's a thousand-franc note you want . . .'

'You know very well it isn't, papa. Listen, doctor . . . You shall be judge. If you've been round the house you'll have seen that it's a mixture of bazaar and museum. There's a bit of everything, some horrors and some quite decent things . . . Father's one of those people who never throw away anything, not even a worn-out suit, and he must keep a box somewhere with all his old buttons . . .'

'You're exaggerating!'

'Maybe. All the same all my old toys are up there . . . I was a spoilt child . . . When we were in Tahiti, toys used to come for me on every boat from France. Father has kept them all . . . They're worth nothing, of course. But now, as it happens, a pal of mine has got a child, and I've promised him the old toys; I've come to ask my father . . .'

The old man gave a slight, sad smile.

'You see, doctor?' he said. 'He sees nothing amiss with coming to rob me of objects which remind me of his childhood and of his poor mother . . .'

'Don't act sentimental!' cut in the young man. 'It's no, then?'

'Take whatever you want,' sighed his father resignedly.

'I've brought a friend's car. It won't take a minute.'

And without the least compunction he rushed into the house and was heard climbing the stairs to the first floor.

'He's a good lad!' the father sighed. 'But he's impulsive. He's soft-hearted. Just because he's promised a friend!'

'Shall we go up and see?'

'See what?'

'The toys he's taking away . . .'

'If you like!'

A few minutes later they found Claude raising clouds of dust in the larger of the two attics. Monsieur Marbe had really been a generous father. Mingled with native objects from every tropical country (there was even a huge stuffed crocodile!) one could make out two or three wooden horses of assorted sizes, a tricycle and some lead soldiers.

'Are you going to take everything?' the father asked, averting his eyes.

And at that point the Little Doctor was almost moved himself.

He became conscious of a curious hesitation on the part of the young man, who was trying to meet his father's eyes. What was happening between them? And why did Marbe ever more stubbornly stare at the other end of the room?

'Yes, everything!'

'Just as you like . . .'

Claude stepped out on to the landing. He had picked up all sorts of trivial little objects, jumping-jacks worth a few coppers, a celluloid flute, a drum with torn parchment, a toy gun.

And yet he did not seem satisfied. He stepped over cases and sacks, shields and piles of arrows. He was looking for something. His brow was furrowed. From time to time he glanced suspiciously at his father.

'Haven't you got enough?' Monsieur Marbe tried to make a joke of it. 'Don't you think that'll do for your pal's son to play with?'

'I was looking for . . .'

He hesitated. Something told the Little Doctor that a sensitive spot had been touched.

'What were you looking for?'

'A wooden trumpet . . . I don't suppose you remember it. A red and blue striped trumpet with a red silk tassel.'

'I don't remember it.'

'Funny . . .'

'Why?'

'I fancy I had seen it . . .'

'Do you think your friend's son really needs . . .'

'It's not that . . . But I remember that trumpet, because it used to be my favourite toy . . . I'd have liked to find it again . . .'

'Keep on hunting!'

Monsieur Marbe's expression, as he looked at the doctor, seemed to say: 'That's what children are like! One does everything for them, and one fine day they turn up with demands, if not insults, on their lips! They carry off all one's souvenirs to give them to a stranger. They don't care if it breaks their father's heart.'

And it would have been very moving, had not Dollent been conscious of something jarring underneath it all. What it was he could not have said precisely.

It was as though beneath the words being spoken other words – the only significant ones – were being implied. He had a clear impression that under the almost farcical comedy a drama was being played out, but a drama to which he did not have the key.

'Have you found it?'

'No!'

And the young man cast a harsh look at his father.

'Do you want to search the house?'

Claude, however, said neither yes nor no. It looked as though he was preparing, for the sake of a wooden toy worth at most three or four francs, to create havoc among the collection of native objects that the former administrator had devoted his whole life to assembling.

Then an almost comic note was struck by Héloïse. From the look in her eyes when she appeared, out of breath from climbing the stairs, the Little Doctor concluded that she had just been treating herself to a stiff drink.

'What are you doing here?' she asked in surprise.

'Claude is taking away his old toys to give to a friend!'

'Good riddance!'

'He's anxious not to forget anything . . .'

'Let him take everything that's in the house. After that we'll be able to clean the place . . . What are you looking for, Claude?'

'A wooden trumpet . . .'

'With red and blue stripes and a big red tassel?'

'Yes . . .'

'It's in your father's wardrobe. I saw it there only the other day . . . I wondered, in fact, why he'd so carefully put away such a tuppenny-ha'penny object among his clothes and underwear . . .'

Monsieur Marbe stood motionless. He had become paler than usual, and beads of sweat stood out on his brow.

'Is it true?' asked Claude, watching him.

'If your aunt says so . . . I don't know . . . It's quite possible that a trumpet may have been put away there by mistake . . . Really, you're a nuisance with this toy business, when I've got other things to worry about . . .'

For the first time he lost his temper. His anger was rising, to the point of rage.

'What I can't understand is that you should choose the moment when I have a friend staying to pester me about your toys, and I wonder if I shouldn't do better to . . .'

'Where's this cupboard, aunt?' the young man asked calmly.

'In his bedroom.'

Without bothering about his father's reactions, he went down to the floor below. Monsieur Marbe followed him; the Little Doctor followed Monsieur Marbe and Héloïse brought up the rear.

'I've always wondered what that trumpet . . .' she was muttering.

The bedroom door was open. Monsieur Marbe opened the wardrobe.

'Have a good look . . . Take it if you find it . . .'

And he gave a bitter laugh, like a man whose most precious feelings have been wounded.

Claude had gone too far to draw back. He hunted among clothes and underwear, and slid his hand behind a row of shoes and espadrilles.

Then came a moment when the scene should have been richly comical. It was when, amidst all this tension, the young man suddenly brandished an object which was absurdly out of keeping with the surrounding atmosphere: a wooden trumpet, such as every toyshop sells, so crudely painted that the Little Doctor almost burst out laughing.

He restrained himself. He glanced at his host, and saw two great tears trickling from the eyes of Monsieur Marbe.

'There's such a mess in the house,' the old man mumbled unsteadily, averting his eyes.

III. In Which the Little Doctor Gives Up Expecting Nocturnal Visitors, and Appeals for Co-operation to an Employment Officer

'You must excuse me for breaking down, doctor . . . If you were a father you would understand . . . Note that I don't hold it against him . . .'

They were under the pergola together; Claude was hastily piling the toys into his car.

'Tonight we'll keep watch and . . .'

'If I'm back!' Jean Dollent corrected him.

'What's that? Are you going away?'

'I've something to do in Nice . . . Don't worry about me . . .'

'But suppose my visitor should come and . . .'

Dollent restrained himself from asserting, 'He won't come!' He had learnt by experience that one must never show too much self-confidence.

Claude now stood before them, having loaded his car.

'I hope you're not too cross with me, papa? I'd given my word! I'm sorry if I upset you . . . But you must admit it was pointless keeping those toys in the house and that they'll be doing more good where there's a child to play with them . . .'

The old man nodded.

'Well, I'll be seeing you . . . I'll say goodbye, doctor . . . Enjoy your stay with father . . . Goodbye, auntie . . .'

Was he feeling ashamed of his persistence? He seemed friendlier than previously, as though relieved of some anxiety.

'Come on! Give us a smile . . . And let's hear no more about it.'

Monsieur Marbe made a great effort, but his smile was a bitter one.

'I must be off. My friends are expecting me.'

'I must be off too. Don't worry about me, Monsieur Marbe.'

'But . . .'

Too late. The young man's car had barely covered two hundred metres along the coast road to Juan-les-Pins when the Little Doctor leapt into Tin Lizzie and started up her snorting engine.

If anyone had asked him then what he was hurrying after like that, he would probably have replied, regardless of ridicule: 'The trumpet!'

And it seemed as though that object must be of some importance, since, shortly before reaching Antibes, Claude turned round. Had he noticed that he was being followed? He accelerated, but the doctor found it hard to increase Tin Lizzie's speed. Then, instead of following the main road into Nice, Claude took the first street to the left, then one to the right, then made a right-angled turn and backed into a passage that seemed scarcely wide enough to take a car.

When, some minutes later, the Little Doctor reached the entrance to the passage, there was nothing to be seen or heard.

He gave up. In spite of the promises he had made himself, he had to go into a bistrot to telephone. He did not even know if Monsieur Marbe's villa was on the telephone; fortunately it was.

'Hello! Dr Dollent speaking. Would you be kind enough to give me your son's address in Nice? . . . What did you say? . . . No, no . . . Don't worry . . . Yes! I shall probably be back . . . You said Hôtel Albion? Many thanks . . .'

'No, Monsieur. Monsieur Claude isn't back . . . He seldom comes in before midnight and sometimes much later than that . . .'

'Thank you . . .'

The fever was on him, that fever with which the Little Doctor was now so familiar, since it recurred every time that, during an investigation, an idea struck him at last . . . an idea which he would pursue the more doggedly because it seemed so improbable.

'Tell me, waiter . . . What sort of workers are free only on Wednesday and Saturday nights?'

'What did you say?'

'I'm asking you in what profession people are only free on . . .'

'How can I answer that? Days off used to be fixed; hairdressers had their day, so did butchers, pork-butchers and so on . . . Nowadays, with all the new social laws, it's too complicated. Most of the time people work in rotation. And here at Nice, with the casinos, you don't know where you are . . .'

And yet he had to work fast. He had to find a solution immediately.

'Waiter!'

'What?' mistrustfully.

'Who's in charge of organizing what you call the rotation?'

'The employment officer, of course!'

'Thank you!'

Ten minutes later he was in the presence of that official, who listened to him with amazement.

'Let me make myself clear, Monsieur . . . The problem is a tricky one. The person I'm looking for is only free two nights a week, Wednesday and Saturday . . . So presumably he must work every other night of the week, at any rate until a fairly late hour . . . I know nothing about your regulations or the organization of shifts, but I understand that everything comes under your control . . . In which jobs do they work at night, in a non-industrial area? Croupiers, casino waiters, bakers, who else, now?'

'There are staff always on duty at the gas and electricity companies. Not to mention the waterworks and . . .'

'Two nights a week, Monsieur! . . . That's what we must be guided by . . . Might I ask you to be good enough to consult your files?'

He was tense, as usual at such moments, quivering from head to foot like a newly-released jack-in-the-box.

'Two nights . . .' muttered the employment officer. 'That's what puzzles me. If it had been one I'd have understood . . . Wait a minute . . . In certain firms they work days and nights alternately . . . But in such cases it's one week on days and the next on nights . . . The only place . . .'

'Go on!'

'The only place would be the Casino de la Jetée . . . And there, it would only be the barmen! . . . Now that you remind me of it, they arrange to have two nights off a week each, and on those days they're on duty in the mornings instead . . .'

'Thank you! . . . Most grateful . . .'

He was off already, and the employment officer was left wondering what sort of crank he'd been dealing with.

As for the Little Doctor, he hurried off to the Casino de la Jetée. He paid the entrance fee and rushed to the bar in the first gaming-room.

It meant drinking again. He wondered, at that point, whether professional detectives had a special allowance for drink, they have to put away so much in the course of their duties!

'A small cocktail . . .'

'Martini? . . . Pink gin? . . .'

'All right, a pink gin . . .'

Then a second, to win the barman's confidence.

'Tell me . . . Are there a lot of you here?'

'A lot of barmen? Oh, a dozen . . .'

'I'm looking for one of your workmates whom I was to meet here and whose name I've forgotten . . . All I know is that he's free this evening . . . He has Wednesday and Saturday nights off . . .'

'A big fellow with a squint?'

'What's his name?'

'Patris . . .'

'And where does he live?'

'I don't know . . . I'll ask the head barman . . . Otherwise there's only Pierrot-des-Iles . . .'

'Could I have his address too? . . . In the meantime, I'll have the same again.'

Three cocktails! But on the other hand, two addresses, one of which was more than promising: Pierrot-des-Iles lived in the Hôtel Albion, in a small street leading on to the Promenade des Anglais.

'A middle-aged fellow, isn't he?'

'Must be more than that . . . Pierrot must be in his fifties . . . But he's knocked around the world so much . . . Including the Pacific; that's why they call him Pierrot-des-Iles . . . Not to mention another island that he's not too keen to talk about, namely Devil's Island in Guyana . . . If it's him you want, you'll find him about eight o'clock in the little restaurant at the corner of . . .'

No, not even gratitude to his informant could make the Little Doctor take a fourth cocktail.

IV. Proving that Fortune, which is Blind, can Sometimes be Deaf Too, which Does Not Suit Everybody

'Could you tell me if Monsieur Claude Marbe is back yet?'

The Hôtel Albion was a newish, second-class hotel, obviously frequented by casino employees, professional dancing-partners and women of the town.

'He came back half an hour ago. He carried up a lot of stuff. But I don't know if he's gone out again . . . Hello, No. 57! . . . Hello! No answer from 57? Thanks . . .'

The porter muttered between his teeth, 'I'm sure I didn't see him go out.'

'Which is Pierrot-des-Iles's room number?'

'32 . . . Shall I ring up to find out if . . .'

'Don't bother . . . I'm expected . . .'

The Little Doctor dashed up the stairs. As he drew near room 32 he heard voices being raised, but failing to make out the words he went to knock at the door. It was opened cautiously. A man whom he did not know stared at him and growled, 'What d'you want?'

At that moment Dollent made out another figure in the room; it was Claude Marbe. Claude recognized him with surprise, and said in a low voice, 'Let him in . . .' Then, suspiciously, 'What are you doing here?'

Phew! The hardest part was over. Now he was in the enemy's territory. And since the two men were there, he was sure he had made no mistake. But what did he know, after all? Nothing, almost nothing!

He knew, to be precise, that for the past three months Pierrot-des-Iles had been hunting for a trumpet in Monsieur Marbe's villa and had not found it; that in desperation he'd had recourse to Claude Marbe and probably offered him a substantial sum of money if he could get hold of the said trumpet.

He knew that the trumpet had at some point been in Tahiti.

Monsieur Marbe had lived in Tahiti . . .

Pierrot-des-Iles had lived in Tahiti before he . . .

The room was ordinary enough, with a narrow washroom attached. The toys were there, lying pell-mell in corners, and one of the horses had got its head broken during the journey. As for the trumpet, it was lying on the bed.

'I'm waiting for you to explain yourself,' said Pierrot-des-Iles in a low, unfriendly voice.

'Well, it's like this . . . I've come to warn you . . . You'd be well advised not to go to Monsieur Marbe's villa tonight. Of course you probably have no intention of going there, since you have at last got hold of the trumpet.'

Pierrot was looking at him with narrowed, inquisitorial eyes. He was a man whom nothing could surprise and who was not easily scared.

'Say, Claude!' he snarled. 'Is it you that's landed me with this fellow?'

'Honestly, I shook him off at Antibes . . . And I wonder how he could have . . .'

'I'll tell you all about it, boys,' the Little Doctor asserted cockily. 'You're furious, aren't you? Didn't the trumpet bring you what you were counting on?'

'You don't happen to be police, by any chance?'

'Me? Not on your life! I'm a doctor . . . And what I'm trying to find out now is why Monsieur Marbe, who's a quiet timid man, was absolutely bent on killing his night visitor, who had never done him any harm or stolen anything from him.'

The two men were astonished, particularly Claude, who gazed at his companion in the hope of some explanation.

'Did you say he wanted to . . .' asked Pierrot.

'Why, he was practising shooting in the dark . . . And as though he was afraid of being charged with murder none the less, he made sure I would be there . . . I'd have served to cover him . . . I was supposed to swear that he had only fired in legitimate self-defence . . .'

'The dirty bastard!'

'I quite agree with you . . . But tell me . . . The trumpet . . .'

'It looks to me, doctor, as though you knew too much and not enough . . . Isn't that so? . . . You realise that after bumming around as I've done I've come to recognize snoopers . . . And I shan't get rid of you till you're wise to the whole story . . . I hate people meddling with my private affairs . . . As for Claude, he knows even less than you do . . . I'd simply offered him ten thousand francs if he'd bring me all the toys there were in his father's house, including the wooden trumpet.'

Pierrot-des-Iles shrugged his shoulders.

'Now it's too late! But the swine's going to have to cough up a good whack of it, or else . . . It's easy enough to act respectable and take advantage of other people's efforts, which they pay for with years of hard labour.

'I tell you, doctor, since that's what you are, I'm disgusted . . . Yes, disgusted . . . And if that fellow Marbe was here . . . Sorry, Claude, but the trick your swine of a father played on me . . .

'I may as well put you in the picture now . . . It was in Tahiti . . . I did odd jobs . . . I used to pick up foreign visitors . . . I had a motor boat in which I took them out shark-fishing . . . One day I'd taken on one, a Yankee . . . On the way, I don't remember why, he opened his wallet, and what did I see? Four ten-thousand-dollar notes.

'As you know, Americans, who are rolling in money, can draw notes of any denomination: ten thousand, fifty thousand, a hundred thousand dollars . . . They only have to ask for them at the bank.

'My passenger, who was on a world tour, explained to me that they were less bulky to carry . . . Well, to cut a long story short . . .'

An uneasy silence fell in the little room. Both Claude and the doctor drew their breath with difficulty.

'Well, a shark got him . . . That needn't concern us now . . . I paid dearly enough for it . . . Fifteen years hard! . . . Penal servitude, if you prefer it, because nobody believed the story of the shark . . .

'Only, as regards the banknotes . . . I sometimes used to visit Marbe, who was a decent fellow and who had a kid . . . I was at his house the day I heard they were after me on account of the Yankee. I had the notes in my pocket.

'I'm no fool . . . I picked up a wooden trumpet which was lying on the floor and pushed my four banknotes into it, rolled up very small . . .

'You realise that at today's rate that would mean about a million and a half francs for me . . .

'Fifteen years hard . . . Goes without saying that you come out without a bean . . . I said to myself: I've got to find Marbe . . . I've got to get hold of my trumpet . . .

'And then three months ago I learned that he'd had a villa built at Golfe-Juan which is a regular junk-shop . . . I took a job at the Casino . . . Twice a week I . . .'

'I know!' broke in the Little Doctor. 'You didn't find the trumpet . . .'

'And I got his son to . . .'

'I know that too . . .'

'The bastard had already . . .'

'I can even tell you the date! It was about two years after he came back to France, while he was living at Sancerre, that he found the banknotes in the trumpet . . . What was he to do? Did he guess straight away that . . .'

'Of course he did! The authorities made a thorough search for those notes, at Tahiti, and notes of that sort . . . But he knew I was inside. He took advantage of that. He built his villa and probably put the rest in the bank . . . Then when he read in the papers that I was out . . . When he began hearing noises at night . . . I must admit I'd been a fool. It didn't occur to me that he'd discovered the hiding-place. I thought a retired administrator could afford to build a villa like that . . .

'I couldn't really go and find the authorities and tell them, "I want to claim the money I stole from the American and hid in a trumpet belonging to . . ." You understand? And the bastard's well aware of it! Only, he's frightened . . .'

Monsieur,

Considering my investigation as closed, and the problem you set me as solved, and furthermore apologizing for not being able to take my leave of yourself and your good sister, I am, yours very truly,

Jean Dollent

What was the point of going back there? To grab Monsieur Marbe by the shoulders and shout at him: 'You knew perfectly well who your nocturnal visitor was and you weren't in the least afraid of the Tou-Papaou! But you dared not face him all alone . . . You dared not kill him all alone . . . You were afraid of the deed and of its consequences.

'So, as he had been warned by your son – in all innocence – of the presence of the police, you thought of calling in an amateur . . .

'A guileless amateur, you must have been told by your friend the Deputy Public Prosecutor of Nevers . . .

'An amateur who would be there to serve as witness in your defence, to swear that you had only fired in legitimate self-protection.

'You disgust me, Monsieur Marbe.

'You made use in your own interest of money acquired through a crime, and you'd be well advised to . . .'

A week went by. No news of Marbe. Just a postcard bearing these words:

'It's going all right! I've got him by the short hairs. PIERROT.' Then, six months later:

'We've settled matters. I'm to marry Héloïse. We're sharing the villa and the lolly. PIERROT.'

This was the Little Doctor's first adventure as a private detective. 'What about the cheque?' Anna asked ironically, for he had implied that there would be a second cheque . . . But that never came, and he never heard any further news of Monsieur Marbe.

The Midwinter Marriage

I. About a Christmas Dinner which was like a Contest of Liars, and a Tavern which was like a Den of Thieves

Rain and yet more rain, in great slanting drifts, in great ice-cold drops, bucketsful, barrelsful, rain tumbling down endlessly from a low black sky, as though the world were about to perish in a second deluge.

Boulogne, seen from the train even before it entered the station, was an expanse of black shiny roofs, with dark streets through which nondescript figures scurried by under umbrellas. It was three in the afternoon and the street lamps were already lighted. As for the Channel, glimpsed for a moment, it, too, was all darkest grey, except for the white crests of rollers, while steam trawlers toiled wearily up the fairway.

The Little Doctor, feeling sick with melancholy, looked out of the window as the train drew up. He saw his friend Philippe Lourtie waiting for him, clad in a fawn raincoat, and his depression deepened.

Could this be the same Philippe Lourtie who, three weeks earlier, on December 1st, had married Madeleine, the girl he had always loved?

'Thanks for coming, old man . . . I knew I could count on you . . . Is this all your luggage?'

'In your letter, you asked me to come and stay for Chrismas night and perhaps a day or two longer . . . I must admit I couldn't quite understand . . . If you hadn't doubly underlined the statement that your happiness was at stake . . .'

The Little Doctor's suitcase was light; his friend took it from him, and said with a sigh:

'Before going home I'd like to put you in the picture . . . If you don't mind, we might go into the nearest café . . .'

The change that had come over Lourtie in so short a time was such that Dollent ventured, suspiciously: 'You haven't taken to drink, I hope?'

'No, don't worry . . . In a few moments you shall know all about it . . . Waiter! I'll have a quarter of Vichy water . . . What about you?'

'Why it's none too warm today, and I wouldn't mind a hot toddy.'

Philippe Lourtie was twenty-eight, two years younger than Jean Dollent, whom every one called the Little Doctor. They had been through medical school together and whereas Dollent had settled in the countryside, near La Rochelle, Philippe Lourtie had taken over a sizeable practice at Boulogne-sur-Mer.

'Don't look at me like that . . . It's rather embarrassing for me to meet you again under the present circumstances . . . Hitherto I'd always thought of you as being a man like everybody else. Then I heard so much from our friend Magné about your extraordinary gifts . . . Now I feel rather as though I were in the presence of a judge or a confessor . . .

'Listen, Dollent . . . You know Madeleine, don't you? In any case you know her father, Dr Gromaire, who's the leading specialist in nervous disorders in Boulogne . . . a famous name and a notable personality.

'Madeleine takes after him in that she's totally unlike most modern girls, who are concerned only with showing off and having a good time. She's a woman with a sense of duty, too. A woman capable of completely sharing the life of a man like her father or myself.

'I was brought up in Boulogne, and we'd been friends for a long time. A few months ago I asked her to be my wife and she accepted. We were married on December 1st and . . .'

The Little Doctor had to make an effort to follow the story, so absorbedly was he contemplating his friend.

True, Philippe had never been a frivolous fellow. He was a hard worker, whom all his teachers – and his fellow-students too, which is less common – considered as one of the most promising of his generation.

But though naturally serious, he was remarkable for his serenity, his calmness, his optimism.

And now, at the outset of his married life, he seemed a deeply troubled man, a prey to the blackest thoughts, so much so that Dollent wondered if he should not be sent as a patient to his father-in-law.

'I needn't tell you that I am neither fanciful nor credulous. As you know, I've always been almost too much of a scientist! So I've already examined all the possible explanations of the facts I'm going to relate, and I must confess that none of them have satisfied me.

'Perhaps, with your flair, or rather that sixth sense which you possess, according to Magné . . .'

They were sitting uncomfortably in the sordid café near the station, surrounded by country housewives waiting for their trains, some of them producing food from their baskets.

'One first fact, to which at the time I paid little attention . . . Our engagement was officially announced about the middle of September.

From then on I began getting anonymous letters, all more or less to the same effect . . . They seemed to me so stupid that I just threw them into the waste-paper basket.

'They said something like this: "*You'll regret it if you marry Madeleine. She's not the nice girl you imagine.*"'

'Did you mention them to your fiancée?' asked Dollent.

'No! They were really too offensive. That sort of petty anonymous spite revolts me, and I considered Madeleine so completely above suspicion . . .'

'Go on . . . You were married on December 1st . . . No incidents?'

'None . . .'

It struck the Little Doctor none the less that his friend had hesitated, that his eyes betrayed a faint unease.

'Since I could not take a long time off, and since I knew moreover that Madeleine had always longed to visit Tunis, we took the plane and spent a week there . . .'

'And did anything unusual occur?'

'That's to say we were as happy as a honeymoon couple can possibly be . . . You know how picturesque that region is . . . We took an interest in native life . . . And then suddenly, on our return . . .'

As the Little Doctor's look grew keener, Philippe hastily went on:

'Above all, don't start imagining anything absurd . . . When I was young, like everyone else I read romantic tales of witchcraft, of spells cast by sorcerers, of secret societies, all that sort of thing . . . I tell you I'm a scientist. And though we visited native quarters and all the places where tourists usually go, nothing untoward ever happened . . .

'On the other hand, the first letter I received when we got back said: "*You refused to listen to me. Your wife is leading a double life. I can soon prove this to you if you say nothing to her about it. Otherwise you will regret it.*"'

'And you still said nothing to Madeleine?'

'Nothing,' Philippe replied somewhat shamefacedly. 'When you've met her you'll understand my attitude. There are some women whom one cannot insult by such suggestions . . .'

'Was this note in the same handwriting as the others?'

'None of them were written by hand. They have always been typed. I can't even distinguish the envelopes from among the quantity of commercial envelopes that I get every day . . . You know I've bought a big practice . . .'

'And then?'

'The second letter after our wedding was more detailed. "*If you want to be convinced of your wife's double life, go this evening about eleven o'clock to the* Tonneau d'Argent, *a tavern on the quayside. She will be there. However, don't be too cockahoop if you should not see her. It will just mean the thing is postponed until tomorrow.*"'

'One minute! Do you have separate bedrooms?'

'I insisted on that. I'm often called out at night, and Madeleine's health is none too strong. I thought that . . .'

'And you went to the *Tonneau d'Argent*?'

Philippe Lourtie hung his head.

'Did you see her?'

'No! But . . .'

He opened his wallet and drew out a rather bad snapshot showing the corner of a tavern where a young woman, obviously highly nervous, was sitting with her elbows on a table, in the attitude of someone waiting impatiently at a rendezvous.

'That's Madeleine. Just look at the people round her. They are the very dregs of the sea-faring world, those who go in for smuggling and illicit trading . . . Don't speak too quickly . . . I submitted this print to a photographic expert. I thought it might be a piece of trick photography, but it isn't . . . It was probably taken without the subject's knowledge, with a Leica, a very powerful small camera easily concealed and requiring very little light . . .

'Furthermore, I went back next day to the *Tonneau d'Argent*. I asked Jim, the proprietor, whether a young woman had been in his place the previous night. He immediately glanced towards the corner where the photo had been taken.

'I showed it to him, and he recognized his customer.

'Why I had not met her was because she had apparently come well before eleven o'clock.

'"Whom did she meet?" I asked.

'"That I couldn't say . . . There's such a crowd in the evenings . . ."

'"Have you seen her at other times?"

'"I couldn't swear to it . . . We're always full of people, women as well as men . . ."'

Philippe called the waiter, threw some coins on the table and picked up the Little Doctor's case. Outside, he hailed a taxi from the rank.

'To the *Tonneau d'Argent*!'

The quays were slimy and reeked of fish, for the herring season was in full swing and truckfuls were being unloaded from the trawlers moored one behind the other.

'I want you to see the place. Afterwards you'll meet my wife and you'll understand my bewilderment . . .'

They went down one step. The long low room, with its smoke-blackened beams, was lit only by a single window with small panes, so that semi-darkness prevailed. It resembled a low-class English pub rather than a French bistrot.

Behind the counter, Jim, who was apparently an Australian and who had lost one eye, heaven knows where, was watching his customers with his remaining eye distrustfully, like someone who knows the people he has to deal with.

The place was almost full. There were practically no fishermen, but plenty of seamen from the colliers in the outer dock, and other more suspicious-looking characters, all indirectly connected with the sea.

'We shall just have to drink beer!' Philippe said. 'You see what sort of a place it is. I made some inquiries. From what I was told, this is where every kind of smuggling takes place, all shady deals, all the dirty intrigues the police don't want to deal with . . . Last week an English sailor came out of here, supposedly drunk, fell into the water and was drowned. He's believed to have been pushed by somebody . . .'

'And you say that Madeleine . . .'

'In that corner, to the left . . . Check up for yourself with the photo . . .

'Note that when I asked her whether she had been out that night she told me she hadn't . . . In other words, she lied to me, whereas I had thought her incapable of lying . . . And that's not all . . .'

Dollent began to feel compassion for his friend, who was really a pitiable sight, in an acute state of nervous distress.

'Listen to this: two days later I got a letter saying: "*You'll see that your wife will ask you if she can go to Rouen on Wednesday.*"'

'And she did?'

A nod.

'She told me she wanted to visit an old friend . . . that she'd probably spend the night with her . . .'

'You didn't follow her?'

'I tried to . . . We've each got our own small car. But I lost sight of her and . . .'

He drew another photo from his pocket. This showed part of a dance-hall or night-club. Madeleine was there again, sitting at a table, wearing the same anxious look, while a young man was leaning towards her.

'This is what I received next day . . . Now Madeleine declared that she'd spent the whole time with her friend . . .'

Around them the smoke was dense, the reek of alcohol almost intolerable.

'Now you're going to meet my wife . . . She knows nothing about my suspicions. I haven't the courage to tell her of them . . . Note that I still trust her . . . Nothing will persuade me that she's unworthy of me . . .

'This is the mystery that I'm determined to clear up, that I implore you to help me clear up . . .

'I needn't add that I've spent whole nights turning over and over the data of the problem in my head . . .

'I want straight away to set aside certain hypotheses which are the first to occur to one.

'First, that Madeleine might have been inveigled into wrong-doing by some unscrupulous relative . . . You see what I mean . . . the sort of situation that was the theme of plenty of the thrillers I used to read. But it's not the case here.

'There's nothing questionable about her background . . . You know her father and so do I . . . Her mother died ten years ago, and she was a respectable lady, incapable of rash or improper behaviour. They've never been abroad . . . There's no dark secret about their past.

'So that one is inevitably reduced to wondering about split personality. I'll tell you categorically that I don't believe in that. It sounds very plausible in books. In reality I have never met a case of this sort, nor has my teacher Dr Gromaire, who has specialized in nervous diseases for over thirty-five years . . .

'Madeleine may not be very robust, but she's healthy in mind and body . . .

'Which leave us wondering why, as a newly-married bride, she should without my knowledge visit a place like the *Tonneau d'Argent* and a sordid night-club in Rouen . . .

'If this goes on, I shall go mad myself!

'Come along . . .'

Philippe Lourtie had a large, comfortable private house. His parents were wealthy, and he had been able to acquire a flourishing practice in Boulogne, so that although still under thirty he already had a large number of patients.

He still did a certain amount of general practice, but tended to specialise in nervous disorders, like his father-in-law, and there was every likelihood that one day he would step into the latter's shoes.

Five o'clock. Night had fallen long since.

Philippe showed the Little Doctor into a drawing-room on the first floor, handed the suitcase to the maid and called: 'Madeleine!'

Who would have suspected at this point that the house was in the throes of a drama? A welcome odour of food pervaded the rooms. And as guests were expected that evening, Madeleine emerged from the kitchen where, like a good hostess, she had been seeing to the finishing touches.

'Forgive me, Monsieur Dollent . . . I am still in my workaday clothes . . . My husband must have told you we were expecting friends to supper and so I'm obliged to . . .'

She was exactly as Lourtie had described her: beautiful rather than just pretty, attractive, even fascinating in an unobtrusive way. Not one of those women whom one turns to look at in the street, but one of those whom one appreciates the more as one gets to know them, and with whom one then longs to spend one's life.

But why was she so nervous? Were they all under an evil spell? Dollent felt like suddenly exclaiming:

'Listen to me, my friends! I wonder what you're playing at? You've got everything to make you happy! Everything's going your way and there you are torturing yourselves, spying on one another, each making the other suffer . . . If we could just have it out, don't you think we should all have a good laugh and feel the better for it?'

But hadn't he just been in the *Tonneau d'Argent*, and hadn't he seen those two undeniably authentic photographs?

'Forgive me for disappearing again, but I've still got some instructions to give, and then I shall have to dress. The maid will show you your room, Monsieur Dollent . . .'

'As for me, I believe I've got two patients waiting downstairs . . . You'll excuse me, Jean?'

And the Little Doctor was left waiting for quite a while in a nondescript room, the sort of spare room that gets furnished with oddments and used as a guest room.

'Provided they're not all in dinner jackets!' he sighed. 'I didn't bring mine.'

He changed. He wandered about the house a bit, particularly into the two drawing-rooms, one large and one small, which were comfortable but unremarkable in any way.

'Everything to make one happy! But not for him; he was on edge. He knew that there was a difficult time ahead of him. Didn't this always happen in such investigations? One knows too much and yet not enough. One has no guiding thread, no solid foundation, no 'dominant factor' as he called it.

So, inevitably, one felt depressed.

'I brought off two or three little things, that's true! But who's to say whether it wasn't by chance? Who's to say if I shall be inspired again?'

What could one do, all alone in a house one didn't know, while one's hostess was busy about her own affairs and one's friend was seeing patients in his consulting-room on the ground floor?

He went down. He wanted to see the waiting-room. He pushed open a door and found himself in a small office where a girl with peroxide blonde hair sat typing.

'I'm sorry,' he apologized.

'Come in, Monsieur . . . You must be Dr Dollent . . . My boss told me about your visit. I'm his secretary, Mademoiselle Odile . . . Can I help you? Monsieur Philippe won't be long . . . His patient is an old lady who comes every week and who's a bit faddy . . . What a depressing town ours is, don't you think?'

'Is Boulogne your home town?'

'Yes . . . I used to live in the same street as Monsieur Philippe.'

He noticed that not once did she say Monsieur Lourtie, which would have seemed more natural.

'He was a grown man when I was still a little girl. I went to Pigier's secretarial school . . . When I learnt that he needed a secretary . . . I've been with him for four years now . . . When he was writing his thesis I used to type out his notes for him . . .'

Might this be useful? He noted in a corner of his memory, as he might have done in the margin of a book: '*Mademoiselle Odile. Pretty, pert, lively. Has known Philippe since childhood. Seems to have thrust herself upon him. Chances are she's in love with him.*'

So what? He didn't have to concern himself with Odile but with Madeleine.

The patient's visit was over. Lourtie emerged, his brow deeply furrowed.

'That'll do, Odile. You can go home . . . Jean, if you'd like to come into my study for a drink . . . What do you like? I'll give them a ring upstairs and ask them to send down a bottle and some glasses.'

And to this the Little Doctor had no objection. It was more out of superstition than from any tendency to alcoholism. In all his inquiries he had been induced to drink more or less by chance, and he was beginning to find the atmosphere of this house somewhat dry.

'Dinner is served, Madame.'

'Will you come through into the dining-room? . . . I warn you that it's a very informal meal . . . We've been married so short a time that we aren't yet very highly organized . . .'

She smiled at her husband, but the smile merely lifted the corners of her lips; her face remained sad and uneasy.

As Dollent had anticipated, all the men except himself were wearing dinner jackets. While the party were taking their seats he made a mental sketch plan of the table. Apart from Madeleine, Lourtie and himself, there were present:

1. Emile Gromaire, Madeleine's father, a man of about sixty-five, with grey hair and bushy eyebrows, accustomed to being obeyed and admired.

Why did Gromaire, who could not have failed to notice the nervous tension of his daughter and her husband, keep on repeating: '*How happy they are! how delightful it is to spend a few hours with such happy people!*'

2. Monsieur Boutet . . . Another doctor! A real gathering of medicos. Monsieur Boutet had been Lourtie's predecessor in the practice. At sixty he had retired, and now divided his time between Boulogne and the Riviera, where he was shortly to go for the New Year holiday.

'*I'm so glad,*' he kept saying, '*to find these children so well. Her trip to Tunisia has done your daughter a world of good.*'

Yet another liar, and he was lying even more when he lavished loving smiles on his wife, because . . .

3. Madame Boutet was not a real woman but a caricature of a woman, tall, dried up and swarthy as a prune, sour, suspicious and spiteful.

'*Aren't these children touching, Albert?*' she murmured to her husband.

But they were not in the least touching, and an atmosphere of unease oppressed the entire party.

4. Samuel Kling. Dollent had met him before; he was a boyhood friend of Lourtie. They had been contemporaries at medical school, had specialized in the same subject and had both worked under Dr Gromaire.

Kling kept casting sidelong glances at each member of the party. A bisque of crayfish had been served; it was obvious from his expression that he loathed crayfish.

'*Delicious!*' he exclaimed. '*Madeleine, you have a wonderful cook, or else you're a wonder at instructing her . . .*'

All of them were lying!

But what was so odd as to become, after a while, positively uncanny, was that they all felt impelled to display artificial good humour and to express a delight which they did not feel.

It was like a stage orgy played by bad actors in some small theatre, where the part of Nero is taken by a lean young man who has dined off one roll, and the courtesans are poor skinny tarts brought in from the street.

'Your flight must have been delightful, *chère amie,*' remarked Dr Boutet, who seemed always to be in terror of meeting his wife's eyes.

And Madeleine, quite obviously thinking of something else, replied off-handedly: 'Oh, delicious!'

Perhaps she had not been listening, and thought the topic of conversation was still the soup?

As for Philippe, he was in agonies. He dared not look at his wife. Sometimes he cast a glance towards his father-in-law.

The Little Doctor surprised one of those glances, and it puzzled him.

'Well, well!' he said to himself. 'It looks as though my friend Philippe mistrusts Gromaire . . . Almost as though he were jealous of him.'

However, a minute later Philippe cast an exactly similar glance at Kling.

'Jealous of Kling too? . . . It must be pathological! Can it be that poor Philippe is . . .'

No! It wouldn't do to jump to conclusions. Everyone was on edge. The weather was partly responsible. For weeks these people had been splashing about in the rain, and keeping the light on half the day, sometimes the entire day.

'This lobster *à l'américaine* . . .' began Dr Boutet.

His wife must have been aching to say something unpleasant, for she interrupted shrilly:

'Why do you say that? You know you don't like lobster!'

II. In Which the Little Doctor Realizes with Embarrassment that it is Hard to Combine Detective Work with Social Success

Was it his fault? Had or hadn't his friend Lourtie fetched him over from Marsilly, in the filthiest of weathers, to discover the truth?

'Sorry, Philippe,' he felt like saying, 'it can't be helped. One doesn't put on kid gloves to search the human soul, and it's not by asking people politely for their opinion that you'll get them to admit the truth.'

One truth, indeed, was self-evident: he had well and truly put his foot in it. Indeed, if he had literally taken off his shoes and calmly thrust his feet into the salad bowl, he could not have been glared at more disapprovingly than when he suddenly remarked with an innocent air:

'By the way, I don't know if you've read in the papers . . . The Americans have just arrested a whole gang of dope-peddlers . . . And do you know who was the boss of this gang? . . . One of the best-known doctors in New York, who ran his own private nursing-home . . . It was under cover of this nursing-home that he managed to procure the dope, under the nose of the police . . .'

You could have cut the ensuing silence with a knife. Nothing could be heard but the beating of rain against the shutters and a distant murmur which must have been the sea. The Little Doctor ought to have stopped there. The face of his neighbour, horrible Madame Boutet, should have told him enough. But how could he, a newcomer, have known what everybody in Boulogne knew, namely that she was a morphine addict?

It struck him that Lourtie was looking at him imploringly.

Madeleine had turned very pale and was bending over her plate, the fork in her hand shaking visibly.

Dr Kling had raised his head sharply as though some creature had stung him, and was staring defiantly at the intruder.

Moreover, Monsieur Gromaire must have disapproved of this impertinent sally, for his gaze was hostile under his bushy eyebrows.

Unfortunately we are all subject at times to a crazy compulsion to make blunders, to do what we are well aware we ought not to do.

Jean Dollent gave a little cough as though to clear his throat, and went on:

'Considering that Boulogne is such a busy port, immediately opposite the English coast, I shouldn't be surprised if it were one of the centres of the drug traffic.'

Silence still reigned, broken only by the noise of forks and the continuous, endless rain.

It was too late to draw back. The Little Doctor was launched. He wanted to make sure, to get some reaction from these people, and so he went on with a derisive laugh:

'I wonder if a doctor might not be running the show here too . . .'

Then Dr Gromaire's gravelly voice was heard:

'I should like to point out to our young colleague,' he said drily, 'that so much heroism is displayed in our profession, the finest and noblest of all in my opinion, that it is unnecessary to dwell deliberately on the exceptional black sheep. You arrived in Boulogne this afternoon, Monsieur Dollent? May I ask you if you found nothing to interest you in our town except the question you have raised?'

What could he reply? What could he do but blush? Never had the Little Doctor been so sharply put in his place, and he juggled clumsily with a big lettuce leaf. Things couldn't possibly get worse; he hoped someone was going to come to his rescue, to switch the conversation on to less burning ground. Wasn't it Lourtie's duty, for instance, to extricate him?

But instead of a rescuer he encountered yet another adversary, and one of considerable stature, in the person of Samuel Kling.

'I believe Dr Dollent arrived here by the three o'clock train?' he began in a voice which presaged nothing good.

'That is so.'

'I am not surprised at his interest in narcotics, since by four o'clock he was already seen emerging from an unfortunately famous place known as *Le Tonneau d'Argent* . . .'

It was impossible to look at everyone at once. It was hard enough to maintain one's self-possession. But Dollent did not fail to notice that Madeleine's eyelids fluttered, that her nostrils tautened, that she held on to the edge of the table as though she were afraid of fainting.

And why did Philippe still not intervene? Why did he let it be assumed that the Little Doctor had been into the *Tonneau d'Argent* all by himself?

'I think that's enough on this subject!' broke in Dr Gromaire, as sharply as though he were about to get up and leave the table.

Fortunately the meal was nearing its end. The last few minutes were painful. Everybody was hunting for something to say. Conversation was forced and insincere, made with the sole purpose of killing time.

At last Madeleine was able to rise and announce with a feeble smile: 'We'll take coffee in the drawing-room, and allow the gentlemen to smoke, shall we, Madame Boutet?'

'I smoke myself, so! . . .'

There was some slight confusion, as usual when a dinner party breaks up. The young bride showed more self-possession than the Little Doctor would have expected, for she managed to pass close beside him and to whisper: 'I implore you! . . .'

What was she imploring him to do? To hold his tongue? Why? What was she afraid of?

Monsieur Gromaire deliberately paid no attention to Dollent, who went over to lean disconsolately against the mantelpiece. He did not notice exactly how Philippe Lourtie and Kling left the room, but he presently heard voices raised behind a door.

Philippe's consulting-room was on the ground floor, and so was his study. But there was a small room next to the drawing-room which served as a kind of private study, and this was where what sounded like a quarrel was taking place.

It was so obvious that everyone listened intently. You couldn't pretend to hear nothing. And they stayed there in suspense, holding their cups of coffee.

Poor Madeleine, still trying to keep up appearances against all probability, exclaimed: 'Fancy arguing over politics today of all days!'

But they were not arguing over politics, and the proof of this was that the only word which could be made out, and which was uttered repeatedly, was Madeleine's name.

In any case, the door was soon flung open violently. Kling, red with fury, crossed the big drawing-room without paying attention to anyone, went into the passage, took his coat and hat and rushed down the stairs.

A few moments later the front door was opened and closed with a noisy bang that echoed gloomily through the house.

'I can't think what came over him . . .' Philippe explained feebly. 'He's a funny fellow . . .'

'He's a very able fellow,' retorted his father-in-law.

'That may be, and I think so too . . . That doesn't prevent him from having the dickens of a temper . . . What can I give you, Madame Boutet? Chartreuse or brandy?'

Everybody was anxious to get out of the place, now that it was too late to mend things. Madame Boutet made the first move, complaining of a headache, and left with her husband, after thanking her hosts for 'a really delightful evening.'

Just at this time, in every church in the world, crowds were gathering round brightly-painted cribs, while the sound of singing and the smoke of incense floated upward.

'Time for me to go home too,' growled Gromaire.

He had scarcely left when Madeleine said with a sigh: 'Will you excuse me if I go to bed? I'm a bit weary . . .'

Philippe and the Little Doctor were left alone together, and poor Dollent was by no means prepared for what he got.

'Did you do it on purpose? Do you realise the position you've got us into? . . . If this is the way you conduct your inquiries, I don't think much of it! I must say that if I'd known . . .'

He did not finish the sentence, but it implied: 'I'd have left you in your dead-alive Marsilly and I'd have looked after my affairs myself!'

What could Dollent say? Should he fly off the handle and retort dramatically: 'Very well! I'm off! Give me back my suit-case . . .'

But that was absurd. It had already been unpacked, the clothes put away in the cupboard; his pyjamas were laid out on the bed in the guest room.

'I'm sorry, old man . . . I thought I was acting for the best . . . I still think it may not have been entirely useless . . .'

'You maintain it told you anything about what my wife does in that damned tavern?'

'I didn't say that . . .'

'Well then?'

'Well, nothing . . . Go to bed; calm down . . . If I were you I'd take a sedative . . .'

And the Little Doctor went to his room in melancholy mood.

He woke as usual at 6.0 a.m. What could one do at that hour in a sleeping house?

Lying with his eyes open, he heard the scullery maid go down first to light the kitchen fire, then a housemaid in the room above washing noisily.

At seven o'clock he got up, while other sounds began to be heard in the house, and once dressed, he left his room, hesitated, shrugged his shoulders, went on to the landing, then down the stairs, drew back the chain on the front door and stepped outside to where, by way of a change from yesterday's downpour, a fine drizzle was falling.

Day was just breaking. People were glumly going off to their jobs. The cranes were working in the harbour. Trawlers were coming in, manoeuvring in the dock while men in oilskins and boots flung out heavy, sodden mooring-ropes.

There was something wrong about this case, but what was it? Why did the Little Doctor, usually so happy when faced with a mystery, feel overwhelmed by an inexplicable depression?

There was something about it . . . maybe it was nonsense, and he would not have dared speak of it to anyone; but there was something about it that didn't ring true, though he could not have said precisely what.

He considered Madeleine . . . Wasn't she exactly the sort of woman he'd have chosen for his own wife?

Philippe, whom he knew so well, was the straightest fellow in the world.

Dr Gromaire's reputation was established, Kling was a brilliant creature, and the Little Doctor had sensed reserves of passion in him.

A passion for Madeleine, he was willing to bet. But there was more in the case than a commonplace love story. Madeleine was too honourable a person to belong to two men. And if Kling had wanted to meet her it would certainly not have been at the *Tonneau d'Argent* . . .

Finally, why had everyone reacted so violently when he had talked about drugs?

He had done so on the off-chance. Remembering the strange tavern and the Rouen night-club, he had reflected that the only possible link between the two must be dope . . .

And he flung out his remark at random, not suspecting that it would rebound so violently on his own head.

Why had Kling and Philippe quarrelled, reiterating Madeleine's name?

'Jean, my boy, I'll tell you what's the best thing you could do, but I know very well that you won't do it . . . There's a good train at ten o'clock . . . You've got time to fetch your luggage and tell your friend Philippe that, decidedly, your detective gifts are not equal to such a complicated situation. Anna will laugh at you a bit when she sees you home again so soon, but at any rate . . .'

Not a bit of it! Instead of acting thus, he was soon standing, up to the ankles in black mud full of fish guts, in front of the *Tonneau d'Argent*. The *patron*, Jim, was just taking down the front shutters. He was wearing oiled clogs, a blue sweater and a seaman's cap.

The damp cold seeped through one's clothes. The Little Doctor went in and propped his elbows on the bar counter, behind which stood a fantastic array of bottles, containing every imaginable sort of alcoholic beverage.

'A really hot toddy . . .'

He looked around at the empty room, which was strewn with dirty glasses and enough fag-ends to fill a dust-bin. What could he learn from the place?

'Tell me, *patron* . . .'

The man's single eye stared at him mistrustfully.

'Do you remember me? I came yesterday with a friend . . .You know, the man who showed you the photograph of a young lady . . .'

'What about it?'

'Oh, you needn't worry . . . I'm not going to ask you any awkward questions . . . I'd just like to know if this young woman often came here in the evenings . . .'

Jim hesitated, and it seemed on the cards that he might pick up his little customer by the scruff of the neck and put him outside. His loose lips were pursed in a menacing grimace and the Little Doctor felt none too confident as he sipped the scalding toddy.

'You know her?'

'Oh, hardly at all.'

'Well, *I* know her . . .' And this, too, he said threateningly.

'And I don't want any trouble, d'you hear? I can deal with our sort of people, sailors and suchlike . . . And I know the gent that was with you yesterday . . . He's a doctor . . . In fact my first wife was a patient of his . . . Well, when I see people like that coming in here . . . And when I see them getting themselves photographed in my place, I can't help wondering . . .'

'One minute . . . You just said . . .'

The Little Doctor's heart had leapt up. At last, a tiny glimmer of light amid the prevailing darkness of this case.

'They got themselves photographed?'

'Don't be an idiot . . . They didn't come with a photographer, flash-lights and so on, like for a wedding party . . . All the same the doctor came in one fine evening and showed me the picture of his wife, asking if I recognized her . . . I didn't need to recognize her, because you could see that corner over there, with the earthenware pot hanging just above the table . . . That's tiresome enough for a start . . . Society people ready to shoot each other up on account of dames . . . That's not the sort of thing I want to see here. But when she came in her turn and . . .'

The Little Doctor was smiling. He was a different man now. His torpor was gone; he had shaken off his depression and anxiety.

'Did she show you a photograph?'

'Sure she did! Her husband's, of course! Taken at roughly the same spot . . . And she asked me, just as he'd done, whether he came often . . .'

'And what did you reply?'

'That I didn't notice my customers . . .'

'What'll you drink, Jim? . . . Yes, I insist on standing you one and drinking your health . . . Say, are there any good trains to Rouen? No? Not at this time of day? What about a car? Are you on the phone? Will you get me a taxi . . . A good fast car if you can . . . It's quite a way to go . . .'

He drank a second toddy while waiting. Jim, who counted on getting a hefty commission on the taxi, insisted on standing him a third, and a quarter of an hour later the Little Doctor was positively euphoric as he settled down in the taxi and it sped towards Rouen.

He could not help smiling as he reflected that Philippe and Madeleine would be wondering what had become of him and would probably be feeling sorry for treating him so harshly.

'Never mind! It'll do them good . . .'

It was a splendid road, but glistening with wet so that the trees were reflected in it as in a mirror. Rouen . . .

'Where shall I take you?'

'To the *Monico* . . .'

The night-club might perhaps have been attractive in the evenings, with its variegated lights, but by day it was pretty squalid. A half-open door with posters on either side, and one panel covered with photographs of practically nude dancing-girls. A dustbin full of paper streamers and balls of cotton wool stood beside the door. A woman was sweeping the stairs.

'Is the proprietor here?'

'Monsieur José must be in the dance hall.'

Dollent found him there, with an electrician who was mending a spotlight. He was obviously a foreigner.

'What can I do for you?'

'One question first of all . . . Are you in your dance hall every night?'

'Of course . . . It wouldn't do for me not to be . . . But I can't see why . . .'

'One minute . . . I'd like to know if recently a young woman – a very respectable young lady – has asked you or one of your waiters to recognize a photograph . . .'

There was no need to press the point. Monsieur José was visibly startled. He hesitated, wondering who this might be.

'That's to say . . .'

'A tall blonde young woman . . . She was sitting in that corner, close to the pillar . . . There was a very dark young man sitting beside her . . .'

'Eusebio . . .'

'Who's Eusebio?'

'The professional dancing partner. He asked her to dance, as it's his job . . . She refused, but she showed him a photo and asked him . . .'

'Did Eusebio recognize the photo?'

'No . . . It was the photo of a man . . . He must have been here, since he was photographed at the bar . . . But nobody noticed him . . . You'd have to question all the hostesses to find out . . .'

'Thank you . . . That's all . . . Goodbye, Monsieur José . . .'

A minute later, the Little Doctor emerged on to the pavement, glad to be out of the sordid atmosphere that prevails behind the scenes in a place devoted to pleasure. His taxi-driver was waiting anxiously.

'Can you get me back to Boulogne by lunch time?'

'If we leave right away and it doesn't rain too hard . . .'

Miraculously, while they were on the Artois plateau not a drop of rain fell, and they even had a glimpse of sunlight, rather pale but none the less welcome.

At midday, they entered the streets of Boulogne, and then, as though at a prearranged signal, the heavens opened and the rain came down.

At ten past twelve the Little Doctor bustled into the Lourties' house and rushed up the stairs to the first floor; he stopped suddenly on reflecting that . . .

He had been so pleased with his two discoveries that he had not immediately noticed that they explained nothing, that the most difficult and most serious business was still to be done.

As he stood there hesitating, somebody leaned over the banister and a soft voice said:

'Come up, doctor . . . I'd like to speak to you a moment . . .'

It was Madeleine, who must have been on the watch for him all morning!

III. Showing that Somebody had Organized, Scientifically, a Regular War of Nerves

'Come in here, doctor . . . This is my study, rather than my husband's . . .'

The study in question was the little room in which the stormy scene between Lourtie and Kling had taken place the night before.

'Sit down . . . I've been waiting to see you all morning . . . My husband is at the hospital, although this is a holiday, and I don't expect him back for another half-hour . . . I wanted to see you before . . .'

She must have taken a tranquillizer, for she was calmer than on the previous evening, but it was an almost terrifying calm, being clearly the result of a strenuous effort of will.

'I know that you're not obliged to answer me. But perhaps you'll take pity on a woman? . . . Perhaps you'll understand that I am prepared to hear anything? . . . I was going to add *to admit anything* . . .'

He stayed motionless, doing his utmost to conceal all that was going through his mind.

'*How long have you been working with him*?'

She asked this question like someone well aware of all its weight and gravity.

'You understand me? . . . I repeat, I am prepared to admit everything . . . I can't stand any more . . . If I haven't spoken to him yet . . .'

'You've not seen him this morning?'

'Philippe has been at the hospital since eight o'clock. He telephoned me to ask if you had come in . . . in which case he'd have liked you to go and see him there . . . Now it's not worth while . . . Well then, Dr Dollent: *how long have you been working with him*?'

The difficulty was to remain unmoved, not to answer, not to smile, to appear as though he were fiercely guarding a weighty secret; and the Little Doctor, to keep himself in countenance, lit a cigarette.

'You don't want to tell me anything, do you? You don't want to betray him . . . But suppose I told you that I know more than he suspects? . . . For instance, take your visit . . . is it natural that a man, only three weeks married, and who's in love with his wife, should invite to stay for several days a friend whom previously he saw barely once a year?'

'I apologize for my intrusion and I swear that if I'd known . . .'

She stamped her foot impatiently.

'That's not the point and you know it very well. Philippe is a terribly busy man, and he's not in the habit of meeting people at the station, even his closest friends . . . But he went to meet you at three o'clock. It was five when you both got here . . . Admit, Dr Dollent, that you went together to the *Tonneau d'Argent* . . .'

'I don't see what . . .'

'Do you think it's natural, then, that men in your social position should have nothing more urgent to do, when they meet for the first time in months, than to rush off to the lowest of dives? Don't you think, doctor, that it would be simpler and more decent to admit everything? . . . I know the temptation must sometimes be very strong . . . I had thought that Philippe's parents had left him comfortably off, if not wealthy; I understand now how he was able to buy a practice as considerable as this and . . .

'It's horrible! . . . It's all the more horrible in that my father is adamant against any surrender of principle . . . You heard him yesterday when, I cannot imagine why, you felt impelled to refer to your traffic . . .'

He repeated, as though shaking off a great burden:

'*Your traffic* . . . You did say *your traffic*, didn't you? . . . And you were referring to the traffic in drugs?'

'But . . .'

She was puzzled and shocked by his sudden exuberance.

'I cannot see how my words . . . Unless you consider such traffic legal and fail to realise the damage that heroin . . .'

'. . . *the damage that heroin* . . .' he echoed again.

'Are you crazy, doctor?'

He had no time to reply. She was listening attentively, and she grew pale. She motioned him to silence, whispering:

'Hush! I hear footsteps in the drawing-room . . . It's Philippe . . . We'll go on with our conversation when . . .'

But Dollent had risen to his feet and he flung open the door.

'Come in, old man . . . Your wife and I were discussing some very serious problems . . . What are your views about the traffic in heroin and cocaine?'

'That again?' Philippe said impatiently; he was on edge, probably from having waited all morning for Dollent at the hospital.

'What are your views about it?'

'Do you really want to know? Haven't you anything else to think about?'

'It's not me . . . It's your wife . . .'

'What are you talking about?'

'Just imagine . . . But wait a minute. We'd better not be disturbed. Madame, would you mind telling your maid that we shan't want lunch for a little while? . . . On the other hand, if she could bring us something to drink . . . I'm not ashamed to add, something pretty strong . . . I've done a lot of work this morning. I've travelled I don't know how many kilometres . . .'

Madeleine and her husband were wholly at a loss; they could not understand what was happening to them.

'Elise, will you bring the port . . .'

'Forgive me again . . . Port is too sweet . . . Could we have some brandy and water?'

And, once he'd been served: 'Now, Madame, would you mind answering some of my questions? We must take it in turns, surely! . . . You were grilling me just now, and I promise you I could hardly refrain from bursting out laughing in your face . . .

'You see, it's very difficult to conduct an inquiry among decent people, because they invariably make the most blunders. Besides, they have reticences which prevent them from bringing certain things into the open . . .'

'I should like . . .' Philippe broke in sharply.

'You shut up! . . . So I come to my first question, Madame; how long have you been getting anonymous letters?'

Madeleine was not the only one to stare at him wide-eyed. Her husband was equally astonished.

'But . . .'

'Come now, Madame, tell me frankly . . . Since your engagement was officially announced, isn't that so?'

'Yes . . . But . . . how do you know?'

'The letters were typewritten. Until your marriage they probably confined themselves to asserting that your husband was not the man you thought him and that he led a double life . . .'

She hung her head, and the Little Doctor began striding up and down in front of the guilty-looking couple.

'That was all that had to be established!' he burst out in mock anger. 'And you both consider yourselves intelligent people! Out of tact, as you would say, you hadn't the honesty to show each other the letters you were receiving or even to refer to them . . . Oh dear no! Caesar's wife must be above suspicion . . . The letters go into the waste-paper basket . . . You shrug your shoulders; you get married; and then one fine day . . .'

Madeleine looked at Philippe. Philippe looked at Madeleine. But the Little Doctor did not allow them time to indulge in this mutual contemplation.

'I must confess right away that I was no more intelligent than yourselves, and that I'm not in the least proud of my investigation.

'On the other hand, we are dealing with somebody extremely clever, such an expert in psychology that I'd like to take my hat off to him right away . . .

'For months you dismissed the anonymous letters that brought no proofs to either of you . . . You got married . . . You had a wonderful honeymoon journey, from which you returned full of confidence and happiness . . .

'What was needed now to cause a rift between you, or at least, at the beginning, to sow doubts in your minds?

'A proof!

'Madeleine – if I may call you so? it makes things easier – must be given a proof that Philippe is unworthy of her. And Philippe must be given clear proof that Madeleine is not the decent woman he imagines . . .'

He fell silent. The maid had just opened the door.

'Can I bring in lunch? Cook says the roast lamb . . .'

'Never mind the roast lamb!' cut in the Little Doctor, as though he had been speaking to Anna. 'Shut the door! Don't come back until you're sent for.'

He poured himself a drink. He was tense. He walked round the narrow room ten times a minute and forgot himself so far as to fling his cigarette ends on the carpet.

'To compromise decent people! To compromise them in such a way as to leave no doubt in any honest person's mind . . .

'I don't say it's a masterly achievement, but I can assure you that the man or woman who thought it up . . .

'To prove to Philippe, for instance, that his wife frequents the most unsavoury spot in Boulogne . . . That involves luring her there . . . But if Philippe sees her there, if they're there at the same time, an explanation becomes possible, and that wrecks our criminal's plans.

'If on the other hand somebody writes to Madeleine: "*Your husband, whom you take to be a serious medical man, a man of integrity, is really an adventurer who lives by drug-peddling . . . For that purpose he frequents a shady tavern, the* Tonneau d'Argent, *where he meets his accomplices . . . You can see him there on such and such a day, at such and such an hour . . . If he's not there, it means that the meeting has been put off till next day . . .*" '

The Little Doctor mimed the scenes like an actor.

'Madeleine goes there. She doesn't see her husband. She determines to go back next day. But next day she receives an authentic photograph, proving that Philippe had really been at the *Tonneau d'Argent* shortly after herself . . .

'Are you beginning to understand the method? There's a double game going on. While Madeleine was waiting for her husband in the dive, she was also being photographed . . . And Philippe, by going there to catch her in the act, provided the opportunity for his own photograph to be taken . . .

'Husband and wife receive a photo of each other. Each of them is convinced . . .

'But frequenting the *Tonneau d'Argent* is not proof enough . . . Something further is needed . . . You're persuaded to visit Rouen, one after the other as before, so as to avoid meeting one another . . . And you are photographed . . . And these photographs . . .

'What d'you say about it? . . . Nothing? . . . I say it's diabolical! And the most diabolical thing is not so much the invention itself as the psychological insight that the plot reveals . . . For in any other milieu, with people of a different sort, the thing would probably not have worked.

'But you two are so intensely, so idealistically in love . . . Madeleine is one of those women that no man would dare insult by a suspicion, while Philippe is a man of such integrity . . .

'So the pair of you will suffer in silence . . . You won't dare look one another in the eyes . . . You'll seek the most far-fetched explanations . . . While gradually mutual mistrust creeps into your relationship. Tension grows; a real war of nerves begins between you . . .

'And you have to keep up appearances, to go on smiling, carrying on as usual and meanwhile telling yourselves that all you thought of as your happiness, your purpose in life, is a sham, a complete sham, as faked as a second-rate stage set . . .'

Madeleine was the first to rise, white to the lips. She just said 'Philippe!'

And as he was about to go up to her and, perhaps, to clasp her in his arms, he paused hesitantly, hid his face in his hands and broke into sobs.

'Philippe! Forgive me . . .'

Ought the Little Doctor to stay there? Wouldn't he do better to leave?

To keep himself in countenance he seized the bottle of brandy and his glass, opened the door and went into the dining-room.

The maid was waiting there resignedly.

'Are they going to be long?' she asked.

'I don't know . . . It depends . . .'

And he poured himself a drink. At that moment the front door bell rang.

A few minutes later Dr Gromaire entered the room and glanced at Dollent with undisguised hostility.

'Are my daughter and son-in-law here?'

He was making for the little study, but Jean Dollent barred his way.

'One moment . . . They're very busy . . .'

'Are you going to stay much longer in Boulogne?'

'Why, since the climate doesn't suit me particularly, I guess I'll go off tonight . . . By the way . . . Our friend Kling . . .'

'Kling is laid up,' growled Madeleine's father.

'Anything serious?'

'He shot himself in the head . . .'

'What?'

'But he missed his aim!'

IV. In Which Jealousy is the Main Theme

They were sitting round the table once again. An extra place had been laid for Monsieur Gromaire. Philippe and Madeleine, their eyes glowing, really looked like a honeymoon couple.

'You know that Kling tried to blow his brains out?' the Little Doctor asked with his most innocent air, as though anxious to put his foot in it yet again.

'Is that true?' Philippe, aghast, turned to his father-in-law.

'It's true . . . But he did not wound himself seriously. Kling is very highly strung, like all people who overwork . . . Last night's scene upset his nerves. When he got home . . .'

Madeleine reddened and looked down at her plate.

'It may be my fault,' Philippe said. 'Yesterday, after Dollent's remarks, he said something that offended me . . . I must admit that at first I thought he'd gone off his head . . . He asked me if I was not ashamed of disgracing the medical profession and deceiving a woman like Madeleine . . .

'I took him into the study to discuss things face to face . . . I asked him what he was referring to . . .

'Now the strange thing, about which I'm still wondering, is that he had made a connection between Dollent's remarks about the drug traffic and our visit to the *Tonneau d'Argent* that afternoon.

' "I've already heard something about that," he told me.

' "From whom?"

' "I shan't answer that question . . . Tonight I believed it must be true. I was shocked that such an unscrupulous man should have married a woman like Madeleine . . ." '

There was silence round the table, and a certain uneasiness in the air. But this time it was Philippe's turn to speak out resolutely.

'I proved to him that I had never gone in for dope-peddling. Then he apologized . . . He confessed what I already suspected, that he was in love with Madeleine and that if I hadn't proposed to her he would have . . .'

Suddenly the sharp voice of the Little Doctor broke in.

'Do you think Kling was capable of writing those anonymous letters?'

And Philippe replied frankly: 'No! He was in love, true, but too sincerely and whole-heartedly to have recourse to such methods. The proof of that is that after confessing his love the poor fellow, still overcome by emotion, attempted suicide.'

'May I ask you an indiscreet question, Philippe?'

The Little Doctor again! It looked as if he was deliberately choosing the most crucial issues!

'Your secretary . . . Odile . . . Has there ever been anything between you? . . . I don't mean only on your part, but on hers . . .'

'When she was fifteen!' Philippe replied with a smile.

'What happened?'

'We were in love with each other, briefly . . . For about a month, if my memory is correct . . . Since then, she's fallen for a violinist who waits for her every evening outside the house.'

'Is it still raining?' the Little Doctor said, as though he had made a great discovery.

'It's the time of year,' Madeleine replied ironically, her interest in life reviving. 'You mustn't come to this part of France in winter if you're afraid of water . . .'

Then, rising from table: 'Shall we go next door for coffee?'

The four of them stood there. Dollent seemed to be hunting for something, although he was not actually doing so. He accepted a cup of coffee, went up to M. Gromaire, to whom he said a few words, and then both of them adjourned into the little study, which was evidently consecrated to mysterious conversations.

'Can *you* think of anyone, Philippe, who bears us enough ill-will to have written those letters?'

Philippe shook his head reflectively.

'No, I can't think . . . Yet it must be someone who knows us, and who knows us well . . .'

'And who wants to separate us from one another . . .'

'Apart from Kling . . .'

'It isn't Kling . . .'

'Or Odile!'

'You must be joking! I tell you that Odile and I . . .'

'Then I really wonder . . .'

The two men came out of the little study, feigning cheerfulness.

'Your little doctor was telling me a story . . . But that's by the way! . . . I've got an appointment at three . . . Incidentally, I forgot to tell you . . . Next week I'm off for a cruise in the Mediterranean . . . Why, yes! My turn for a holiday . . .'

He was not happy, not happy at all. And as he took his leave, he turned an anxious gaze towards the Little Doctor. The latter nodded.

'I promise!' he seemed to be saying.

What was the good of relating to Philippe and Madeleine the confession he had just heard?

Gromaire had lived only for his daughter. The thought that a man, one of his own pupils, was going to take her away from him . . . that they would be happy together, without him, and that he himself would now be nothing but a useless old creature – those were the words he used.

Perhaps the fact that all his patients were extreme neurotics, that all his life he had been almost exclusively in contact with people who were half crazy, had diminished his own responsibility.

The matter no longer concerned the Little Doctor.

'It's still raining!' he sighed.

'Doesn't it rain at La Rochelle?'

'Not like here!'

And suddenly, to avoid the questions that he felt imminent, he burst out: 'After all, I've had enough of this dump! . . . What did I come here for, when all's said and done? Nothing at all! To help a pair of idiots – forgive me, Madame – who weren't capable of sorting out their own affairs . . . Because a madman or a crank took it into his head to write them anonymous letters and send them photographs . . .

'You won't catch me at it again, my dears! Particularly as the parlourmaid has taken away the brandy-bottle . . .

'So what about it? Can't one even get a drink in this house?

'That's your bad luck! . . . No, don't insist . . . I'd rather go and have one with Jim at the *Tonneau d'Argent* . . .'

And the young married couple were grateful for his clowning, which spared them from having to talk seriously about something of which they were now ashamed.

Not to mention the fact that they dimly guessed that the Little Doctor was in possession of a secret, and one of which they would be wiser to remain for ever in ignorance.

Isn't it often the case that the most honourable, upright men are the ones who allow themselves to . . .

Dr Gromaire tramped along the quayside, his hands behind his back, his shoulders hunched, under the rain: *he had definitely lost his daughter.*

The Corpse in the Kitchen Garden

I. In Which the Little Doctor is Visited by an Authoritarian Young Lady and Hears About the Discovery of a Mysterious Corpse

'Ten drops three times a day, d'you hear?' shouted the Little Doctor to old Madame Tatin, his last patient that evening.

She nodded gently, smiling as the deaf do. Had she understood anything? It didn't matter, since the medicine was quite harmless.

As usual, Jean Dollent showed his patient out by the little door that gave directly on to the road. As usual, too, he went to open the other door, the one into the waiting-room, to make sure nobody was left. The waiting-room was dark. At first he could not clearly distinguish the girl who now got up and walked deliberately into his consulting-room.

When he saw her in broad daylight, straight and slim in a finely tailored suit, he involuntarily knit his brows, for this was the first time that his humble country surgery had been graced by the visit of such a pretty girl or of anyone so elegant.

'Please forgive the untidiness,' he stammered. 'I've seen about twenty patients this afternoon and . . .'

If only he'd had time to put on a clean lab coat and comb his hair!

The stranger, meanwhile, sat down on the arm of a chair the seat of which was cluttered with objects. She took a cigarette from a monogrammed case, lit it with a gold lighter, and then began:

'Your locum is free for the time being? . . . Dr Magné, isn't it? I inquired before coming here . . . I know that when you're busy with an investigation he looks after your practice . . . Now I want to take you away with me this very evening . . .'

To say that he was surprised would be an absurd under-statement. Amazed would still be too weak. His eyes were literally starting out of his head as he looked at the young lady who, although only in her early twenties, was ordering him about with such offhand self-assurance.

'Forgive me, Mademoiselle . . . I'm a doctor and not a detective . . . I may have happened by chance . . .'

'And suppose chance offered you once more the opportunity to exercise your gifts? I suppose you've heard about the mysterious corpse at Dion?'

This was a village forty kilometres from Marsilly and three or four from Rochefort. Despite his passionate interest in crime reports, the Little Doctor had not had time to read the papers during the last few days.

'I'm sorry, but I haven't heard about it . . .'

'In that case, I'll tell you what happened at Dion and when you've heard my story you shall come along with me. Let me first of all give you these two thousand-franc notes by way of surety . . . I went to Niort today on purpose and sold a ring to get the money . . . I want you to make this inquiry on my behalf and no one else's.'

'Poor fellow!' the Little Doctor couldn't help thinking, as he tried to picture the man who would some day be this young lady's husband. 'He won't have much say in running his own life!'

But a few minutes later his mind was full only of the story which she was quietly telling him, with a simplicity and clarity rarely met with in statements to the police.

Time passed; Anna looked in to ask, with a curious glance at the girl who was now seated on the edge of the desk, smoking one cigarette after the other:

'What time d'you want dinner?'

Dollent's eyes met those of his visitor. He would have liked to put up some resistance, if only so as to provoke her. But against his will he replied:

'I shan't dine at home . . . I shan't be back to sleep either . . .'

Shortly afterwards the girl climbed back into a luxurious car which she drove herself, while the Little Doctor, having changed his clothes, followed in Tin Lizzie.

The corpse had been discovered by Cogniot, better known at Dion as Cogniot-the-Stutterer. It had been six days ago, on the first Tuesday in April. At half past six in the morning, Cogniot, his feet in sabots and his pipe between his teeth, had gone into the kitchen garden pushing a wheelbarrow he had just taken from the shed. It was a bright fresh morning.

The kitchen garden was huge, and as carefully tended as a public park. It was enclosed on three sides by a whitewashed wall covered with espaliers. The fourth side was taken up by the house of the proprietor, known locally as the château on account of its size.

The château had been bought about fifteen years earlier by some very rich people, the Vauquelin-Radots, who spent the greater part of the year there.

Cogniot was their gardener. His wife looked after the poultry.

There were four other servants: a man who acted as butler and valet, a cook and two maids.

'All that lot for three bosses!' Cogniot would sigh, shaking his head.

At half-past six he was perfectly calm, thinking only about the manure he was going to spread on the flower-beds. A minute later he was racing towards the house, uttering shouts for help which sounded most peculiar because of his stammer.

Cogniot had just discovered, among the lettuce seedlings he had recently planted out along the walls, the body of an unknown man, whom he had never seen and who looked quite unlike the sort of person usually met with in that part of the world.

Not only was the man dead, but there was a large blood-smeared knife lying not far from his body, and, heaven knows how, blood had spurted on to the whitewashed wall.

The Little Doctor, who was now speeding along the road to Rochefort, had been told all this by the girl, Martine Vauquelin-Radot, niece of Robert Vauquelin-Radot, the owner of the big house at Dion.

The local constable had come, then the Mayor, then the Rochefort police, and finally the D.P.P. All day long they had trampled poor Cogniot's vegetable plots, and he had never stuttered so much in his life, for he'd had to tell his story at least twenty times.

'I was going along, you see, with my barrow and my pipe, and I was thinking to myself it was going to be a bad year for slugs, when . . .'

The corpse had been photographed from every angle. The papers had published photographs and a detailed description. Nobody had seen the man. Nobody knew him. It looked as if he had dropped from the sky to die, with a knife through his heart, in that quiet kitchen garden.

Death had occurred, according to the forensic pathologist, at about nine the previous evening.

The fingerprints specialist, who had examined the knife, was even more categorical: there was not a single print on the handle, which, being of wood, might have been expected to show clear prints.

But the dead man had not worn gloves!

'And yet suicide is the only plausible explanation,' said Monsieur Vauquelin-Radot. 'I cannot see who could have come into my kitchen garden to kill a man there . . .'

'Can you explain, on the other hand, how a man whom nobody knows should have come here on purpose to commit suicide by stabbing himself, which requires unusual strength of mind and is practically impossible without leaving finger-prints?'

But there were some even more fantastic details in the case.

To begin with, the dead man himself: the sort of person he seemed to have been, since nobody had seen him alive. He must have been about fifty; he was very thin, in poor health, his body worn out by excesses, malnutrition and alcohol, according to the somewhat pompous statement of the Rochefort pathologist, who was the father of eight children and president of a temperance society.

He wore his silvery hair very long, '*à l'artiste*', and had a pointed beard under which he sported a black *lavallière*, a loose bow tie like those worn by Montmartre painters of an earlier generation.

On the Butte of Montmartre, between the Sacré Coeur and the Rue Lepic, he would not have attracted attention. But at Dion! . . . Could one assume that he was really an impoverished old painter, a bohemian photographer, or some seedy cabaret singer?

The same question recurred constantly, whatever hypothesis was envisaged: 'what was he doing at Dion? and why had he climbed over a wall – true, it was not a very high one, nor topped with broken glass – to enter the kitchen garden of Monsieur Vauquelin-Radot?'

Finally, how had he come there *without a centime in his pocket?* For the pockets of his suit, which was very worn and shiny with age, were completely empty. Neither tobacco nor cigarettes, nor a purse, nor any of the small articles that the most poverty-stricken men carry about. Not even a handkerchief!

There was just one thing: a wallet which, to judge by its shapelessness, he must have been carrying around for years. And this wallet, originally no doubt crammed with papers of every sort, contained only a single sheet.

What importance was to be ascribed to it? Should one believe, as did the examining magistrate, that this paper was the hub of the whole affair?

It was a message composed of letters cut out of a newspaper and stuck side by side:

'*Monday nine p.m., you know where. Discretion and mystery.*'

Did not the last words in particular suggest the idea of a hoax, or the work of a romantic schoolboy? Unfortunately the man had in fact died on the Monday evening at nine o'clock.

Was it by means of this message that he had been lured into the kitchen garden of the big house at Dion?

Nobody had seen him go through the village. And yet the weather had been fine, and in spite of the darkness some people had been enjoying the evening air on their doorsteps.

No bicycle had been found, and the stranger had not taken the bus. On the whole, the investigation had not been badly done. For instance, the man's clothes had been most carefully examined: it was found that all labels had been removed from them, and there was no evidence to be got from the leaky, down-at-heel shoes.

An inspector had questioned the staff at Rochefort station. One of them had a vague recollection of seeing a traveller corresponding to the description of the dead man alight from the Bordeaux train at 5.0 p.m. on Monday afternoon. The traveller had handed in a third-class single ticket from Bordeaux to Rochefort.

And the Little Doctor automatically registered this in a pigeonhole of his memory:

'A single ticket! So the man did not intend returning to Bordeaux, at any rate not immediately . . .'

That was all, at least as far as anything positive was concerned. But it was only the beginning of the drama. Martine's frown had deepened, and she blew out a puff of smoke from her nostrils. After a brief silence she went on:

'Doctor, I am convinced that this man was my father, Marcel Vauquelin-Radot . . . And although I am not yet in a position to bring a charge, I suspect my uncle Robert of having lured him to Dion in order to murder him . . . That is why I wish you . . .'

It was an order, given without the slightest hesitation.

'. . . I wish you to make a personal inquiry on my behalf, independently of the official investigation which is too much subject to my uncle's influence . . . My uncle is a rich man . . . After his marriage he became one of the principal directors of the Suez Company . . . His name and his titles impress the officials and even the magistrates . . . He writes books on history and he hopes one day to be elected to the Institut . . .'

Contrary to his original intention, the Little Doctor did not go to Dion that night. It was too late. He was hungry. He began by dining in comfort at the buffet of Rochefort station, then, having reserved a room at the hotel, he did what he had so often done during his investigations: he went into bistrots, with the firm determination to avoid drinking alcohol, but with a will-power by no means equal to it.

'Tell me, waiter . . . Were you on duty last Monday?'

'Yes, Monsieur . . . You're going to ask me if I saw a fellow wearing a big bow tie . . . It's the third time this week I've been asked that question.'

Rather annoying . . . Still, he kept it up, and at the sixth bistrot, which had a garrulous *patronne*, he had some luck.

'I know what you mean . . . An artist, wasn't he? I was really upset when I saw his picture in the paper . . . And I said to Ernest, who delivers lemonade on a Wednesday, that you'd have thought the poor man suspected what was coming to him.'

'Did he look unhappy or anxious?'

'I couldn't tell you precisely . . . No, but he had funny little eyes. He was drinking like someone who wants to forget his worries . . .'

'Did he drink a great deal?'

'Three double brandies . . . Look, here are the glasses . . . He emptied them at one go, then he'd stare down at the floor and mutter something to himself . . . Unfortunately I couldn't catch what he was saying . . .'

'What time was it?'

'When he left? Exactly ten past seven. I remember because he looked at the clock and said out loud: "It's time, if I want to be there at nine."

'That's all I know. I thought the police would come and question me before now . . . You are the police, aren't you? . . . Oh, I've always been on good terms with the police . . . I'm respectable, I am . . .'

Next morning at seven o'clock the Little Doctor's car drew up in front of Dion's only inn, the Two Chestnut Trees, opposite the church.

If he had been asked what he intended to do, he'd have found it hard to give an answer, for he had not the slightest idea.

It was seven days, now, since the events had taken place. Tuesday again . . . The body of the stranger, after being subjected to the final humiliation of an autopsy, had been buried in the graveyard at Rochefort. No mourners followed the hearse, and the grave was marked only by a number.

The man's clothes and the piece of paper with the message were at the office of the Clerk of the Court.

What remained to serve as basis for an investigation? A substantial middle-class residence, the gate of which he could see just before the first bend in the road, a spacious house with tall windows, five steps up to the front door, and a neat little park in front; on the left, the gardener's cottage. The kitchen garden was at the back, with a flower garden as well, and one could see why the local people called this property the château.

'I could do with a bite!' said the Little Doctor to the landlord of the inn. 'A bit of sausage, some brown bread and a glass of white wine for instance . . .'

'I'll go and see if the pork-butcher's is open. You don't mind garlic in the sausage?'

After all, he was unlikely to meet yesterday's young lady again, and so he ate garlicky sausage, while the morning life of the little square – which was shaded not merely by two, but by six chestnut trees – went on as brightly and simply as usual.

Suddenly, when for some minutes he had been listening to voices without paying attention to them, he gave a start on hearing someone stuttering. It was outside the baker's shop close by the inn. The stutterer, who was none other than Cogniot, was protesting furiously, as though bad luck had made a special target of him.

'It can't go on like this!' he grumbled, with much repetition of syllables. 'Because if they're trying to make a fool of me, I won't set foot in their blasted garden again . . . It was bad enough finding the dead man there . . . All day Thursday I was looking for my surveying-chain, to straighten the paths . . . I knew exactly where I'd left it . . . So I went into the shed, I slid my hand along the shelf: no chain . . .

'In the evening I went into the second garden to sow my seeds and I nearly stumbled . . . On what? on my chain which was lying stretched out there! . . . I went to pick it up, wondering who'd had the nerve to take it without my leave. And at the end of the chain I almost fell into a hole a metre wide, just at the foot of the fig tree . . .

'Then I got real mad . . . I ran into the house and asked who had taken the chain and who had dug the hole . . . Nobody knew . . . They all put on an innocent air, including the butler . . .

'So then this morning . . .'

He was choking with indignation, and when that happens to a stammerer!

'Give me a glass of white, Eugène! . . . This morning I went as far as the stream to see if the cress had grown . . . That's a place right down the far end of the estate, where one doesn't go every day . . . What did I find? The pegs I use for my tracing line, stuck in Indian file a metre apart . . . Rather like when navvies are marking out a trench . . .

'Well, I rushed up to the house again . . . I gave them a piece of my mind . . . I said if I'm not in control of the garden, and people can mess about in it without my leave, I'll give in my notice.

'And all of them looked even sillier than the day before. Auguste, the butler, swore nobody had set foot down there.

'All the same I'd like to know what this funny business means, and whether it's likely to go on . . .'

'Excuse me,' the doctor's clear voice cut in.

Everyone looked at him. The villagers were beginning to get used to policemen and they must have taken him for one.

'Since last Monday, had you gone back to the two places you have just mentioned? Think carefully . . .'

'As regards the stream, I'm sure of it . . . I didn't work down there all week . . . As to the fig tree, I might have gone past it, but not close by . . .'

'So that the hole may have been dug since Monday night? And the chain laid out? . . . and even more probably, the pegs stuck in beside the stream . . .'

'Are you telling me it was the dead man?'

And Cogniot, who clearly was not fond of corpses, grimaced and shuddered as though overcome with nausea.

'If only that chap had chosen somewhere else to die . . . When I think of it . . . Just where I'd planted my lettuce seedlings . . .'

He turned round. The sound of a horse's hoofs was heard. The Little Doctor thought for one moment that it was a *gendarme* on his rounds, but he noticed that the gardener looked abashed, and then hurried into the baker's shop. A minute later the horseman appeared: he was a man of fifty-five to sixty, tall and lean, every inch the French provincial aristocrat.

He rode past with a casual wave of greeting to the group, from which the gardener had now vanished; it was the gesture of the lord of the manor acknowledging his peasants.

'Is that Vauquelin-Radot?' queried Jean Dollent.

'Don't you know him? He goes for a ten-kilometre ride almost every morning. Sometimes the young lady's with him. They have two fine horses . . .'

'Who looks after the horses? Cogniot?'

'No . . . He doesn't know enough about it . . . It's an old fellow called Martin, who used to be a company sergeant-major in the cavalry; he lives at the end of the street, and goes to the stable every morning and every evening . . .'

'And where is the stable?'

'Just beyond the house . . . You can't see it because the road bends . . . A little one-storey building that opens straight on to the street and on to a courtyard at the back . . .'

Cogniot poked his head out.

'All the same, I'm going to ask the boss by and by if he's the joker who's been digging holes and pinching my pegs . . . Sure, I'll speak to him . . . And I'll tell him straight, I will; I'll say: "Monsieur . . . Monsieur, for fifteen years now I . . ."'

The Little Doctor had stopped listening. True, he had heard of frightful family dramas. Within his own sphere of action at Marsilly, he had come across fierce hatreds provoked by petty questions of material interest – an ordinary party wall, for instance, or the clearing of a ditch!

But how could one conceive that this rich, distinguished-looking man, a future member of the Institut, who had just gone by on his daily ride, could in cold blood have lured his brother into a trap by a trick so commonplace as to be puerile, with ridiculous words cut out of old newspapers?

And then the stabbing of the victim with a heavy, common knife! The handle wiped clean, the body left lying in the garden plot, the blood on the white wall . . .

The village was bright and spruce as a toy village, perfect, even to the cheerful ring of the blacksmith's hammer on his anvil and the warm odour of new bread issuing from the baker's shop . . . The château was the very picture of a happy home, where luxury was simple and unostentatious. The man who chose to live there, when he could have afforded a more showy way of life elsewhere, must have an appreciation of happiness of a deep and quiet sort, of order and of good taste.

But how was one to explain the hole under the fig tree, the pegs, the surveying-chain laid out in the garden?

And finally, how could the other man, whom nobody had recognized and who came from heaven knows where, have been Marcel Vauquelin-Radot, officially reported dead five years previously?

With her astonishing forthrightness, Martine had told him all that she knew, all that she thought.

'There were just the two brothers, my father Marcel and my uncle Robert . . . Apparently my father squandered his inheritance . . . When I was born and my mother died in childbirth, he decided to go off to the colonies to start a new life, and entrusted me to my uncle . . .'

'Who was still a rich man?'

'Particularly as he had just married the daughter of a major shareholder in the Suez Company . . . I must admit right away that I never knew my father . . . I've only seen a portrait of him as a child with his brother . . . I was brought up by my uncle and aunt . . . I was quite a big girl when they explained to me, as a mysterious secret, that my father had not behaved quite honourably – that he had done foolish things, even in Africa when he took refuge there – that at Dakar, finally, he'd had to choose between jail and a mental hospital . . . Had he really gone out of his mind through drink?

'That was what they told me . . . Then, five years ago, there was that terrible accident of which you must surely have heard . . . There was a fire in the hospital at Dakar . . . All the patients, except two or three – and my father was not one of these – were burnt alive . . . I went into mourning . . .

'And now . . .'

Was it the way she had been brought up by her uncle, that quintessential representative of the upper bourgeoisie, which had given this girl such self-possession? She faced things as calmly as she was now facing the Little Doctor.

'They tried to prevent me from seeing the body they found in the kitchen garden . . . I managed to get close to it, however . . . My uncle gave me a nasty look . . . When I saw the face I felt a sort of shock . . . I'm not saying I felt the call of kinship, for I'm a modern girl and I don't believe in that sort of thing.

'Then I thought about it . . . There was another detail that struck me . . . For the past week my aunt has been supposed to be ill, and has kept to her own room . . . It started on the Sunday, the day before the stranger came . . .

'Suppose my uncle had been planning something, he could have . . .'

It was terrifying to hear her calmly uttering such monstrous charges!

'You suggest that your uncle could have made his wife ill by some means or other?'

'Or got her to pretend to be ill . . .'

'What sort of woman is your aunt?'

'She's a feeble creature . . . Always depressed for no reason, always studying medical books and dosing herself; she thinks she's got cancer and that she hasn't long to live . . . The X-rays are all negative, but she accuses the doctors of conspiring to deceive her . . . You must conduct an inquiry *for my sake*, because I've got to know . . .'

Sitting at a small green-painted table on the terrace of the little inn, opposite the church and the six chestnut trees, whose pale green leaves were just burgeoning forth, the Little Doctor wondered whether . . .

Had she not admitted that her father had been a ne'er-do-well, a reckless adventurer, and had finally been shut up in the mental hospital at Dakar?

If he'd been crazy, wasn't it possible that his daughter? . . .

And in that case, if she were mentally deranged in any degree, was the doctor not playing a deplorable role? For here he was, after all, in the position of suspecting a man of having murdered his brother in the most shocking circumstances imaginable.

What was he to reply if that man should challenge him: 'Aren't you ashamed, as a doctor, of accepting two thousand francs from a girl you've never set eyes on, to undertake a job of this sort?'

For it was the truth. Strictly speaking, he had intended to return to his visitor the two thousand-franc notes she had laid on the desk. Then, when she was leaving, preoccupied by what he had heard, he had forgotten all about them. It was Anna who had picked them up when the doctor himself was about to leave, and there had been a certain contempt in Anna's voice as she remarked:

'I see that Monsieur's doing nicely for himself in his new job . . . It would have taken a lot of visits at twenty francs a time . . .'

He had made up his mind. He had not promised to set about his inquiry in any particular fashion. Well, by and by, when he'd seen the horseman ride back, he would ring at the gate of the château. He would ask to see Robert Vauquelin-Radot. He would introduce himself. He would tell him . . .

The truth, to be sure! Except, of course, that he would not mention the girl's approach to him.

The telephone bell rang in the bistrot. The *patron* listened in perplexity for a while; then finally he came out on to the terrace, saying with some surprise: 'You're wanted on the phone.'

'Me? That's impossible . . .'

'There's nobody else on the terrace, is there? . . . I was told: "*Fetch the gentleman who's on the terrace . . .*"'

He hurried in.

'Is that you, doctor? I saw you from my bedroom window . . . Yes, I'm the person who came to see you yesterday . . . Listen! I think *he suspects something* . . . When I got back he immediately noticed that I was not wearing my ring. I pretended I'd lost it . . . Then he thought of something I'd not have believed him capable of . . . He went to check the mileage on the indicator of my car . . . He came back looking very grim . . . He ordered me to go to bed . . . Then he added that, until this business was finished with – those were his very words – he requested me (and when he makes a request!) not to leave the house . . .'

'Thank you . . .'

'What are you intending to do? If he suspects we know one another, I wonder what he's capable of doing . . . I'm beginning to be frightened . . . Listen, doctor . . .'

The Little Doctor frowned, guessing what would follow.

'Perhaps it might be more prudent to give up . . . or to postpone this . . .'

Such is the contrariness of human nature that, whereas a minute earlier Dollent had been wondering what hornets' nest he had got into, and his only longing had been to escape from it, now the mere fact that he was asked to do so was enough to make him determined to stay on!

'Are you there? Did you hear?'

'Yes . . .'

'And have you decided . . .'

The line was cut off abruptly. Had someone come into the room – the ailing aunt, or the horseman himself, who might have returned home by some other route?

'I think I'll have lunch here, *patron* . . . Have you got something nice for me?'

'Well, you know, we don't . . . Just a fricandeau of veal with sorrel . . . Some sardines to start with, if you like . . . That's all I can offer you . . . You'd do better if you went on to Rochefort.'

But here again he showed his obstinacy. And at eleven o'clock he was ringing at the gate of the château.

II. A Lively Altercation between a Gentleman who is Not Easily Upset and a Little Doctor who Feels the Ground Giving Way under his Feet

As it happened, Jean Dollent had occasionally visited the homes of those rich provincial bourgeois who are often more inaccessible than the aristocracy of old. So why was he somewhat scared of the Vauquelin-Radot residence and its owners?

When he rang at the gate, he was kept waiting a long time, and he gazed up in vain at the windows; not a single curtain twitched. Had Martine stopped keeping watch?

At last the door opened. The butler walked majestically down the steps of the perron, crossed the few yards of gravel to the gate, and then frowned.

'What do you want?' he asked, his glance critically scrutinizing the Little Doctor from head to foot.

'I want to speak to Monsieur Vauquelin-Radot.'

'I'm sorry, but Monsieur sees nobody at this time of day. Monsieur is working. If you will leave your card, Monsieur will probably give you an appointment . . .'

'I should like you to take him my card immediately, and I think he'll see me . . .'

The butler opened the gate, and even, reluctantly, allowed this intruder to enter the hall, where a soft half-light prevailed. Then he knocked discreetly at a carved oak door, disappeared into a room and presently returned with a spiteful gleam in his eye.

'As I warned you, Monsieur is sorry, but he cannot see you.'

'One minute . . . Would you give me back my card?'

And underneath his name he wrote: '. . . *who knew Marcel Vauquelin-Radot at Dakar.*' He'd chance it! Perhaps he would not have done so but for the insolence of that flunkey and the oppressive atmosphere of solemnity that pervaded the house. He was on his mettle.

'Take back this card to him and you'll see that . . .'

'Just as you please!' the butler seemed to imply. 'You'll regret it!'

And indeed the Little Doctor was presently to regret having rushed recklessly into the most unpleasant fix he had ever had to cope with. The start had been encouraging, though, and he thought he had scored a point.

'Kindly follow me . . .'

The open door revealed a huge library with tall windows overlooking the garden. Robert Vauquelin-Radot, whom the doctor had seen that morning in his riding-habit, was now wearing a black silk dressing-gown and sitting at a large desk with his back to a blazing wood fire.

It was positively irritating . . . It was too perfect . . . That anyone, in this age of unrest, should go on living just as in the most peaceful of bygone days . . . The morning ride . . . The manservant in striped waistcoat . . . This monumental fireplace and those thousands of beautifully bound books . . . That well-tended garden glimpsed yonder, even the carefully sleeked, splendid silver hair of the master of the house, even his over-sumptuous dressing-gown . . .

Vauquelin-Radot did not rise. From afar, he watched Dollent coming towards him over an immense carpet of Savonnerie workmanship, and he maintained absolute calm. Only a slight gesture of his well-kept hand motioned his visitor to a chair facing the desk.

'How old are you, doctor?'

Dollent had come to ask questions and not to answer them. So was considerably disconcerted.

'I'm thirty . . .'

'You studied medicine in France?'

'At the Faculty of Bordeaux.'

'So you left that town about five years ago . . . Consequently . . .'

He was playing carelessly with the visiting-card and he let it fall to the ground, somewhat contemptuously:

'I wonder why you thought fit to lie to me . . . It is obviously impossible that you should have known my poor brother in Dakar since, at the time when you might have visited that town, he was already dead . . . I am sorry, doctor . . .'

He stood up to show that he considered the interview at an end, while the Little Doctor's ears turned crimson.

'I apologize for making use of a rather crude and admittedly tactless stratagem to gain admittance here . . .'

The other man was carefully cutting the tip of a cigar for himself, not offering one to his guest.

'I know I have no right to meddle with an affair that does not concern me. Nevertheless, a man has been killed and I presume that, like everyone else, you are anxious for the matter to be cleared up . . .'

'The law has the necessary powers to . . .'

'I respect the law as much as you do, but on several occasions I have happened to discover the truth where the experts were baffled. That is why I venture to insist and to ask you . . .'

'I'm sorry, Monsieur!'

He was being well and truly dismissed, and this time very curtly. The Little Doctor, feeling the floor give way beneath him, had no alternative but to beat a retreat, when suddenly the door was flung open: Martine came in, wearing a light-coloured dress and smiling cheerfully. She exclaimed: 'Why, Dollent! . . . How are you, my dear?'

Then, turning to her uncle: 'You never told me you knew my friend Dollent! . . . We've often met in friends' houses, he and I . . . We've played bridge and tennis together . . . So then, doctor, you've looked in to say hello to me? I hope you're going to stay to lunch with us?'

'Martine!'

Vauquelin-Radot's imperturbable composure made his bearing really impressive.

'I shall be obliged if you will go back to your room . . . The doctor is anxious to leave . . .'

Now she seemed abashed herself, which made the Little Doctor feel he had somewhat got his own back. Then as she was leaving she glanced at him as though to say: 'Why didn't you listen to me? You see what you've brought upon yourself!'

But Dollent's troubles were not yet at an end. Scarcely had the girl disappeared when Vauquelin-Radot said drily:

'You live at Marsilly, don't you? I wondered what my niece was doing there yesterday . . . Some friends recognized my car in the village . . . Now I understand . . . And I must press you all the more insistently to leave this house. I don't know what Martine has told you . . . I'm not asking you to tell me and I don't want to know. Goodbye, Monsieur!'

Thereupon he pressed an electric bell which rang in some distant part of the house. At the same moment the bell of the front gate was heard ringing. The butler went to open the gate before answering his master's summons.

Footsteps and voices sounded in the hall. The visitors must have been important people, since the flunkey let them into the house directly. The library door opened.

'Monsieur, the examining magistrate wishes to know if you will see him . . .'

'Show him in . . .'

Dollent did not know what magistrate was in charge of this case. He felt a gleam of hope and he was not disappointed. As he was making for the door he encountered a tall fellow who recognized him and exclaimed:

'Dollent! . . . What are you doing here? . . . I might have guessed this business would interest you . . .'

There was an awkward silence. Behind the magistrate, whom Dollent knew of old, came a clerk and an inspector from Rochefort.

'I am obliged to bother you yet again, Monsieur Vauquelin-Radot, to get clear about certain details . . . I see you know my friend Dollent . . . You must have heard of his amazing flair and I assume . . .'

'Monsieur Dollent forced his way into my house and I have requested him to leave!' the master of the house replied coldly.

Everyone now felt ill at ease. The magistrate persisted, in spite of a warning glance from Dollent:

'We should greatly have valued his co-operation in our inquiry, and I wonder if under the circumstances . . .'

'I am sorry, *monsieur le juge*. An unknown man has been found dead in my garden, and the law does not entitle me to deny you access to my house nor to prevent you from questioning my domestic staff and myself. None the less a man's home is his castle, according to the old French tradition, and if this gentleman persists I shall be forced to have him thrown out by my servants . . .'

It was the most unpleasant moment the Little Doctor had ever been through in his life. He felt the blood rush to his face, then back to his heart again, leaving him pale and voiceless.

He could have . . . What could he have done? Rushed at the man to strike him? But not only was the man in his own home, and consequently within his rights, but moreover since he was a couple of heads taller than Dollent such a gesture would have been ridiculous.

Dollent went out. He collided with the framework of the door. And he had the unpleasant surprise of encountering there the butler who must have overheard everything, and who offered him his hat with an ironic expression, murmuring: 'This way . . . If Monsieur will kindly . . .'

Should he jump into his car and go home to Marsilly? And try to forget this humiliating adventure?

But for one thing, he had left Tin Lizzie outside the inn. And when he reached the terrace Dollent felt impelled to go in for a drink. He had not only one but three. And thus his mood had time to change. His gaze hardened.

'It's between the two of us now, Monsieur Vauquelin-Radot!'

But how could he investigate a case from which the interested parties excluded him so categorically? Should he wait until the magistrate emerged and ask him for the essential information?

'You've not forgotten my fricandeau?'

'It's simmering, Monsieur . . . It'll be ready in an hour . . . Can't you smell it?'

A man was trudging across the square, an enormous leather bag by his side and a uniform cap on his head.

'Louis!' he called out as he came in. 'A letter for you . . . One letter and a bill . . . Say, have you got relatives in Algiers? Will you keep me the stamp for my kid's collection?'

As the Little Doctor, who had been immersed in thought, raised his head and looked at the country postman with the long ginger moustache, the dazed expression vanished from his face, his eyes narrowed and a very keen look came into them.

'What'll you have, postman? I'm tired of drinking by myself . . .'

III. Showing the Usefulness of Philately and the Advantages of Having Old Maids as Postmistresses

'It's not that I'm bored here, but it's time I went . . . You see, I've got two villages to serve, more or less, seeing that Dion includes a hamlet two kilometres away . . .'

'I happen to be going there!' the Little Doctor broke in, on the off-chance.

'You're going to Morillon? To which house? There are only four of them . . .'

'I'm just going to have a look at the neighbourhood . . . Shall I take you in my car?'

'Well, you'll have to stop several times on the way because of my round . . .'

And thus Tin Lizzie performed an official task that morning, taking the mail from Dion to Morillon.

'Has your son a nice collection?'

'Well, we've made a start . . . You see, we're in a good position . . . When I see a foreign stamp on a letter I ask people to let me have it . . . I know everybody . . . I don't often get a refusal, except from the baker who collects stamps himself . . .'

'And I expect the big house gets a great many letters?'

'Oh, a great many! The Vauquelin-Radots give us as much work as all the rest of the village put together . . .'

Among the four houses of Morillon, one was a grocery-cum-bar, and the Little Doctor felt the need to quench his thirst and his companion's.

'You see there isn't much to visit . . . Now I've got to go home . . .'

'I'll drive you back . . . There's not much to visit, as you say . . . On the other hand it would amuse me to look at your son's collection . . . I'm a collector myself . . . Perhaps we might arrange some swaps with our duplicates?'

By midday he was at the postman's home, where the man's wife was waiting to give him his lunch.

'You'll take a glass of wine? . . . Look, here's the album. We haven't sorted everything yet . . .'

A moment later, Dollent had already noticed five stamps from Dakar.

'Are they quite recent?'

'Oh no . . . For quite a long period the château people got a letter from those parts every month . . . That's what gave me the idea of asking the butler to set the stamps aside for me . . . Then that stopped . . . Look, here's a stamp from Conakry that arrived soon afterwards . . . Five years ago . . . I remember that because an old army pal of mine was at Conakry at the time and he wrote to me the same week . . . I said to myself: "Monsieur Vauquelin-Radot and I have friends in the same part of the world."'

When the Little Doctor left, half an hour later, he had at least the basis for an investigation.

For whereas the mail from Dakar had ceased abruptly (presumably after the fire at the mental hospital) a letter from Conakry, some hundreds of kilometres further south, had arrived shortly afterwards, then one from Matadi, even further south in the Belgian Congo.

After that the journey became interesting to follow. It looked as though the man who wrote these letters was travelling along the African coast at a slowish rate, ending up at the Cape, from whence letters had come over a space of two years.

After that, nothing more from Africa. On the other hand, a stamp postmarked Hamburg a few weeks later. Now the German shipping lines that travel along the African coast start from Hamburg and end up there.

The Hamburg stamp was only two years old. Then came a Belgian one, from Antwerp.

Another port! After Antwerp, however, there were no more foreign stamps from the Vauquelin-Radots' mail.

'How about my fricandeau, *patron*?'

'Here you are, here you are . . . By the way, the gentlemen from the D.P.P. have just left . . . Do *you* think they'll discover anything, and are we ever going to know whose body was found in the kitchen garden?'

'Yes, most likely . . . Very good, your fricandeau! . . . Tell me, is the postmistress at Dion a nice person – there's a woman in charge there, I suppose?'

'She's an old maid, a regular cat! . . . As she has hardly anything to do she spends all day peering out of her window and she knows everything that goes on in the village . . . I wondered at one time if she didn't perhaps open the letters, she knows such a lot . . .'

'Could you tell me, Mademoiselle, how much it costs to send a money order by cable to Dakar?'

'It depends what sum you want to send . . . Dakar? Wait a minute . . . It's a long time since . . .'

She was a huge woman, with a beard and moustache, mischievous little eyes and an insatiable curiosity, as was proved by her next question:

'Didn't you lunch at the château?'

'No. Why?'

'Because I saw you go in there about eleven . . . They so seldom have visitors . . . Actually I find it rather surprising, rich as they are, for there isn't much going on at Dion and if I had their money . . . Dakar . . . You said a thousand francs? . . . And no written message on the telegram? Eighty-two francs . . . About the same rate as to Conakry.'

'Oh yes . . . I forgot that you must have cabled money orders to Conakry . . .'

'How do you know?'

'My friend Vauquelin told me so . . . He had a friend out there . . . A friend who hadn't had much luck . . .'

'He can't have stayed there long, for he only had the one money order for five thousand francs. I remember, because that was the first time I'd ever had to telegraph a money order to Africa. Here, people send them by post in the ordinary way . . . You have to be in a great hurry to . . .'

'But after that you had other money orders, didn't you? Matadi . . . Then . . .'

'So you're a friend of Monsieur Gélis too? Just fancy, at one point I thought he must be a gentleman doing a world tour . . . I wished he'd send Monsieur Vauquelin-Radot picture postcards instead of letters, then I could have seen what those places are like . . .'

'Always for five thousand francs?'

'The one to Matadi was for ten thousand, if I remember right . . . I had a lot of bother with that one, for I had to convert it into Belgian money, and all that business of exchange . . . Afterwards there were British pounds . . .'

'When Gélis was at the Cape . . .'

'That's right! I see you know the story . . . He stayed there nearly two years . . . Almost by every boat there came a letter in his handwriting, a very odd hand that I could recognize a long way off . . . It was so irregular, with the lines running into one another, one could hardly read it . . . Then there came a letter from Tenerife, written on headed paper from a German boat . . .

'"I say," I thought, "the gentleman's coming back to Europe . . ." If anyone sent me all that money I'd take advantage of it to visit China and Japan – because at that time the yellow people weren't at war . . .'

'Hamburg, Antwerp . . .'

'That's right . . . He seemed to be coming back by short stages. He was taking his time. And the money orders weren't so big, except for the last but one, the one to Antwerp, which jumped suddenly from a thousand to ten thousand . . . Afterwards there was a letter from Brussels, two or three from Paris, and finally, barely a fortnight ago, one from Bordeaux. It was so badly written that if I hadn't known the address by heart I'd not have been able to read it . . .'

'Did Monsieur Vauquelin-Radot send back a money order?'

'No . . . There wasn't anything more . . . Well, now, what's the address of your friend in Dakar?'

'On second thoughts, I'd rather wait a little . . . It costs so much to cable money . . .'

What a look he cast at Monsieur Vauquelin-Radot's mansion as he drove past in Tin Lizzie!

Was he mistaken, or did he really see a hand waving from between the curtains at a first-floor window?

'It's me! Don't let me disturb you . . . Tell me, Duprez, what did you think of the reception I got?'

He had reached Rochefort. He was sitting in the study of his friend Duprez, the examining magistrate, and Duprez was looking at him in some astonishment.

'You seem terribly excited, old fellow! . . . I must admit that I can't understand your passion for these criminal cases . . . Honestly, if it weren't my job, I'd rather go off for a game of golf myself . . .'

'Anything new?'

'Not really . . . Curious discoveries in the garden . . . A crazy story of a surveying-chain and a hole . . .'

'I know.'

'And another about pegs stuck in as though to . . .'

'I know that one too. As though to mark out a particular place, or more precisely as though to recognize it again, isn't that so? . . . Enough to make you think someone was trying to dig up some treasure or other in the garden . . .'

The magistrate's surprise increased.

'I thought of that!' he admitted. 'But I'm a bit suspicious. We're only too liable to be influenced by all the detective stories that are so popular . . . Let me tell you that I know at least twenty landlords in the region who fancy that there's a buried treasure on their lands and spend vast sums on organizing excavations . . . It's a chronic sickness in rural areas . . . If one farmer happens to dig up a few old gold coins in his fields, then for hundreds of miles around . . .'

'What has Vauquelin-Radot to say about it?'

'That he never heard of any treasure, or anything of the sort. That of course he himself has never gone in for digging holes in his garden or pinching his gardener's surveying-chain . . . Don't you think perhaps that character drinks rather too much and that his imagination may have . . .'

'Did Vauquelin suggest that?'

'No! With me he's invariably polite but nothing more . . . He answers yes or no . . . Today was my third visit to the place, and consequently my third conversation with him . . . I must admit he seemed a bit weary . . . Was that the effect of your visit? He's lost none of that characteristic Olympian calm which will make him such a splendid Academician. And yet underneath that calm I thought I sensed a kind of secret unease . . .'

'What was he doing at nine o'clock that Monday evening?'

'That's the oddest part of it . . . He says he doesn't remember . . . According to him, when dinner is over (and it's always over by about half-past eight) he takes the air for a few minutes on the terrace or in the garden . . . After which he goes back into his study, where he spends about an hour correcting his proofs . . .'

'Who is on the ground floor at that time of night?'

'The domestic staff are in the right wing of the house, quite a long way from the study, which you have seen and which, between you and me, is pretty splendid . . .'

'And the women?'

'They usually stay in a sitting-room on the first floor. The girl reads or writes letters . . . Her aunt, who's always tired, dozes in an easy-chair . . .'

'And nobody heard anything unusual?'

'Nobody . . . I inquired whether the windows had been open. As it's so early in the year, they were not . . .'

'What about the Cogniots?'

'They go to bed at half-past eight, for they have to get up very early . . .'

'And Martin, the man who looks after the horses?'

'He does his last round at eight o'clock, waters the horses and goes home after locking the stable door . . .'

'One more question, Duprez . . . Which way was the corpse facing?'

'Wait a minute . . . I've a whole pile of photographs taken by the finger-prints man . . . See here . . . He was facing the wall . . . The dark mark you see, about the level of a man's chest, is a blood stain . . .'

'Was the blow struck from in front or from behind?'

'From in front, with unusual force, according to the pathologist, and in particular with unusual precision. The heart was pierced immediately and the blood spurted out abundantly, making the mark you see . . .'

'It must have been dark at nine o'clock . . .'

'Of course . . .'

'And nothing peculiar struck you? These photos are excellent, but I'd still like to see the place . . .'

'Now that you make me think of it . . . An idea of the inspector's – I've been given as an assistant in this inquiry a highly intelligent, well educated young fellow – he noticed that the whitewashed wall, which is made of friable stone, bore scratches at the level of the bloodstain, as though a first blow had been struck which had not hit the victim.'

'Many thanks . . . No identification, I presume?'

'None. As you have seen, the photograph was published in all the papers . . . Apart from the proprietress of a small bistrot at Rochefort, who came this morning to report to the police that she'd been questioned by a man whose behaviour, on reflection, she had found suspicious . . .'

'That was me!'

'So you know the position . . . Nothing else . . . Monsieur Vauquelin-Radot is beginning to grow impatient, and he gave me to understand, this morning, that if we went on bothering him thus he would use his influence in high places to put a check on . . . As for you, old chap, I don't think you're very wise to go on prowling round that château, as they call it . . . After the way you were treated this morning!'

'Have you questioned the girl?'

'We questioned her as well as everyone else . . . She knows nothing . . .'

'I was forgetting the most important point . . . The labels had been taken off the dead man's clothes, hadn't they? . . . Can your experts say whether this had been done recently?'

'If you mean on the night of the crime, I can say categorically no. If you mean a few weeks earlier, yes.'

'Thank you . . .'

'Can you understand anything about it?'

'Everything, unfortunately!'

'What do you mean? Why unfortunately?'

And the little Doctor gave a wry smile. 'Because!'

'Won't you tell me?'

'Not just now . . . I'm bound by professional secrecy myself!'

'I say! What about me? All I've just been telling you?'

And Dollent replied, without turning a hair: 'That's not the same thing!'

IV. In Which the Little Doctor, Having Apparently Developed a Liking for Humiliations, Scores a Success in a Most Unexpected Way

'Hello! Can I speak to Mademoiselle Martine, please?'

'I don't know whether Mademoiselle is awake . . . Who is speaking?'

'Tell her it's her friend.'

It was eight in the morning. The Little Doctor was at the Two Chestnut Trees inn, and the village square, that sunny morning, still looked like a picture-book scene.

'Hello, is that you, doctor? Why are you being so stubborn? You frighten me . . . You'll end by . . .'

'Hello! Your uncle hasn't gone out riding this morning. I've good reason to think he's uneasy and in rather a bad temper . . . Are you afraid of him?'

'That's to say . . .'

'When you've done what I'm going to explain to you, he'll be furious . . . He'll repudiate you . . . You'll go through a very unpleasant few minutes . . . But the truth is worth it, isn't it?'

'I don't know now . . .'

'You're to speak to him . . . You're to tell him I have just telephoned you . . . That you're sorry you ever approached me . . . That I've turned out to be very different from what you expected . . . In short, that if he won't receive me and accept my conditions, the list of certain money orders sent by cable will be handed to the police this morning . . .'

'But . . .'

'If you refuse to help me I shall go myself and . . .'

He hung up. He waited half an hour and, if the truth must be confessed, he displayed more intemperance than ever. So much so that the innkeeper began to look with some suspicion at a customer who got drunk so early in the day.

Back to the garden gate . . . The Little Doctor's legs were shaking somewhat as he reached out for the brass handle that would set the noisy bell ringing.

Exactly as on the previous day, the butler appeared at the top of the steps, but he must have been given specific orders, for he stepped forward and opened the gate, with a certain haughty stiffness.

'Will you announce me . . .'

'Monsieur is expecting you!' Auguste said curtly. 'This way . . .'

The same man, in the same dress, was sitting at the same place in the huge library. But he displayed an even more marked contempt, together with an obviously unfeigned weariness which verged on despondency.

'I shall not ask you to sit down, doctor . . . I presume this won't take long . . . How much?'

'Fifty thousand.'

'And what assurance can you give me that you'll keep silence afterwards?'

'It depends on how anxious you are for me to keep silence. The sum, actually, will depend on that too . . .'

'Did you really know my brother?'

'No!'

'Have you ever corresponded with him?'

'No!'

'Did you know any of his former friends?'

'No!'

The three 'noes' were spoken firmly and cheerfully.

'In that case I don't understand how you . . .'

'How I knew that it was your brother Marcel who died last Monday at nine in the evening, in your kitchen garden?'

'My brother was insane, did you know?'

'That's a fact. At any rate I have every reason to assume that it's a fact . . . For one thing, official mental hospitals do not readily take in people who are still of sound mind . . . And then his handwriting . . .'

'Do you know his handwriting?'

And Monsieur Vauquelin-Radot glanced instinctively towards a small safe in the wall to the right of the fireplace.

'I can give you an inventory of the letters in that safe, Monsieur . . . From Dakar first . . . Weren't those letters from Dakar written by the head of the mental hospital to keep you informed about your brother's health? . . . The last of them must have been an official announcement of his death . . .

'But then there came a letter from Conakry, the writing on which you can't have failed to recognize, although it was signed Gélis . . .'

'You . . . did you break into the house?' stammered the master of it, so surprised that he forgot to be haughty.

'Oh no . . . After Conakry, Matadi . . . After Matadi . . . Shall I quote the sums you sent your brother, who was constantly pestering you for money? Each time, I suppose, he promised to mend his ways, to disappear for ever into the bush, and that you'd hear no more about him . . .'

'That's quite true . . .'

'Only then he would start drinking again, possibly gambling, and the next letter would be a fresh request for money . . . Definitely, Monsieur Gélis was just as bad as Monsieur Marcel Vauque . . .'

'Be quiet! You said fifty thousand francs . . . I'll sign a cheque and . . .'

'Hamburg!'

'What?'

'Hamburg, I said . . . Antwerp . . . Paris . . . Bordeaux . . . I'm just giving you the list of the requests for money and the cabled money orders . . .'

'Can't we have done with it, doctor?'

'No, Monsieur Vauquelin-Radot . . .'

'You think fifty thousand francs is not enough and you're presumably hoping . . .'

'There *is* something I'm hoping for, indeed . . .'

'I warn you that . . .'

'Do go on . . .'

'. . . that if you keep this up I shall inform the legal authorities at Rochefort . . . I shall tell the magistrates . . .'

'Do so!'

'You defy me to do so? Just as you please!'

He uttered the last words with all the upper-class self-confidence he had shown the day before.

'Hello! Mademoiselle, will you give me the . . .'

The Little Doctor calmly laid his hand over the instrument.

'It's not worth while . . .'

'Why?'

'Because you did not kill your brother . . . Because you could not have killed him unless you had been insane yourself . . . Because your brother was lying facing the wall, less than thirty centimetres from it, and it would have been impossible for another person to have thrust the knife into his breast . . .'

There was an impressive silence.

'Sit down, Monsieur Vauquelin-Radot. Do you know, I never imagined your class-conscious pride would go so far as to . . .

'But if you like . . . do you mind if I smoke? . . . I shall give you a few hints which will perhaps prevent you in the future from despising a village doctor.

'Needless to say we can forget about the fifty thousand francs you mentioned earlier.

'Yesterday an honourable man who was only seeking the truth came to see you in all honesty and you unhesitatingly threw him out. Today in order to gain admittance to your study and extort a few minutes' conversation from you I had to pose as a blackmailer . . .'

He had sat down, not on yesterday's chair but in a deep armchair, and had crossed his legs. That was a slight gesture of revenge, by way of a start.

'Notice that in this whole case I'm not interested in you so much as your brother. You followed the easy, ordinary path . . . Rich, well-considered, even wealthier through your marriage, you have gone in for the sort of historical writing that requires no genius, and you have gained honour and glory thereby.

'Your brother, meanwhile, having less self-discipline, lapsed into a feckless and disorderly existence from the first . . . As a result of what excesses or what disease he became partially if not totally insane I need not speak, since I assume that you are not asking for my professional medical opinion.

'The fact remains that he became a human wreck and that once that wreck was shut up in a mental hospital at Dakar you felt more at ease, since you need no longer fear that any scandal might besmirch the name of Vauquelin-Radot . . .

'Then there was that dreadful fire . . . And the fact that your brother had escaped, unbeknown to everyone . . . and that once at liberty he had asked you . . .'

A flat, calm voice said, 'Do you know, doctor, what he asked for?'

'Money . . .'

'A million to start with! And do you know what he threatened to do? To come and take away his daughter, whom he knew I had adopted and whom my wife and I considered as our own child . . .'

'You sent him five thousand francs . . .'

'I sent small sums to prevent his committing any further follies . . . He was becoming increasingly wild . . . I felt he was capable of anything . . . His letters, which I have here . . .'

'I know . . .'

'You shall read them . . . Should I have had him committed again? I felt sorry for him . . . I hoped he would manage to settle down somewhere. But instead, he became constantly more threatening, more demanding, and kept talking of taking away Martine . . .

'When I saw that he was coming closer . . .'

'Hamburg!'

'Yes, Hamburg . . . Then Antwerp . . .'

'You were afraid of the scandal . . .'

'Less on my own account than on Martine's . . . I offered him larger sums of money if he would consent to stay out of the country . . . But then, as his madness increased, he began asking for millions . . . The letters are there . . .'

'So you've said . . .'

'What would you have done in my place? I sent him twenty thousand francs and told him he'd get no more. And it was then that . . .'

'That he came closer . . . Bordeaux . . . And that he began to brood over revenge . . . In his mind you were the enemy, the profiteer of the family, the man who had not only wealth but his daughter, and society's respect into the bargain . . .

'I have studied psychiatry, Monsieur . . . He sought revenge, *a mad man's revenge* . . . He wanted to create a drama that would ruin your peace and your honour.

'He displayed a madman's lucidity in his attention to the slightest details . . . An anonymous corpse . . . anonymous clothes . . . and a strange letter making an appointment to meet in your kitchen garden.

'And that was still not enough to focus attention on you . . . He complicated things, showing himself to be really mad, probably a future victim of G.P.I. He got there early and discovered the tool-shed; he took into the garden the surveying-chain, the pegs and a spade, and he dug a hole . . .

'How could the inquiry fail to arouse the interest of the Press when it was so mysterious?

'And then he killed himself, as he had long ago decided to do. But he killed himself in such a way as to make it look like a crime. He wiped the handle of the knife with his jacket . . . He pressed the handle against the wall, with the blade against his chest close to his heart.

'He was wearing no gloves . . . Who would believe that the absence of finger-prints was not necessarily a proof of murder?

'He hated you, as I said . . . He belonged to your clan, to your world, but your clan and your world had relegated him to mental hospitals. And he held you alone responsible . . .'

'Tell me, doctor . . .'

It was the Little Doctor's turn to speak categorically: 'Be quiet!' he ordered. 'You were so afraid of a scandal for yourself and your family that you kept silent and . . .'

'Do you think it would have been better to let Martine know that her father . . .'

'And to jeopardize your election to the Institut?'

Monsieur Vauquelin-Radot hung his head.

'You are very hard, doctor . . . Scandal must always be avoided as far as possible and I cannot see how it could have been preferable . . .'

'That's all I had to say to you, Monsieur. I am not in charge of the investigation, as you so correctly pointed out yesterday . . . I only entered your house by cunning, playing the role of a blackmailer, otherwise I should surely have been thrown out, as I was yesterday . . .'

'What are you going to do?'

'Nothing . . . Go home . . .'

'And? . . .' He was hesitant, not knowing how to put the question. 'If you should meet your friend the examining magistrate?'

'He's in charge, isn't he? I'm not even a witness . . . As for the cheque . . . Later on, when this business has been forgotten – since I presume nobody's going to elucidate it – I wonder if it would not be desirable for your brother's body . . . I understand the Vauquelin-Radots have a family vault at Versailles . . . Those thousand francs . . .'

'One minute, doctor . . .'

'Excuse me, I'm in a great hurry.'

The situation was now reversed, and the Little Doctor was evading the other man's pursuit.

'You really must allow me to . . .'

Dollent, in the hall, summoned the butler: 'My hat and coat . . .'

'At least do me the pleasure of . . .'

'No ceremony, please! Very kind of you, Monsieur Vauquelin-Radot. But my duties . . . I'm a very busy man . . .'

And as a final treat which he'd promised himself, he called out in presence of the astonished butler:

'Good-day to you!'

And he tripped lightly down the steps to the gate, and leapt joyfully into Tin Lizzie which, for once, started off without more ado.

The Dutchman's Luck

I. What Happened to Mynheer Van der Donck after a Good Dinner and a Visit to Luna-Park

When Superintendent Lucas left the 'reports' conference, held each morning at the Quai des Orfèvres between the Director of the Police Judiciaire and the chiefs of the various squads, he was carrying a slim blue file; he waved it from afar, with a wink, to the Little Doctor, who sat quietly waiting.

It was August. Jean Dollent had decided to spend in Paris the fortnight's holiday he allowed himself, and to take advantage of it to learn something about the methods of the Police Judiciaire. As it happened, Superintendent Lucas was a native of Charente, and the Little Doctor had had an introduction to him from friends.

'Come and see me every morning about nine o'clock. There's sure to be a case that'll interest you one of these days.'

And now Lucas led his young companion along an endless corridor.

'Let's pretend to be having a chat,' he whispered, and he drew Dollent's attention to a glazed partition behind which was a waiting-room. 'Have a look at the man in there . . .'

In the little room a man was seated, a tall, strongly-built man whose rubicund face, shining with sweat, wore that expression of boredom that all faces assume after a long period of waiting.

He had obviously had leisure to go round the room ten times, to get up and sit down again, to study the black-framed photographs of detectives who had died for their country and the hideous mid-nineteenth-century clock that occupied the place of honour on the mantelpiece.

He had got as far as the green baize table and was staring at it conscientiously.

'Have you had a good look at him? Come along . . .'

Back in his office, Lucas asked: 'What d'you think of him?'

'H'm . . . He's a northerner, probably a foreigner . . . He hasn't been in bed all night and he's not a nervous type, for he's bearing the agonies of waiting more calmly than I should . . . What has he done?'

The Little Doctor was rather anxious, and as humble as a

schoolboy in front of his teacher.

'Steady on! Do you think the only people who come here are those who've done something? . . . Now settle down in that corner . . . Don't move!'

Superintendent Lucas rang, and told the messenger: 'Send in Monsieur Kees Van der Donck.'

The sun was high in the sky already. The wide open window let in the sounds from the embankment and the reflected shimmer of the Seine as it flowed between its stone walls. Coaches full of foreigners passed from time to time, and on the Grands Boulevards, the night before, the Little Doctor, who was more accustomed to the quiet of Marsilly and La Rochelle, had heard every sort of language spoken.

'Sit down, Monsieur Van der Donck . . . I apologize for keeping you waiting, and I'm obliged to you for having so kindly held yourself at our disposal.'

'It's a very tiresome business,' sighed the big man, whose eyes, in a pink blunt-featured face, were strangely childish.

'I know what you mean . . . Very tiresome . . . I see from this file that you are a Dutchman . . .'

'From Amsterdam . . . I'm an importer of colonial products, particularly from the Dutch East Indies . . .'

'You've been in Paris three days . . . Last night you dined by yourself in a big restaurant in the Champs-Elysées . . .'

'I dined too well,' the Dutchman pointed out; there was something quaintly naive about his facial expressions. 'It's all the fault of French cooking and French wines . . . In Holland we're not used to . . . After dinner I felt very merry, and as it was too warm to go to the theatre I thought I'd visit Luna-Park . . . It's really very exciting . . . There were a great many pretty Parisian girls there . . . They were having a good time, they were laughing a lot . . . I was laughing myself . . . And that was how I met Annette and Simone, beside the swings, all of us laughing . . . I only know their first names . . . Two very nice young ladies . . . Very merry, very amusing. We visited all the attractions. We went into all the booths. And from time to time we went for a drink at the bar.'

'You often went to the bar?' murmured the Superintendent, who was the quietest, most smiling of men.

'Often, yes . . . And this morning I've a bad headache . . . That doesn't matter . . . A hangover . . . what d'you call it? *gueule de boa* . . .'

'*Gueule de bois*, yes . . .'

'Does it mean a serpent's mouth?'

'Not exactly . . . But go on.'

'The last time we went to the bar I noticed a girl watching us as if she wanted to enjoy herself too . . . I went up to ask her, and actually I knocked over a little table on the way, because I wasn't walking very straight.'

'And you went on having a good time with your three girl friends?'

'It's a little awkward to explain, Superintendent . . . The other two, Annette and Simone, were just having fun, as you might say . . . They were nice girls that lived at home . . . But the third, Lydia her name was, she wasn't a French girl. She told me she was a dancer . . . But I don't know . . .'

'In short, about midnight you packed your first two girl-friends off in the métro and stayed alone with Lydia?'

'We went into the Hôtel Beauséjour, near by, in the Avenue de la Grande-Armée . . .'

'One question, please. You are staying at the Grand Hôtel in the Boulevard des Italiens. Why did you not go back there with the young woman?'

'Oh, Superintendent . . . At the Grand Hôtel I'm a respectable gentleman and I shouldn't like . . .'

'Let's go on . . . You stayed about an hour in the hotel . . . I suppose you gave your girl-friend a present before leaving?'

The Little Doctor, who never took his eyes off the Dutchman, saw him redden and look disconcerted for a moment.

'I don't remember . . . No, I don't believe so.'

'And she didn't ask for anything?'

'She'd been drinking too . . . We had a drink together before going into the hotel. When I left I wanted to walk a bit . . . I was nearly at the Arc de Triomphe when I noticed that I hadn't my wallet with me.'

'In which pocket do you usually keep it?'

'In my back trouser pocket . . . Here . . . See, here it is.'

'So you went back to the Hôtel Beauséjour. You went up into the room. Lydia was fully dressed . . .'

'Yes . . . Lying on the bed . . . Or rather across it . . . I thought she must have fallen asleep when she was about to leave . . . I tried to shake her . . . That was when I saw some blood and I realized she was dead. Her skull had been smashed in . . .'

'Didn't you call anyone?'

'I went downstairs and left the hotel.'

'Excuse me . . . Had you found your wallet?'

'Yes, on the floor . . . It had fallen out of my pocket . . . At the corner of the avenue I asked the constable on duty where the nearest police station was. I went there . . . I showed the sergeant my papers . . . I told him the young lady was dead . . .'

'That's all you know?'

'It's quite enough, isn't it? . . . I'm dreadfully afraid of my name being published in the papers . . . In Holland they're very strict about behaviour . . . It would be very bad for my business if it became known . . .'

'Were you intending to return to Holland soon?'

'In two or three days . . .'

'You may have to wait a little longer . . . I must ask you not to leave Paris before I give you the word. You may go now, Monsieur Van der Donck.'

'My name won't appear in the papers?'

'I see no need for that at present.' He rang. 'Joseph! Show this gentleman out . . .'

'Well, doctor, you see the sort of case we get landed with in the summer time . . . What's your opinion?'

The Little Doctor scratched his head in considerable embarrassment.

'You are said to have a remarkable gift for nosing things out, by highly individual methods. I don't know what crimes you've had to deal with, down in the country. This is an absolutely standard case. What are you going to do? You have the same data at your disposal as we have . . . Sorry, I forgot one document: the passport of Lydia Nielsen, born in Hungary, a cabaret dancer or night-club hostess, twenty-two years old, unmarried, recently resident in Brussels, where she worked for some time in a night-club called *Le Pingouin* . . . According to her passport Lydia Nielsen arrived in Paris yesterday, but we don't yet know in which hotel she was staying . . . I'll give you the information as soon as I get it, for the Lodgings Squad are at this moment busy showing her photograph to all hotel managers.

'As for the cause of death: Lydia Nielsen had been hit on the head with unusual violence and her skull was split open . . . If you're not too squeamish, which is unlikely since you're a doctor, I can show you a photograph on which one can make out fragments of brains spattering the wall-paper.

'I was about to forget one detail . . . When I asked Van der Donck whether he had given the girl a present it was because, apart from the passport and various trifling objects, her handbag contained nothing but one fifty-franc note and some small change.

'I'll leave you to it, doctor. Come along here whenever you like. All my files are at your disposal and I shan't conceal anything from you about the progress of the inquiry.'

There was a hint of irony in the closing words, but it was a friendly irony and the Little Doctor could not decently take offence at it.

'By the way . . . if I should not be here when you call, ask for Inspector Torrence, who always works with me . . .'

Well, when he was back on the embankment, where the heat, at ten in the morning, was already stifling, the Little Doctor did not feel his customary zest. This case was unlike any of those he had elucidated hitherto, and possibly he was somewhat overawed by the vastness of Paris and the teeming life around him.

What line were the police likely to take? For it was obviously pointless for him to follow the same course. In the first place, the room in the Hôtel Beauséjour would have to be carefully examined; and for this task the finger-prints experts were better qualified than he was.

The night porter at the hotel must be questioned, and information sought about all the guests who had stayed there that night. Lydia's movements since her arrival in Paris must be traced; the Superintendent had spoken of this.

What next? Information would be sought by telegram from the Netherlands police about Monsieur Van der Donck, and from the Belgian police about the girl's stay in Brussels.

He was really disheartened. For the first time he was conscious of his own smallness amid a vast world. The atmosphere of Paris crushed him. The immensity of the task involved in even so commonplace an investigation as this one made him doubt his own capabilities, dependent as he was on his brains alone.

He tried to make use of his usual method, which consisted in establishing, prior to any research or deduction, a clear and simple basis, a certain number of undoubted truths.

'Van der Donck arrived in Paris three days ago . Lydia arrived there on the very day of the crime . . .'

If they had known one another beforehand and had arranged a meeting, would they have chosen so noisy a spot as Luna-Park and would the Dutchman have come to the rendezvous accompanied by a couple of girls?

Lydia had followed her companion into the nearest hotel. He left her after one hour, which might be considered normal. And again, there was nothing surprising about his going back to look for his wallet.

Was Lydia already dead when he left her the first time?

In that case, would he have returned and then gone to inform the police, whereas he could quite well have disappeared without a word?

He had not given her anything . . . But he had specified that the young dancer was almost as drunk as himself.

Lydia had been fully dressed when they found her. Why had she put on her clothes again?

If someone had come into the room to kill her, what was his object, and why had he not removed the wallet, which, lying on the floor, must have been clearly visible?

The Little Doctor had reached the Grands Boulevards, and he looked up admiringly at the huge façade of the Grand Hôtel; after a moment's hesitation he went through the revolving door and found himself among the milling crowd in the reception hall.

Should he speak to the porter? What could he ask him? Information about Van der Donck? On the left side of the hall he noticed a luxurious American bar, and the sight of it made him thirsty. A moment later, perched on a high stool, he had ordered a cocktail and was deep in thought.

'Monsieur Dollent! Monsieur Jean Dollent wanted on the telephone!'

A pageboy was calling his message all over the place, and for some minutes the Little Doctor remained unaware that he was the person referred to. How could anyone have known that he was here?

'Monsieur Dollent . . . Booth number 7 in the basement, on the right . . .'

'Hello! Is that you, doctor? Lucas here . . . I'm sorry to interrupt your investigations . . .'

It was such a bad beginning that Dollent nearly replied with an expletive.

'I wanted to let you know straight that I've got an interesting fellow in my office . . . He came rushing up as soon as Lydia's picture appeared in the papers . . . Would you mind jumping into a taxi?'

Five minutes later the Little Doctor was at the Quai des Orfèvres. In Lucas's office he found a tall, thin young man, wild-eyed, his hands clenched tensely.

'Come in, doctor . . . Let me introduce René Fabry, who's a bank clerk in Brussels . . . You're twenty-two, aren't you, Monsieur Fabry?'

'Twenty-one . . . Lydia and I . . .'

His lower lip was quivering, his Adam's apple moving up and down, and he had the greatest difficulty in restraining his sobs.

'It's like this,' Lucas explained to gain time. 'For nearly two months now Monsieur Fabry has been Lydia's lover . . .'

'We loved each other!' corrected the young man, his eyes flashing.

'That's what I mean!' resumed Lucas without any sign of irony. 'They loved each other. It seems that Lydia was not at all the sort of woman one might have thought. She was a respectable girl of good family who only became a cabaret dancer to earn her living . . .'

'Her father was a Hungarian officer!' the young man broke in.

'You see, doctor! Of course Monsieur Fabry and Lydia did not live together. Monsieur Fabry lives with his parents. But they often met in the afternoon . . . In the evenings Monsieur Fabry went to the *Pingouin*, but he could not wait for his girl-friend until four in the morning, on account of his job . . .'

'I knew she went straight home . . . I followed her twice . . .'

'Now tell us how you discovered that Lydia had disappeared.'

'I went to her place yesterday afternoon . . . She had a furnished apartment in the Bourse district . . . Her landlady told me she had just gone out carrying a suitcase, and had taken a taxi. The landlady had heard her give the order: "Gare du Midi . . ."'

'Now from the Gare du Midi she could only have been taking the train to Paris.

'I spent hours in agony. I had no dinner. Then I decided to go off myself. I left a message for my parents. I wrote a letter to the Bank, apologizing for taking my holidays without giving due notice . . . I caught the midnight train and reached the Gare du Nord this morning, shortly before seven.'

Still admirably concealing his irony, the Superintendent said to the Little Doctor: 'Monsieur Fabry was hoping to find his girl-friend in Paris . . . He hadn't got her address. He wasn't even sure she was there . . .'

'I'd have found her!' the young man proclaimed proudly. 'I'm convinced that if she hadn't been killed . . .'

'So you never heard of Monsieur Van der Donck?'

'Never.'

'And Lydia never referred to a Dutchman in your presence?'

'She didn't bother about men, once she was outside the *Pingouin* where she was obliged to . . .'

'Of course, of course! . . . And you're sure she was not the sort of woman who would go to a hotel with a man she did not know?'

'Absolutely not, and I can't . . . I won't allow . . .'

'Keep calm . . . The doctor and I are quite ready to believe you . . . Considering your relations with the victim . . .'

'I would have married her . . . And if my parents had refused their consent . . .'

'So you maintain that Lydia must have been the victim of a plot . . . That was what you told me just now.'

'I repeat that there's no other possible explanation . . . Perhaps she was involved in politics . . . maybe espionage?'

'You know nothing about that?'

He reddened, annoyed at not knowing.

'No . . . Lydia was secretive, like all Hungarian women . . .'

'Would you be kind enough to tell me at what hotel you are staying and where I can contact you?'

'Hôtel Maubeuge, near the station. It's the first time I've been to Paris and . . .'

'What d'you think of that, doctor?'

'What do you?' Dollent retorted sullenly.

'The same as yourself, that's to say, nothing so far . . .'

With a touch of sarcasm, Lucas added: 'The fact is that luckily we in the Police Judiciaire don't do much thinking, do we? By the way . . . We've traced the Paris address of our young woman, whom René Fabry makes out to be such an innocent . . . She put up at the Hôtel Cristal, in the Rue Fontaine, a hotel which, between you and me, is chiefly frequented by ladies of easy virtue, night-club hostesses and the shadier sort of gentlemen . . . Her room has been searched. In her dressing-case was found a sum of ten thousand francs in Belgian notes, which seems to rule out the idea that she might have picked up a stranger for the sake of the customary remuneration.

'Apart from that, nothing unusual . . . A case full of the sort of dresses these girls wear . . . dancers' tutus, make-up, picture post-cards from girl-friends in Istanbul, Cairo, Tunisia, Venice, Cannes . . .

'Finally I rang up Amsterdam myself. Monsieur Van der Donck is well known and respected there . . . He's a bachelor, and travels a great deal on business and for pleasure . . . He's not expected back there for several days, for this is the time of year that he devotes to an important European tour . . .

'That's all, doctor . . . Now you know as much as we do . . . I wish I could say as much . . .'

'What does that mean?' retorted Dollent, frowning.

'That I'd like to be sure I knew as much as you do . . . Considering your previous exploits, I can't believe that you haven't already formed an opinion, and that from one deduction to the next . . .'

Well, well! It wasn't worth quarrelling about it. Of course, smiling Superintendent Lucas, aware that he had all the power of the police machine behind him, was right. And the Little Doctor, country cousin that he was, could not hope to try to emulate the speed and ingenuity of the official police.

'I'll leave you to your investigation, doctor . . . Good luck to you!'

Dollent had walked all the length of the corridor and was about to start down the stairs when Lucas ran after him.

'Psssttt! One word more . . . I nearly forgot the most important thing . . .'

He was being ironical again, that was obvious. He held a scrap of paper in his hand.

'This was found in the dancing-girl's handbag . . . A scrap from a menu, as you can see. On the back a pencilled number: 658 . . . That's all . . . You must admit that I'm playing fair with you, keeping nothing back, even inadvertently.'

'Can you let me have this paper?'

'With the greatest of pleasure.'

An hour later, on account of that scrap of paper torn off the bottom of a menu, the Little Doctor was comfortably installed in the fast train to Brussels, though somewhat annoyed at having to pay for a seat in a Pullman because it was the only train available at that time.

'The police are lucky, they don't have to worry about money,' he sighed, thinking of what he had just paid and what he'd have to spend in the Belgian capital.

In which he was badly mistaken, as Lucas would certainly have told him had he been there. And Lucas would doubtless have added:

'Remember that my men, when they take a taxi, are almost always certain that their fare will not be refunded!'

At all events Dollent was conscious of having used his reasoning powers, if only for one brief moment. The proof of which was that the others – the Police Judiciaire people – had seen nothing interesting about that scrap of paper.

The printed part, which presumably bore the name of the restaurant, was missing. It was the bottom of a page. The writing included the words: *Shrimp mayonnaise: 8 francs.*

This made the Little Doctor raise his eyebrows. He had only visited Belgium twice, but he remembered the particular fondness of its people for such dishes as shrimp, crab or lobster mayonnaise.

He had dashed up to Montmartre before taking the train, and had gone into a restaurant.

'Tell me, *maître d'hôtel*, which restaurants include shrimp mayonnaise on their menus?'

The funny thing was that he had happened on a head waiter who hailed from Brussels and who replied with the raciest of accents:

'That's Belgian, that is, for sure!'

As for the number . . . The Little Doctor would not have liked to explain to Lucas the way his mind had worked. That number reminded him of a trip to Rome . . . He had stayed at the Hotel Excelsior, in room 432 . . . The lift attendant had explained to him that in grand hotels all the rooms on the first floor have numbers beginning with one hundred, those on the second floor with two hundred, and so on.

During that holiday Dollent had met a charming hostess in a night-club – she was Greek, not Hungarian – and had begged her to spend the night with him.

'We can't leave before closing time,' she had said. 'Wait for me . . . Let's drink something meanwhile . . .'

In the space of two hours he had had seven or eight hundred lires' worth of champagne supper. And it was only 3.0 a.m.!

'When do you close?'

'Not before five o'clock; six or even later if there are still people here . . .'

He could not afford to stay so long, at the rate he was spending money.

'Promise to come along then,' he had urged hopefully, for the Greek girl seemed to be the soul of sincerity.

'Where?'

'Hotel Excelsior . . .'

'Write down your room number . . .'

What a night! Until seven in the morning he had waited, in his silk pyjamas, going round and round the room, and had seen day break gradually and the sun rise above the roof-tops.

The Greek girl had never come!

'I say, waiter, would you tell me . . .'

The Pullman waiter had just served tea.

'How many big hotels are there in Brussels with at least six floors?'

'There's the Métropole . . .'

'I know . . .'

'Then the Palace, near the Gare du Nord . . . The Astoria . . . The . . .' He made rapid notes. There were eight hotels. But a minute later there were only seven, for the waiter came back to explain that he'd made a mistake, and that one of these hotels had only five floors.

What might Superintendent Lucas be doing meanwhile? And what sort of face would he wear if, next day, the Little Doctor came back with . . .

He was agog with excitement at the thought of returning by the same comfortable train, with the problem solved, of landing at the Gare du Nord, jumping into a taxi, and remarking casually to Lucas:

'It's done . . .'

'What's done?'

'Everything . . . Here's the solution of your case . . .'

His eyes half closed, the Little Doctor day-dreamed with a smile on his lips, while the first houses of Schaerbeek filed past.

II. In Which a Certain Young Man in Love would Doubtless Lose his Illusions if he were to Eavesdrop, and In Which the Little Doctor Shows Himself a Good Loser

'Can you help me, porter? . . . I'm looking for a friend of mine who I believe is staying here. If I'm not mistaken his room number is 658 . . .'

This was at the Métropole, the third hotel that Dollent had visited that afternoon. It struck him that the porter was wearing an unnecessarily mischievous expression and was looking past him at something. At the same moment he felt a tap on his shoulder, and although his conscience was fairly clear he gave a start; the shock was unpleasant enough to make him realize what effect such a sensation might have on a criminal.

A cheerful voice said, with a guttural Brussels accent, 'I bet you're the doctor, aren't you?'

A short plump fellow with a ruddy face and a round pouting mouth winked at the porter as he said, 'Thanks, Jefke . . . I'll deal with it now.'

Then, still tapping Dollent on the shoulder: 'It struck me, you know, that you'd be wasting your time questioning Jefke and all the rest . . . They're chatterboxes, those fellows. So if you'd just come and have a drink with me, good beer with no froth on it . . .'

'I beg your pardon, but . . .'

'Sorry! Stupid of me, I forgot to introduce myself: Inspector Snoek of the Belgian Sûreté . . . My old colleague Lucas gave me a call to say you'd surely be arriving and I was to make things easy for you.'

He dragged the Little Doctor to the terrace of a huge café close to the hotel, and gave his order to the waiter: 'Two stunners!'

A minute later they were brought glasses which must each have held a litre of beer.

'Now, if you want to ask me anything . . .'

Inspector Snoek drew a stout notebook from his pocket and laid it on the marble-topped table, apparently prepared to extract from it every conceivable sort of information.

'Who occupied room 658 at the Hôtel Métropole?'

'You really don't know? Then you must be pretty smart, and I wonder how you worked it out! It's Kees Van der Donck, of course! He has a suite here by the year . . . The sixth floor of the Métropole is more or less reserved for good customers, bankers, stock exchange people, diamond merchants, industrialists who come to Brussels at regular intervals and who like things the way they're used to them . . . Their rooms are kept available for them by arrangement . . . Some of them even leave luggage here all the year round. If you were to take a walk up there you'd see trunks standing all along the corridor . . .'

'Did Van der Donck have luggage?'

'Two big trunks in which, when he arrived from Amsterdam bringing only his little leather briefcase, he would find everything he needed, clothes and underwear. There are a number of people who move about like that, doing the round of the Stock Exchanges, Brussels on Monday, London on Wednesday, then over to Cologne or Düsseldorf on Friday . . . Your good health!'

The Little Doctor noted a mischievous twinkle in the eyes of this boisterous, informal acquaintance.

'What else would you like to know?'

'Did Lydia Nielsen visit the Dutchman in his rooms at the Métropole?'

This time he got another tap, not on the shoulder but in the stomach.

'You're no fool, you know, for an amateur! Only it's not possible, for once, to give you an answer . . . Seeing that almost every night she was creeping about the hotel like a mouse . . .'

'Have you questioned the people at the *Pingouin*?'

'Sure we have! . . . Your good health! . . . It seems there was nobody like Lydia Nielsen for getting on to a good thing . . . You get my meaning? . . . Inside, as cold as a fish in a fridge . . . But outside, a regular teaser, she'd have hotted up the whole fire brigade . . . She'd keep the poor fellows on tenterhooks until four or five in the morning and they were always left with twice as many champagne bottles under the table as they'd really drunk . . . Afterwards, if they were worth while, she'd join them in their hotel . . . sometimes the Palace, sometimes the Métropole . . . All the night porters were used to seeing her turn up at dawn, still wearing evening dress . . . She'd give them a wink and hurry into the lift . . .'

'What about the night of the 6th?' queried the Little Doctor.

'Van der Donck had already been in Brussels for several days . . . In the afternoon he received some visitors in his apartment . . . That night he came back early, about eleven o'clock, saying that he was leaving by the first train next morning. He settled his bill before going up to bed . . .'

'And his two big trunks?'

'He said nothing about them . . . The night porter, whom I questioned, thinks he remembers Lydia coming that night, but he can't swear to it. He doesn't recall seeing the Dutchman leave, either . . . There's nothing extraordinary about that, seeing that about that time he goes into his little den and warms up his coffee . . . Is that all you wanted to know, doctor?'

And Dollent, seeing an even livelier gleam in his companion's little eyes, thought to himself: 'You, my boy, with your innocent airs, are wondering whether or not I'm going to ask you a certain question . . . Well, here goes! Is this the one you were expecting?'

Out loud, he asked: 'Are the two trunks still in the corridor?'

'Only one of them.'

'What happened to the other?'

'Waiter! Two more stunners! What happened to the other? Well, it went off by train . . . When he got to the station about 6.0 a.m. Kees

Van der Donck telephoned the Métropole . . .

'"Send the larger of the two trunks to Paris!" he said.

'"To what hotel?" the porter asked.

'"To the left-luggage office at the Gare du Nord . . . As for the receipt, you can send me that poste restante . . ."

'"To what post office?"

'"Post office number . . . number 42."

'Now I fancy you know as much as I do! You're lucky, you know, to be Superintendent Lucas's blue-eyed boy! . . . Here in Belgium, if you were to try and run your own little investigation, I fancy the bosses would send you packing . . .'

At nine o'clock that evening the Little Doctor was already at the Gare du Midi, looking for a seat on the Paris train. Could he honestly say Lucas had not been decent to him?

He had, to all appearances, made things easier, since he'd got a Belgian policeman to meet Dollent and give him all the information he needed. But hadn't this meant treating him too condescendingly, as if he were a child? The train doors were being slammed. A newsboy was running along the platform.

'*Paris-Soir. . . L'Intransigeant . . . Le Soir . . . La Dernière Heure . . .*'

He took the whole bundle at random; a few minutes later, as the train passed through the suburbs of Brussels, he was sitting in the dining-car and, as he waited for the first serving of dinner, he unfolded the first of the papers.

The Luna-Park Affair

An unexpected development

A young Belgian fires point blank at the Dutchman Kees Van der Donck

'Our readers will not have forgotten the strange affair at Luna-Park, reported in previous issues. About 3.0 p.m. this afternoon the death of Lydia Nielsen was the occasion of a second sensational affair, this time at the bar of the Grand Hôtel, Boulevard des Italiens.'

The bar at which the Little Doctor had been drinking that very morning! The waiter brought him the regulation *consommé madrilène*, but he did not touch it.

'A young man had just asked for Monsieur Van der Donck, and the porter, acting, as he thought, for the best, informed the visitor that the Dutchman was probably in the bar.

'What makes the subsequent happenings all the more remarkable is that at that very moment a detective was present in the reception hall of the hotel: Inspector Torrence, who was responsible for discreetly keeping an eye on Kees Van der Donck.

'He watched the young man. He saw him speaking to the barman. Then he saw him apostrophizing the Dutchman, who had been drinking for some little while and who, according to the barman, was already somewhat tipsy.

'We can only guess at the words that passed between the two men. At all events, a minute later the young man briskly pulled out a gun from his pocket and fired twice, then tried to fire a third shot but fortunately was unable to do so, his revolver having jammed.

'While the victim was bending over the bar, wounded in the right leg by one of the two bullets, the murderer, who is of Belgian nationality, let himself be arrested without offering resistance.

'At the time of going to press, the condition of the Dutch business man is satisfactory, the bullet not having hit any vital organ.'

'What did you say, Monsieur?'

The Little Doctor looked up in surprise. 'Did I say something?'

And the head waiter of the dining-car restrained a smile as he apologized: 'I beg your pardon . . . I thought you were speaking to me.'

What could he have been saying out loud without realizing it? He was thinking desperately, in the vain hope of co-ordinating these data which seemed to lack all coherence.

Why had Van der Donck, who seemed to know Lydia very well, even in the Biblical sense of the word, pretended in Paris to treat her as a casual pick-up?

Why had he taken her into a third-class hotel, whereas in Brussels he had no hesitation about receiving her in his room at the Métropole, although he was better known there than in France?

Why had the Hungarian girl, accustomed as she was to a certain degree of luxury, accompanied him into the Hôtel Beauséjour, the haunt of second-rate street-walkers?

Why. . . ?

He was still running through his chaplet of why's, with a furrowed brow, when he got off the train at the Gare du Nord. It was one o'clock in the morning. The huge hall was almost empty. Dissatisfied and with an aching head, the Little Doctor was about to rush off to bed in his hotel near the Gare d'Orsay.

'What about it?'

He gave a start. He had recognized the friendly, faintly mocking voice.

'Did you have a good journey? Have you brought back masses of useful information?'

Superintendent Lucas took him amicably by the arm and led him towards the exit.

'You're not vexed with me? . . . I guessed you would go to Brussels and I wanted to make things easier for you . . . Besides, you yourself asked me, didn't you? to let you study official police methods . . .

'Well, you may have noticed that we have no method . . . We mistrust arguments and theories . . . Patiently, like the good civil servants that we are, we collect as much information as possible by ordinary means. And it seldom happens that among all this information we fail to find something that puts us on the right track.

'Shall we have a beer?'

'Thank you, no; no beer!' His stomach still felt bloated with Inspector Snoek's 'stunners'.

'I wanted to bring you up to date with what has happened during your absence . . .'

'I've read the papers!' the Little Doctor retorted crossly.

'Then you know about as much as we do . . . I put young René Fabry through a preliminary questioning, but I got nothing out of him . . . He's as stubborn as a mule . . . He's determined to speak only in the presence of his solicitor . . . Meanwhile he's at the station . . .'

'And Van der Donck?'

'At the Beaujon Hospital . . . I've seen him . . . He can't account for the action of that lunatic, as he calls him.'

'Did you ask him what René Fabry had said to him before firing?'

'Of course . . . And do you know what he replied?

'"That'll teach you to rob girls of their honour!"

'Let's have something to drink all the same, shall we? If you don't want beer . . .'

And they sat down at a terrace table. It was a mild night. Couples passed by slowly in the shadows. Taxis were on the prowl. Coaches loaded with foreigners were making their way up to Montmartre.

After a first brandy-and-water the Little Doctor ordered a second, and began to feel better. It seemed to him that he had a sharper perception of the life around him, the life of a great city of four million inhabitants, not to mention those who, like Lydia, like Van der Donck, like René Fabry, came from the four corners of the earth to deal with their personal affairs there.

Lydia was Hungarian, Van der Donck was Dutch, young Fabry was a bank clerk from Brussels; and the three of them had landed up in Paris. Paris happened to be the scene of the dénouement of a drama which had begun heaven knows where, perhaps at the Hôtel Métropole in the Place de Brouckère, perhaps in the *Pingouin* night-club . . .

'Waiter! A brandy-and-water . . .'

Lucas glanced at him out of the corner of his eye, but the doctor paid no attention.

'What I'd like to know . . .' he began suddenly, after swallowing half of his third brandy.

Then he fell silent, with a shrug. Was his companion really telling him all that was in his mind?

'What would you like to know?'

'Nothing . . . Or rather . . . The Beaujon Hospital is the one in the Rue Faubourg Saint-Honoré, isn't it?'

Lucas frowned. He himself would have liked to know what the Little Doctor had at the back of his mind.

'Well, I'm going to bed.'

'So am I.'

They were both cheating. The proof of that was that the Little Doctor took a taxi and said, in a loud voice: 'Quai d'Orsay . . . the corner of the Rue de Beaune.'

Lucas took another taxi. 'Follow the car in front of you . . .'

In the Place de l'Opéra, Jean Dollent opened the sliding panel that divided him from the driver. 'Beaujon hospital! Quick as you can!'

When he got there the Faubourg Saint-Honoré was dark and deserted. He rang the bell. The heavy door swung open and the porter stared him up and down.

'I'm a doctor . . . I want to see one of your patients urgently . . . Will you call the intern on duty?'

'One moment. Will you wait here?'

He was reminded of his first house job at Bordeaux, and he recognized the familiar odours, the same white figures of nurses moving noiselessly down the corridors.

A young doctor in a white coat came up to him at last.

'You wanted to speak to me?'

'I am Dr Dollent . . . I'd like to have a few words with one of your patients, Kees Van der Donck . . . Since his condition is not serious, I assume . . .'

'You're unlucky, doctor; the Dutchman has been put into a private room . . . there are orders for nobody to see him . . . I must add that the police must have good reasons for this, since they have put an inspector on duty in the corridor . . .'

Dollent had just noticed that the young doctor was looking past him at something behind his back. He turned round: Lucas was there, calmly smiling.

'You should have told me just now that you wanted to talk to Van der Donck . . . It was I who gave orders that nobody was to disturb him . . . But if you're really anxious to . . .'

He showed his card to the intern, who had to give in.

'This way . . .'

Passages, stairways, dim lights, more nurses and, at the far end of the longest corridor of all, a youngish man with a hat on his head sat smoking a stubby pipe.

'Well, Torrence?'

'Nothing, Chief . . .'

'You've got the key?'

The detective drew it from his pocket and handed it to his boss. Lucas opened the door.

'Come in, doctor . . .'

Dollent took barely one step into the room. The window was open and a draught was blowing in. Not only was the bed empty, but it had been stripped of its sheets; tied to the foot of a wardrobe, they were hanging out of the window, knotted to one another.

'What a pity!' sighed Superintendent Lucas. 'This is a really tiresome business. What will people think of me tomorrow when they learn that Kees Van der Donck, in spite of his injuries, insisted on climbing out of the window? . . . Torrence, didn't you hear anything?'

'Nothing, Chief . . .'

'You didn't leave your post at all? You didn't go to flirt with the nurses?'

'No, on my honour, Chief . . .'

'Well, you're in the wrong all the same . . .'

'? . . .'

'You should have taken the elementary precaution of removing his clothes from the room . . .'

'But you never told me . . .'

'You fellows need to be told everything, to have everything foreseen for you . . . You ought to know your job better, for heaven's sake! . . . You can go to bed now . . . I don't see any point in guarding an empty room . . .'

This time Lucas and the doctor separated at the corner of the Quai d'Orsay and the Rue de Beaune, and Dollent really did go to bed.

III. In Which the Little Doctor Stakes Everything and Risks Being Charged with Forgery, Misappropriation of Documents, Theft and Receiving Stolen Goods . . . Not to Mention an Even Graver Charge

As someone has said, if it weren't for the vanity which is the mainspring of human behaviour and which inspires us to heroism, we should still be living in caves.

The Little Doctor was up at six as usual. Thus, except for the dustmen, he was practically alone in the streets of Paris.

He was determined, however, not to let himself be humiliated by Superintendent Lucas, but to prove that his detective gift, which was already recognized in his own part of the world, was by no means dulled by contact with the capital.

For two whole hours he wandered along the embankment, and he seemed to be concerned only with the sight of the barges gliding downstream. Actually, he was thinking, 'If only there are some letters for me by the first post!'

Then he went in search of a chemist's shop, and to find one open he had to go as far as the Rue Montmartre, which gave him the pleasure of crossing the Halles. The two small phials he bought somewhat surprised the chemist's assistant, particularly when he demanded, in addition, a brush of the sort used for painting sore throats.

'Any mail for me?' he inquired, just as eight o'clock struck, at the reception desk of his modest hotel.

'Three letters, *monsieur le docteur*.'

He went upstairs to his room. He did not bother to open the letters but, dipping his paintbrush in each of the phials, he wiped it twice over the words 'Jean Dollent', which disappeared as though by magic.

After which he wrote, slowly and carefully with his tongue between his teeth: 'Kees Van der Donck'.

He was feeling very tense. Before a quarter of an hour had passed he entered Post Office no. 42 like a whirlwind and stopped at the poste restante position.

'Is there anything for me?'

'What name?'

'Kees Van der Donck.'

'Have you your identity papers?'

'I've left them at the hotel . . .'

'In that case . . . Unless you can produce two postmarked envelopes . . .'

He showed them, and was rewarded with a handsome letter on the headed notepaper of the Hôtel Métropole, addressed to Van der Donck.

'Eighty centimes to pay . . . plus fifty for the poste restante . . .'

Well, Lucas and the official police would just have to lump it! After all, they'd made a fool of him in the first instance!

Less than ten minutes later a taxi deposited him at the Gare du Nord, where he rushed to the left-luggage office brandishing the consignment receipt which he had found in the envelope . . .

'I've come to collect my trunk . . .'

They examined the receipt, turning it over and over, and the Little

Doctor began to quake.

'Go to the Customs . . .'

He had to run off again, like a child playing puss in the corner, from one hall to another, and eventually a clerk showed him an enormous cabin trunk standing in a corner. A customs officer was waiting.

'Have you got the keys?'

Damn! He hadn't thought of the keys!

And . . . and a sudden idea flashed through his mind . . . *The man who had rung up the Hôtel Métropole to get the trunk sent off had not thought of the keys either* . . .

At that his last scruples vanished.

'Actually, I've lost the keys of this trunk . . .'

'You could send for a locksmith . . .'

'It's not worth it . . . The trunk's an old one . . . I'm sure that with a pair of pliers we could break open the lock and . . .'

'Have you got pliers?' the customs officer said curtly.

He had none with him, obviously! And he began darting through the station premises in search of a pair of cutting pliers.

It was like the sort of dream in which you think you're being followed and your legs are so limp that you can't put one foot in front of the other.

Perhaps Lucas and his men . . .

He cast ceaseless glances towards the street. His heart was in his mouth. But he had the pliers. He had just borrowed them from an odd-job man for twenty francs.

He rushed up. 'Here you are. The lock just needs forcing . . .'

'Well, it's your look-out,' the customs officer's look implied.

The metal ripped . . . It only remained to open the trunk which, like all cabin trunks, stood upright.

'There we are!' he said triumphantly. 'You can look now, *monsieur le douanier* . . .'

He stepped back a couple of paces, pale-faced, his hands trembling. This was agonizing . . . What if he had made a mistake? What if he had committed all these offences only to . . .

'Look here!'

The enraged customs officer was sniffing. 'What's inside here? It seems to me . . .'

At the same moment he opened up the two sides of the trunk and a dead body fell into his arms.

'Look out! Don't let him get away! He's a murderer . . .'

The Little Doctor was not trying to escape, but the people around him could not believe that he would let himself be caught so easily. Perhaps they thought he was armed? In any case, owing to the panic, he could have made his escape ten times over if he had wanted to.

'Send for the police . . . Telephone to . . .'

He sat down on a case and lit a cigarette. What chiefly astonished those who were staring at him in horror was the contented smile that flitted across his lips.

'Take him first to the railway police station . . .'

There he was kept waiting a good quarter of an hour, under the eye of two constables who were ready to hit out at him at the slightest suspicious movement.

And he still went on smiling!

'Hello, Police Judiciaire? We have just arrested a certain Van der Donck who was trying to take out a trunk from the left-luggage office . . . Now this trunk . . . What's that? . . . All right . . . Very good, Chief!'

There were two or three hundred people outside; there was even a press photographer, who had been waiting at the station for the arrival of some film star, and who turned this opportunity to good account by taking close-up shots of the Little Doctor.

'Put the handcuffs on him . . . Fetch a taxi . . . Take him straight to Police Headquarters . . .'

It was a queer experience to drive through Paris thus, handcuffed, between two policemen whose belts were crushing his ribs. And then to go in through the great stone gateway at the Quai des Orfèvres . . .

'This way . . . Quiet, mind! or else . . .'

It was lucky that nobody had thought it necessary to put him through the third degree!

'Who's it for?' asked the doorman, looking the prisoner up and down.

'Superintendent Lucas . . .'

'I'll let him know . . .'

At last he was going to be left in peace! They would take off the handcuffs that bruised his wrists! And above all, his moment of triumph was near!

'The Superintendent says to put him in No. 2 cell for the time being; he'll see him presently.'

'Excuse me,' Dollent tried to protest. 'Tell the Superintendent that . . .'

'Come on! This way . . .'

And they shut him up in a cell which was one metre in width and two in length, and which was lit only through a grating.

For a whole hour he fretted and fumed. After that he sank into dejection. Finally he recovered self-possession and began to rehearse what he was going to say presently.

'Obviously, Superintendent, you were able to move heaven and earth, to send policemen into every hotel in Paris, to have hundreds of people interviewed and to get all the information you wanted from the Belgian Sûreté in the minimum time, just by a telephone call.

'Whereas I, a mere amateur . . .

'Would you like me to tell you, my dear Superintendent, if I may so address you, what struck me most in Van der Donck's story?

'It was the fact that Lydia Nielsen was fully dressed when he found her dead . . .

'He had not been gone more than a few minutes, since he had only walked up the avenue as far as the Etoile, where he noticed that his wallet was missing . . .

'But the woman whose dead body he found was fully dressed, with her stockings neatly pulled on, and if she was not wearing a hat it was because the blow she'd received on her head had knocked it off . . .

'From what I know of that sort of woman I'd have expected Lydia to spend the rest of the night in the room . . .

'I wanted to ask you at the time if the bed had really been unmade, if it still bore the imprint of *two* bodies, but I didn't do so because I didn't want to arouse your suspicions . . .'

A policeman was on duty behind the peep-hole, but Dollent paid no attention to him, and just as certain prisoners prepare their defence, he was preparing his triumphant explanation.

'Van der Donck did not expect to meet Lydia Nielsen, and she was not in Paris just by chance.'

He seemed to be waiting for someone to challenge him, but there was nobody in his cell.

'From that point I conjectured that they had not gone to the Hôtel Beauséjour for the obvious purpose, but solely to settle their accounts . . . Lydia had not undressed, nor had the Dutchman . . . After a few minutes' conversation he must have struck her, possibly with one of the candlesticks, or one of the fire-irons in the room . . .

'Then he waited, prudently, so as not to arouse the night porter's suspicions by too brief a stay . . .

'He went off . . . He thought he was safe . . . He was walking up the Champs-Elysées; nobody suspected him of the crime . . . Then, suddenly, he noticed that he'd left his wallet behind in the room . . . It must have slipped out of his pocket while he was making a strenuous movement . . .

'To leave it there would be to give himself away . . . To go back and fetch it would be even more dangerous, for it was possible that the alarm had been given . . .

'It seemed better, since he looked like an honest man and even a simple one, to act the simpleton to the end, to go back into the room, to inform the police, to make himself out to be one of those unfortunate foreigners for whom "Gay Paree" proves a source of every kind of trouble . . .

'But, you will ask me, why murder Lydia Nielsen?' He felt a painful twinge of hunger, but he disregarded it and carried on his soliloquy:

'Because Lydia Nielsen knew . . .

'What did Lydia know?

'That I could not tell, Superintendent, and it was in order to find out that I went to Brussels, where I had a somewhat ironical reception from your friend Inspector Snoek – and, by the way, I wish he were here now to offer me one of those "stunners" which I didn't sufficiently appreciate . . .'

The key turned in the lock. The door opened. The policeman merely growled: 'Come along!'

IV. In Which the Race is Practically a Photo-finish

'What? You here? . . . Officer, take off Dr Dollent's handcuffs . . .'

'That'll do!' growled Dollent. 'As though you didn't know that I was the prisoner in No. 2 cell . . .'

Lucas waited until the guards had gone.

'I confess I did,' he said.

'In that case you'd better fetch me up a glass of beer and a sandwich . . .' He added mistrustfully, as Lucas was telephoning:

'You haven't caught him, have you?'

'Who?'

'The murderer of Van der Donck . . .'

'Caught him? We never lost him . . .'

'But last night at the hospital . . .'

'I counted on his getting out of the window . . . Come in; put the tray down here . . . Thanks . . .'

There were four glasses topped with creamy froth and two thick ham sandwiches, into one of which the Little Doctor set his teeth.

'As to your methods, my dear doctor, although I admire the speed with which you got results, I'm obliged to point out that we could scarcely afford to use them ourselves . . . Forgery, misappropriation of correspondence, aggravated by the theft of a trunk . . . and finally, if we're to carry your case to its conclusion, attempted theft and concealment of a body . . . Quite a list!'

'All the same I put you in possession, within twenty-four hours, of the body of Van der Donck . . . I mean the real Van der Donck . . .'

'That's true . . . And perhaps we shouldn't have found it until two or three days later . . . On the other hand, we have the false Van der Donck under lock and key . . .'

Basically, they were full of admiration for one another, but they felt bound to assume a surly manner.

'What was your starting-point, doctor? Rational argument! For instance, it was an admirably subtle process of reasoning that led you to room 658 at the Métropole. We, on the other hand, got there by a different method . . . I asked the Brussels police to put me on the track of Van der Donck . . .'

'You've means enough at your disposal!'

'The shot fired by that idiotic lover – René Fabry, I mean – almost led us on to a wrong trail . . . None the less I had our Dutchman watched, and I said to myself: "If he's got something on his conscience he won't stay long in hospital".

'And that's what happened . . . One of my men was waiting for him in the Beaujon garden . . . He followed him to Le Havre and arrested him a few minutes before the mail boat left for South America . . . What I'm wondering now is how you, doctor, knowing so little . . .'

The Little Doctor wiped his mouth, for he had just eaten both sandwiches and drunk two of the glasses of beer. He was looking longingly at the third, which had not been touched.

'I simply put myself in other people's shoes,' he asserted. 'And if I had been Monsieur Van der Donck . . .'

'Go on!'

'If I had rooms reserved for me all the year round in several capital cities, I would not telephone from the Gare du Midi at six in the morning to ask a porter to forward a trunk to Paris . . . Particularly to the left-luggage office! . . . And particularly giving a poste restante address for the receipt . . .'

'Why aren't you drinking?'

'I thought that was for you . . .'

'Oh no! Three beers for you and one for me . . .'

'Your good health! . . . I suppose the bogus Van der Donck is some well-known crook . . .'

'He's the Dutch ex-convict Peter Krull . . .'

'Right! He stops off at the Métropole . . . He knows that his compatriot is staying there and that he always carries a considerable sum of money with him . . . At night he goes into Van der Donck's room and murders him . . . Just as he's about to hide the body in one of the trunks standing in the corridor, Lydia Nielsen, whom he does not know, turns up unexpectedly . . .

'There's the flaw that always ruins the cleverest crime, the mistake thanks to which justice always prevails in the end . . . Peter Krull, as you call him, had not suspected that his compatriot had a date with a cabaret dancer that night . . .

'To keep her quiet he gives her ten thousand francs . . . She goes off . . . He leaves the hotel himself, without being seen by the night porter . . .

'But he reflects that it won't be long before the trunk gives out a tell-tale odour . . . He telephones . . . He has it sent to Paris, to a station cloakroom where it may remain for weeks without being examined . . .

'He goes to Paris himself, takes a room at the Grand Hôtel and enjoys a night out in his own way . . .

'Until the moment when he finds himself face to face with Lydia Nielsen . . . Had she, on second thoughts, decided that ten thousand francs was not enough payment for her silence? From what we know of her, it's highly likely. She had come to blackmail Krull . . . She probably expected to find him in some Montmartre night-club; instead of which she meets him sooner than she expected . . .

'At that point he gets rid of his two little girl-friends . . . Under pretext of settling accounts with Lydia he takes her into a nearby hotel and kills her . . .

'And bad luck dogs this Dutch murderer. He leaves his wallet behind in the room! . . . He has to go back . . .'

'I say, doctor!'

'Yes?'

'D'you know you're very bright? D'you know you have reconstructed the facts with almost perfect accuracy?'

'That's only natural . . . When you follow an argument through and when you put yourself in the other person's skin . . .'

'Talking of which, you put yourself so thoroughly in the murderer's skin that you were the one they handcuffed and who spent several hours in cell No. 2 . . .'

'Thanks to your . . .'

'I'll admit that it was because I didn't want to see you triumph . . . I was expecting news from the detective who was trailing the false Van der Donck . . . I wanted to impress you . . .'

'Same here!'

'You found the trunk . I should probably have found it in a few days . . .'

'And I should surely have got as far as Le Havre . . .'

'But the boat would have left!'

The Little Doctor muttered, musingly: 'Maybe!'

He was deep in thought. His brow was furrowed as though in the throes of an investigation. But the question he was trying to answer, this time, was, 'Whose results were more important, mine or those of the P.J.?'

He was seeking a truthful answer to the question. He was frowning, oblivious of his companion, who concluded good-naturedly:

'There now! You're a champion, doctor! Next time it'll be my turn to go to Charente and take a lesson from you . . . Promise to get in touch with me over your first case . . . And meanwhile, suppose we treated ourselves to one of those meals that a gourmet doesn't forget?'

Only René Fabry remained in prison. He stayed there three months, before appearing at the assize court, where he was acquitted.

Meanwhile the bogus Van der Donck, Peter Krull, told the French police who were taking him to the frontier, where Inspector Snoek was waiting for him:

'I don't give a damn! *je m'en fous*, as you say . . . There's no death penalty in Belgium . . . And as my first crime was committed there, you've plenty of time to wait before I come back to France to account for my second . . .'

With his pudgy features and his little blue eyes, he still looked the best-natured fellow in the world!

Popaul and his Negro

I. In Which the Little Doctor, on a Luxury Liner, Visits Tropical Forests without ever Leaving the Port of Bordeaux

'Do you like plenty of ice?'

'Very little . . . Thank you . . .'

Dollent had to exercise strenuous self-control not to give vent to childish exultation. Could it really be he, the Little Doctor of Marsilly, with his drab grey suit, his untidily knotted tie, his much-rained-on old hat, was it really he who was sitting in this first-class saloon, panelled in rare woods, reclining at ease with his legs crossed, a glass of whisky with a lump of ice in it within reach of his hand and, between his lips, a millionaire's cigar?

True, the boat was not on the high seas. What he could see through the portholes, in the hazy sunlight, was just the wharf of Bordeaux, and what he could hear was not the throbbing of the engines, nor the ocean rollers, nor the rush of water against the hull, but the clatter of the cranes unloading the liner *Martinique.*

And what a select company surrounded the Little Doctor, what important personalities were full of attentions for him! The old gentleman with a goatee beard, constantly wiping his pince-nez, was a director of the Company; the tall grey-haired fellow in a white coat, lavishly braided, was the captain of the ship. The others were officers, the purser, the ship's doctor.

A few months earlier, when he pursued an inquiry, the Little Doctor had been obliged to creep in between the legs of officials like a small boy, and had often nearly been thrown out.

How could he so swiftly have gained a reputation as a solver of puzzles? It was firmly established today; even Anna, his ever-grumbling housekeeper, had been deeply impressed on reading the telegram:

Earnestly request you undertake immediate investigation on board liner Martinique now in port Bordeaux stop. Have agreed with police which will provide all facilities stop. Your own conditions accepted in advance.

His little car, Tin Lizzie, white with dust, stood on the quayside, between the docks. And the gentlemen who were entertaining him had doubtless been somewhat surprised, if not disappointed, when the great detective they were expecting turned out to be a slender, excitable young man who looked less than his thirty years and was dressed without any sense of decorum.

The director was the first to speak, as though at a board meeting.

'The tragic event which has taken place on board this ship, doctor, and which is extremely mysterious, is liable to prove highly damaging to the Company which I represent. Moreover the police, obliged to follow certain supposedly scientific methods, has effected an arrest which, if maintained, will do us even greater harm.

'That is why we are asking you to do your utmost to discover the truth without delay. The *Martinique*, as you know, provides a regular service along the western coast of Africa, between Bordeaux and Pointe-Noire, calling at all French colonial ports. She docked here this evening. In theory she should leave again in two days, but there is a possibility that the authorities may detain her at Bordeaux if the mystery has not been elucidated in the meantime.

'The staff of the ship is at your disposal. So are our funds . . . Now I only have to wish you good luck and leave you to work in peace with our friends here . . .'

Thereupon the gentleman in the pince-nez and goatee beard, satisfied with his speech, solemnly shook hands with the Little Doctor and the captain of the ship, made a vague gesture of farewell towards the less important characters and went off towards the limousine which was waiting for him under the accommodation ladder.

'If you'll kindly tell me the facts, Captain?'

'Gladly . . . I'll begin with the end, that's to say with what happened last night. The *Martinique* was due to berth yesterday, Tuesday, about six in the evening. A strongish swell in the gulf of Gascony delayed us; then, as we were coming up the Gironde coast, a storm broke out, so violent that visibility being practically nil we struck a sandbank. That's the risk in estuaries. We thus lost about three hours, and when we reached Bordeaux the customs office was closed.'

'You mean the passengers were unable to disembark?'

'Exactly . . . They had to wait until this morning to . . .'

'Excuse me . . . How long had these passengers been on board?'

'Those who embarked at Pointe-Noire had been on board for three weeks.'

'And were friends or relatives waiting for them on the quay?'

'Yes, indeed . . . That quite often happens . . . I needn't tell you that it invariably provokes some resentment . . . Fortunately we had only some twenty first-class passengers . . . By September the holiday season is over . . . It's the day after tomorrow, on the outward journey, that we shall be full.'

'So the incident took place right here, in port?'

'I should like to give you a more or less exact idea of the atmosphere . . . Night had fallen . . . All the passengers were on deck, waving handkerchiefs, looking at the lights of the town, using their hands as megaphones as they called out messages to the people waiting for them on shore . . . Before the visit of the customs and the quarantine service, which took place at six o'clock this morning, nobody was allowed to land . . .'

'And nobody landed?'

'Nobody could have landed! The harbour police and the customs officers were keeping watch all along the ship . . . And now consider that most of the passengers had been away from France for more than three years, some for ten years . . . A mother, on the wharf, was showing her husband a child whom he had never seen and who could talk already . . . As I said, tempers were rising. There were a few attempts to sneak off, which were quickly checked. It was then that Cairol, better known in Equatorial Africa as Popaul, fixed matters in his own way.

'"I'm treating everyone to champagne!" he announced. "Meet in the first-class bar."'

'Excuse me,' the Little Doctor murmured, like a good little schoolboy. 'I'm not familiar with luxury liners. Where is this first-class bar?'

'On the upper deck . . . I'll show you presently. Most of the passengers accepted . . . Only a handful of them went off to bed. Bob, the barman, served not only champagne but a good many whiskies and cocktails . . .'

'One more question before you go on. Who is this Cairol, known as Popaul?'

The Captain's instinctive reply produced an involuntarily comic effect. 'The corpse!'

'Forgive me . . . But before being a corpse?'

'A fellow as well known in Bordeaux as on the African coast. A timber-cutter . . .'

'I'm very sorry, Captain, but I don't even know what a timber-cutter is . . . I suppose it's not just a lumber-jack?'

The officers smiled, and the Little Doctor maintained the calm and innocent expression of a well-behaved child.

'Timber-cutters are generally pretty adventurous fellows . . . They obtain from the Government concessions of several thousands of hectares in the equatorial forest, often a long way from any centre . . . They settle in there, recruit native workers as best they can and cut down mahogany and gaboon trees . . . These have to be transported by river as far as the coast. It's not unusual for timber-cutters to make several millions of francs by this means . . .'

'Was this the case with your Popaul?'

'He made fortunes on this scale on three or four occasions . . . After which he would come back to France and spend in a few months all the money he had made . . One incident will give you an idea of the man . . . It was four years ago . . . He'd just come back to Bordeaux with his pockets well lined . . . It was pouring with rain . . . From a café opposite the theatre Popaul watched the ladies in full evening dress and the gentlemen in tails on their way to a gala performance . . .

'Then, for a joke, Popaul hired all the taxis in Bordeaux and lined them up in a procession. At the close of the performance he drove past at the head of hundreds of cabs while the ladies and gentlemen tried in vain to hail them . . . The poor things had to go home in the pouring rain while Popaul . . .'

'Did he go back to Gabon?'

'I was bringing him home for the fourth time, rich again, or so he said . . . He brought along with him a negro whom he jokingly called "Victor Hugo" . . . A fearful-looking Bantu . . .

'Popaul never behaved like other people. So he took a first-class cabin for his negro, next to the luxury cabin he occupied himself . . . He brought him into the first-class dining-saloon to eat at his own table . . . I tried to make him see sense, but in vain . . .

' "I'm paying, aren't I?" he would say. "And so long as Victor Hugo doesn't spit into the dishes . . ." '

'Where is this "Victor Hugo" now?'

'He's disappeared . . . I'm coming to that presently . . . I don't know if you can picture what this sort of voyage is like. Apart from Popaul and his negro, we had only very respectable people on board, mostly senior civil servants, and including a general . . .

'All along the coast the heat is stifling and even in the bar you have to keep your sun-helmet on because of the reflected glare.

'Usually bridge and *belote* help to kill time, with a certain number of whiskies and apéritifs . . . There's a lot of drinking on board these liners . . .

'Needless to say, Popaul and his negro caused a sensation . . . I'm sorry you never met the man . . . He was vulgar, of course . . . A big fellow with a bony face, bold eyes, boisterously high-spirited, who could down a bottle of pernod or picon without getting intoxicated . . . He was still handsome, at forty . . . He despised officials and made fun of their habits . . .

'All the same he impressed people; he would sit down uninvited at anyone's table, order drinks all round, tell stories, slap people familiarly on the thigh, all in such a way as to disarm resentment . . .

'When we held our traditional little party on board, he spent twenty-two thousand francs on champagne and cigars . . . I believe this box in front of you is the last we've got left . . .

'As for women . . .'

A slight smile flitted over the Captain's lips, and he glanced at his officers before going on to say: 'I don't want to say anything derogatory to the opposite sex, of whom I am a great admirer . . .'

That went without saying! The Little Doctor had already noticed that the Captain must have been something of a ladies' man.

'I don't know if idleness and the heat had anything to do with it, but there's no doubt that Popaul's vulgarity was not unattractive to some of our lady passengers . . . When you like, I'll give you certain details which will probably be helpful to your inquiry, for I need hardly add that on board ship nothing concerning the trivial intrigues that take place there escapes the notice of the staff . . .'

'I fancy I'm beginning to sense the atmosphere of shipboard life,' the Little Doctor murmured. 'Would you just mention the women who have been in contact with Popaul?'

'First, Madame Mandine, the beauty of Brazzaville. Her husband's an administrator . . . They were both coming home on leave for six months.'

'What sort of person is Monsieur Mandine?'

'The serious, not to say boring sort. He plays bridge from morning till night and grumbles because meal-times interrupt the game . . .'

'Who else?'

'Mademoiselle Lardilier, of course . . .'

'Why do you say *of course?*'

'Because she's the person they've arrested . . . I may have confused you by telling you the story sometimes from the beginning and sometimes from the end . . . I don't know if you're going to understand it . . .'

'Tell me about the critical events, as they took place.'

'I'll go back to last night . . . Most of the passengers were in the bar, drinking . . .'

'Was Madame Mandine among them?'

'Yes . . . And her husband had managed to arrange a bridge four, in a corner, with the general and two other people . . .'

'And Mademoiselle Lardilier?'

'She was there too . . .'

'And her father? For I assume the young lady was not travelling along the African coast all by herself?'

'Her father, Eric Lardilier, is owner of the Lardilier warehouses, which are to be found in every port in Gabon . . . You don't know Africa? Then I'll explain the precise meaning of the word "warehouse" . . . These are huge establishments, where every sort of thing is bought and sold: native products and machinery, cars and provisions, clothes, tools, even boats and aircraft . . .'

'A rich man, then?'

'Very rich . . .'

'Did Popaul and Eric Lardilier know one another?'

'They couldn't help knowing one another, but I never saw them exchange a word . . . Monsieur Lardilier displays a certain contempt for adventurers who, in his opinion, damage the reputation of our colonies . . .'

'Was Monsieur Lardilier in the bar?'

'No . . . He had gone downstairs to bed early.'

'And now, the crisis, please?'

'At a certain point, about one in the morning, Popaul left his guests saying he'd be back immediately . . . He looked as if he were just going to fetch something from his cabin . . .'

'Was his negro with him?'

'No, "Victor Hugo" must have been in the cabin fastening up the trunks . . . That reminds me of one detail I'll mention presently . . . Popaul, as I said, had just gone downstairs . . . It was then that a steward, Jean Michel, who's been with the company for many years and is completely trustworthy, was, in the course of his duties, going along gangway B on to which Popaul's cabin gives. The cabin door was open. The steward glanced in automatically . . .

'He saw Mademoiselle Lardilier standing in the middle of the room, holding a revolver in her hand . . .

' "What are you doing?" he exclaimed in horror.

'He went in. The bathroom door was open too. On going in there he discovered the body of Paul Cairol, known as Popaul, lying beside the bath in a pool of blood.

'He immediately gave the alarm . . . The doctor was the first to arrive. He declared that the passenger, who had been shot through the chest, had only been dead a few minutes. It was the doctor's idea to wrap a handkerchief round the revolver which Mademoiselle Lardilier, in a daze, had just put down on the table.

'I informed the authorities . . . The inquiry was begun immediately, in order to enable the passengers to leave this morning . . . You can imagine what a night we had, with questioning going on in this very room . . .'

'But the negro?' the Little Doctor persisted.

'We couldn't find him anywhere . . . Neither the customs officers nor the police had seen him leave the boat . . . As most of the portholes were open on account of the heat, it's probable that he climbed through one of them on the port side and swam ashore.'

'What does Mademoiselle Lardilier say?'

'Antoinette . . .' the Captain began, then bit his lip. He corrected himself:

'She and I were good friends . . . That's why I've just called her by her first name . . . She was questioned for over an hour and they got nothing from her except the following statement, which I'm beginning to know by heart:

' "*I was going to my cabin to fetch a Spanish shawl, because the night was getting cool, when I passed in front of Monsieur Cairol's open door . . . To my great surprise I saw a revolver on the floor . . . I picked it up and I was going to call someone when a steward came in . . .*

' "*I don't know anything. . . I never realized there was a dead body in the bathroom . . . I had no motive for killing Monsieur Cairol . . .*"

'The unfortunate thing,' sighed the Captain, 'is that her fingerprints were the only ones found on the gun, which is definitely the one that killed Popaul. Here's a copy of the report of Mademoiselle Lardilier's interrogation. If you'd like to glance through it . . .

Q. During the voyage, you saw a good deal of M. Cairol?
A. So did most people on board.
Q. Some witnesses assert that you often walked on deck with him late at night.
A. I never go to bed early . . . I used to take a stroll with him sometimes, but so I did with the captain. All the same, I didn't kill M. Cairol or anybody else.

'Is this correct, Captain?'

'Perfectly correct . . . I may add that Mademoiselle Lardilier used frequently to come to my office for a drink . . . all most respectable . . . It's quite usual on board ship, where entertainment is in short supply and flirtations are not taken very seriously . . .'

'So she used to flirt both with Cairol and with yourself?'

'You could say so . . .'

He smiled. The Little Doctor resumed his reading.

Q. When you reached gangway B you met nobody?
A. Nobody . . .
Q. And yet the murderer could not have been far away, since, when the doctor arrived, much later on, Monsieur Cairol had only just died?
A. I'm sorry. I've nothing to add. I shall answer no more questions.

'A little more whisky? . . . Please do . . . So Antoinette Lardilier has been detained by the police . . . in other words she's practically been arrested . . . Her father is furious . . . He's an important customer of ours and he's been whipping up all the exporters of

Bordeaux against us . . . It was my idea to appeal to you, doctor, for I've followed a number of your cases . . . I don't believe Antoinette is guilty . . . I'm convinced that there's far more in this business than a straightforward story of love or jealousy, and that's what I want to talk about now.

'These gentlemen, whom I have asked to stay so that you may more easily check the truth of my story, will bear me out.

'There was something suspicious about Popaul's attitude, ever since he came on board at Libreville . . .

'Of course he had always been unconventional and wild . . . He was a notorious bluffer . . . He loves, or rather loved, spectacular attitudes . . . After three years alone in the forest with his negroes he was enjoying life to the full, with an aggressive sort of avidity.

'None the less I'm convinced that, this time, he was not in his normal state of mind . . . He himself remarked, referring to his negro: "American gangsters have their bodyguard, don't they? Since I'm in quite as much danger as they are, I'm entitled to have my own." Isn't that correct, gentlemen?'

'Quite correct.'

'He let fall other remarks, particularly when he'd been drinking too much, which was an everyday occurrence. Among others, I remember this one word for word:

' "This time my fortune isn't in any bank and I'm in no danger of having half of it taken from me by the Treasury, as happened last time I came back to France . . ." '

The Little Doctor, still polite and demure, queried: 'Can you guess to what he was referring?'

'No . . . What is particularly odd is that he referred to several millions. He asserted that he'd never need to go back to Africa . . . When he saw the coast for the last time he called out: "Goodbye for ever!"

'Then, on another occasion, the barman Bob heard him say: "If I get to Bordeaux alive, I'm going to enjoy life . . . And this time it'll be for good!" '

'I suppose, Captain, that your Popaul couldn't have been carrying several million francs in banknotes about with him?'

'Quite impossible!' the Captain declared categorically. 'Where could he have got hold of such a sum in notes? The Libreville bank hasn't that amount available. All payments there are made by transfer, and as little cash as possible is kept . . . And yet . . .'

The Captain was pondering. The ship's doctor now intervened for the first time.

'I've good reason to think Popaul carried his wealth about with him!' he said. 'I remember one detail. It was shortly after our call at Grand-Bassam. He had drunk a great deal that night, more than usual. Next morning he came into my cabin looking worried.

' "I'd like you to sound me, doctor," he said. "It would be such a shame, now that I'm stocked up for the rest of my days . . ."

'And as he bared his chest he explained: "This morning I felt some sort of twinges on my left side . . . Say, it couldn't be heart disease, could it?"

'I reassured him . . . He got dressed again . . . Just as he was putting on his linen jacket, he noticed a small crocodile-skin wallet which had fallen out of the pocket . . . He picked it up quickly and said, with a mocking laugh:

' "Good Lord, I nearly left my fortune in your cabin! Rather a high fee for a consultation! . . Besides which, you'd not have known what to do with it . . ."

'Now the wallet was quite flat . . . It can't have held much . . .'

'Did you tell the police about this visit?' asked the Little Doctor anxiously.

'I must admit I never thought of doing so . . . It was what the Captain was saying that reminded me of it.'

'Tell me, Captain . . . Being solely responsible, after God, for this ship, you must have been present at the examination of the body, the searching of the cabin and of the man's clothing . . . Did you notice this wallet anywhere?'

'No! I saw a big brown leather wallet containing all sorts of papers and a passport . . . But nothing else.'

'Do you know where the Mandines are spending their leave in Europe?'

'At Arcachon . . . They own a small villa there . . .'

'Forgive me for being indiscreet . . . Did Madame Mandine occasionally visit your office for a drink?'

'That has happened . . .'

'Do you think her relations with Popaul were no more than a mere flirtation?'

The Captain, slightly embarrassed, finally smiled.

'Madame Mandine is a highly-sexed woman, as they say . . . When you see her husband, you'll understand why . . .'

'I understand. Thank you. I suppose that Monsieur Lardilier's home in France is at Bordeaux?'

'Quai des Chartrons, less than five hundred metres from here . . .'

'Did he board the ship at Libreville?'

'No. His chief warehouse is at Libreville, but he was staying with his daughter at Port-Gentil, the next port of call.'

'Did Popaul know that Lardilier was going to be a passenger?'

'I couldn't say . . . The two ports of call are very close to one another. Navigation is tricky in that region, and I had no time to bother about my passengers . . .'

'Perhaps the purser can . . .'

The purser put in his word. 'The very first day, Monsieur Cairol asked what passengers we were taking on at various ports of call. I showed him the list . . .'

'And you noticed nothing unusual about his reaction?'

'It was some time ago now . . . I wasn't expecting a tragedy at the end of the cruise . . . Yet, I could almost assert, although not on oath, that he gave a funny sort of smile . . .'

'A satisfied smile?'

'I find it hard to answer . . . And yet . . . I don't want you to set too much store by what I'm going to say . . . I think it was an ironical smile . . . no, a sarcastic one rather . . .'

'And he said nothing?'

'He said something which did not surprise me, coming from him, but which in retrospect may be significant:

' "So we shan't be short of pretty women!" '

'Thank you, gentlemen!' the Little Doctor said gravely, uncrossing his legs. And for the first time he felt it incumbent on him to assume an almost solemn air.

'May I ask you, doctor, if you have any ideas and if you think . . .'

'I shall tell you in twenty-four hours' time, Captain . . .'

He would have burst out laughing to see himself taken so seriously, had he not been thinking:

'Dollent, my little man, it's all very well to have impressed these fine gentlemen and to have become a sort of national celebrity. Only now you've got to discover something! No more lolling in a first-class saloon drinking excellent whisky on the rocks and smoking luxury cigars. Two hours from now you're likely to have made an utter fool of yourself and to be running back to Marsilly with your tail between your legs . . .'

He felt cheerful none the less. Perhaps it was duc to the sunshine, the unfamiliar atmosphere of this fine liner, the white uniforms all round him and the scent of adventure which he'd been breathing in ever since he came on board?

After all, why should he worry? Somebody had killed Cairol, known as Popaul; that was a fact. Was he going to show himself stupider than the murderer? Wasn't his guiding principle the saying which he had considered pinning up over his bed:

'*Every murderer is an imbecile, since murder never pays!*'

Since he did not consider himself stupider than an imbecile! . .

'Has "Victor Hugo" been in Europe before?'

'Never!'

'Does he speak French?'

'A dozen words . . . Popaul and he spoke Bantu to one another.'

'Are there many Bantus in Bordeaux?'

'About a hundred . . . All known to the maritime authorities, because in order to bring a negro in from Equatorial Africa you have to pay a large deposit . . . ten thousand francs.'

'So Popaul paid ten thousand francs to bring "Victor Hugo" with him? . . . I suppose it won't be long before the police get hold of the negro?'

As though at a prearranged signal, the steward now announced:

'It's Inspector Pierre, sir . . .'

And the Inspector entered, greeting the company and casting a respectful glance at the Little Doctor, whom he must have known by reputation.

'I've come to tell you that we've caught the negro. He was hidden on board an old lighter, moored close to the wharf . . . He's trembling all over . . . They're looking for an interpreter to question him.'

'May I ask you one thing, Inspector?' put in Jean Dollent. 'The revolver . . .'

'Well?'

'Do you know to whom it belonged?'

'It's a Smith and Wesson, a powerful gun, but none of the passengers admits to having owned a Smith and Wesson . . .'

'It's not an easy weapon to get hold of, is it?'

'It's rather cumbersome . . . Only experts . . . At fifteen feet it'll kill a man outright, whereas your little Browning . . .'

The doctor emptied his glass, wiped his mouth, and after a moment's hesitation dipped his hand into the cigar box.

His practice at Marsilly never provided havanas of this quality!

II. Revealing the Apparent Stupidity of 'Victor Hugo', and Showing the Little Doctor Searching in Vain for a Certain Object

The scene, at times, reached such a peak of absurdity that it became sublime. The Little Doctor and Inspector Pierre dared not look at one another for fear of bursting out laughing, while the ship's captain was constantly obliged to turn his face away.

Chance had certainly played its part. Where what was needed was the most patient man on earth, chance had produced Superintendent Frittet, a hot-blooded, black-haired little man with an aggressive moustache, storming and swearing with the sonorous accent of the Toulouse region.

'Last night . . . dark . . . Last night . . . You here . . . waiting for master . . . master sahib . . . master sahib come down . . .'

The cabin was spacious and sunlit, and still full of Paul Cairol's trunks. The bathroom door stood open. The Superintendent was yelling. The interpreter was yelling even louder, and finally a gleam of understanding lit up the eyes of "Victor Hugo". He made his way into the bathroom. Everyone followed him. He went up to an enamel hook fastened to the wall beside the bath, on which a bath-robe of gaudily coloured towelling was still hanging.

'Here!' he said.

Whew! He had understood at last. The Superintendent pressed him further, however, and he nodded. He had been in the bathroom when his master had come down. He had been finishing the packing, and had gone to fetch the bath-robe and toilet articles . . .

'May I?' said the Little Doctor, going up close to the negro.

And he ascertained that from that position it was impossible to see into the cabin.

'What's he saying? Translate what he's saying!'

For now "Victor Hugo", so long mute, was speaking volubly and there was no stopping him.

'What's he saying?'

'He says that suddenly his master came in . . . He was walking fast, like someone who's forgotten something important . . . Then there was a tiny noise, like a hiccough, and the white man fell forward . . .

'Paul Cairol was shot in the back!' the Inspector said to the doctor in a low voice. 'That seems to confirm the negro's sincerity.'

The Superintendent was pressing the interpreter: 'And then? Ask him what he did, whom he saw . . .'

'He saw nobody . . . He bent down . . . There was blood everywhere . . . Then he was so frightened that he jumped through the porthole . . .'

Just then Jean Dollent felt something hard under his foot. He had stepped back to leave room for the Superintendent and his two negroes. He was almost behind the door. He bent down and picked up a small tube of black steel, which he handed to Frittet, murmuring in a quiet, innocent way that contrasted strangely with the tumultuous scene that had just taken place:

'Tell me, Superintendent, isn't this what they call a silencer?'

For that was what it was, and the policeman himself had not often had occasion to examine one so closely, since this American gangsters' gadget is hard to get hold of.

'That's why nobody heard the shot . . .'

The two negroes were wondering why nobody was taking any notice of them. Actually, the case had suddely developed a new aspect.

Already the fact that the criminal's weapon was a Smith and

Wesson had set the Little Doctor pondering. But now this redoubtable weapon had assumed a far more sinister character through being provided with the latest type of silencer!

Who had gone into that cabin last night and . . . ?

'I'd like to ask you a few more questions, Superintendent . . . I have been assured that nobody had landed from the boat. But is it equally certain that nobody came on board?'

'The police and the customs officers have said so categorically.'

'I was thinking . . . Considering that "Victor Hugo" was able to disappear by climbing through the porthole and swimming ashore, couldn't a man have come in a boat and . . .'

'We are six metres at least above sea-level . . . Unless we assume that such a man brought a ladder, or somebody threw him a rope from on board . . .'

Then the Little Doctor smiled, and the irascible Superintendent wondered why. The strange thing was at the very moment when Dollent was abandoning his hypothesis of a murderer from outside he sensed that this idea had impressed the policeman, who was about to start off along that trail. It would lead nowhere!

Something had clicked in the Little Doctor's mind, and now he had a foundation to work on, a basic truth: *if Popaul was afraid, it was not of anyone coming from outside.*

Otherwise, why, during the entire cruise, when they were on the open sea and nobody could come on board, would he have taken so many precautions, keeping his negro beside him from morning till night, even in the dining-saloon? And why was it at Bordeaux, precisely, that he had relaxed his vigilance?

'I wonder,' Dollent said under his breath, as though talking to himself, 'why, when he was enjoying a drink upstairs, he rushed down so suddenly?'

The luggage was still there. The Superintendent's gaze followed that of the Little Doctor.

'I searched everything last night,' he hastily declared. 'I must mention that in the dead man's pocket we found a revolver . . .'

'A Smith and Wesson?'

'No . . . A large-bore cylinder revolver . . . There's another in the drawer of this trunk . . .'

'And you didn't anywhere find a small crocodile-skin wallet? I may be giving you a pointless task, Superintendent. Nevertheless I think a meticulous search of this cabin and the bathroom would be advisable . . . Meanwhile the two negroes can be shut up in the next room.'

The search went on for nearly an hour, and the Captain, considerately, sent for drinks. Dollent turned to the steward and said:

'Were you on duty on this gangway last night?'

'Yes, sir.'

'When you gave the alarm, can you specify which people came along first?'

'I'm afraid I didn't notice . . . I was very upset . . . It was the first time I'd seen a sight like that . . . I remember that the surgeon . . .'

'But the passengers? . . . Was Monsieur Lardilier one of the first to appear?'

'No! I could swear to that . . .'

'Why?'

'Because in the middle of all the upheaval I heard a bell ring. I wondered who could be calling for me at such a moment. I went into the corridor to see. The light was on above Monsieur Lardilier's door. I knocked and went in. He was in bed, very cross, and he asked: "Who's making all that noise? Not only are we kept on board an extra night, but we're prevented from sleeping! Tell the Captain . . ."'

'Did you tell him what had happened?'

'Yes. He put on a dressing-gown and followed me . . .'

'Did you see Madame Mandine?'

'No . . .'

'I attended to her,' the ship's doctor put in. 'When she heard of Monsieur Cairol's death she came down, like all the rest . . . But she didn't get as far as this; she fainted on the staircase. I brought her round, and had her taken to her cabin by a stewardess.'

Then Superintendent Frittet sighed: 'I may as well tell you right away, that line will take you nowhere. I questioned the passengers and the crew that same night, while the events were still fresh in people's minds . . . I came to the conclusion that it's impossible, on board a ship, to establish what everyone was doing at a given moment . . . Except for the four bridge players, who couldn't have left their table . . .'

'Excuse me!' retorted the Little Doctor. 'You're obviously not a bridge player, Superintendent. In a four of bridge there's always a dummy, one of the players who can leave the table for the few minutes that the game lasts . . .'

His little eyes were gleaming. It amused him to send the policeman after various hares, and particularly to see how eagerly he started in pursuit of them.

'You think that? . . .'

'I think we shan't know anything until we've found the little wallet I told you of . . . I think, furthermore, that we shan't find it ourselves. We're not sufficiently at home on board ship for that . . . It's you, Captain, and your ship's engineer, who must help us. Let's see. If you were the occupant of this cabin with its bathroom, and had a small wallet to hide, how would you set about it?'

They explored every hypothesis. They tapped all the tiles on the bathroom walls in turn; they dismantled the four ventilators and part of the plumbing.

'May we take these trunks to pieces, Superintendent?'

'Well . . . You'll have to explain to the Department of Public Prosecution . . .'

They cut the trunks to shreds to make sure they contained no hiding-place. They examined the heels of all Popaul's shoes.

'Messieurs, it's really not possible that . . . Let's all put ourselves in the dead man's place . . . He has a wallet to hide . . . It's a matter of life and death . . .'

He was getting impatient himself now. He could not admit defeat. He cast his eyes around in search of inspiration. Then the Captain's voice was heard.

'If it was a matter of life and death, how do we know the murderer didn't take away the wallet? Moreover, doctor, it seems to me that we've gone a long way from Mademoiselle Lardilier, who was actually here with the murder weapon in her hand when the steward . . . I must remind you, after all, that her finger-prints are unquestionably there and . . .'

'Of course, of course!' growled the Little Doctor. 'I think I'm going to take a turn in town to clear my head . . .'

The Captain caught up with him at the end of the gangway.

'Just one word more, doctor . . . I think I'm expressing the wish of the Company . . . I don't know whether you'll discover the truth, and I hope you may . . . But in any case I should like you to give Monsieur Lardilier the impression that you're acting on behalf of his daughter . . . I'd like him to know that we've done our utmost to clear her . . . You see what I mean?'

The man was clearly in love with Antoinette Lardilier, and he was blushing slightly as he moved away.

III. In Which the Little Doctor becomes Garrulous and, Suddenly Seized with a Liking for Advertisement, Visits Newspaper Offices

'I must apologize for disturbing you; it's because I am convinced that your daughter did not kill Paul Cairol . . . The Company, being anxious to discover the truth, have asked me to undertake an investigation conjointly with that of the police . . . I thought I could not do better than to visit you in the first place . . .'

The man was heavily built, with a thick head of hair and suspicious eyes. The Little Doctor was in his drawing-room in the Quai des Chartrons; outside, the full sun was beating on the windows, but only slender streaks of light filtered though the closed shutters.

'You are an old colonial hand, if I may venture to use that expression . . .'

'I'm sixty-two years old, and I spent forty of them in the colonies . . . I'm not ashamed of the fact that I'm a self-made man, by dint of labour and patience and also of strength of will . . .'

'Did you know the man they call Popaul?'

'I did not know him and I never wanted to know him. If you had lived in Africa you would realize that it is men of his sort, vulgar adventurers and sensualists, who do the greatest harm to a decent colonial system . . .'

'I shall venture to ask you an indiscreet question, Monsieur Lardilier . . . Please understand that it's only due to my anxiety to find out the truth . . . In view of your opinion of that buffoon Popaul, I wonder why you allowed your daughter . . .'

'I know what you're going to say . . . I don't expect you have any children, doctor . . . My daughter, who lost her mother fifteen years ago, has spent most of her life in the colonies, where there's much greater freedom than here . . . She's the only thing I have in the world . . . So I needn't tell you she's a spoilt child . . . When I ventured a remark about Paul Cairol she merely replied: "Can I help it if he's the only person on board who's fun?" And I know her well enough to realize it would have been useless to insist.'

'So you were a reluctant witness to an incipient flirtation?'

The business man frowned. 'Why do you speak of a flirtation? Can't a girl play at deck-quoits or *belote* with a man without something further being suspected? If that's your idea, doctor, I'd rather tell you right away that . . .'

'No, no, don't get worked up, old man!' thought Jean Dollent. 'My passion for detective work has frequently got me chucked out of this sort of home. I'm not going to risk it again. This time I shall be sweetness itself.'

And he replied out loud, with an air of the utmost candour:

'Forgive me . . . I said more than I meant . . . I was simply repeating something that the Captain . . .'

The other man flared up at this.

'Very nice of your Captain, particularly as he himself continually pursued Antoinette with his attentions! . . . And if it had only been Antoinette that he pursued! But he was always hanging round the ladies on board, and now he dares to . . .'

'He's undoubtedly got a weakness for the fair sex . . . But I wanted to talk to you about more serious matters. You see, I've come to the conclusion that Popaul must have been concealing something in his cabin, and that it was on account of that thing that he was killed. If I can manage to prove that, your daughter will almost certainly be exonerated, for it's most unlikely to have been a love-letter. Do you see what I mean?'

'What makes you think that?'

'Oh, just an idea, of course . . . But I have certain intuitions . . . Thus I might tell you . . .'

His loquacity and self-assurance were intolerable. To see him, no one would have guessed that this pretentious fellow had really solved certain supposedly impenetrable mysteries.

'You have travelled by sea a great deal, Monsieur Lardilier. Believe it or not, this morning was the first time I've been on board a real liner . . . Apart from the cross-channel steamer from Boulogne to England . . . That's why I'm putting the question to you: if you had to hide a small wallet, or just a sheet of paper, in a luxury cabin like Popaul's what place would you choose?

'That's the whole question! When I've succeeded in answering it, the police will have to release your daughter with their humblest apologies.'

'A wallet?' repeated Lardilier. 'What sort of wallet?'

'For instance, a small crocodile-skin wallet . . . We searched the cabin this morning . . . We almost demolished the bathroom and dismantled the bath . . . We searched the negro's room too . . .'

'And you found nothing?'

'Nothing! Now, I refuse to believe, as the Superintendent does, that the murderer had time to get hold of that wallet and make away with it . . . The fact that your daughter came on the scene . . .'

'My daughter maintains that she saw nobody . . .'

'I know, I know . . . I've read her statement . . .'

'Don't you think it's truthful?'

'Absolutely truthful . . . That's to say . . .'

'That's to say what?'

'Nothing . . . You haven't answered my question, Monsieur Lardilier. If you had to hide a . . .'

'Why, I don't know . . . Under the carpet?'

'We looked there . . .'

'On top of a wardrobe?'

'We hunted there . . .'

'In that case . . . You must excuse me; I've got to see my daughter's solicitor, who is expecting me at two o'clock . . . When I think that they had the audacity to shut her up like a criminal! . . . Thank you for your visit, doctor . . . If I can be of any further use to you . . . A cigar?'

'No, thanks . . .'

Too many cigars! Too many whiskies! He was quite lively enough as it was. Seldom had he felt in such high spirits. Seldom had he displayed such boisterous good humour, and he astonished the sub-editor of the *Petite Gironde* with his chatter.

'I thought you might like to have a little information about last night's crime . . . Officially the police probably don't give you very much . . . But since I'm in charge of an unofficial inquiry . . .

'Believe it or not, I've come to the conclusion that the whole matter revolves around a scrap of paper . . . Do you want to take notes?

'Here you are, then: Paul Cairol, known as Popaul, was on his way home from Gabon with a fortune of several million francs, so he said.

'He was frightened . . . He knew some danger was threatening him . . .

'Now this treasure worth several million francs was kept in a small crocodile-skin wallet . . . One day he dropped this wallet in the doctor's cabin, and that was how . . . Am I going too fast?

'So then, somebody on board wanted to get hold of that wallet, or rather of the document it contained . . .

'During the whole voyage, this person was keeping watch, but our Popaul was on his guard and couldn't be caught napping for a moment.

'Why, on the last night . . . Or rather let me put the question differently: *Why did Popaul, who had been drinking and making merry at the bar, suddenly rush down to his cabin?*

'Wasn't it because he suddenly realized he'd been taken off his guard? If he'd had the document on him, he'd have had nothing to fear . . .

'Here, then, is my hypothesis . . . After he had dropped the wallet in the doctor's surgery, Popaul realized that it was dangerous to keep it on his person, particularly when he was wearing linen garments . . . He sought some *safe* hiding-place . . . He found one, for he was a man of some imagination . . .

'You'll agree, surely, that his adversary must also have been someone to be reckoned with, otherwise he'd have promptly been eliminated from the contest.

'In other words, the safe hiding-place had to be one that this opponent was *incapable of finding*.

'I'll put my original question again: Why was it at Bordeaux, when the vessel was in port, that Popaul suddenly became uneasy, and hurried down to his cabin, where he was to meet his death?

'That's all . . . You can use these disclosures in your paper . . .'

Ten minutes later he was climbing the stairs to the office of the rival paper, *La France de Bordeaux et du Sud-Ouest*, where he put on the same act, telling the whole story over again with additional embroideries:

'I maintain that my argument inevitably leads us to . . .'

A really exciting day! That splendid boat, gleaming white in the sunshine, those uniforms, those friendly officers, and he himself feeling so agile, so subtle, with such a sense of manipulating people's destinies!

He had never bestirred himself so much in all his life. His shirt was clinging to his back. Although it was September already, the asphalt seemed to be melting in the streets, so that the ground was as soft as a thick carpet.

'Police station!' he ordered his taxi driver.

For he had left Tin Lizzie on the wharf.

'I've taken the liberty, Superintendent . . . See now . . . I'd like to ask you two small favours . . . First of all, to have a discreet watch kept on Popaul's cabin and on his servant's.'

'That's already been done.'

'Why?'

'Because it's the rule . . .'

And the Little Doctor smiled. He had his own good reasons for wanting a watch kept over those cabins!

'Will this watch be kept up all night? Good . . . Now a second request, which is somewhat trickier: I presume you are keeping the negro under your eye?'

' "Victor Hugo" is in one of our cells . . . That's another of our principles: until anyone is proved to be . . .'

'Well, that's just it; I should like you to release him . . . Let me make it quite clear, I'm not asking you simply to abandon him to his fate . . . You release him . . . You put one or two of your best detectives on his heels . . . I don't imagine "Victor Hugo" will be cunning enough to escape them.'

'Do you expect he'll lead you somewhere?'

The oddest thing about Superintendent Frittet was that each time he assumed that sly manner, that's to say each time he thought he had seen through the other person's secret intentions, he was on the wrong tack!

'There's no hiding anything from you,' the Little Doctor sighed without a trace of irony.

'I see things differently . . . I'm sure it's a pointless task . . . "Victor Hugo" is too stupid to be an accomplice or to . . . However, since the Company has asked us to give you every possible help . . . Is that all you wanted?'

'While you give your instructions about the negro, I'd like to use your telephone.'

He called the sub-editors of *La Petite Gironde* and *La France de Bordeaux*.

'Is your layout ready? You're coming out in an hour's time? . . . Will you add a few lines to your article? I assure you they're sensational: The negro whom Popaul had brought with him as bodyguard and nicknamed "Victor Hugo" will be released in an hour at the least . . . You don't see the importance of it? Believe me, it's of the utmost importance . . . Particularly if you add that, since he speaks no French, he will probably go to meet the man who acted as interpreter for him this morning in a certain back-street in the harbour which is frequented only by Blacks . . . what did you say? It'll appear in your current issue? Thank you . . .'

And the Little Doctor drew from his pocket one of the magnificent cigars provided by the Company, for he had taken the precaution of removing a few of them.

IV. Which Proves that a Man who has Staked his Life Once and has Won may be Forced by Circumstances to Stake it Again and Lose

'Funny job!' he reflected cheerfully. 'To think that there are people who earn their living doing this from morning till night!'

'This' was what is known as shadowing. For three hours at least he had been on the heels of the extraordinary "Victor Hugo", trying not to be seen, sometimes exchanging a wink with the two policemen who meanwhile were responsible for officially watching the negro.

Poor negro, really! He was as bedazzled by the great city as an owl is by the bright August sun. And ten times at least he had narrowly escaped being run over by a tram or knocked down by buses or taxis.

He did not know where to go. He cut a comical figure in the old suit provided for him by Popaul, which looked even more dilapidated after its immersion in the Gironde, and people turned round to look at him.

Moreover, he was presumably penniless. Nobody had thought of giving him any money. He zigzagged about at random, staring about him with bewildered eyes, and when he had to cross a street he dashed forward like a madman, so that it was often difficult to keep track of him.

Fortunately, he caught sight of the ships' funnels in the distance, beyond the Quincunxes. They represented the only part of the white man's life that was familiar to him, and as the Little Doctor had foreseen, he turned his steps towards them.

Other negroes were lounging on the quayside, but they were more civilized negroes, who had come under Arab influence and belonged to a different, more highly developed type than the poor Bantu, who dared not address a word to them.

He kept walking along the quayside. He would inevitably reach the corner that the Little Doctor had noticed, opposite the last docks, a tangle of narrow streets inhabited solely by black bunkerhands and all the scum that had drifted thither from Africa on one boat or another.

The two newspapers had come out over an hour ago. This was all to the good. Without them, Dollent would have been obliged, as in the case of Lardilier, to seek out each of the passengers of the *Martinique* and each time to repeat his long rigmarole, the story of the secret hiding-place and so on. Now, thanks to the papers, all the passengers were acquainted with his idea about the crime. Inevitably, therefore, one of them . . .

If it were Mandine, would he have time to get here from Arcachon? And if it were Madame Mandine? If it were the Captain himself? . . . If? . . .

Enough of that! The Little Doctor was play-acting, decidedly; he was cheating himself for fun. He knew perfectly well who he expected to see turn up. Or rather, there were just two people to choose from.

Since Antoinette Lardilier had said nothing . . . For she could not have failed to meet the murderer. *Since she had let herself be shut up rather than utter a name* . . .

Whom could a girl be trying to shield in this way? Her father, of course; but equally, her fiancé or her lover . . . Now the Captain of the *Martinique* . . .

There was nothing to do but wait . . . And a new comic scene was taking place not far from the Little Doctor, who had some difficulty in remaining concealed. On the terrace of a small bistrot, so filthy that it looked more Eastern than French, "Victor Hugo" had recognized the negro who had acted as his interpreter. He stood there on the edge of the pavement, staring at him stupidly.

The other negro beckoned to him, with all the authority conferred on him by his *bois-de-rose* trousers, his white cap and his role as an established French citizen.

What could they be saying to one another? One could only guess from their gestures and expressions.

'So they've let you go?' the interpreter was asking.

'I don't know . . . They told me to "clear out".'

'Sit down . . . You've got some money, I hope?'

And the other, who had no money, gesticulated despairingly.

'You let a white man bring you to France without demanding money from him? You're daft . . .'

The Little Doctor could only roughly reconstruct this conversation, particularly as night had fallen and he was too far off to discern the facial expressions of the two men.

Suddenly he gave a start. He had just noticed, on the other side of the street, the Captain of the *Martinique*, who had changed from his white uniform into a navy blue one; he stood there, apparently quite at his ease, smoking a cigarette and gazing in the direction of the bistrot.

Unhesitatingly, the Little Doctor got into a parked car, where he was hidden from view.

The two negroes were now sitting side by side at a small table, exchanging remarks which must have had a certain tartness, to judge by their ever more vehement gestures.

As for the detectives on the quayside, they were absorbed in studying the posters advertising a great international fair.

'He'll go! . . . He won't! . . . He'll go! . . . He won't . . .'

It was like a game of cat and mouse . . . To think that by a simple process of reasoning, but of reasoning faultlessly, one had been able to . . .

'He'll go . . .'

It seemed most likely . . . You could sense that the Captain was about to cross the street and accost the two negroes.

Then he suddenly stopped short . . . The Little Doctor looked over at the terrace and caught sight of a short square figure entering the bistrot.

It was Eric Lardilier. He had gone inside. The *patron*, doubtless on his orders, went out to fetch the two negroes, presumably so as to avoid a scene on the terrace . . .

'Well, Captain?'

The Captain looked at the Little Doctor in surprise. And immediately he exclaimed excitedly: 'So you thought of it?'

'Of what?'

'The hiding-place! . . . Because of your persistence, I've been worrying all day and saying to myself: "If I had a document to hide, where would I . . ." So that eventually I had an idea. It occurred to me just now, as I was reading the newspaper . . .'

'The paper that said "Victor Hugo" had been released?'

'Yes . . . Well . . . if I'd had a document to hide and if I'd had a negro with me, I . . .'

At that, the Little Doctor left him standing in the middle of the street and rushed into the bistrot, beckoning the two detectives to follow him.

At a poorly-lit table, Monsieur Lardilier was sitting with the two negroes and trying to make them understand something. On seeing the door open, he started to rise, but it was too late.

'Good evening, Monsieur Lardilier . . . I see that several of us have had the same idea . . .'

'But . . . I . . .'

'Come in, *messieurs* . . . You know Monsieur Lardilier, don't you? He's had a brilliant idea . . . The man is anxious to save his daughter, and you can understand that . . . He thought . . .'

The Captain had come in too. The *patron* wondered what was happening, and a couple of Arabs prudently made themselves scarce.

Suddenly the Little Doctor addressed the Bantu interpreter.

'Ask him where his master hid the paper . . .'

The man, taken aback, was at a loss for words, and "Victor Hugo" seemed ready to take flight.

'Search him, you fellows . . . Not his pockets, it's not worth while; they've already been done when you arrested him . . . Feel the lining of his jacket, the padding on the shoulders, the turn-ups of his trousers . . .'

He broke off and seized Lardilier by the arm.

'I was sure you'd give me an idea . . . *Supposing on board ship one has to conceal a document and* . . .'

He asked the detectives: 'Any luck?'

The jacket was lying on a chair, practically reduced to rags.

'Take off his trousers . . .'

Never mind about modesty! There were no ladies present and surprisingly enough, "Victor Hugo" was wearing underpants.

'Anything?'

'I think I can feel something thickish . . . Wait a minute . . . Yes, here's a paper . . .'

'Look out . . . One of you two watch the door . . . Give me that paper . . .'

For two pins he would have run off with it, he was so afraid of disappointment.

'Is there a telephone here? . . . No? . . . Then I'd better read this document out loud, so that if it were destroyed there would still be witnesses . . . You come here, *patron* . . .'

The ink was faint, the paper still wet after the previous night's soaking.

'*To whoever finds this letter . . .*

'It must be taken at all costs to the authorities, not here in Gabon but in France . . .

'This is the last wish of a dying man . . . In an hour or less I shall be dead . . . I am alone with four dull-witted natives in a hut in the depths of the forest, five hundred kilometres from any town . . .

'Nobody can save me . . . I have no medicines . . . So I'm done for . . .

'My name is Bontemps, Roger Bontemps, partner of Eric Lardilier. When he

came to France he made me put all my money into a business he was starting in Gabon . . .

'I feel the fatal spasms already . . . I must be quick and put down the essential points . . .

'We both made a great deal of money, he in Africa and I in France, where I was in charge of our registered offices . . . Why did I listen to him when he asked me to come out to inspect our warehouses? And particularly when he suggested this visit to the forest . . .

'It was to last forty days . . . This is the fifteenth. It was he who gave me the quinine tablets . . . The one I have just taken contained not quinine but strychnine . . . I opened the others. Six more of them contained poison . . .

'So I was doomed in any case . . . Because Lardilier wanted to remain sole proprietor of the business . . .

'I'm cold . . . I'm in a cold sweat . . . My last wish is that he should be sentenced and . . .'

'Captain, would you kindly send for a car? I don't trust this gentleman . . .'

'Some ice?'

'No thanks. No more whisky either . . . I must confess, Captain, that I never drink . . . except during the course of my investigations, because there's always some reason then for drinking something.

'I presume you don't require any explanations? . . . Our friend Popaul hadn't needed, this time, to cut down many mahogany or gaboon trees in order to make money. He had merely had to find this note, somewhere in a hut abandoned in the heart of the forest.

'He realized that he had just made his fortune and that this bit of paper was as valuable as those more elaborately embellished ones issued by the Bank of France . . .

'It was blackmail, to put it crudely . . .

'Dangerous blackmail, because a man who had already killed another in order to keep the whole pile for himself would not hesitate . . .

'As for the hiding-place, you practically found it yourself . . . The negro! . . . That was why he never let him out of his sight! And why, when he failed to see "Victor Hugo" in the bar, he suddenly rushed downstairs apprehensively.

'A bullet in the back . . .

'The poor Bantu never saw the murderer . . . He made his escape through the porthole, wild with terror.

'And Antoinette, suspecting her father . . .'

'Do you really believe she was in league with him?'

'I believe she didn't know what was really going on. But her father had urged her to become intimate with Cairol . . . it was one way of finding out . . .'

'I must confess that I believe she's honest . . .'

'So do I . . . That was why, noticing Popaul's excited state, she followed him . . . She must have seen her father. She couldn't have failed to see him . . . He'd put on gloves to fire the revolver . . . And then she automatically picked it up, before discovering the body.

'What did Lardilier risk by letting her be suspected? She would never have been found guilty on such circumstantial evidence . . . At worst the murder would be considered as a "crime of passion" and Popaul as a vile seducer . . .

'Meanwhile, Lardilier would manage to get hold of the famous letter . . .

'That was why I kept on telling him about the crocodile-skin wallet . . . And also, since I wasn't certain that he was the murderer, why I talked to the Press at some considerable length . . .

'The man who had killed Popaul to get hold of the document was bound either to return to the cabin or to go after the negro, so as to . . .'

'Have a cigar?'

'No, thanks! I've smoked so many cigars since this morning that I'm feeling queasy. As for your investigation . . .'

'You've carried it out so skilfully that . . .'

'I beg your pardon! The result I reached was just the reverse of the one you were hoping for: to placate Monsieur Lardilier, the Company's most important customer, and . . . I say! I ought to ring up Anna . . . I told her I'd be away two or three days . . . But Tin Lizzie will get me back there by tomorrow morning.'

'The Company has asked me to present you with . . .'

'What?'

'Why, there's been so much talk of crocodile-skin wallets . . . So that's what we chose . . .'

What the Captain of the *Martinique* did not add was that it contained some fine notes issued by the Bank of France, of the category that people like Popaul describe as *grands formats*.

The Trail of the Red-Haired Man

I. In Which the Accountant Georges Motte, Having Good Reason to Consider Himself a Lady-killer, Keeps an Unusual Appointment

The first time Anna got in touch with the Little Doctor he was at a farm where they were on the telephone and where he was attending a doddery old man.

'Hello, Monsieur? . . . Anna here . . . There's somebody in the waiting-room who's in a great hurry . . .'

'Is he injured?'

'Not so as you'd notice . . .'

'Is he sick?'

'Perhaps inside . . . In any case he won't keep still . . . He told me to get in touch with you at all costs by telephone, because every minute matters . . .'

'All right, I'll come.'

He did not hurry, for all that. He was used to patients who summon you urgently and sometimes get you up in the night because of a nose-bleed or a pimple on the backside.

An hour later, Anna called him again, this time at the home of a seedsman where there was a case of measles.

'He's driving me crazy with his restlessness . . . I think if you keep him waiting much longer he'll do something dreadful . . .'

'I'm coming . . .'

And he made his way back leisurely, with Tin Lizzie purring gently, reaching home a good hour later. Before he had even opened the door of his consulting-room a man appeared, wild-eyed, and the Little Doctor understood why Anna had been so scared.

He had never seen anyone in such a nervous state before, and the sight made him realise the meaning of the word terror. The man was literally terrified out of his wits. At the same time his nerves were so over-strained that he could no longer control his facial expressions, and his features twitched convulsively.

'Are you . . .' he burst out, surprised maybe to see so small and unimpressive a man.

'I'm Dr Dollent, yes . . .'

'You're really the one they call the Little Doctor? You carry out investigations?'

'That's to say . . .'

'Shut the door, doctor, I implore you. You're sure nobody can hear us? And do you think your servant is capable of holding her tongue, of forgetting that she's seen me, of forgetting me for ever? I've come from Paris. I've been travelling all morning. And I spent last night wandering through the streets . . . I don't remember having eaten . . . I don't know . . . It doesn't matter . . .'

Dollent took a flask of brandy from his medicine cupboard and poured out a glass of it for his strange visitor, hoping to calm him down a little.

'My adventure is beyond belief . . . I don't think anything like it can ever have happened to any man . . . Yesterday I was happy, I was a respectable person, well thought of by my employers, married, soon to become a father . . .'

'One moment. Don't you think you'd better tell me things in the right order?'

Even had he been calm he would have been noticeable, for one thing on account of his height, which was well above the average, but particularly on account of his flaming red hair and his freckled face. His eyes were blue as forgetmenots.

'In the right order, yes . . . I'll try . . . I'm sorry. You're sure no one is listening at the door?'

'Quite certain . . .'

Actually he was certain of the contrary, because Anna, having seen such a phenomenon, would surely be unable to restrain her curiosity.

'In the right order . . . My name . . . I'm Georges Motte, twenty-eight years old . . . I got married two years ago . . . I'm an accountant in an insurance firm in the Rue Pillet-Will, near the Grands Boulevards . . . Did I tell you I've had a house built at Saint-Mandé and that's where I live . . . On a mortgage, of course . . . I've fifteen years to pay . . . Where had I got to?'

His knees were patently trembling, his lips looked dry.

'Yesterday . . . Good heavens, when I think it was only yesterday. What time is it? Five o'clock? Who knows whether by now the concierge mayn't have discovered . . .'

'Discovered what?'

'The corpse . . . you don't understand? I'm so sorry . . . I wanted to tell you everything at once and I'm getting muddled . . . Yesterday, at just this time of day it must have been, for our office closes at five, I was on the Grands Boulevards . . . Before catching my train back I usually have a bite to eat in a self-service bar at the corner of the Rue Drouot. Do you know it? . . . I've a big appetite . . . Even when I was quite a youngster . . .

'I was there at five o'clock as usual . . . I was eating a pâté sandwich and looking round me without thinking of anything in particular. And suddenly I noticed that a woman was staring at me and smiling.

'Please don't take me for a womanizer. Up till now my wife has been all I wanted . . .

'But that woman! I immediately wondered what she was doing in such a humble bar . . . I suppose you sometimes go to the cinema? You've seen those great American film stars, vamps as they call them?

'Well, doctor, I had just encountered a vamp!'

Jean Dollent was anxiously wondering whether to burst into laughter or to go on listening seriously to the man.

'What did she do to you?' he asked non-committally.

'In less than an hour she made me forget who I was, what I was . . . I don't even know how we started talking to one another, but a few minutes later we were sitting together on the terrace of a big café . . . It was hot . . . I've never seen the boulevards looking so beautiful . . . I think I forgot to mention that she had a foreign accent. I couldn't say from what country . . . I'm no good at languages . . . She was well dressed, but not quite like a Parisienne . . .

'She was very beautiful, very mysterious . . . When she looked at me and those moist lips parted I felt I was capable of doing anything to . . .

'We took a taxi . . . She wanted to drive round the Bois de Boulogne with me . . . The sun was setting, very red . . . I felt her hand in mine, her body close to mine . . . I leaned over and tried to kiss her . . .

' "This evening," she whispered.

' "Shall I see you this evening?"

' "All night, if you're good . . ."

'Can you believe it, doctor? Do you think I'm capable of arousing such a sudden passion?

'Unfortunately *I* believed it!

' "I'm not as free as I'd like to be," she admitted. "Too many people take an interest in me . . . We shall have to be very careful . . .".

' "What am I to do?"

' "*At eight o'clock tonight, at eight o'clock exactly, go to no. 27b Rue Bergère . . . It's not far from the place where we met.*"

' "I know it . . ."

' "*I hope the concierge won't see you . . . But if she were to ask you where you're going, tell her: To see Monsieur Lavisse.*" '

Georges Motte was at last speaking less jerkily, and the Little Doctor was able to study him at leisure.

'She went on: "*Monseur Lavisse is one of the tenants of our house. As he has a good many visitors you won't be noticed . . . Go up to the sixth floor . . . This is the key of my flat; take it, go in and if I'm not there, wait for me . . ."'*

'And did you go?' asked the Little Doctor, knitting his brows. 'Didn't you think it very odd?'

'I assumed it was love at first sight . . . You may despise me and laugh at me, but that's the truth . . . I rang up my wife, or rather the dairy-woman next door, since we aren't on the telephone, to say I had extra work at the office and I shouldn't be back that night . . .

'Then I walked through the streets of Paris, looking at the time on every electric clock I saw . . . I was practically crazy . . . I thought myself the luckiest of men . . .

'At eight o'clock exactly I turned up at no. 27b Rue Bergère. The concierge was standing on the doorstep knitting, just like in a country town.

'"To see Monsieur Lavisse!" I called out as I went in.

'I noticed that she looked at me with curiosity, but I paid no attention to that . . . On the stairway I met two other tenants going out, a young couple on their way to the cinema, maybe . . . They stared at me too. With my red hair, I'm used to being stared at . . .

'I opened the door on the sixth floor . . . I saw nobody . . . I felt nervous about going in . . . I was less confident already . . . I don't know what I was frightened of, but the fact is that I *was* rather frightened.

'Next to the entrance hall there was a peculiar drawing-room, very orderly but full of strange furniture, Chinese I believe . . . And a great many curios . . . Then through an open door I could see another room full of more curios in glass cases . . .'

'You went all round the flat?' queried the Little Doctor, who no longer felt like laughing.

'I'm afraid I did . . . Little by little . . . As nobody came, I peeped in here and there . . . There were six rooms, plus a kitchen, and in every room there were curious pieces of furniture, not only Chinese but from othe countries, and antiques, carved crucifixes, lamps, armour . . . If it had been on a ground floor I'd have thought I was in an antique dealer's shop . . .

'I did something of which I'd never have thought myself capable, for I'm inclined to be timid . . . There was a bottle of spirits on a table, and a tray with glasses . . . I poured myself a drink. Then I waited. Nine o'clock . . . Ten o'clock . . .

'I began to wish I was back home in Saint-Mandé . . . I kept thinking of my wife, who's expecting a baby in three months . . . I said to myself: "If she's not here in ten minutes . . ."

'And then I allowed her another ten minutes . . . And so on. Then suddenly I heard a sigh.

'A real sigh, as though somebody was waking up . . . I looked all round: nobody . . . I was seized with panic . . . I nearly ran away.

And then I thought I heard a man speaking indistinctly . . .

'I'm not particularly brave . . . But the voice came from behind a door, a cupboard door . . . I opened it, and I'm still wondering how it was that I didn't scream . . .

'In the cupboard there was a man, an old man, covered with blood, his eyes open, his mouth half open too . . .

'When the door gave, he rolled out on to the carpet . . . I distinctly saw his hand open and his fingers contract . . . Then they became stiff . . . His eyes ceased to move . . . I realized that he had just died there in front of me, and that all the time I'd been waiting there unawares, he had been dying . . .'

'Have a drink!' the Little Doctor said calmly, filling the man's glass.

'What do you think about it? Isn't it incredible?'

'Incredible, indeed . . .'

'My one thought was to run away . . . I went out of the apartment, and I don't know if I left the key in the lock . . . Downstairs the door was shut . . . I called . . . I had to go on calling for a long time . . . Then a light went on . . . A wicket opened and a pair of round, sleepy eyes stared at me in amazement.

' "Oh, it's you," the concierge finally muttered. She pressed a button . . . there was a click and the door opened, and I found myself in the street . . . I'm sure a policeman turned to look at me . . . I walked and walked . . . And I kept thinking . . . I said to myself that the concierge had seen me go in at eight o'clock and come out at midnight, and that she would undoubtedly give a description of me . . .

'I was thinking very clearly . . . I didn't know one could be so clear-headed at such moments . . . I remembered the bottle and the glass on the table . . . Wouldn't my finger-prints be on them? and on the door knobs and all the objects I had touched?

'Who would believe me when I told my story? . . . Wouldn't everyone assume I was the murderer of the old gentleman whom I didn't even know?

'I was nearly out of my mind . . . Luckily there was no train back to Saint-Mandé, so I had time to think while I was walking through increasingly empty streets . . . I don't know how many kilometres I covered.

'There are strange chances in life . . . That very morning a colleague in the office had been talking about you . . . I don't know what case he was discussing, but I said, if you'll forgive me: "I don't much like detectives."

' "The Little Doctor isn't a detective," he retorted. "He's a puzzle-solver, which is something different."

'This came back to me during the night . . . I went to the Gare d'Orsay and inquired about trains to La Rochelle . . . I wrote a line to my wife, saying that my employers were sending me on a tour of inspection in the provinces, which has actually happened once . . . Then I wrote to the head clerk to say that owing to a death in the family . . .

'And so I'm here . . . I don't know if people noticed me during the journey . . . I haven't dared buy a newspaper . . . It's obvious that at any moment now the entire police force will be out looking for a man with red hair . . .

'And the red-haired man is me! My life is at stake, all because of an adventure which . . . which . . .'

'An adventure which, indeed!' the Little Doctor echoed comically, scratching his head. 'What do you propose to do?'

'To hide until you've found out the truth! I'm not rich, I've told you . . . But I've got a life insurance on which I can borrow up to ten thousand francs.'

'I'm not concerned about that, but about you.'

The red-haired man must have had a strange conception of the doctor's profession; at all events, he announced ingenuously:

'While you go and investigate, couldn't I stay here? I'll pay for my keep, of course . . .'

And the Little Doctor, after reflecting, suddenly declared:

'On one condition . . . that you'll stop in the room I shall show you and won't try to get out of it . . . Besides, you may as well know that Anna will have orders to lock you in . . .'

'Why?'

'Because! Take it or leave it . . . Have you a photo of yourself?'

'There's one on my identity card.'

'Give it me . . .'

'You're not going to give me over to the police, are you, doctor? Note that I came here of my own free will, that I told you everything frankly and that . . .'

'Come along . . .'

He went up to the first floor and ushered his visitor into a room which was occasionally used as a guest room.

'You'll be brought some supper . . . Above all, don't mistake Anna for a film vamp . . .'

Poor fellow! He did not know whether to be delighted or terrified, to show gratitude or resentment.

'As soon as I've anything to report I'll ring you up . . . Anna will bring the telephone into this room; the flex is long enough . . .'

No one was more surprised than Anna, when he came down and warned her:

'On no account let him go out . . . Even if he shouts . . . even if he threatens you . . .'

'He's not armed, I hope?'

And the Little Doctor could not have been as confident as all that, for he went back into the room and asked his new lodger to turn out his pockets.

'Thank you . . . I shall be in Paris by eleven o'clock, if I take the auto-rail as far as Poitiers and catch the Bordeaux express . . . Be patient . . .'

II. In Which the Little Doctor Astonishes Superintendent Lucas with his Black Magic

Superintendent Lucas of the Police Judiciaire, to whom Dollent had sent a wire, was waiting at the station, surprised by this unexpected visit from the Little Doctor, and even more by his excitable manner. Dollent began by demanding a meal at the station buffet, and displayed a remarkable appetite for so small a man.

'Tell me, Superintendent, if you find the door of an apartment open, have you the right to go in?'

'Not unless I have been sent for . . . Or else I should need a search warrant, and nobody can give me one at this time of night. Even if I had one in my hand I should legally have to wait until sunrise . . .'

'That's a bore,' the other grumbled with his mouth full. 'And if you knew for certain that a crime had been committed in that apartment?'

'At a pinch, I might assume responsibility for . . .'

'Let's go then!'

'Go where?'

'To 27b Rue Bergère. The home of a gentleman called Lavisse.'

'The collector?'

'I've no idea.'

'There is an Etienne Lavisse, a collector who is well known to connoisseurs the world over . . . He's a former expert on *objets d'art* who now lives alone surrounded by his collections . . . Rue Bergère, it's bound to be him, for I know he's never been willing to live more than five hundred metres from the Hôtel des Ventes, the auction rooms where he spends his days . . .'

Suddenly, belatedly, he realized the oddity of the situation.

'By the way, how does it happen that you've come all the way from Marsilly to tell me . . .'

'Let's go, anyhow! I'll explain later.'

The concierge took a long time opening the door to them, and an even longer time putting on a petticoat and a shawl to receive them.

'Monsieur Lavisse? No, I haven't seen him today . . . It's surprising, come to think of it, for he hasn't been down to take his meals, as he usually does, at the restaurant round the corner . . .'

'Will you come up with us, Madame?'

'Well, there's no lift and it's on the sixth floor . . .'

As Georges Motte had said, the key was still in the lock, and when they opened the door they saw that the lights were burning in several rooms – the lamps that the red-haired man had switched on the previous night and had not thought of turning off.

'It's funny . . . It looks as though . . .'

Then the concierge gave a scream. She had been the first to discover the lifeless body of her tenant lying on the drawing-room carpet.

Lucas could not help casting a curious glance at the Little Doctor. However could he have . . . ?

'He has been savagely stabbed with a knife,' the Superintendent declared after examining the body. 'Tell me, doctor, can you establish the approximate time of death?'

And Dollent, without bending down to look, said briefly: 'Last night about midnight.'

Then he turned to the concierge: 'You've something to say, haven't you? A man came last night to see Monsieur Lavisse at eight o'clock precisely . . .'

'That's right . . . And he was . . .'

'Red-headed!' the Little Doctor amused himself by completing her sentence.

'That's quite true . . . I told my husband I'd never seen such red hair . . . He stayed there late . . . When he came down . . .'

'At midnight . . .'

'Did Monsieur Lavisse often have visitors?'

'Very seldom! And never at night. He used to go to bed very early. During the day he sometimes came back with elderly gentlemen, often foreigners, who were interested in his collections . . .'

'Have any been lately?'

'Not for three or four days.'

'And yesterday, before the red-haired man, did nobody ask for Monsieur Lavisse? You didn't notice a man and a woman in the stairway? A very pretty, well-dressed woman, the sort of woman you see in films?'

The concierge shook her head.

'I'm very sorry, my dear Superintendent, but I'm bound by professional secrecy . . . Later on, when it's all over . . . What I can tell you is that it's an extremely tricky business and we'd better be prudent . . .'

'I think that when we've laid hands on this red-headed man . . .'

How could Lucas understand the subtle smile that played on the Little Doctor's lips?

Next day the murder of Etienne Lavisse came like a bombshell to the world of collectors and the Salle des Ventes, and by 10.0 a.m. the police were keeping order ouside the house in the Rue Bergère.

Two experts who were also friends of the deceased spent hours going through the apartment, examining every object, and thus the Little Doctor, who was no connoisseur, learned that Lavisse had had no special predilection except for quality. He was as ready to buy a Flemish painting as cloisonné enamel or Japanese ivories.

By four in the afternoon the experts were at last able to declare:

'The ten finest pieces are missing, the easiest to transport which are also those that have the greatest commercial value. At today's prices the objects assumed to have been stolen are worth four or five million francs . . .'

'Was Monsieur Lavisse very rich?' the Little Doctor asked in some surprise.

'He owned nothing but his collection. Apart from that, he lived economically, almost like a poor man, taking his meals at a *prix-fixe* restaurant. You must realise, moreover, that, apart from what has been taken away, all that you see here represents much careful research and great taste, but relatively little money. Scarcely half a million altogether . . .'

'Had Monsieur Lavisse any relatives?'

'He was an elderly bachelor . . . But he had a sister who lives in the Vendée . . .'

Lucas noted her name and address, so as to send her the news, although she must presumably have learnt it already through the papers and the radio, which had reported the case at great length.

From a bistrot, Dollent rang up Marsilly and spoke to Anna, who displayed unprecedented ferocity.

'Aren't you ashamed of treating me like this?' she cried. 'Me who've never done you any harm, who've looked after you like a baby! . . . Leaving me alone in the house with a murderer . . . Yes, I know what I'm talking about . . . If you think I haven't read the papers and recognized the red-haired man . . . There can't be many of that colour . . . And he's not going to get any fancy dishes from me . . . He'll get what's coming to him, that's for certain . . .'

'Is he calm, Anna?'

'I've no idea.'

'What does he say?'

'He doesn't say anything.'

'Listen to me, Anna . . .'

'I don't want to listen to anything, and when you come back I shall hand in my notice . . . That's all you deserve . . . As for knowing what he's doing, that's out of the question, seeing as how I only open the door wide enough to put his plate on the floor.'

'You're sure he's still there?'

'Yes, worse luck! He's been making enough noise walking up and down ever since this morning . . .'

All the papers headlined in heavy type:

The Trail of the Red-haired Man.

And the police would undoubtedly receive masses of anonymous letters about all the red-headed men in Paris and the surrounding region.

'Is that you, Lucas?'

'Yes . . . Dollent? . . . No, absolutely nothing new . . . And besides, considering the way you're behaving with me, I wonder if I hadn't better drop you completely!'

'And what if I were to give you the description of a woman who's involved in the case? Listen . . . A sort of film vamp . . . It's not a joke . . . A sort of film vamp . . . A strong foreign accent . . . Dresses very well, with a touch of eccentricity . . . The kind of woman that every man turns to look at in the street . . . I'd like to know if she hasn't been observed recently in the neighbourhood of the Salle des Ventes and the Rue Bergère?'

'All right!'

'Thank you; goodbye . . .'

A taxi took him out to Saint-Mandé, where he soon located Georges Motte's trim though undistinguished little house. He rang the doorbell. A young woman, unmistakably pregnant, opened the door, and it was clear that she had not connected her husband with the notorious red-haired man.

'I wanted to speak to Georges Motte . . . He's an old Army pal . . .'

'Unfortunately my husband is away for a few days. The Company have sent him into the provinces to do some checking-up.'

'You don't know where he is?'

'Not exactly . . . On these occasions he visits a number of towns, sometimes all in one day . . . But please come in . . .'

It was neat and pretty and respectable, with furniture which must have been bought on the hire-purchase system.

'I'll come back in a few days.'

Whew! Lassitude was setting in . . . For hours and hours he had been as tense as a bow-string. He had not slept . . .

And once back on the Grands Boulevards, he felt unsteady, his head empty and his mouth dry. He lacked the energy to go and dine, and he retired to sleep in the first hotel he came to, after eating a sandwich in the self-service bar at the corner of the Rue Drouot.

Meanwhile the whole of the French police force was out hunting for the red-headed man!

III. *In Which Anna Keeps Cool, and the Little Doctor Picks Up the Trail of an Interesting Lady called Betty*

'It would be worth living in Paris for this alone,' the Little Doctor reflected, 'to see the sun rise over the great avenues!'

But how many Parisians watch the sun rise? For the first time in his life the Little Doctor had the pleasure of waking up in the heart of the city, in a hotel picked at random, and the sight before him, in the light of dawn, made him as merry as a lark; so much so that while he shaved he sang like a lark.

He promptly learned that not everyone is equally enraptured by the early morning light, for his neighbours on both sides began knocking on the walls simultaneously.

The more fools they; he would stop singing. He could think just as well without singing. For Jean Dollent was thinking. He gazed out at the broad, almost empty roadway, where the earliest buses were passing and taxis were driving up in a long string to take their places in the cab rank. A municipal watering cart seemed to be tracing elaborate patterns on the asphalt. And two hundred metres away women were swilling the floor of the self-service bar where poor Georges Motte . . .

It wasn't hard to imagine the scene. A few hours hence, when offices and workshops closed for lunch, midinettes and salesgirls, typists and clerks would descend on the self-service bar like a flock of hungry sparrows, with the same shrill chatter.

But soon, when the first pangs of hunger were appeased, wouldn't each of them look up from his plate and observe the others' faces, greeting with a smile some other's smiling lips, tousled hair, laughing eyes?

'Less poetry and more analysis,' the Little Doctor scolded himself; he had finished shaving and was sitting on the window ledge. It was unlikely that a woman looking like an American film vamp would have gone unnoticed. If she had entered that bar, she must have been looking for something or somebody. Why had she chosen Georges Motte?

There was a mischievous twinkle in the Little Doctor's eyes, for he sensed that it would not be long before he had an answer to these questions.

'Let's see now . . *If Georges Motte is to be believed*, Etienne Lavisse had been stabbed and shut up in the cupboard before eight o'clock in the evening. Now it's more than likely that the crime was not a premeditated one. In such cases the murderer seldom uses a knife, particularly a sort of dagger picked up on the spot and belonging to the collector himself. The number of blows, moreover, inclines one to believe that the man who struck them acted under the influence of surprise and fear . . .

'He did not take the trouble to make sure that Etienne Lavisse was really dead . . .

'So that for hours on end that cupboard was the scene of a silent death-agony . . .

'Before eight o'clock . . .

'Now it was at five o'clock that the "vamp" made the acquaintance of the red-headed man, took him to the Bois de Boulogne, excited him and made an appointment to meet him at eight o'clock in the old collector's apartment.

'Had the poor man already been attacked by five o'clock?

'Medically, it's quite possible . . .'

This argument and the consequences that could be drawn from it were only valid, obviously, if Motte had been speaking the truth.

At that precise moment there came a knock at the door. A chambermaid told him: 'You're wanted on the telephone . . . The phone is at the end of the passage, near the staircase . . .'

'Is that you, Monsieur?'

Anna, when she wanted to, was capable of putting on an angelic voice which exasperated the Little Doctor, because he knew it always meant she was going to say something tiresome.

'Yes, it's me . . . Nothing's happened, I hope?'

'No, Monsieur . . . I just wanted to let you know he's gone . . .'

'What's that? How?'

'I don't know . . . I slept in my room as usual, and I had put your revolver on my bedside table. This morning I went to take him his breakfast . . . I opened the door a crack . . . I laid the tray on the floor . . . Then, as I heard nothing . . . He wasn't there! . . . I'd just as soon, you know!'

The Little Doctor had turned pale, and he hung up without thinking of replying to whatever Anna was asking him. A minute later he had an even greater fright. He had moved two steps away when the telephone bell rang again. He lifted the receiver automatically.

'Hello . . .'

'Hôtel des Italiens? Can I speak to Dr Dollent?'

'Dollent speaking . . .'

'Hello! Lucas here . . . I thought you were probably not far from the phone, for I heard that someone was on the line from Marsilly . . .

Were you telephoning your home? . . . No bad news, I hope?'

Could he possibly have . . . It sometimes happens that a crossed line enables one to overhear a conversation . . .

'No bad news, no . . .'

'Well, I'm very glad. For my part, I've got some information for you . . . If you like I'll give it you over the phone to save time, for I've a busy day ahead of me . . .

'Firstly, it's been established that Etienne Lavisse left the auction room about four o'clock that day . . . Hello! Are you listening? I thought that would interest you, because usually he didn't go home until much later. When one of the auctioneers commented on it, he admitted that he wasn't feeling very well and was going home to bed. He wasn't ill, but he was liable to stomach trouble and it had been a very hot day . . .'

'Thank you,' said the Little Doctor without enthusiasm.

'Another piece of news, probably more important. Will you note a name? Jean-Claude Marmont . . . Got it? . . . He's the victim's nephew, the only son of the sister who lives in the Vendée and who has come to Paris this morning . . . Jean-Claude Marmont is twenty-four, and he's vaguely connected with film-making . . . Hello? Are you listening? He was second assistant to a producer . . . He frequents the Champs-Elysées bars and, so I gather, gaming houses . . .'

'Well off?'

'His mother's quite well off . . . A big country house near Luçon . . . She used to send him subsidies, but not proportionate to our young man's needs . . .'

'His uncle?'

'For over a year had refused to see him . . . He'd been fleeced too often.'

'Is that all?'

'Don't you think that's enough? I've given you two important pieces of information for breakfast, and you grumble . . . If you like I can supply you with the list of all the red-headed men we hear of . . . Eighteen so far . . . And I'm in duty bound to send policemen in all eighteen directions . . .'

'Thank you . . .'

'I say, doctor, it strikes me . . .'

'What?'

'Aren't you well? . . . Are you suffering from the heat too?'

'You haven't given me the address of Jean-Claude Marmont? . . . Hôtel de Berry, Rue de Berry . . .'

He went there, but with an utter lack of zest. The police were bound to have gone there first and extracted from the staff all that there was to extract. He went in, however, and approached the head porter.

'I'm sorry to bother you, but I should be grateful if you could give me a piece of information.' (Here a hundred-franc note, folded up small, passed from Dollent's hand to the porter's.) 'I'd like to know whether Jean-Claude Marmont, who lives in this hotel, has had a visit recently from a red-haired man . . .'

The porter stared with some surprise at the note in his hand and then at his questioner.

'It's funny,' he said.

'What's funny?'

'You don't belong to the police, because . . .' And he showed the note, implying that detectives of the Police Judiciaire are not in the habit of paying cash for information received.

'As it happens, a sergeant I know came here an hour ago and asked me exactly the same question.'

'What did you answer?'

'I told him no!'

'And is that true?'

'It's absolutely true . . .'

'Did he ask you nothing else?'

'No . . . He seemed to be in a hurry . . .'

'And suppose I were to ask you a second question . . .' (which was accompanied by a second hundred-franc note). 'Suppose I were to ask you what sort of women used to visit Jean-Claude Marmont? For I presume a young fellow of his age . . .'

'I couldn't tell you very much. Except that the latest was called Betty, Miss Betty . . .'

'Did she often come?'

'She only came twice, but she used to telephone . . . That's how I know her name.'

'A pretty girl, with a foreign accent, looking like a film star?'

'That's just what I'd have said if you'd asked me to describe her . . . She's gone off on a journey . . .'

'How do you know?'

'Because the day before yesterday Monsieur Marmont, who sometimes borrows a little money from me, came running downstairs about six o'clock in the evening . . . He'd just had a telephone call.

' "Albert," he said to me, "lend me a few notes, will you, and make it snappy? I have to take my girl-friend to catch a train . . ." '

'And you don't know which station he went to?'

'I don't know . . . He came back about midnight . . . Since then, he's hardly been out . . . I think this morning he had a phone call from his mother.'

The Little Doctor, looking anxious and dissatisfied, had already reached the corner of the Rue de Berry and the Champs-Elysées, when he turned about and once more pushed the revolving door of the Hôtel de Berry.

'Tell me, Albert . . . Have you ever seen this Betty with another man?'

'No, sir . . . I've only seen her twice, and both times it was with Monsieur Marmont.'

'You've never heard mention of a friend or a . . .'

'Perhaps you're thinking of her brother? He rang me up once to say "This is Miss Betty's brother. Will you tell Monsieur Marmont, when he comes in, to meet us in the usual place?" '

Two pages came in carrying luggage. A lady dressed all in black was entering through the revolving door; she was clearly up from the country. Her eyes were red and she held a handkerchief in her hand.

'My son's room, please . . . Jean-Claude Marmont . . .'

A young man emerged from the lift. He had probably been watching from the window. He, too, looked sad, even downcast. His eyes were even redder than his mother's. He embraced her at some length, saying in a low tone:

'Poor mother . . . Who would have thought . . . Come with me . . .'

The porter and the Little Doctor exchanged glances. Then Jean Dollent heaved a sigh, shrugged his shoulders as though getting rid of a burden, and went out.

A few minutes later he might have been seen at a table at the *Select*, where, although it was still early in the day, he had ordered a brandy-and-water.

'Will you bring me the directory, too?'

A second brandy-and-water, then a third.

'Let's see . . . Antiques and Curios . . .Samuel . . . Jérôme Lévy . . . Guillaume Benoit . . .'

He selected the address that was nearest. It was not far from the Elysée, a private house of several storeys full of antique furniture, wood panelling, and sculptures that drew customers from all over the world.

'Monsieur Guillaume Benoit? . . . No, I'm very sorry, I've not come to buy anything . . . I'd simply like to ask you for some information. Superintendent Lucas told me you were kindness itself . . .' That was untrue, but it couldn't be helped!

'Are you also concerned with the Lavisse case?'

'Why do you say *also*?'

'Because an inspector came this morning . . .'

'What did he ask you?'

'Whether the objects stolen from my unfortunate colleague . . . for we all considered him as a colleague, and we frequently had occasion to seek his advice . . . Whether the objects stolen would be easy to sell.'

'And what did you reply?'

'That it would be practically impossible to get rid of them in Europe, where these pieces are too well known and where immediate warnings were issued to all dealers and connoisseurs . . .'

'Why do you specify *in Europe*?'

'Because in America, where the market is much wider than here and where money changes hands more readily, it's easier to find a collector who's not too particular about the provenance of a rare piece . . .'

'May I now ask you a second question? . . . You would naturally be familiar with Monsieur Lavisse's apartment?'

'I have often been there to visit my old friend.'

'Would someone who was not a member of your profession, an average amateur, so to speak, have been capable, in a very short time, of picking out amongst all the things that were there the few most valuable pieces?'

The antique dealer's brow darkened.

'No, I don't think so, and it's odd that you should have asked me that question . . . We were discussing it yesterday at the Salle des Ventes . . . For instance there was an engraved emerald which is a unique piece worth at least four hundred thousand francs, but which a layman would have taken for a stone of no value . . . Similarly there was a fifteenth-century reliquary which few thieves would have chosen in preference to the gold snuff-boxes of the Napoleonic period which stood in the same case . . . Might I ask you on whose behalf you are inquiring? No doubt on that of the insurance company? . . . And yet I believe our poor friend's latest acquisitions were not insured . . .'

The Little Doctor left without saying either yes or no, and a little later he tackled the most exhausting and discouraging task of his whole day.

IV. In Which a Six-storey House is Gone Through Floor by Floor, One Household After Another, One Tenant After Another, and In Which the Red-headed Man Comes into the Picture Again

Lucas, even graver and more worried than the Little Doctor, had been hunting for the latter since ten that morning, and it was already one in the afternoon. He had made telephone calls all over the place, and as a last resort, even before having his lunch, he had returned to the Rue Bergère and asked the concierge:

'You haven't seen the person who was with me yesterday?'

'A dark, excitable little gentleman? He's been in the house over an hour . . . He must have reached the third . . .'

'The third what?'

'Third floor . . . I must say he's got patience and he's not afraid of bothering people. He knocks at everyone's door . . . He questions everyone, even six-year-old children and old folks that can't leave their armchairs . . .'

It was quite true. But even here the Little Doctor had not been first in the field. When he called on the ladies' tailor on the first floor, on the left (the place was in semi-darkness and there was a sickly smell of wool) he had been told:

'Your colleague has already been here this morning . . .'

What was the point of saying that he didn't belong to the police?

'I suppose you want to know if we met the man in the photograph on the stairs?'

'Oh, I see . . . My colleague showed you a photograph . . . It was of a red-haired man, wasn't it?'

'No . . . A rather thin young fellow with long hair . . .'

Jean-Claude Marmont! So the police were neglecting no trail, since a detective had already ascertained that Jean-Claude Marmont, whose photograph he had managed to procure, had not been in the house on the day of the crime!

'Since my colleague visited you, we have received further information . . . What I'd like to know is whether between four and five o'clock you met any unknown person in the stairway of the building . . .'

It was tedious, it was discouraging! Some people were suspicious and reluctant to speak; you had to drag the words out of them one by one. Others, on the contrary, were eager to tell you all about their affairs and particularly those of their neighbours!

When you undertake an investigation of this sort, you come to realise what a wide variety of human lives are contained in a Parisian apartment block. The tailor . . . The dentist on the first floor right . . . The retired officer on the second floor, and his daughter with her husband from the Ecole Polytechnique . . . The lady living alone, who . . . whom . . .

His prescription-pad in hand, Jean Dollent took the occasional note, asked questions, gave thanks, apologized, took his leave and knocked at the neighbouring door.

He was just emerging from the last apartment but one, the fourth floor left (furs imported direct from Russia, wholesale and retail), when he found himself face to face with Lucas.

For some reason, a sort of clash could be felt between the two men;

all their friendliness seemed to have disappeared. They looked each other up and down. The Superintendent's normally ingenuous gaze had hardened and his bearing stiffened, while the Little Doctor gave a cough to keep himself in countenance and hung his head.

'I've been looking for you for the past two hours, Monsieur Dollent. You won't be surprised, I'm sure, if I say that I must ask you for certain explanations?'

'All right!' the Little Doctor sighed, closing his prescription pad. 'I suppose we can talk more comfortably in your office?'

Out in the street, he ventured: 'Couldn't we have a drink? . . . It was so stuffy in that house . . .'

He had two. Lucas, watching him, waited for the right moment to say:

'This morning on the telephone I mentioned eighteen red-headed men. Now I have the pleasure of informing you that we have a nineteenth . . . And he's the one I have arrested. Don't you want to know why?'

'I don't care.'

'I'm going to tell you, none the less . . . I had him arrested because it was the *gendarmerie* of Nieul, three kilometres from Marsilly, who discovered him this morning, hiding in a little wood . . . The La Richardière wood, you must know it, being from that part of the world . . . The coincidence struck me as odd, to say the least . . . Don't you think you owe me an explanation and . . .'

'Maybe . . . But not until we've done some work,' sighed the Little Doctor.

They were in a taxi, and the driver had been directed to go to the Quai des Orfèvres. Lucas was complaining with bitter resentment.

'I'm most disappointed, doctor . . . And the word isn't nearly strong enough for what I feel . . . Like some of my colleagues, I admired your unconventional methods . . . In an earlier case I had practically given you a free hand . . . During this one, I repressed my curiosity and trusted you, though it meant assuming grave responsibilities myself. I went even further; only this morning I gave you over the telephone all the information I possessed . . .

'And yet, I must admit, I felt uneasy . . . When I called you, you happened to be having a conversation with Marsilly . . . I overheard nothing, but I was struck by the fact . . . When, at about ten o'clock, the *gendarmerie* of La Rochelle informed us that a red-headed man . . .'

'I know . . . I know . . .'

'And is that all you have to say?'

'Who's paying for the taxi?' asked the Little Doctor, as they alighted in front of the main gate of Police Headquarters. 'Wait a minute . . . I've got change . . .'

And they went in together under the archway.

V. In Which the Little Doctor and Superintendent Lucas Collaborate Uneasily, while the Red-headed Man, in Jail at La Rochelle, Writes to Beg his Wife's Forgiveness

In Lucas's office the windows were wide open, overlooking the Seine, and the continuous sunshine made one's head reel.

'It's a great pity, Superintendent, that you should have come an hour too early, for in another hour I think I'd have been able to present you with a complete report. Now, before answering, I shall have to ask you to be patient . . . And if you want to arrest the murderer of Monsieur Lavisse, you will even have to allow me to carry on the investigation from this office . . .'

As Lucas gave a start of surprise at such audacity, the Little Doctor, sitting down in a crimson plush armchair and lighting a cigarette, began gravely.

'For the time being I'll pass over the rather unkind insinuations you've just made, and I don't think I shall bear you a grudge on that account. I must confess that I feel very hesitant, being as it were faced with a matter of conscience . . .

'It's your advice that I'm asking for.

'Did it ever happen to you, Superintendent, in the course of an investigation, to feel convinced that you were right, that you were on the right tack, that you were moving towards the truth? . . . Note that I'm speaking of a moral, not a material, certainty . . .

'I'll put it differently. Has it ever happened to you, while everyone else was hurrying along a particular trail, to hang back, feeling that truth lay elsewhere, and to persist in that attitude?

'And in that case, have you ventured to assume responsibility when everyone was against you?'

Poor Lucas was wondering what his interrogator was getting at, and hesitated to commit himself.

'Has it happened to you, in a word, when there was, say, a thirty per cent chance of being wrong, to carry on regardless?'

'Frequently . . . If one didn't gamble on a seventy per cent chance . . .'

'That's what I wanted you to say . . . And yet you're an official! You're running a big risk!'

'We run the risk of being censured, and sometimes more than that . . .'

'In that case, Superintendent, will you be kind enough to ring up the Compagnie Transatlantique?'

The Little Doctor was not bluffing; this was no joke. There were even great drops of sweat on his forehead.

'Hello . . . Yes . . . Police Judiciaire here . . .'

And, to Dollent: 'What shall I ask them?'

'Whether a boat sailed for America the day before yesterday, and at what time . . . And also at what time the boat train left the Gare Saint-Lazare . . .'

'Hello . . . Will you kindly tell me . . .'

'I've got your information. The *Normandie* sailed from Le Havre two nights ago on the night tide, that's to say at 1.0 a.m. The boat train taking the passengers to Le Havre left the Gare Saint-Lazare at half-past ten . . .'

'When does the *Normandie* reach New York?'

'In two days' time . . .'

'Can you get in touch with the ship in the meantime?'

'Yes, by telephone . . . The *Normandie* and its passengers can be contacted by day and by night by wireless. There's even a telephone at the head of every bed, just as in luxury hotels . . .'

'And suppose I'm wrong?' the Little Doctor queried instinctively, speaking to himself rather than to the Superintendent.

Lucas was by now scrutinizing him with less hostility, but more uneasily. Wasn't this amateur going to involve him in some disastrous step?

Suddenly the Little Doctor raised his head.

'Would you be kind enough to make one more call? This time to La Rochelle . . . To the jail . . .'

'But . . .'

'Ask them what Georges Motte, who was arrested this morning, is doing . . . If he's written a letter, it mustn't be sent . . .'

This was one of the Little Doctor's happiest achievements, particularly because it was of a purely psychological order. Since poor Motte had been arrested . . .

'Well?'

'The warder tells me he's writing a long letter to his wife.'

'You gave instructions that it should not be posted?'

'*Until further orders, yes!*'

And the Little Doctor, casually taking his prescription-pad from his pocket, laid out some sheets of paper on the table.

'I presume the statements made by people who mistook me for a policeman are valueless? So we shall have to . . .'

He looked up as an idea struck him.

'I've got it, Superintendent . . . If the *Normandie* has wireless telephony it must also have the radio . . . There'll undoubtedly be a broadcast announcement of our red-headed man's arrest . . .'

'Most likely, if it hasn't already been done . . .'

'In that case I must ask you . . . I must beg you to take a chance . . . Call the *Normandie* immediately . . . I'm sure that among the first-class passengers there are a young woman and her brother . . .'

'What are their names?'

'The woman's first name is Betty . . . She looks like a sort of film vamp . . . Her brother, I'm pretty sure, is not her brother, but that's not important . . .'

'Is that all you can give me by the way of description?'

'That's all, except that the brother is very dark and has a small dark moustache . . .'

Lucas lifted the receiver without much enthusiasm.

'Thank you, Superintendent . . . I only hope now that I haven't got you into any sort of trouble . . . If you could send for some sandwiches we'd be able to talk quietly and I could explain to you . . . You see, I've such faith in my line of argument, it's based on such solid foundations that . . .'

To the Little Doctor's amazement they got through to the *Normandie* before even finishing their sandwiches. In other words, it took less time to make contact with a ship at sea than with Marsilly!

'The purser has promised to take the necessary steps . . . He'll ring us back within the next hour . . .'

'Thank you . . . What struck me, you see, was that the man was red-haired . . . I don't know if you remember a case that made a great sensation two years ago . . . I think it was you yourself who were in charge of it . . . A body had been thrown out on to the roadside from an aubergine-coloured car . . . During the next fortnight some twenty or thirty aubergine-coloured cars were reported, and the police had no end of trouble . . .'

'As I well know!'

'If Georges Motte hadn't been red-headed I'd not have believed a word of his story, and I'd have brought him along to you . . . For if he had committed a crime he might quite well have come to see me so as to clear himself in advance . . . Knowing that his prints were in the apartment, he would thus get credit for frankness by telling me that story . . .

'But he's red-haired, quite exceptionally red-haired . . . Moreover it is proved that he remained for several hours in the apartment with a dying man behind a cupboard door . . . And that he deliberately left his finger-prints all over the place!

'Note that this might have been a piece of supreme cleverness . . .

'However . . . In the first place there is the fact that the woman he describes really exists, and that she was quite recently the mistress of Lavisse's nephew, Jean-Claude Marmont . . .

'There's the fact that it was five o'clock when this woman . . .

'You'll understand it all, Superintendent . . . I don't know who this Betty is . . . I don't know who her brother, or her so-called brother, is . . . But I've every reason to think they are adventurers on a big scale . . .

'They frequent places of entertainment . . . They make the acquaintance of Jean-Claude, who claims to be a film producer . . .

'Jean-Claude, who is short of money, refers with some bitterness to his eccentric uncle, who accumulates useless wealth and who refuses to see his nephew . . .

'They question him; they get all the necessary information out of him. Whether he's in league with them or not, I cannot say . . .

'The fact remains that they merely plan a robbery . . .

'And here you have the evidence of two children, a little girl of nine and a boy of eight . . . They live in the house in the Rue Bergère; they often play on the staircase . . .

'On the day of the crime, shortly after four o'clock, they saw a dark-haired gentleman go up to Monsieur Lavisse's apartment and let himself in with a key . . .

'Now these children had already seen the same man a few days earlier, but he had not gone in . . . He had merely rung at the door, when nobody was at home . . .

'*On this occasion, he had come to take an impression of the lock!*'

'Hello! . . . A call for you from the *Normandie* . . .'

The Little Doctor showed enough strength of mind to remain in his armchair, watching the Superintendent, who was saying:

'Yes . . . What? Siryex? . . . And you're sure he's very dark, with a small dark moustache? . . . His sister? . . . Yes . . . Well, give the ship's detectives the order to search their luggage . . . I'll confirm it by telegram presently . . . Thanks . . . Agreed . . . Goodbye . . .'

The Little Doctor did not wait for an explanation, but went on with his account:

'Our dark man, Betty's brother or pseudo-brother, undertakes the job . . . He has his information. He knows that Lavisse never comes home before six o'clock and that a boat is leaving for the States that very night . . . Unfortunately for him and for the collector, the latter is suffering from stomach trouble and comes home earlier than usual. He finds an intruder in his home . . . The thief strikes him, shoves the body into a cupboard and joins Betty in a nearby café . . .

'They've got the swag, and *it's not five o'clock yet.* But no doubt the body will soon be discovered . . . the alarm will be given, all exit routes barred . . . ports, roads, boats, frontier-posts . . .

'It's not five o'clock yet, and the Grands Boulevards are at their busiest.

' "We must lay a false trail!" Betty declares. "*A false trail that will keep the police busy until we've landed in New York . . .*"

'Had she read the story of the aubergine-coloured car? . . . The real murderer is dark . . . Somebody more noticeable is needed . . . a man whose trail is easy to follow . . . a man who won't be able to clear himself of suspicion for a long while . . .

'She goes into a self-service bar, by herself . . . She notices a man *with flaming red hair* . . . He'll do to keep the police busy while the couple quietly land at New York with their treasure . . . He's a simple soul, and so much the better . . . A drive round the Bois, and he's infatuated . . .

'So he'll go to the appointed place at the very time when, on a summer evening, *the concierge will be sitting outside her door.* He'll wait . . . He'll leave his finger-prints everywhere . . . He won't leave until late at night, when the front door is closed, so that the concierge will see him once again . . .

'In the meantime the guilty pair . . . The boat train . . . The *Normandie* . . .'

'But Jean-Claude Marmont?'

'An accomplice, I fancy . . . Not of the murder, but of the robbery, in so far as he suggested the job . . . The proof is that Betty rings him up and he takes her to the station with her supposed brother . . . I'm prepared to bet that at this point the couple don't confess that they have murdered his uncle . . . They promise him his share . . . They probably give him an advance so as to compromise him and force him to keep quiet . . .

'It's only on the following day, when he reads the paper, that he learns that he's been a party to a murder, and that is why, just now, he was even more distressed than his mother.'

There was a pause. The Little Doctor seemed weary; he kept his eyes fixed on the telephone, which remained obstinately silent.

'It's only deduction, isn't it?' he murmured with a forced smile, as though in self-excuse. 'Note that if I'm right, that woman's a genius . . . For while you were all following the trail of the red-haired man . . .'

The Superintendent was annoyed, but did not betray it.

'Are you sure the ship's detectives? . . .'

'They're our own men, and chosen among the best . . . You told me just now that the man Motte is married and that his wife is expecting?'

Feeling a pang of remorse, he rang up the news agency.

'About the bulletin I gave you recently . . . It's not gone out yet? In that case suppress it . . . Announce instead that a couple of sensational arrests are imminent . . .'

There was nothing to do now but wait, in front of a silent telephone. And that was the most tedious and intolerable part of it, particularly for the Little Doctor who, by the end, was dying of thirst and would have welcomed any sort of drink to calm his nerves.

At last, at 5.0 p.m., the telephone rang.

'Yes . . . Oh . . . What did you say? . . . Yes, send them by telephoto . . . Of course . . . They're still protesting? . . . Oh, yes . . . The confirmatory wire . . . I'll see to it . . . Thanks!'

It was disturbing to think that the voice came from a ship on the high seas and that the background noise was not that of the waves but of the band playing for a *thé dansant* on board the *Normandie*!

'Well, Superintendent?'

Lucas looked up and assumed a severe expression.

'Well, doctor . . . You have . . .'

A silence which seemed endless . . .

'You have gambled on a seventy per cent chance and you've won . . .'

'What?'

'The stolen objects, which being small in size take up very little room, were discovered in a false-bottomed trunk . . . in the cabin of Alfred Siryex, a Turkish national, who was travelling with his sister Betty Siryex . . . In a few minutes we shall receive their finger-prints by telephotograph and we shall know . . .'

'I told the Chief that you were the one . . . He wants to see you . . . This is the first time in eight years that we've managed to catch Fred Stern, red-handed. He's the biggest American specialist in that field . . . His sister, who's not his sister but his mistress, has been protesting in vain, but . . .'

The Little Doctor was smiling passively, nodding his head as he listened to the congratulations of the Director of the Police Judiciaire. Lucas now watched him anxiously.

'Say, doctor . . .'

The Little Doctor went on smiling, with such an artificial smile that . . .

'Doctor!'

'Let me sleep,' sighed Dollent. 'I was so afraid . . . I was so unsure that . . . When you went up to the Finger-prints Department and the . . .'

His speech was so blurred that his words were barely distinguishable.

'. . . the Records Department I went down to . . . to the corner bistrot and . . . I can't remember . . . six, seven . . . I think I had seven brandies and water . . .'

He was too drunk for anything further to be comprehensible.

'Seventy degrees . . . No! Seventy per cent chance . . . Oh, yes . . . The degrees were . . .'

He slept for two hours in the crimson armchair in Lucas's office and woke up somewhat ashamed of himself.

'Do you know that you've just brought off the most successful investigation in your whole career?' they asked him when he awoke.

'Have I?'

And then, promptly: 'Where's my redhead? . . . I hope he hasn't told his wife anything? . . . The only time the poor fellow has ever . . . And she's expecting a baby! . . . Fancy, he offered me the ten thousand francs of his life-insurance . . . By the way, Superintendent . . . I'm thirsty . . . I don't know what's happening, but I've such an almighty thirst . . . Shall we go and have a beer?'

The Disappearance of the Admiral

I. In Which we Immediately Realize that the Admiral is not a Real Admiral, and Learn that a Man can Disappear in Broad Daylight, in the Middle of a Street, Without Leaving a Trace

Facts are facts, and all the arguments on earth can never alter them. However much the people of the little town went on repeating that the Admiral's disappearance was impossible, it was none the less true that the Admiral had disappeared, from the middle of the street, in broad daylight, you might say in full view of everybody. And the Admiral was not one of those skinny fellows capable of swarming up a drainpipe or slipping down a grating; he was a fine figure of a man, weighing some ninety kilos, with a pronounced paunch.

It would be unwise to name the town, on account of local susceptibilities, but we can mention that it is one of those sunny little towns in Provence somewhere within the quadrilateral Avignon, Aix, Marseille and Nîmes.

One of those towns where everyone knows everyone else and when some man ventures along the scorching pavement, with his panama on his head, you can hear the whispers behind shuttered windows:

'Hullo! there's Monsieur Taboulet going to meet his wife at the station. Lucky he's got a high-crowned hat, for goodness' sake, to hide what's growing on his forehead . . .'

White houses. Green shutters. An avenue, the Mall, shaded by pale plane-trees. Bead curtains in front of the doors to keep out flies.

The thing happened on Wednesday June 25th, in the full heat of midsummer, when the mistral had not blown for a month. Most men were now wearing their linen or alpaca suits, and the tax-collector and a few others were even sporting tropical helmets.

Just at five o'clock in the afternoon, as on every other day, the Admiral came out of the restaurant *À la Meilleure Brandade*, situated at the corner of the Route Nationale and the Rue Jules-Ferry.

Now the Route Nationale does not pass directly through the town centre, but somewhat higher up. The Rue Jules-Ferry runs downhill to the avenue, where the Post Office and the Bank are situated.

The Admiral, at sixty-eight, was still in his prime. His complexion was ruddy, his beard silky and, unlike most men today, he was not ashamed of his paunch but on the contrary displayed it with a certain pride. Perhaps because his thighs were fat, he walked with short steps in a kind of majestic waddle.

'Why, it's Marius in person!' had once exclaimed a Parisian visitor passing in company of some pretty women.

The Admiral had not taken offence; quite the contrary.

'Will you take a bet that he's Tartarin?' had ventured a schoolboy who was a stranger to the town.

And the Admiral had not minded that either. He was not Marius, nor Tartarin, nor indeed was he an Admiral. But in his younger days he had been a good deal at sea as cook's assistant on board liners, and ever since then he had worn a naval officer's cap.

It was he who had founded the restaurant *À la Meilleure Brandade.* Then, when he was past sixty, he had handed it over to his niece, who had married a Northerner, a man from Lyons, and he lived with them.

At five o'clock, then, the Admiral was toddling down the Rue Jules-Ferry. This street is only three hundred metres long, and the evidence as to what happened in the space of under ten minutes is somewhat vague.

'*It was just five o'clock – I looked at the shop clock – when the Admiral went past,*' asserted Monsieur Pichon, the hatter, whose shop, in the Rue Jules-Ferry, is next door to the restaurant.

So there was no mistake about the start of this strange expedition, for no one ever doubted the word of Monsieur Pichon, former deputy mayor and town councillor and President of the town's Festival Committee.

And then? . . . Three houses lower down is the tobacconist's shop kept by old Madame Tatine. It is also a haberdashery and a newsagent's. That day, as Tatine was suffering from her rheumatics, her son Polyte was serving in the shop.

'The Admiral came in a few minutes after five, as usual. He took the paper and his packet of cigarettes and he said:

' "Fine weather, laddie! Reminds me of Madagascar . . ." '

For whether it was windy, rainy or scorching hot, the ex-ship's cook was invariably reminded of some foreign part.

At the bottom end of the street, just where the Mall begins, the game of bowls was in full swing. This, moreover, was the object of the Admiral's walk, for his daily habit was to take up his stand beside the players without saying a word, waiting for some disagreement in which he would inevitably serve as umpire.

The game took place close to the Post Office, so that everyone could see the time on the electric clock. Now Monsieur Lartigue, the fishmonger, who had just thrown the jack and considered it had gone too far, whereas his opponent declared the throw was in order, looked up along the Rue Jules-Ferry.

'*Pity the Admiral's still too high up along the street!*' he remarked.

And four of them, at least, saw the portly Admiral, who at that moment was half way down the street, exactly opposite the third lamp post.

It was five past five. The game went on. Monsieur Lartigue, who was a shocking grumbler, made another dubious throw, looked around for the Admiral and said in some surprise: 'Why, he's vanished!'

And indeed the Rue Jules-Ferry was empty, half in shade and half in sunlight, and there was literally not a cat to be seen on the pavements.

Note that no street, not even a lane, gives on to the Rue Jules-Ferry.

The Admiral had not reached the bottom of the street.

Neither had he gone back up it!

When the Little Doctor got out of his car in front of the *Meilleure Brandade*, he was covered in sweat, dust, oil and grease, for he'd had some serious trouble with Tin Lizzie, who was no longer in her first youth.

In the dining-room of the restaurant he saw, at first, only a black-eyed, Spanish-looking little maidservant who seemed to be examining him with audacious irony.

'Can I have a room?'

'I'll call Monsieur Jean . . .'

This was the *patron*. He appeared, wearing a white jacket and cap. A tall fellow of thirty to thirty-five, thinnish and not particularly cheerful of aspect.

'I hear you want a room . . . For several days?'

And the Little Doctor retorted aggressively: 'How d'you know it's for several days?'

'I don't know at all . . . It was just a manner of speaking . . . Would you like to go up at once and have a bit of a wash?'

The maid, whose name was Nine, took him up to the first floor. She still wore the same ironical expression, and the Little Doctor did not care for it at all.

Hadn't he been wrong to desert his practice at Marsilly yet again in answer to a somewhat ridiculous challenge? For nobody had sent for him. He knew nothing about this business except through the newspapers, which had not been very informative. On the other hand, two days previously he had received an anonymous letter which said:

'You may think yourself clever but I bet you're incapable of finding out what's become of the Admiral.'

It was a queer sort of hotel! One wondered how the proprietors made their living, for there was not a guest to be seen. Yet eight tables were laid for dinner, as though people were expected.

To the right of the dining-room there was a smaller room, a café-bar which again was empty of customers.

Finally, sitting at the cash desk was Madame Angèle, as Nine called her – the proprietor's wife and niece of the Admiral.

'Can one get anything to drink in this house?'

Monsieur Jean came in person to serve him.

'A *pastis?* . . . I don't know if you're a connoisseur, but this is the real stuff . . . Your good health . . .'

Monsieur Jean had poured himself a *pastis* too, and duly clinked glasses with his customer.

The opalescent beverage did not make him any more cheerful, and he sighed as he looked out at his terrace, shaded by an orange-coloured awning and surrounded by oleanders in green tubs.

'Do you always have as many guests as this?' asked the Little Doctor jokingly, feeling the need to take his revenge for the heat and for all the bother he'd had with Tin Lizzie.

'Sometimes fewer,' retorted Monsieur Jean promptly, 'sometimes more. In the past, in the old man's time, we did well . . . Cars didn't go so fast and they kept on breaking down . . . Now they rush past at a hundred kilometres an hour and don't bother to stop . . .'

'How long have you been running the business?'

'Since I got married, six years ago . . .'

Dollent frowned, intrigued by the glance that the man had just cast at the young woman over there at the cash desk.

'Hullo,' he thought. 'This gentleman doesn't seem too happy in his married life.'

'On the whole, then,' he said out loud, 'you're rather sorry you settled here?'

'I'm sorry in a sort of way, and yet I'm not . . . If it weren't for the bother we've had here during the past week . . Didn't you read in the papers?'

'No . . .'

'The old man, who used to live with us, has disappeared . . . I went to report to the police . . . Would you believe it, they didn't take me seriously and barely made a pretence of an investigation.

' "Monsieur Jean," the Superintendent told me, "according to statistics about thirty thousand people disappear every year in France. They all turn up again some day, at least nine-tenths of them . . . Just fancy, if the police had to go hunting for those thirty thousand people who aren't happy where they are and go off without giving warning . . ." '

'Was your uncle not happy here?'

'Monsieur, he was in clover!'

Why did he say this in such a gloomy tone?

'Contrary to what some people imply, – for there are always spiteful neighbours! – he'd had the best of the bargain . . . For when his niece married me, Monsieur Fignol, whom everybody calls the Admiral, was practically ruined . . . Only people didn't know that . . . He had made some queer investments which were to have brought him in thirty per cent, but which had swallowed up all his savings . . . The business was mortgaged . . . I took it over and undertook to keep the old man and feed him for the rest of his days. I even used to give him a little pocket money for his cigarettes and his game of cards . . .'

'Had he no money of his own?'

'Don't you think twenty francs a week is enough for a man of his age, who's settled down quietly? Another little *pastis*? . . . On me this time . . . Well, there you are! He's disappeared, and the worst of it is what happened next . . .'

'What did happen next?'

'You're not from these parts, are you? Otherwise you'd have known . . . Twice in under a week the hotel has been burgled . . . And don't tell me about the gang from Marseilles who, so they say, have been pillaging the neighbourhood . . . How could the Marseillais have known the house so well? . . . These thieves managed to get in, to go back and forth, open doors and cupboards without being heard . . .'

'Did they take much?'

'All my uncle's belongings . . . Old suits, worn-out suitcases not worth anything, a briefcase in which he kept his letters, I don't know what else . . .'

'And the second time?'

'That was the second time. The first time they took nothing, they merely searched the room . . . Well, I thought, now the police would at last take the thing seriously . . . Not at all! Quite the contrary!

' "You see," they said to me, "your uncle can't be dead, since he's been back to fetch his things . . ."

'I must point out that the Admiral, who weighed ninety kilos, couldn't have gone up the stairs without making every step creak! And that as far as I could make out, the burglar or burglars got in through a window on the first floor, climbing up a vine . . .

'And so I maintain, Monsieur – and I don't know who you are – that it's not worth being a tax-payer in this country if our money goes to keep up such a lot of slackers as our police force . . .

'I maintain, Monsieur, that the Admiral has been murdered, because if he were still alive he'd have been found, particularly as the Rue Jules-Ferry isn't a long street and we know all the people that live there.'

'Could he have been taken away in a car?'

'In a car?' the other exclaimed contemptuously. 'Do you really believe – but perhaps you're from Paris – that cars go up and down the Rue Jules-Ferry all day long? Apart from the baker's van in the morning, and the insurance agent who lives at no. 32 and has his own car – no, Monsieur! No car went down the street that evening.'

'Jean!' a woman's voice called.

The Little Doctor turned towards the cash desk and saw Angèle, the proprietor's wife, displaying real terror. An alert-looking small boy stood waiting beside her.

'Will you excuse me? It's my wife again! She can never manage without me. If she could have me on the end of a chain . . .'

Monsieur Jean went over to the cash desk reluctantly. He and his wife spoke in low voices. Then she held out an envelope, and he seized it.

'Well, for heaven's sake! . . . Can't you give that kid a nickel to go away?'

Paying no further attention to his wife, he came back to the Little Doctor's table.

'It's another hoax,' he grumbled. 'Look what my uncle's supposed to have written to us . . . To crown it all, it's his own writing . . .

> *"Dear Jean and Angèle,*
> *Don't worry about me. I've gone into the country. I'll be back in a few days.*
>
> *Marius Fignol."* '

'Did the boy bring this letter?'

'Yes. He's the postman's son. When he was sorting the mail, the postman recognized the Admiral's writing and sent his boy with it right away to save time . . .'

'What does the postmark say?'

'The letter was posted right here, at the main office in the Mall.'

For the past few moments the Little Doctor had been watching Monsieur Jean closely, and then glancing at the cash desk. But the object of his attention was not Angèle; it was an inkpot on which were smears of violet ink.

'I say . . .' he broke in, drawing another letter from his pocket.

'What?'

'Why did you send for me?'

'Who, I?'

'Yes, you . . . Admit that it was you who wrote me this note and that the reason you've been telling me all this is that you knew perfectly well who I was . . .'

The innkeeper still hesitated. He had reddened, and his hand was shaking as he picked up his glass.

'I don't know what you're talking about . . .'

'Read this! . . . Will you show me a specimen of your handwriting? Do you want me to submit this to an expert?'

'No . . . It's not worth while . . . I'm sorry, doctor . . . I wanted you to take the matter up, because I've heard so much about you . . . I thought that if I told you things the way they are, you wouldn't accept . . .'

He averted his head and confessed: 'And I said to myself that a famous man like you would ask for no end of money . . . I'm not rich . . . And so . . .'

'So you thought of a way to secure my collaboration free of charge!'

'Of course I shan't charge you for the room or meals . . . Nor even drinks! . . . You can drink as much as you like . . . And if you find my poor uncle I'll find one or two thousand-franc notes somehow . . .'

A skinflint, that was quite clear! Not merely a skinflint, but one cunning and ingenious enough to have thought up the trick of the anonymous letter.

'You will stay, won't you? I apologize for having done this . . I was in a panic . . .'

'May I have a word or two with your wife?'

A cloud seemed to darken the eyes of Monsieur Jean.

II. Concerning an Unhappy Household and the Petty Larcenies of the Admiral

'I would rather you left me alone with her, Monsieur Jean . . . I presume you've got plenty to do in the kitchen at this time of day.'

The Little Doctor propped his elbows on the cash desk and studied Angèle closely. She seemed quite young, and yet no more cheerful than her husband.

'This letter is in your husband's handwriting, isn't it?'

'Yes . . .'

She was frightened. She was trying to understand.

'He used this means to bring me here to look for your uncle . . . Does that surprise you?'

'I . . . I don't know . . .'

'I suppose you all three got on well together?'

He knew the reverse was true. He only had to look at her!

'We got on all right, yes!' she sighed.

'Except when there was a quarrel . . .'

'*They* used to quarrel sometimes . . .'

'Why?'

'In the first place, because my uncle didn't like people from Lyons and said my husband talked "mincing", which is bad for business in the Midi . . . But it's not Jean's fault if he hasn't the right accent! . . . Then he thought Jean didn't put enough garlic in the *brandade* . . . And a whole lot of small details . . .'

'Your husband, meanwhile, must have resented the expense of the Admiral's keep . . . Wasn't that so?'

'A bit, maybe . . .'

'Were there violent scenes between them?'

'Not violent . . . But there were scenes . . . Particularly about the till . . .'

She turned round to make sure that Jean was not listening through the kitchen door, which was ajar.

'I got the blame, to begin with . . . During the week hardly anyone comes, but on Sundays we sometimes have twenty or thirty customers . . . That brings in money . . .'

'And was money often missing?'

'How did you know? . . . Almost every Sunday money was missing, and it was always a hundred-franc note . . . At first my husband, who's terribly jealous, believed that I took the money to give a lover . . . I, who practically never leave the house . . . Even if I wanted to, for heaven's sake . . .'

A deep sigh! Decidedly, the household was not a happy one! Perhaps little Madame Angèle would not have been sorry to seek consolation with some strapping fellow from her own part of the world.

'One evening he caught my uncle slipping his hand into the till . . .'

'I can imagine the scene!'

'Poor Uncle didn't dare say anything! Everyone respects him in the town, and yet he was as shamefaced as a child caught misbehaving, and he didn't say a word . . .'

'You don't know what he used to do with that money? I'm going to ask you a rather delicate question . . . Was the Admiral still spry enough to be interested in girls . . . you get my meaning?'

'Oh no . . . He'd got over all that long ago . . . He liked eating and drinking, playing *manille* and watching the bowls players . . . But as for anything else . . .'

'The letter you've just received is really in his hand? You're certain it's not a forgery?'

'Nobody could have copied his writing so well . . .'

At that moment Nine, the little maid, turned on the wireless, in the hope perhaps of attracting custom. But Angèle frowned. The radio set, indeed, emitted only whistles and a cacophony of sounds.

'Nine! I've told you not to turn on the radio until the set's been repaired . . . Hasn't the electrician been yet?'

She sighed, wearily; everyone in this house seemed to be overcome with weariness!

'The electrician promised a fortnight ago to come and mend the radio set, and there's been no sign of him . . . On the other hand he spends every afternoon playing bowls on the Mall . . . Nine! Customers outside . . .'

A couple on a tandem cycle had just sat down on the terrace, and the woman had got badly sunburnt, so that her face was the colour of a ripe tomato.

'Two lemonades . . .'

'Tell me, Madame . . . Since the Admiral disappeared there have been no more thefts from the till?'

'No . . . not since . . .'

'Hadn't your uncle any friends in this street?'

'Only Monsieur Béfigue, the chemist . . . But for the past three weeks he's been in hospital in Marseilles, after a car crash . . .'

'So the Admiral would have had no reason to go into any house in the Rue Jules-Ferry?'

'Only the tobacconist's . . . He would just pop in and out again . . . He knew he was expected on the Mall . . . About half-past five they always play the big match, between champions, and my uncle was umpire . . . He was secretary of the Society of Jolly Bowls-players . . .'

She kept glancing around anxiously. Her husband, tired of waiting, emerged from the over-heated kitchen, mopping his face with a napkin.

'Has she told you anything interesting? Do you know what really baffles me? I've been thinking it over in the kitchen. By the way, you're having stuffed shad this evening . . . What really baffles me is this letter . . . You'd think the murderer had seen you come, or known you were coming, and was trying to make you go away again . . . If my uncle had really gone into the country – which he never did! – how could the letter, which was posted today, have been put into the letter-box in the Mall? Eh? Answer me that one, please!'

He turned round sharply. Somebody had come in and was sitting near the electric fan, in a place which seemed to be reserved for him.

'Oh, so here you are, Superintendent! . . . Are you still going to say I'm making things up?'

The Superintendent was wearing an alpaca suit and a straw hat, and smoking a pipe with a long slender stem.

'I've said nothing yet . . . And first I'd like to drink a nice cold *pastis* . . . Not the *pastis* off the shelves, eh? The other sort, the one you keep under the counter . . .'

In other words, illicit liquor.

'Is it true you've had a letter from the Admiral?'

'How did you know?'

'Isn't it our job to know everything? . . . Even things that other people don't know yet . . . For instance, that the Admiral's clothes and belongings have been fished out of the river . . .'

Angèle gave a start.

'Has Uncle been drowned?'

'I didn't refer to your uncle, but to the clothes and cases that disappeared out of his room a few days after he did . . .'

'And the clothes he was wearing?'

'We haven't found them yet,' the police officer replied brazenly. 'They're probably still on him . . . Only I warn you; I've been in this job thirty years . . . I'm due to retire in two years . . . Well, the man who makes a fool of me isn't born yet . . .'

It sounded like a threat; to whom was it addressed? The Little Doctor tried to guess, but failed.

'I don't see why anyone should try to make a fool of you,' sighed Monsieur Jean.

Then Dollent decided to take the air, particularly since the clock showed 5.0 p.m., the time at which a week previously, the Admiral had left the house.

The pavement along which he walked was in the full sun. He glanced for a moment at the enormous red opera-hat hanging in the air which served as the hatter's shop-sign, and inside the shop he caught sight of a little gentleman with a goatee beard, who would undoubtedly notice everything that went on outside.

Then three private houses. Then the narrow shop-front of the haberdashery, which also sold tobacco and newspapers.

'A packet of Gitanes . . .'

In contrast with the glare outside, it was as dark as a vault in here. A young man reached up and grabbed a yellow packet. Around him was the traditional lay-out: illustrated papers, dailies hung over a wire rail, boxes of embroidery cotton, balls of wool, the wire lattice in front of the counter for tobacco, stamps, tickets for the National Lottery, and in a corner, lollies and other cheap sweets for children.

'There's another thirty centimes change for you . . .'

The young man hunted in the drawer of the till, then put down the coins on the counter.

Five houses further on, a brass plate announced: Insurance. Then, next to it, a bailiff's escutcheon sign.

Everybody seemed to be asleep in this street!

A shop front painted black, with a green jar on the right and a yellow one on the left, and a door in the middle: Béfigue, pharmacist and chemist. It was open, in spite of the absence of Monsieur Béfigue, who was still in Marseilles following his accident. And wafts of music from a radio set emanated from it.

In the doorway stood a young man of about twenty, in round horn-rimmed glasses, proudly wearing the white coat that gave him something of the look of a doctor in a hospital.

Not a nook or cranny in the street. Not a hoarding, not a patch of waste ground. More houses, the workshop in which a cobbler sat wielding his awl, a grocer's which also sold vegetables.

Finally, a hundred metres from the Mall where the white shirts of the bowls players gleamed brightly against the blue shadow, a somewhat larger building inscribed: 'Provençal Distillery'.

Five minutes later, the Little Doctor, smoking endless cigarettes, seemed to be following with unflagging interest a bowls match about which he understood absolutely nothing.

On the previous Wednesday, the Admiral had not got as far as this! The street was not a long one, and yet he had never reached the end of it!

There was nowhere to hide! And no one, particularly a man known to the whole town, could have passed unnoticed there.

And nevertheless . . .

With its patches of dazzling light and its patches of almost violet shadow, with the pale trunks of plane-trees and the slight rustle of leaves, the brightness of the men's shirts and the leisurely pace of life that was due to the heat, the little town, looked at from where he stood, seemed like a setting for *Carmen.*

III. In Which, among so many Lovers, the Little Doctor Begins to Feel Lonely, but soon Becomes Everybody's Confidant

The window gave on to the courtyard, which was bright and colourful, with flowers growing in pots, and from the first pink light of dawn birds could be heard singing in a lime-tree behind the house.

But that morning the Little Doctor was not interested in nature. A different sight had aroused his interest. As he got out of bed a window had opened, just opposite his own, revealing an untidy room, an unmade bed, and above all revealing Nine, the little maidservant, getting dressed.

About the same time, Monsieur Jean went down into the courtyard, in his morning dishabille, with slippers on his bare feet; he flung a few handfuls of corn to the hens and doves, and stood there, hands in pockets, as though waiting for something . . .

What he was waiting for was Nine, who came down next. She could be heard grinding the coffee and poking the fires, then she swiftly crossed the courtyard with a jug in her hand and entered a kind of shed.

A minute later, Monsieur Jean also made his way into the shed, in a seemingly casual manner.

The Little Doctor smiled and stayed at his observation post. Nine emerged first, dishevelled, with a livelier flush on her face, carrying a jug full of white wine. As for the innkeeper, he stayed a few minutes longer, and for the sake of appearances came out carrying an armful of logs.

During this time Angèle was dressing in another room, but the Little Doctor could not see her clearly, for she had not opened her window.

Steps sounded on the stairs, and there was a knock at his door.

'Come in . . .'

It was Nine, bringing his breakfast on a tray.

'I didn't send for you,' he protested. 'How did you know I was up?'

She smiled mischievously.

'I could see you behind your curtains. So I thought this was the best time to speak to you without Madame hearing us . . .'

She was an odd girl, lively, cheeky, with her hair still ruffled, and radiating sensuality. Under her linen overall she was obviously scantily dressed, if at all, and the Little Doctor turned away his head with a sigh.

'How old are you?' he asked, sugaring his coffee.

'Eighteen . . . But I don't want to talk about myself . . . It's about that bitch . . .'

'What?'

'The one over across there, who's getting dressed . . . Look, from here I can see her sticking powder on her weaselly face . . . I wanted to warn you, because with her hypocritical airs she's capable of taking you in . . . To see her, always so quiet and resigned-looking, you'd think butter wouldn't melt in her mouth . . . But before she was married she was the worst sort of trollop who'd go after anything in trousers, including married men.'

It was hard not to smile when he pictured the scene in the shed, which he had practically witnessed!

'I believe that's why her uncle was glad to get her married; he was afraid that one of these days it would be too late . . . You see what I mean? . . . And she's as devious as they come . . . You've seen her . . . Last year it was with the pork butcher in the Rue Haute . . . This year it's with the chemist's assistant . . .'

'The one in Béfigue's shop?'

'Yes, a good-for-nothing fellow, Tony they call him, always up to no good with Polyte from the tobacconist's . . . Well, a married woman like her, in charge of a business like this, isn't ashamed of running after that Tony . . . Because it's she who does the running! . . . On the slightest excuse she's off to the chemist's shop to get an aspirin or a cough-drop . . .'

'Does her husband know?'

'Sure he knows . . . That's why they don't sleep together . . . If it wasn't for the business, they'd have split up long ago . . .'

'And you'd have become the boss's wife, maybe?'

She didn't turn a hair. She seemed to be wondering for a moment why he had been so categorical. Then she looked out of the window, saw the shed door still ajar and smiled.

'You saw us? . . . There's no harm in it! . . . Considering that *she* started it . . . I'll tell you something further . . . I'm sure the old Admiral wasn't the only one who took money out of the till. He used to take it, that's for sure . . . I saw him at it more than once . . . But just fancy what the mistress must have pinched to pay for her boyfriend's ties and white suede shoes! . . . Do you know, if it weren't that the Admiral had lost all his money, I'd be inclined to think . . .'

'That it was your *patronne* and her chemist's assistant who got him out of the way?'

'Sh . . . She's going downstairs . . . I've got to go down too . . . As for what I've told you, you can do what you like about it . . .'

And the Little Doctor was left alone in the sunlight with his *café au lait.*

So Monsieur Jean was Nine's lover, and apparently wanted to marry her!

And Angèle was the mistress of the chemist's assistant, after being a lot of other men's. Was she, too, envisaging possible re-marriage?

What was the role of the missing Admiral in this imbroglio? What had either of the two couples to gain from his death?

He no longer had any fortune, and he was reduced, like a young delinquent, to pinching hundred-franc notes from the till! The restaurant no longer belonged to him, nor did the house.

And he had no authority there; he was apparently treated like an unwelcome lodger.

Was Monsieur Jean miserly enough to have got rid of him in order not to have to go on feeding him for a few more years, and to save the twenty francs pocket money he handed out each week?

This was what amused the Little Doctor: twenty-four hours previously he knew nothing about this house, and now it had come to life before his eyes, he was able to examine its remotest crannies, to guess at all its intrigues and each individual's meanest secrets!

The previous evening, in a bistrot near the Mall, after the bowls match, the fishmonger, with whom Dollent had struck up an acquaintance by standng him a drink, had declared:

'That Monsieur Jean's no good. *He's not even from these parts!*'

Which, on his lips, amounted to a verdict of Guilty.

Having finished breakfast, he went down and found the *patron* tidying up the café. He was no more cheerful than on the previous day. He worked without zest, like a man with a secret sorrow.

'You weren't visited by burglars last night?'

Monsieur Jean made sure his wife was out of hearing.

'What has the girl been telling you?' he asked. 'You mustn't take too much notice of what she says . . . She's young, you understand? She gets ideas into her head . . .'

He was watching the Little Doctor, who was repressing a smile.

'All the same you're on pretty good terms with her, aren't you?'

'If that's what you're thinking of . . . You know how things are . . . It doesn't mean anything.'

'And your wife's relations with the chemist's assistant?'

'I guessed she would give you the whole story . . . I'm not saying it's not true . . . All the same there's no proof . . . She sees a good deal of him . . . But that has nothing to do with her uncle's disappearance . . . Look! See what they've done . . .'

And he showed the Little Doctor a local paper in which Dollent's photograph spread over two columns on the front page. It had been taken the evening before, while he was watching the game of bowls.

'Famous Detective Joins Hunt for the Admiral'.

'Note,' Monsieur Jean insisted, 'that I never told them anything. It's incredible how news spreads here . . . And meanwhile our poor uncle . . . Between ourselves, doctor, what do you think? Is he dead or isn't he?'

Dollent turned round and saw Angèle, who had come in noiselessly and was listening to them.

'I'll answer that question tonight,' he said. 'I must go and buy some cigarettes and look in at the chemist's for an aspirin . . . I've got a headache . . .'

'I shall go and do my shopping,' announced Monsieur Jean. 'What do you say to a nice aïoli for lunch?'

'Doctor! . . .'

He was about to go out, as he had said, but this time it was Angèle who detained him. Her husband had left. Nine could be seen in the kitchen, washing the floor.

'What have *they* been telling you?'

'Nothing . . . They talked about this and that . . .'

'About me, I'm sure . . . They both detest me . . . So much so that I sometimes wonder if it's not me they'd have liked to get rid of . . .'

Decidedly, if people sometimes made love in this house, there was a good deal of hatred there too!

'My husband only married me because he thought my uncle richer than he really was . . . When he realized that apart from the restaurant there wasn't any money, he was furious and he practically claimed he'd been cheated . . . As for that slut, he's been hanging round her for long enough . . .'

She hesitated, glancing at him furtively.

'I bet they talked about Tony? . . . If they said there was anything between us, they were lying . . . Tony's a decent fellow who loves me . . . But so long as I'm married he respects me too much even to kiss me. Besides, the other two would be only too glad! . . . It would give them the chance to ask for a divorce, with me as the guilty party, and I'd be thrown out without a penny . . .'

Phew! the Little Doctor was beginning to weary of this charming family and the unsavoury dealings which seemed to be an integral part of its way of life.

'You can see that it would be in their interest to get rid of me, doctor! They may have found my uncle an embarrassment . . .'

For pity's sake! He felt the need of fresh air and sunshine, of contact with real life again! He went out. He was immediately immersed in the warmth of a summer morning and the familiar, reassuring sounds of the little town.

His first call was at the tobacconist's, and there behind the counter he found Polyte, still unwashed and unshaven, his muddy complexion and the rings round his eyes suggesting late nights and habitual self-indulgence.

'So it seems it's you who are going to find the old fellow?' he jeered, pointing to the morning paper.

'I'm trying to,' the Little Doctor answered modestly. 'You must have known him well, didn't you? since he came in here every day.'

'I wasn't here every day myself . . . If you think it's a man's job to be selling stamps, little packets of snuff, ribbons and lottery tickets . . . If it wasn't that my mother's ill . . . What did you want? Cigarettes, same as yesterday?'

'Some Gitanes, yes . . . I suppose your mother stays in the room at the back of the shop?'

'She's upstairs in her bedroom . . . Her legs are too swollen for her to go up and down stairs . . .'

'Do you close early?'

'Eight o'clock. After that, there's not a living creature in the street:'

'You must get bored in the evenings, in a little town like this?'

'I go to Avignon with my friend on his motor-bike.'

'Tony?'

'That's right . . . He's got an old motor-bike . . . I sit pillion . . .'

'And you're off to the bright lights!' the Little Doctor teased him.

He was about to leave, but changed his mind.

'Tell me . . . It's easier to speak frankly with you than with the family . . . Don't you think the Admiral may have had some secret vice?'

Polyte scratched his head, repeating thoughtfully: 'Some vice?'

'I wonder what he could have done with his money . . . Sometimes he spent two or even three hundred francs a week . . . He didn't drink . . . He was past the age for going after girls . . .'

'It's funny,' muttered Polyte. 'You're sure he spent as much as that? . . . I say! . . . Could he have put something on the tote?'

The hatter was standing on his doorstep, just beneath the gigantic opera-hat which served as his shop sign, and he greeted the Little Doctor, obviously eager to engage in conversation. The whole town knew Dollent now, thanks to the paper which had printed his picture on its front page.

'Lovely day, isn't it? . . . It's going to get warm presently . . . So it seems you're going to find our friend the Admiral? . . . Won't you come in out of the sun for a minute?'

In some of his investigations the Little Doctor's greatest difficulty had been in persuading people to talk. In this one, on the contrary, he could foresee the moment when he would have trouble keeping them quiet. How many more people were going to waylay him as he walked down the Rue Jules-Ferry?

'A drop of white wine, doctor? . . . For it seems you're a medical man? . . . There's something I wouldn't have confided to anybody but yourself, for they're such scandalmongers around here! . . . The Admiral and I, we were old friends . . . In winter, when the weather was bad, he used to come in here and we'd have a chat, just as we're doing now . . .

' *"They've got it in for me because I've no more money,"* he once told me, speaking about you know whom. *"But they might well have a surprise one of these days . . . Then they'll start buttering up old Uncle instead of begrudging him his food and drink . . ."*

'That's what he said to me, doctor . . . I thought maybe he was expecting a legacy? . . . Or that he'd got a stake in something profitable in the colonies, which he was always talking about?'

At that moment Polyte went by, still untidily dressed and with unkempt hair. Dollent leaned forward to see where the youth was going, and saw him precipitately enter the chemist's shop.

After listening a little longer to the hatter's confidences, Dollent went on down the street. He met Polyte on his way home, and the youth gave him a casual greeting.

The Little Doctor now entered Monsieur Béfigue's dispensary, as Polyte had done; the chemist's assistant seemed to be expecting him.

'What do you think of all this, doctor? Isn't it a shame that one can't live in peace in a little town like ours?'

Like Polyte, he was pasty-faced, which was not surprising considering that they were both given to spending half the night in Avignon.

'Do you live in the house?' asked the Little Doctor.

'No . . . I shut the shop at night, and in the absence of Monsieur Béfigue and of his wife, who's gone to join him in Marseilles, the house is empty. I have a room a little further down, at the cobbler's house, which you must have noticed as you went by . . .'

'Did the Admiral often call at the chemist's shop? Was he in the habit of taking medicine?'

'Never . . . If you'll forgive me, he hadn't much use for doctors or pill-sellers, as he called them . . . And when Monsieur Béfigue was not at home I've never seen him come into the place . . .'

It was pointless trying to hide or to make a mystery of his doings. He went into the cobbler's shop.

'I know what you're going to ask me . . . My friend the Superintendent has already asked me the same question . . . No, I don't remember seeing the Admiral go past last Wednesday. Usually I look up when he goes by along the pavement, because I know it's his regular time . . . But sometimes I'm too busy . . .'

'Is Tony's room on the ground floor? Has it a separate way out?'

'Go and look for yourself . . . Just go through the kitchen . . . It's the room on the left . . . You have to pass through the shop to go in and out . . .'

The room was empty and untidy, and the cobbler's wife was busy turning the mattress, amid a cloud of fine dust.

One had constantly to revert to the one indisputable truth: on Wednesday June 25th at five o'clock the Admiral had left the *Meilleure Brandade* and started off, as he did every day, down the Rue Jules-Ferry.

The hatter had seen him pass. The Admiral had gone into the tobacconist's and Polyte had served him.

Then the chemist's assistant, too, had seen the former ship's cook go past. And from below, the bowls players had caught sight of him in front of the chemist's shop.

That was all!

But the Admiral, who seemed to have no material needs, was in the habit of dipping into the till!

The Little Doctor, as he crossed the Mall with his hands in his pockets and underwent everyone's gaze with a jaunty air, was far from suspecting that a second disappearance was imminent.

IV. How the Rue Jules-Ferry Seemed Anxious to Beat the Record for Mysterious Disappearances, and how the Little Doctor, Ignoring the Rest of the World, Paused to Contemplate an Official Poster

'No, môssieu!' had wearily sighed the proprietor of the bar which accepted bets for the Pari Mutuel Urbain. 'Your Admiral was not bright enough to back horses, and besides, he never used to set foot in here, seeing as how he belonged to the top end of town . . .'

One o'clock! The Little Doctor was now sitting in the dining-room, where there were only four customers besides himself, a couple with two children.

'Sit properly . . . Don't eat with your fingers . . . You're not to take your little brother's meat . . .'

The usual harangue! . . . The room was hot . . . The aïoli wasn't bad, the rosé wine went to one's head . . .

From time to time, Monsieur Jean thrust his white-capped head through the chink of the kitchen door. Nine, in a black dress and white apron, went about waggling her neat bottom, reminding the doctor of that morning's scene. As for Angèle, at the cash desk, she was red-eyed, as though she had been crying.

At what point, exactly, did it happen? Actually, he did not see her get up or leave the room. He preferred to watch Nine and . . .

It was the time when all the shutters in any self-respecting meridional town are closed against the scorching heat of the streets, and when the ground seems to be steaming.

'Will you take coffee, doctor?'

'Yes, yes . . .'

He had even practically decided to have a siesta like everyone else. He did not expect, as he sipped his coffee, to see Monsieur Jean suddenly emerge and ask the maid: 'Where is Madame?'

Still less did he expect the hullabaloo that ensued! Angèle had, in her turn, vanished. In vain they searched every room in the house, and combed the neighbouring streets.

Not only had she disappeared, but she had taken nothing with her, no hat, not even her handbag . . .

The hatter was still asleep under his fig-tree in his little courtyard. The tobacconist's was shut, and Polyte replied to their inquiries from a first-floor window.

The shutters of the chemist's shop were not closed, but the lever-handle on the door had been withdrawn and a cardboard clock indicated that the dispensary would not be open until half-past two.

Through the window they could see into the back of the shop, where Tony was quietly eating his lunch and reading a paper. When he saw people there he got up in surprise, and came through the shop to open the door a crack.

'What's up?'

'Have you seen my wife?' asked Monsieur Jean, who was ready to explode.

'Your wife? . . . And why should *I* have seen your wife? I'm fed up with always hearing about *your* wife!'

It looked as though the two men were coming to blows, but nothing happened; one of them retired into the semi-darkness of his den, the other set off towards the Mall, dragging the Little Doctor with him.

'Have you seen my wife? . . .'

Was anybody in the restaurant looking after the family with the two children? Probably not. People were accosted in the street:

'Have you seen my wife? . . .'

Nobody had seen her, and yet she had unquestionably disappeared, just like her uncle the Admiral.

'Say, doctor, do you think that . . .'

Monsieur Jean turned round, surprised to find nobody at his side, and saw the Little Doctor immobilized in front of an old poster in the window of a tobacconist's in the Rue aux Ours.

'I think . . .' Dollent began, frowning. Then, in sudden excitement:

'I think we must act quickly, for heaven's sake! . . . Your wife . . . your wife . . . Show me the way to the police station at once . . .'

He was gesticulating like a marionette, and not walking but running. He muttered disconnected phrases: 'If they should ever find her . . . Is it far?'

'The first street on the left . . . I wonder . . . Luckily the Superintendent lives over the station . . . He'll be having his nap, but we'll wake him up . . .'

Monsieur Jean's prediction was right.

'What d'you want? What's come over you to wake people up at such a time of day? . . . Oh, so it's you, Mr Detective? . . . Have you found our Admiral?'

'Yes . . .'

'Eh? . . . What's that?'

'Well . . . that's to say I think we're going to find him . . . But we must act quickly . . . For I wonder if he's still alive . . . Bring some men . . . three, four, five men . . . All the men you can . . .'

'I've only got four, and one of them's on leave . . .'

'Never mind . . . Come on . . .'

He led the little posse towards the restaurant *À la Meilleure Brandade.*

The official poster which had held his attention had proclaimed:

National Lottery. Yachting Section.
Today June 25th. Drawing at 3 p.m.

The draw was to take place at Dieppe.

'Where are we going?' queried the Superintendent. 'You're not going to tell me the Admiral is hidden in his own home?'

Not at all! In fact the Little Doctor passed the restaurant without stopping and then halted for a moment outside the tobacconist's.

'Leave a man here . . . He's to stop *anybody* coming out . . .'

And he went on down the Rue Jules-Ferry.

V. Showing how a Man's Life was Saved by the Mislaying of a Scrap of Paper

Through the windows of the closed shop, the chemist's assistant could be glimpsed in the back room, still reading his paper at the table beside the remains of his meal.

'Either the Admiral and his niece are there,' the Little Doctor declared with feverish excitement, 'or I'm going to make an utter fool of myself and I'll vow never again to undertake the smallest investigation.'

The Superintendent, mistrustfully, knocked on the window. Tony came up, looking surprised, found the lever-handle and put it back, asking:

'What's up now?'

'I'd like to have a look round the house.'

Tony cast a venomous look at Monsieur Jean, as if to say: 'What have you been telling them now?' But out loud he remarked:

'Look wherever you like . . . The house doesn't belong to me . . . Only you'll have to deal with the boss when he gets back, and I fancy he'll kick up a row . . .'

The Superintendent embarked on a conscientious search of the various rooms, while Tony, with a contemptuous expression, remained in the dispensary, pretending to arrange bottles.

The Little Doctor hesitated for a moment, then shrugged his shoulders. He was a puzzle-solver, as he liked to say, but not a detective, still less a policeman. It was therefore not his job to . . .

If the Superintendent's precautions were inadequate, so much the worse for the Superintendent!

'What about this door? What do you think it is?'

They were in a vaulted cellar, and they had reached a further door fastened with a solid lock.

'I believe,' the Little Doctor put in, 'that this is the place where the chemist keeps dangerous products, such as large bottles of sulphuric acid . . .'

'We haven't got the key . . . Sergeant, go and ask the chemist's assistant if he has the key to this room . . .'

The Little Doctor had foreseen the sequel. The chemist's assistant had already vamoosed silently, at least as far as the cobbler's, for after that he had started up the noisiest of motor-cycles and dashed off along the Route Nationale.

'Fetch a locksmith, sergeant . . . We shall catch the man later . . . But I think something's moving inside here . . .'

Something was definitely moving, for a few minutes later, when they had forced the lock, they beheld two human beings: the Admiral, bound hand and foot with ropes, a gag on his mouth, but plenty of life in his eyes; and Angèle, who appeared to be in a faint.

'Is she dead, do you think?'

'Carry her out into the courtyard . . .'

She was neither bound nor gagged, but a characteristic smell told the doctor that she had been chloroformed.

'Can *you* understand anything about it?'

'Yes,' he replied in all simplicity.

'You're not going to claim that you knew what we were going to find here?'

'I did!'

'So you want us to believe that in the space of twenty-four hours, merely by drinking *pastis* with Tom, Dick and Harry, you have . . .'

'Well, yes, it's like that, Superintendent . . . I might have been mistaken . . . I warned you of that . . . And yet there were so many chances that my deductions might have been correct! . . . You see, what gave me the hint was that the radio set at the *Meilleure Brandade* was out of order . . .'

Success is always delightful, of course, but Dollent's pleasure would have been far greater if those who witnessed his triumph had been capable of appreciating it, people like Superintendent Lucas, for instance!

They had all forgathered in the bar at the *Meilleure Brandade*, and the Admiral had put away so many tots to aid his recovery that he was half asleep. As for Angèle, she had come round quite a while ago, but was still pale and avoided meeting people's eyes.

Polyte was there. The policeman had pounced on him just when, on hearing his friend's motor-cycle, he had tried to rush out and knock down the representative of law and order.

As for Nine, she stood in the background, casting imploring glances at the Little Doctor.

'One must first inquire,' the latter was saying, 'what an elderly man, all passion spent, can get for a hundred francs. He doesn't gamble, he doesn't drink, he's no longer interested in what they call the fair sex. And yet he finds it necessary to remove hundred-franc notes from the till at regular intervals.

'This man, you will note, had ruined himself by making rash investments. Note, moreover, that he told his friend the hatter that one of these days he might become rich again . . .

'The answer is a simple one: the Admiral, knowing that he would never make his fortune otherwise, used regularly to buy tickets for the National Lottery, unbeknown to his niece and her husband.

'He bought them at the nearby tobacconist's, at the same time as his cigarettes, and he hid them heaven knows where . . .'

Why was Nine making such urgent signals to him, and what did they mean? He went on:

'Now that Wednesday, the day they drew the lots, the radio was not working in the restaurant . . . Moreover, for some weeks past, the old woman who keeps the tobacconist's shop had been replaced at the counter by her good-for-nothing son. It was he who sold the ticket to the Admiral . . . And his radio was working. By five o'clock, he knew that the Admiral had won an important prize . . . How much was it, Polyte?'

'One million,' the youth growled reluctantly, staring at his handcuffs.

'One million . . . The idea of getting hold of that million . . . The Admiral knows nothing about it yet . . . He goes into the shop as usual . . . He probably asks, knowing that they have the radio in the house:

' "I suppose I haven't won anything?"

'Polyte can do nothing in that narrow shop, too close to the restaurant, apart from the fact that the old lady, up on the first floor, might hear everything.

'So Polyte replies: "I don't know . . . I couldn't follow the report. But my friend Tony in the chemist's shop is listening to it. If you'd like to go and ask him from me . . ."

'The two young men, who spend most of their nights in shady

haunts in Avignon and Marseilles, get together . . .

'The Admiral comes in . . .

' "Come this way . . . I've got the list in the back-shop . . ."

'As the Admiral bends down to look at the paper they chloroform him . . .

'The two rascals hope he'll have the ticket on him . . . In that case he's done for; they'll kill him . . . He'll disappear for good; they will go to Paris to claim the million francs and get across the frontier with enough to live riotously for a certain time . . .

'Now as it happens the ticket is not in the old man's pockets. They shut him up in the cellar. They question him. They terrorize him . . . But he refuses to tell his secret . . .

'Hence the two burglaries, in an attempt to find a scrap of paper worth a million francs . . .'

At this point the Admiral raised his head and glared defiantly at his nephew. Nine, meanwhile, made fresh signals to the Little Doctor. But he disregarded them.

'This, then, ladies and gentlemen, is the sort of struggle which went on for about a week in that cellar . . . On the one hand, an old man determined to keep his secret . . . He must have understood that once in possession of the ticket the other two would have no choice but to kill him . . .

'Then they took fright . . . They were scoundrels, true, but they are amateurs, and amateurs are always clumsy. In order to put an end to the inquiry they thought it was a bright idea to force their prisoner to write a letter saying he had gone into the country. And they got rid of the stolen cases and the clothes taken from the old man's bedroom by throwing them into the river, from which they were quickly recovered . . .

'They were just small-scale rascals . . . And they still hadn't got the lottery ticket!'

He felt Angèle's eyes upon him, and also Monsieur Jean's.

'A woman guessed everything, as a result of my talks with her. She even guessed before I did . . . She hurried to the chemist's shop . . . She was anxious to prevent a murder, to force Tony to release her uncle . . . For Madame Angèle was that woman . . .

'I might add . . .'

No, he would say no more. It was pointless to explain that people are never either as good or as bad as one believes. Angèle might be capable of taking a lover, but she was not capable of letting that man kill her uncle! Tony, for his part, was capable of making love to her, but not of giving up the chance of wealth for her sake.

'He chloroformed her, to save time!' the Little Doctor boldly summarized the story. 'And meanwhile the famous lottery ticket, worth a million francs, had still not been found . . .

'And our two scoundrels were going to be obliged, in the end, to kill two people *without gaining anything thereby* . . .

'That was the situation, messieurs, at two o'clock this afternoon, when I stopped in front of a poster announcing the final draw of the National Lottery . . . Some tradesman had forgotten to take it down from his shop-window, and it was thanks to this oversight . . .'

Everyone turned to the Admiral, who was growling under his breath and who finally managed to bring out the words:

'The worst of it is that I can't remember . . . A million! . . . To think that a million's going to be lost unless . . .'

He clasped his head in his hands.

'Usually I hid the tickets on top of the wardrobe . . . This time . . . what can have happened this time?'

Nine was desperately trying to attract the Little Doctor's attention, and he turned to her at last. She was like a schoolboy lifting his hand to ask leave to be excused.

'May I go up into my room for a moment?' she asked.

'On condition that I come up with you.'

'Come if you like . . .'

They climbed the stairs in silence. The bed was still unmade. She pulled a book from under the mattress.

'I think it's in here,' she declared. 'I saw something like a National Lottery ticket, but I didn't take any notice of it.'

She rubbed up against him coyly.

'I've got something to confess . . .. The Admiral always used to bring back books . . . how shall I put it . . . naughty books . . . And I used to take one up to my room sometimes to read in the evenings . . . When you mentioned a lottery ticket just now I remembered the last book I borrowed . . . Look! it's still there . . . The Admiral must have used it as a book-mark and forgotten it . . .'

It was quite true! The million francs were there, in the shape of a common, badly printed scrap of paper!

The chemist's assistant was arrested by the Carcassonne *gendarmerie*, and the odd thing was that he would probably not have attracted their attention if he had not been exceeding the speed limit on his motor-cycle.

The Admiral cashed his million francs.

And the Little Doctor incurred much odium in the house where, at the time of the crisis, he had been everybody's confidant.

Monsieur Jean suddenly proved himself a model husband and nephew-in-law . . .

His wife was all smiles for him and even more for her uncle . .

Nine became, once again, just a conscientious little maid-of-all work, and if she still met her employer in the shed she did so with greater secrecy.

Nobody was left now to pinch notes out of the till!

Even old Madame Tatine had resumed her place at the counter of her shop, in spite of her swollen legs.

A grand banquet was held at the *Meilleure Brandade* in honour of the new millionaire. The bowls players were there, and the hatter, and everybody from the upper town . . .

But nobody pressed the Little Doctor to stay, and he went off disconsolately in Tin Lizzie. A grudging word of thanks was all he'd got. He knew too many things . . . He had become an embarrassment . . .

'You know,' Monsieur Jean tried to explain, 'at moments like that, when one's nerves are on edge . . . one exaggerates, one says things one doesn't mean . . .'

Dollent was already far away when the banquet took place, and the second place of honour, after the new millionaire, was allotted to the police Superintendent.

'Since we are fortunate enough to have at the head of our town's police force a man whose shrewdness . . . whose coolness . . . whose professional skill . . .'

It's too much to expect popular acclaim as well as inner contentment!

'No serious illnesses?' was all Jean Dollent asked Anna, when he got back to his home and his practice.

'Two children born in the middle of the night . . .'

'Thank goodness I wasn't there!'

He had acquired a splendid tan from his trip to that confounded Midi!

The Communication Cord

I. In Which Etienne Chaput, Whose Appearance Matches his Profession, Tells of a Young Woman's Eccentric Behaviour

Of all the Little Doctor's cases, this business of the communication cord probably came closest to the 'perfect crime' dear to all criminologists. And yet that case began like a crude farce. During all the time that Etienne Chaput was speaking, waving his short, flabby, sweaty hands, Jean Dollent often found it hard to keep a straight face. The man fitted his role so perfectly!

Never had the Little Doctor been confronted with such a realistic specimen of the humbug: his face, his hands, his whole body were so limp that it looked as though, if he got any more heated, Etienne Chaput would begin to melt!

To crown it all, the man made church candles!

Everything was against him, his bleary eyes with bags under them, his layered chins, his dewlaps and a paunch bulging under the waistcoat across which lay a heavy watch-chain.

In short, he was the very image of the sly, unpleasant bourgeois, miserly and prudish, cowardly and depraved, as he is still portrayed in some old-fashioned stage productions.

And what had happened to him? Exactly what one would have expected from his appearance: he was actually accused of having made an indecent assault on a lady, on the 8.45 p.m. Paris–Marseilles express train, during the night of October 12th.

'If you knew me, doctor, you would realise the absurdity of such a charge . . . Nobody could lead a more open and upright life than myself . . . I've been married thirty-two years, and my wife and I have never had the slightest disagreement; we have always lived in the same apartment in the Rue du Chemin-Vert . . . The landlord and our neighbours will all tell you what a model couple we are . . .

'My candle factory is in the Rue d'Alésia, and I go there every morning and every afternoon . . . You must realise that in my line of business, one's conduct must be irreproachable . . .

'We sell our candles wholesale to all religious communities, and we supply the majority of convents . . .

'I was on my way to Marseilles to arrange about the supply of candles for the forthcoming pilgrimage to Notre-Dame de la Garde . . .

'I had taken a second-class couchette, for you know business is none too good just now . . . My wife had come to see me off at the station with Bobby . . .'

'Is that your son?'

'No, our dog . . . Alas, heaven has not granted us children, but we adore animals . . . I swear to you, doctor, by all that I hold most sacred . . .'

And the little Doctor was on the point of interjecting facetiously:

'Such as Bobby?'

But he restrained himself, for the limp man now wore a dramatic expression. He was mopping his brow; he was breathing with difficulty, as though he were asthmatic.

'I swear to you that things happened just as I'm going to relate them . . . Before the train left, I took advantage of being alone in the compartment to take off my shoes and put on my felt slippers. Then I removed my collar and tie and my jacket, and I put on the flannel jacket that I always take with me when I travel . . .'

What a seductive scene this must have been!

'I hoped I should remain alone in the compartment, for there were not many passengers on the train . . . Unfortunately a young woman, who seemed to have been looking for a place for some time, opened the door and asked me whether the couchette opposite mine was free.'

'A pretty woman?' inquired the Little Doctor.

'Pretty, yes . . . Although I'm no great connoisseur of feminine beauty . . . Very blonde hair, possibly dyed, I don't know . . . A fur coat . . .'

'Any luggage?'

'I don't remember . . . Wait a minute . . . She had a small light-coloured suitcase . . . Yes, that was all . . . The train left almost immediately and my fellow-passenger also took off her shoes, then her hat and coat . . . She settled down on her couchette, and I immediately noticed her lack of modesty . . .'

'What do you mean by modesty?'

'A lack of decency, if you prefer . . . She could quite well have lain down without showing me her legs as she did. I was shocked, and turned towards the wall . . .'

'Did you fall asleep at once?'

'No . . . I always find it difficult to sleep . . . It was very hot in the compartment . . . The guard came by and punched our tickets . . . Before leaving, he turned down the light, but one could still see fairly well . . .'

'Were you still facing the wall?'

'No. I can't lie long on my right side . . . I kept closing my eyes and opening them again . . . My neighbour, lying on her couchette, was smoking one cigarette after another, and this bothered me, because I'm a non-smoker . . . She didn't appear to want to sleep . . . I noticed that she kept looking at the time on her wrist-watch . . .'

The stout man sighed, crossed and uncrossed his legs, and then drew a deep breath, with a faint wheezing sound at the back of his throat.

'I don't know how long we had been travelling. I had already dozed off once or twice . . . All I know is that my eyes were open . . . The young woman was sitting up on her berth and staring fixedly at her watch . . . Then suddenly, without even looking at me, she got up and pulled the communication cord with all her might . . .'

'For a moment I thought I must be asleep and dreaming . . . But the train began to slow down . . . There was a grinding of brakes; people were running up and down the corridors . . .

'I sat up . . . Before I could find words to express my astonishment the door opened and the guard came in.

' "What's up? Who pulled the cord?"

' "I did, *monsieur le contrôleur*," the young woman said quite coolly. "I was frightened. Just imagine, this person took advantage of my being asleep to assault me with the obvious intention of . . ." '

The Little Doctor managed to control his amusement. And yet the candle-manufacturer, round-eyed and open-mouthed with indignation, offered an extremely comical sight.

'On my honour, doctor, I pinched myself to make sure I wasn't dreaming . . . I, who hadn't stirred from my berth! . . . I who hadn't even spoken a word to the woman . . . I who . . .

'I tried to protest, and I could see that nobody believed me . . . Everyone looked at me with disgust . . . All the passengers had been surprised by the stopping of the train; they were standing in the corridors and jostling one another to get a sight of me . . . I thought they were going to lynch me, such was their contempt and indignation . . .

'However the train started off again . . . I could vaguely overhear the woman's conversation with the guard.

' "Where are you travelling to, Madame?"

' "Laroche-Migennes . . . I'm going to visit my sister, who's expecting me . . ."

' "We shall be there in a few minutes . . . Will you kindly repeat your statement to the special superintendent there, and sign your complaint . . . Your name is?"

' "Marthe Donville, 177 Rue Brey, Paris."

'The Guard looked at me with such contempt that I felt quite weak.

' "As for you, give me your name and address . . . Your ticket is for

Marseilles? When we get there you shall come with me to the Superintendent, who will decide what is to be done . . ."

'That's what happened to me, doctor . . . I have been strictly truthful about the whole story, I have exaggerated nothing . . . I had never seen this woman before. I shall probably never see her again, for she gave a false address . . .'

'How do you know that?'

'At Marseilles they merely drew up a report and let me go about my business. I thought it over . . . I racked my brain to try and understand . . . Then I reflected that this woman, if she wasn't crazy, must have acted as she did in order to blackmail me . . .

'As I told you, doctor, my business is of a somewhat special character, and you will readily understand that a scandal of this sort would alienate all my customers . . . It would mean not only disgrace but ruin . . . As for my poor wife, if she believed me capable of such an act, I think it would kill her . . .

'I therefore wanted to implore this creature to break off proceedings by withdrawing her complaint . . . I went to the Rue Brey, to the address she had given . . . But the Rue Brey is a very short street behind the Etoile, and it has no number 177 . . . Nevertheless I questioned all the concierges in case I had misheard the number . . . I was prepared to offer her money, a considerable sum if need be . . .

'All this was exactly ten days ago, doctor . . . I have had no news of my so-called victim . . . On the other hand I was summoned to my local police station, where a number of questions were put to me . . .

'When I asked what was happening I was told that things were taking their course . . .

'I feel I'm living with a rope round my neck . . . At any moment I expect to be faced with the official charge which will create the inevitable scandal . . .

'Is it possible, doctor, that an honest and hard-working man's life can be destroyed because a crazy or designing woman has chosen to . . .

'To whom could I turn? . . . The police are firmly convinced of the truth of this woman's fabrication . . .

'I thought of you . . . I took advantage of a long over-due visit to the diocese of La Rochelle to call on you and beg you to help me . . .'

He was speaking wheezily and mopping his perspiring face. When he had left, the Little Doctor looked with some distaste at his own hand, which had been clasped by the moist, flabby hand of Etienne Chaput.

How could a man's physical appearance correspond so closely to his occupation? One might almost think that a connoisseur of physiognomy had chosen this candle-manufacturer from among the millions of Parisians to play that dubious role on the Paris-Marseilles express, on the night of October 12th!

The onset of winter brought cases of bronchitis and flu, but the Little Doctor, who had undertaken no investigations for several months, once again rang up his colleague Magné and entrusted his practice to him.

He would have liked to go to Paris to take the same train, the *rapide* 19, that Etienne Chaput had taken.

But for the job he envisaged he needed his old Tin Lizzie, which took him to Laroche-Migennes without too much difficulty.

Here he learned that Laroche-Migennes is, as it were, at the hub of the entire P.L.M. network, and in the railway offices he became acquainted with a language hitherto unknown to him.

No. 19 was referred to familiarly as though it were a flesh and blood human being, then, when he asked where this No. 19 had been at 22.31 hours, the time when the unknown woman had pulled the communication cord, he received the laconic reply:

'Kilometre 139 . . . Just short of Cézy level crossing.'

'I'm sorry to be such a nuisance . . . Of course that's when it's due . . . But are you sure there's never any delay?'

'Never on the Paris-Laroche section . . . If the train's delayed, it's after Dijon . . .'

The railway officials must have taken him for a policeman, for they proved obliging and even went to fetch the record of train No. 19 for the night of October 12th.

'Here you are . . . Everything as usual . . . The train was exactly up to schedule when, at 22.31 the alarm went off . . . The train stopped a few seconds later, that's to say at about three hundred metres from the place where the cord had been pulled . . . That's what you wanted to know, isn't it? . . . When No. 19 drew to a halt, the head of the train had just reached the level crossing at Cézy . . .'

The Little Doctor noted it all down carefully, like a conscientious student. Then he went over to the platforms and began a lengthy examination of the railway staff. Not for the first time, he was made aware that the simplest information is the hardest to obtain.

It took him nearly two hours to ascertain:

1. That the woman known as Marthe Donville had repeated word for word to the police official in charge of the station the story which she had told the guard on the train:
2. That her hair was in fact very blonde, probably bleached, and that she was fairly well dressed;
3. That her fur coat, according to the Superintendent, was cony, not worth more than fifteen hundred to two thousand francs at most;

4. That she was in fact carrying a small fibre suitcase of a light colour, such as are sold in all travel-goods shops and multiple stores;
5. That she did not seem anxious to lodge a complaint, but that when the police official insisted she had signed her statement in a somewhat uneducated hand;
6. That she had subsequently made her way to the exit . . .

The Little Doctor questioned the man who had been collecting tickets on the night in question. He had noticed the young woman, because not many passengers leave the station at Laroche-Migennes, where most people change trains.

'Was anyone waiting for her?'

'I didn't see anyone . . . It was pouring with rain . . . Outside the station there was only an old cab that waits there every night until midnight . . . But this woman didn't take it . . . Nor did she go to the hotel in the square . . . She turned right, walking fast, as though she knew her way about the town.'

No one had seen her again, and it was in vain that Dollent, like an authentic police detective, visited all the hotels in Laroche, in none of which had any young woman stayed that night, nor anyone registered under the name of Marthe Donville during the past fortnight.

Could it be that the woman had not been lying, but had really gone to her sister's? And if that sister was married, her name would be different and it would be impossible to find her.

But why had she given a false address in Paris?

The Little Doctor had reached this point in his reflections, and had just gone into a café for a hot toddy, when he gave a start; he had just recognized a customer who sat there reading a newspaper.

It was his candle-manufacturer, Monsieur Etienne Chaput, who came to greet him, quite unabashed, holding out a limp hand.

'It occurred to me last night that I might be able to help you, and since business is quiet just now I took the train . . . I knew I couldn't fail to find you here . . . Well, doctor, have you found anything yet?'

His forced smile made his face look even flabbier.

II. In Which the Little Doctor Follows a Trail Patiently, like a Swimmer against the Stream, and Begins to Sense that He is Being Fooled

'I don't want to be in the way!' Etienne Chaput protested. 'If you like I'll stay here . . . You must just let me know when you need me . . . I won't interfere at all. In any case I've brought my salesbook along and

I shall take advantage of whatever spare time I have to bring certain accounts up to date . . .'

Dollent had taken a room at a second-class hotel, the *Cloche d'Or*, and by eight o'clock next morning was out on the trail.

It was a grey, damp day. The trees had already shed most of their leaves and the roads were thick with mud.

Since there was no main road running parallel to the railway, the Little Doctor was obliged to venture into the lanes in quest of his 'kilometre 139'. But before reaching it he questioned the gate-keeper at the Cézy level crossing.

'Do you remember the night when the express train No. 19 stopped at your level crossing? Could you tell me if, about the time when the train drew up, a car was parked somewhere nearby?'

'There was no car!' the man asserted without the slightest hesitation. 'You notice cars at night because of the headlights. And I'd have noticed it all the more because the crossing stayed closed longer than usual.'

'You saw nobody get off the train?'

'You know, from here, I can only make out the engine. There must have been a brakesman running alongside the train with a red light . . .'

It would have been too much to expect, of course! Had he really hoped the gate-keeper would say: 'Yes, there was a powerful car waiting near the gate . . . I saw a shadow gliding alongside the train . . . A man got into the car, which dashed off at top speed as the gate opened . . .'

'Is Kilometre 139 far from here?'

'About as far as the little wood you can see on the right . . . But you're not allowed to go along the railway line; you'll have to walk through the copse.'

He did so. He was determined to pursue his investigation patiently, to check the slightest details with great care before embarking on any far-fetched deductions.

Leaving Tin Lizzie on the road, he started off down a narrow path where wet brambles caught at him as he went past, amid the depressing surroundings typical of a railway cutting – telegraph poles, blackened ballast and bare tree-trunks, and weeds growing as thickly as on a waste land.

For at least a quarter of an hour he had been floundering along, and the water was coming in over the tops of his shoes, when the landscape changed quite abruptly. A clear stream was flowing on his right, and it must have been full of crayfish. It was edged with willows. Black and white cows were grazing on a gently sloping meadow, and the roof of a farm was outlined against the cloudy sky.

Then suddenly there was a road, not a tarred main road but a good, well-kept country road. Through the trees, the Little Doctor thought he could make out some swings, and he hurried on until he came to an attractive house-front, a gable displaying an advertisement for some apéritif, and green-painted benches on either side of the door.

Au Rendezvous des Fins Pêcheurs, said an inn sign bearing an artless representation of a salmon trout, such as was assuredly not to be found in the stream.

'Anybody there?' he called out. 'Hello there! *Patron!* . . .'

He was amazed to see a handsome girl come out of a room at the back. She was tall, well made, with a pile of dark hair, a firm bosom and shapely hips. She had presumably been busy with housework, for she was wiping her hands on her apron.

'What is it?'

'Well, I shouldn't be sorry to drink a glass of white wine . . . Besides, there's such an appetizing smell about that I'd rather like to lunch here, if you don't mind . . .'

'Léon!' the woman shouted, turning round. 'Come here a minute . . .'

She made no attempt to serve him, but stood there hesitating; and a thin man, who seemed only half awake, even at that time of the morning, scrutinized the stranger with a certain insolence.

'This gentleman would like to lunch here . . .'

Léon looked at the road, saw no car, and asked brashly: 'How did you come?'

'On foot!' the Little Doctor calmly replied. 'The countryside is delightful, and I'm enjoying a ramble. I asked Mademoiselle . . .'

'Madame! She's my wife!'

'. . . I asked Madame, then, to bring me a jug of white wine . . .'

'Go and draw some out of the barrel,' the man said to his wife.

'I suppose that at this time of year you don't get many visitors . . .'

The man made no answer, but his piercing gaze never left the Little Doctor's face.

'A friend from Paris told me: "Since you're going into the neighbourhood of Cézy, don't fail to have a meal at the *Rendezvous des Fins Pêcheurs*. It's the best inn in the whole region . . ."'

'Your friend told you that?' the man queried with a touch of sarcasm.

'He must have come to dine here recently . . . Let me try and remember . . . It was . . . let's see . . . about ten days ago. October 12th, I fancy.'

'Then it was the gentleman who sat in that corner,' said Léon, taking the jug of wine from his wife's hands. 'You remember him, Germaine? A short stout man with a very high colour, wearing plus fours?'

'That's him,' agreed the Little Doctor. 'I don't remember if he came in his car or if . . .'

'In his car . . . A grey American eight-cylinder car, wasn't it, Germaine?'

From that moment, the Little Doctor began to feel ill at ease. He could not have defined the cause of his disquiet, but he had the impression that strange glances were passing between the landlord and his wife.

Furthermore, things were going too smoothly; replies were coming too readily, and perhaps in rather too much detail.

'I can tell you what your friend had to eat . . . First some cold salmon; we had some left over from the day before . . . Then a mushroom omelette . . . With all the rain we've been having, there's no end of mushrooms in the fields . . .'

Why did he assume an almost threatening tone to say *no end of mushrooms in the fields*?

And why did his wife, who must have had work to do elsewhere, stand there with her arms folded, swaying from one foot to the other?

'Didn't he stay the night here?'

'No . . . He was expecting a friend . . .'

'And what time did the friend turn up?'

The man and his wife exchanged glances. It was the woman who replied:

'About half past ten, maybe eleven.'

'Did he come by car too?'

'No, on foot . . . He was soaking wet . . . He was cold . . . He drank three glasses of rum straight off, then they went away together, asking me the best route for Luchon . . .'

'Luchon, on the Spanish frontier?'

'Yes . . . They were both going to Spain, as far as I could make out.'

'Did the man who came on foot have any luggage?'

'Just a brief-case, the sort businessmen always carry . . .'

The Little Doctor was on edge, and his ears had turned crimson. He had never so clearly felt that he was being made a fool of. But what could he do? He had asked questions. He had been given answers. How could he tell whether the story had been invented for a special reason, or whether the answers were genuine?

'Have you come to the neighbourhood for a rest?'

'For a few days, yes . . .'

'In that case, if you'd like a room . . .'

'I'm not sure yet . . . It's possible . . . By the way, when it left here would the grey car have gone over the level crossing at Cézy?'

'No, it was going in the opposite direction . . . As for your lunch, we'll do our best to please you . . . You won't be treated as well as your friend, for we've no more salmon . . . What would you say to some crayfish done in a court-bouillon, followed by a nice slice of roast lamb with beans? . . . Is there some cheese left, Germaine?'

While he spoke, the Little Doctor, who was in the mood for noting details, made the following observations:

1. The landlord of this inn was not unlike the proprietor of some bistrot in the neighbourhood of the République or the Bastille. It's true that a good many of those gentlemen retire into the country, where they condescend to become innkeepers.
2. Germaine was even less of a rustic type than her husband, and one could sooner picture her dressed in bright colours, perched on high heels and wearing make-up, than in a servant's apron.
3. Both of them repeatedly gave the impression that they were expecting a visit from the Little Doctor, and that the answers to all his questions had been prepared in advance.
4. Finally, a detail which was somewhat alarming: the nearest house was the farm whose roof could be seen over six hundred metres away; nobody, not even Chaput the candle-manufacturer, knew where Dollent was, so that if he should disappear . . .

He felt a chill between his shoulder-blades, and recalled, for no precise reason, a story he had read as a child about travellers venturing into a Spanish inn which was really a nest of brigands . . . Hadn't somebody just mentioned Spain?

The innkeeper was smiling: 'A little more white wine? It's a local vintage . . . Your friend enjoyed it very much . . . By the way, what was his name? Robert? . . . No! . . . Don't *you* remember, Germaine?'

It was an invitation to the Little Doctor, who did not trouble to reply. The other man went on – and his irony was now patent:

'A good fellow, he was! And a gourmet . . . He enjoyed life! . . . I wonder what's become of him . . .'

Was it a warning? Was Léon playing at cat and mouse with his guest?

'He promised to send us postcards . . . But perhaps you've had news of him? . . . I'm trying to recall his name . . . Let's see . . . Etienne?'

A brief, piercing glance.

'Etienne? . . . No, more like Germain . . . here's to your good health . . . Germaine, you'd better start seeing to lunch . . . Meanwhile I'll keep monsieur company . . . Unless he'd rather have a bit of a walk to get up an appetite?'

What did it all mean? Was a threat being followed by a hint that there was still time to get out? Or did all these intentions exist only in Dollent's mind?

Doesn't it sometimes happen that appearances are deceptive, that an over-excited imagination may mislead one into taking the simplest and most modest of places for a haunt of dangerous criminals?

'Do you like your meat rare? *Saignant*?' called out Germaine from the kitchen.

No! The Little Doctor didn't want to let himself be scared, and yet even that suggestion of blood . . .

Was he getting goose-pimples, like a frightened little girl?

III. In Which the Little Doctor Plays a Quiet Game of Belote, but In Which a Four of Jacks is not enough to Allay his Anxiety

The crayfish were excellent, the lamb was tender and tasty. Meanwhile the landlord, true in this respect to the tradition of country inns, did not leave his guest alone for one moment and allowed him no respite. Was it because he had nothing else to do, or did each of his remarks, on the contrary, conceal a secret meaning?

Curiously enough, the Little Doctor, although accustomed to rural solitude, had never experienced the anguish of isolation as keenly as today. The leaden grey sky, the dripping, leafless trees may have contributed to it.

Behind those trees, barely a hundred metres away, the black implacable line of the railway embankment with its rows of telegraph wires and crows wheeling overhead.

'Funny what fancies one gets . . .'

The innkeeper was speaking in disconnected phrases, like someone who has nothing to say but is simply trying to keep the conversation going.

'When you came in just now, I thought you were looking for your friend . . .'

A quick, furtive glance.

'I said to myself: here's somebody who's going to take the 2.17 train to Lyons to catch the connection with Luchon . . .'

Was this by way of a warning? After all, the place wasn't at the end of the world! Five or six hundred metres away there was a level crossing and a gate-keeper with his wife and children . . . And about the same distance away, towards the hill, a farm with cattle . . .

'You see how mistaken one can be,' went on the man, in no way put out by the silence of his guest, who was eating hungrily. 'You told me you wanted to sleep here, didn't you? By and by Germaine will get the best bedroom ready for you. You'll see how quiet it is here in the country . . . You'll hardly even hear the trains go by . . .'

Jean Dollent gave a start. He thought he had heard footsteps outside. And yet nobody entered the inn. On the other hand, all sounds had ceased in the kitchen.

'Will you take cheese? . . . No? . . . What do you plan to do this afternoon? In my opinion, it's going to rain . . . When you see the sky darken over there, it's a bad sign . . . In any case, if you've nothing better to do, we might try a game of three-handed *belote* . . .'

'I have to go to Laroche . . .'

'Oh, you have to go to Laroche? . . . That's right, I was forgetting you had a car . . . You left it by the level crossing, didn't you? . . . Let's hope the gate-keeper's kids, young rascals, haven't been playing with it . . .'

Dollent had no further doubt. All this was being said intentionally, and he found it hard to go on with his meal with apparent serenity.

He felt all the more uneasy when Germaine came back into the kitchen a little later with muddy shoes. It was she who had gone out. He reckoned that she'd had time to go as far as the level crossing and back.

He was having his coffee when the telephone bell rang. He noted with relief that the instrument was not in a box but on the wall in the dining-room. The landlord picked up the receiver. It was obviously a long distance call, for he had to wait a few minutes before it came through.

'Hello . . . Yes . . . It's me . . . Yes . . . Yes . . . Of course . . .'

Why did he keep staring at the Little Doctor as he made these monosyllabic replies? Was it just mechanically, because one's got to look at something? He displayed no surprise, no emotion. He gave more than ever the impression of a resolute, self-confident man, who knows exactly where he is going.

'Yes . . . That's agreed, then . . . Germaine sends her love . . .'

And as he hung up, he murmured for the benefit of his customer:

'That was my sister-in-law asking for news.'

Dollent was tempted to put in: 'Her name is Marthe, isn't it?' But he restrained himself, and sat sipping the calvados he had ordered.

His experiences today recalled a childhood memory. At his parents' home there had been some curious jars in which a layer of honey was spread. Flies went in, and when they touched the honey they would flounder there for hours before becoming completely engulfed in it.

Never before had an investigation given him such a sense of secret anguish. Never before, when tackling a criminal case, had he realized that he was at risk.

Here he saw, or rather felt, the threat of danger everywhere.

'I'm going as far as Laroche!' he announced, lighting a cigarette. 'Shall I settle up with you now?'

He added, with a touch of irony himself: 'In case I don't come back!'

'Don't bother! *You'll be back*!'

'May I go up to my room for a minute to have a wash?'

'Germaine! Take monsieur to no. 3.'

He felt no need for a wash, but he had just determined to take his precautions, at the risk of seeming a fool if he was mistaken.

On a sheet of paper torn from his prescription pad, he wrote:

'Monsieur le commissaire,

'If I am not in your office by four o'clock, will you send a taxi to the inn *Aux Fins Pêcheurs*, a little way beyond the Cézy level crossing along the railway line.

'If, moreover, you have no news of me by six o'clock, I think you had better inform the *gendarmerie*, so that they can make a raid on the said place.

'My name is Jean Dollent. A telephone call to Superintendent Lucas of the Police Judiciaire will confirm that you can trust me completely.

'It might be as well, finally, to have a certain Etienne Chaput followed; he is staying at the *Hôtel de la Cloche d'Or*.

'Believe me, Superintendent. . . .'

And on another note he wrote:

'Please convey this letter urgently, by any possible means, to the address indicated. Enclosed a hundred-franc note for the messenger. It's a matter of life or death.'

'Are you going out too?' asked the Little Doctor in some surprise, when, on returning to the public room, he found the *patron* wearing a soft hat and a raincoat.

'Why yes, I'm coming along with you as far as the level crossing. A little walking's good for the digestion . . .'

When they got there, Dollent's car was still parked by the side of the road where he had left it.

'Don't you often have trouble with that old jalopy?' queried the innkeeper.

'Not too often,' replied the Little Doctor, getting into his seat. 'Goodbye for the present . . . I'll be back by evening . . .'

'Have a good trip!'

But he pulled the self-starter in vain. The engine was dead. He got out, opened the bonnet, but could see nothing wrong. Had somebody discharged the accumulators? Had a wire been cut, somewhere out of sight?

'Shall I give you a hand?' the innkeeper offered ironically.

'No, thanks . . . I think something's badly wrong . . .'

He lingered none the less, opened the tool-box and scattered the tools on the ground. His mistrusted the gate-keeper, who was standing in his doorway. He hoped for other help, and he was not disappointed, for after a few minutes a car came over the level crossing. It slowed down on account of the bend in the road. He rushed out to meet it, and jumped on to the running-board.

'I've had a breakdown,' he shouted. 'Would you be kind enough to call at a garage for me . . .'

And at the same time he dropped his letter on to the knees of the driver, who appeared to be a commercial traveller.

'Well, there we are! . . . I think I shall just have to give up my drive to Laroche and go home with you . . . You suggested a game of three-handed *belote*, and if your offer still stands I really shan't be sorry to kill time . . .'

'A tierce!'

'What value?'

'High . . . Diamonds . . .'

'It's yours . . .'

The game continued in the dimly-lit room, with all the traditional phrases creating a familiar hum; the atmosphere was typical of so many inn-parlours in bad weather, and outside, as the *patron* had foretold, a drizzle had begun to fall, veiling the landscape.

'I trump you . . . Double belote . . . Clubs high, spades high . . . If it hadn't been for that eight of hearts I'd have taken all the tricks . . .'

Was the Little Doctor losing? was he winning? Several times already he had made mistakes, and he almost forgot to declare four jacks!

From time to time he turned to look at an ancient clock whose hands were moving jerkily forward and whose brass pendulum caught a gleam of light with each swing.

'Let's see your four jacks . . .'

And while playing he was striving to think clearly.

One point was indisputable: the innkeeper, Léon as his wife called him, knew perfectly well why Dollent was here, and had made it plain to him.

But hadn't the man also given him to understand that he would do better to take himself off towards Luchon and the Spanish frontier? Didn't this mean that the air in the neighbourhood of Cézy was unhealthy for inquisitive people?

The breakdown of his car had undoubtedly been caused by Germaine, when she had disappeared during lunchtime.

So they must have wanted to prevent the doctor from returning to Laroche. Why?

What was the telephone call that Léon had received from his sister-in-law?

'They know I'm on the right track!' he thought. 'They probably know who I am, or at any rate they take me for a policeman. It looks as if they were trying to gain time. Couldn't this be so as to get rid of me more easily under cover of darkness?'

He was unarmed. He had never carried a gun, and to tell the truth, he was somewhat scared of firearms. Léon was bigger and stronger than himself. Furthermore, he would have the advantage of being able to take his opponent by surprise when he chose to attack.

Half past three. From time to time Léon got up to fetch the bottle of calvados from a shelf and refill the little glasses.

Then all three pricked up their ears as they heard the sound of a car. Could the police superintendent have sent that taxi already?

The car was driving slowly, as though on purpose. It passed even more slowly in front of the inn, and then Dollent saw that it was indeed a taxi, but that there was somebody inside it. Pressed against the window was the heavy, unpleasant face of Monsieur Chaput, the candle-manufacturer.

The car did not stop. It probably did not go far but turned round at the next crossroads, for a few minutes later it drove past again in the opposite direction, still just as slowly, with the fat man inside on the lookout. He seemed to be trying to discern what was going on in the inn.

'Your cards!' said Léon, to recall the Little Doctor to the game.

He was quite calm. He pretended not to have noticed the car. But when it drove past for the third time he frowned.

'What does he want, that great lump? . . . I declare fifty . . . Is he going to spend all afternoon driving back and forth? . . . Your turn, Germaine . . . Is my fifty okay?'

There was tension in the air now. That car had become as exasperating as some big fly that buzzes round one's face in August, when one doesn't know where it is going to alight. Would it ever stop?

Then there came an interruption in the rhythm, during which the car was not seen; it coincided with a telephone call, which Léon answered.

But this time, while he was speaking, his eyes grew sterner and his face assumed an expression scarcely compatible with that of an honest innkeeper. He uttered monosyllables like threats:

'Yes . . . Okay . . . Yes . . . Right . . . Yes . . .'

He returned to his seat.

'Whose deal?'

But before he had distributed the cards the telephone rang once more. He displayed renewed irritation, but the Little Doctor had the impression that this time he was putting on an act.

'Dr Dollent wanted on the phone!' he said.

'You're sure it's for me?'

'So long as you're Dr Dollent . . .'

The doctor picked up the receiver, and immediately recognized the hesitant voice of the candle-manufacturer, which was almost as oily as his person.

'Hello! . . . I thought best to telephone you, for I don't like the look of that inn much . . . I wanted to tell you, doctor . . . Are you there? . . . I think it would be better not to proceed any further in this business . . . I've thought it over . . . I've received certain information . . . Needless to say I shall reimburse you . . . We didn't fix a fee for your collaboration, but if you will meet me in town I will hand over ten thousand francs for your expenses . . . Are you there? . . . You're not answering . . . Hello?

'Hello!' the Little Doctor repeated. He did not know what to reply, being thus taken by surprise.

'I beg you not to go any further . . . It was my fault . . . The police tell me that the charge will not be maintained, or rather that it will not be brought at all, since the plaintiff gave a false address . . . In point of fact there is no longer any plaintiff . . . And in that case it is unnecessary to . . .'

Dollent never batted an eyelid. He cast an apparently casual glance at the couple who sat waiting there, holding their cards.

'I was told that your car had broken down . . . That's to say I noticed it standing beside the level crossing and I made inquiries . . . That was how I learned that you were at the inn . . . If you like I'll send a taxi to fetch you and . . .'

'Come and fetch me yourself!' the Little Doctor said firmly.

Then, to cut short the fellow's long-winded explanations, he hung up.

'Spades trumps? My trick,' he said, sitting down in his place and examining his cards.

IV. In Which Three-handed Belote becomes Four-handed Belote, and In Which the Little Doctor, Seduced by Calvados, becomes Disgracefully Tipsy

It all happened quite amiably, and anyone who had gone into the room would certainly have noticed nothing unusual, except perhaps that Monsieur Etienne Chaput, having decided to spend some time in the inn, was wasting his money by keeping his taxi waiting.

He came in like some innocent thirsty traveller, and after a gesture of greeting to the card-players he sat down in the opposite corner.

'Some beer!' he replied when Germaine inquired what he wanted to drink.

He mopped his brow; he tried to convey to the Little Doctor by signs:

'Here I am . . . Now you've only to go out with me and get into my taxi . . .'

But something suspicious, to say the least, was happening to that taxi. The innkeeper at one point got up, left the room, went out to the taxi driver, handed him a hundred-franc note and said something to him; whereupon the taxi drove off in the direction of the town.

The strangest thing, however, was that the fat man, Etienne Chaput, did not even protest! He sat there in his corner, round-eyed, his forehead damp with anguish.

The Little Doctor, however, was smiling.

'Perhaps Monsieur would like to make a fourth?' he said pleasantly. 'Four-handed *belote* is much more exciting than three-handed and . . .'

'I play so badly, you know . . .'

Moreover he was so worried that a few minutes later the cards were shaking in his hand!

'Would you mind leaving the bottle on the table, *patron*? The calvados is excellent . . . It's years since I drank any like it . . . Your health, ladies and gentlemen . . . Let's hope I get another four jacks . . .'

Ten minutes past four . . . Half past four . . . It was still raining, the sky was growing darker and night was about to fall . . .

The atmosphere must have depressed the Little Doctor, for he had frequent recourse to the bottle of calvados, so much so that the others began watching him with some anxiety. His eyes grew brighter, his voice shriller, and he kept jumping about like a jack-in-the-box, and making jokes that were not always in good taste. The main object of his attack was Etienne Chaput, on whom he lavished scathing abuse.

'Do you know what our little party reminds me of?' he remarked, when he had already drunk a good deal. 'Of three professionals fleecing a sucker . . . For our friend, you must admit, is a typical sucker . . . If he makes a lot of money I'm sure it all goes into the hands of pretty girls who know all the tricks . . . And I suppose they convince him that he's loved for his own sake!'

'Tierce!' mournfully declared Etienne Chaput, who now felt he had fallen into a trap.

But what could he do? Wasn't he practically a prisoner? No car outside; an empty road, glistening wetly, and trees, an endless railway cutting . . .

'Tierce again . . . King!'

The hands were moving forward on the pale clock-face. Half past four . . . Five o'clock . . . Then the Little Doctor, with a sudden spurt of energy, seized the bottle of calvados.

'Your glasses are absurdly small, Madame Germaine . . . When I like a drink I can never resist . . .'

He was swallowing such huge gulps that he turned pale and began coughing frantically. Then he tried to pick up his cards again, but they looked a blur.

'A cup of coffee?' suggested Léon.

'Coffee? . . . Coffee for me? . . . I'd rather have calvados . . .'

This time they stopped him grabbing the bottle. He got up to seize it by force and rolled on to the floor. He struggled to his feet, laughing derisively.

'I want to go to sleep,' he then announced thickly. 'Where's my room? Bring me my room at once, or I won't stay any longer in this hole . . .'

The landlord took him by the shoulders and helped him up the stairs to the first floor, laid him down fully dressed on the bed and remained a few minutes listening to his hoarse drunken breathing.

Without moving from his bed, the Little Doctor took off his shoes, then, with infinite precautions, crossed the room as far as the washbasin. He had already noticed that the downstairs room had no proper ceiling. Above the exposed beams there was only the thin layer of wood of the bedroom floor. Already he could hear the murmur of voices below him.

But he was drunk, drunker than he had ever been. With fellows like Léon it would have been useless to make a pretence of drinking, and he had really swallowed over half a litre of spirits.

A minute later, he did what he used to do after drinking bouts in his student days. He thrust a finger down his throat and, without too much difficulty, brought up all that he had swallowed.

None the less his face was still bathed in sweat, his tongue felt coated, his eyes seemed to be starting out of his head.

He lay down at full length on the floor and pressed his ear to the boards, just above the table where they were playing *belote*.

He heard Léon's voice speaking with repressed fury:

'Are you crazy, landing us with this fellow? . . . We're not on the train now and it's a bit harder to get rid of a stiff . . .'

'You're sure he's asleep?' asked Germaine.

'He's dead drunk . . . But go and see if you like.'

Dollent had time to go back to bed and start snoring loudly. He felt the woman bending over him, and he realised that she was as tough as Léon, if not more so, for she took the precaution of feeling his pockets.

He even wondered . . . Didn't it perhaps occur to her to put an end to him right away and have done with it?

He felt he must not open his eyes or move. The worst moment came when, while withdrawing his wallet, she tickled him, and he had never found it so hard to keep still.

Finally, a few moments later, she moved away, locked the door from outside and went down the stairs.

As for Dollent, he jumped up and lay down on the floor again.

V

Etienne Chaput was as cowardly as his physical appearance suggested; he was morally as slimy as his skin; and he was greedy into the bargain.

His words betrayed him:

'It wasn't my fault . . . When the job was done and you left me in the lurch . . .'

'We didn't leave you in the lurch, you fool . . . We sent you ten lovely notes . . . Ten grand . . .'

In other words, ten thousand francs, exactly the sum which the candle-manufacturer had, in his recent telephone call, offered the Little Doctor to call off the search.

'You sent me ten grand, that's true . . . But you know the job brought you in about a million . . .'

'So what?'

'It's not fair . . . It wasn't what Marthe promised me . . .'

'What did my sister promise you, fathead?' Germaine's voice took on a coarser note. 'In the first place it was her fault for bringing in an imbecile like you on the job . . . When she comes I shall tell her so . . . The very idea!'

'She promised we should share . . .'

'Share what?'

'The money from the job . . .'

'What job?'

'The job you were going to do when the train stopped . . . She said something about mailbags and I don't know what else . . . She needed someone to help her get the train stopped . . . She thought of me because I used to see her every week . . . I kept her, in a sort of way . . .'

'You don't say! What used you to give her?'

'Two hundred francs a time . . . I met her on Wednesdays in a brasserie on the boulevards . . .'

'Cut it out!'

Thus, the Little Doctor made a mental note, Etienne Chaput was really ignorant of the whole business . . . Like many men of his sort, he used to meet the woman Marthe every week in a tavern on the Grands Boulevards; he was certainly not alone in enjoying her favours.

But since, for her performance in the train, she needed somebody apparently respectable, she had picked on him . . .

She must have sensed, long ago, that the candle-manufacturer's honesty would not be proof against the temptation of big money.

And yet she had not told him the whole truth. She had only mentioned a mail robbery, whereas really . . .

If the Superintendent had been there, the Little Doctor could have told him all the rest of the story; meanwhile, however, he preferred to listen to what was being said down below, in this inn which was undoubtedly quite as nightmarish as the Spanish tavern he had read about in his childhood.

'. . . she swore to me that I was in no danger . . . that afterwards there'd be a tidy sum to share out . . . Those were her very words . . .'

'Well, you unspeakable fool, I'll tell you what danger you're in . . . You're in danger of losing your life, d'you hear? . . . That'll teach you to try and put something over on me . . . You're a real bastard to have called in a private dick and . . .'

'I only wanted to put him on your trail . . . I didn't know anything about it . . . I thought there might be something going on up here, but I couldn't make the inquiry on my own . . .'

'You were scared!'

'I wanted to find you again to ask for my share . . . It's only fair, since I was a partner . . .'

'Partner, you say? Hear that, Germaine? . . . When people that call themselves respectable start doing the dirty, they're beyond anything! Monsieur wanted to blackmail us! And since Monsieur – just look at his mug! – didn't dare go to the cops, he hunts out a quack who goes in for private investigations . . . You've seen the doctor; he's a pretty specimen, isn't he? . . . Monsieur sends him after us, just as you'd set a dog to pick up a trail . . . Then when the trail's been found he calls him back . . . He says; "Sorry, my mistake . . . Here are ten or twenty thou' for your expenses . . ."

'Isn't that it? . . . Eh, fat-face, you dare tell me it wasn't like that?'

And the 'fat-face' replied, humbly but stubbornly:

'I wanted my share . . .'

'Well, you'll get your share, but not your share of what you think . . . Your share of the work, sure . . .

'The mailbags were just a dodge of Marthe's to take you in . . . The real job was to bump off a well-heeled Englishman who was travelling on the *rapide* 19 to Marseilles and there taking the boat for India.

'We knew he'd a whole pile of English bank-notes with him – *sterlingues* – so somebody got on the train with him in Paris . . .'

That somebody being, of course, Léon himself, the Little Doctor could have sworn. For although to begin with he had suspected a large and well-organized gang, he was now convinced that the gang consisted of three people only: Léon and the two sisters, Marthe and Germaine.

And Dollent could not help feeling a certain admiration for this temporary innkeeper, who, without making a single slip . . .

Meanwhile, had his note been conveyed to the police? Or had the motorist chucked it into the ditch? Had the Superintendent taken the whole thing for a hoax? It was nearly six o'clock, and there was no sign of the taxi he had asked for . . .

'Just before Montereau, where the train crosses the Seine, we tipped the Englishman overboard, and down he went into the water, with a heavy weight on his feet . . .'

The Little Doctor felt sure he heard the candle-manufacturer groan.

'That was quite a job, you know . . . Only we had to make sure of getting away with the notes before coming to a big station . . . That was why the train had to be stopped . . . The man . . . Well, the one who . . .'

'It was you?'

'If they ask you, I'd advise you to say you know nothing about it. That's all! We sent you ten thou', and that was a tidy sum, it'll enable you to treat yourself to good-looking tarts like Marthe, two or three times a week, till the end of your days . . .'

Dollent could scarcely believe in the reality of his surroundings. And yet outside the windows the rain was falling, the trees were shivering in the wind, the occasional train passed . . .

'I didn't know . . .' moaned Monsieur Chaput.

'What didn't you know? . . . That we were going to bump off a man? . . . Your neck's beginning to feel uneasy, isn't it? . . . Not to mention that for a chap of your build it'll need a good sharp blade . . . Your neck's going to ache a good deal more, by and by . . .

'Oh, so you landed us with that doctor of yours . . .

'Well, now, you've got to get rid of him for us . . . Let's see how you're going to set about it . . .'

'By giving him a considerable sum of money,' Chaput suggested.

'You think everybody's like yourself? None of that nonsense, my boy . . . You can just go up into his room – it's no.3, the number's painted on the door. We'll give you a knife, or a gun, just as you like, or an axe if you'd rather . . . It doesn't matter if he screams, out here . . . After that you'll go and dig a hole in the ground somewhere . . .'

'I can't . . .'

'What?'

'I implore you . . . I'm not a murderer . . . I'd never be able to . . .'

'But you'd be quite able to pull the chestnuts out of the fire, surely? . . . Come on, my beauty . . . If you didn't make us feel so sick we'd lend you a hand . . . But it'll be a joke to watch you doing it all by yourself . . .'

'You can't force me to kill a man . . . If you'd just let me talk to him for five minutes . . . I'll give him what money's needed out of my own pocket . . . I'm not a rich man . . . Nowadays candles aren't . . .'

'Time to burn one now, wouldn't you say? . . . Come on! If you wait till he wakes up, there might be trouble . . . D'you want a glass of calvados before getting down to work? . . . Or a glass of rum, like in the condemned cell? . . . No? . . . Well then . . .'

The Little Doctor felt sick with disgust. The man was weeping and beseeching. He must have gone down on his knees, to judge by the sounds heard from the first floor.

'I tell you I'm incapable of it . . . The mere sight of blood . . .'

'Take a hammer then.'

It was ten minutes to six. The Little Doctor had already glanced out of the window, and decided to venture on the five-metre drop down to the terrace, at the risk of breaking a leg.

'Made up your mind?'

'If I must . . .'

Dollent might have thought he had witnessed the lowest depths of human meanness and cowardice. Presumably, down below, they were putting a hammer or some such tool into the hands of the obese Etienne Chaput, who must have been shaking in every limb.

And yet, just as he was moving towards the staircase, he halted.

'*If I do it, shall we go shares*?' he asked.

The window was already open. Dollent reckoned that by taking a longish jump he could land on soft ground. He was waiting, wanting to see the expression on the candle-manufacturer's face when he opened the door.

This satisfaction, however, was denied him. He first heard the bell of a bicycle speeding down the hill, and a moment later three bicycles stopped in front of the inn and three gendarmes alighted, their silver braid gleaming in the darkness.

'Don't let anyone out!' Dollent shouted from the window.

He was angrier than he had ever been, furious at having encountered a sample of humanity which nauseated him, and which was going to put an end to his optimism for some time to come.

He wished the door would open so that he could tackle Etienne Chaput himself and . . . He didn't know what he would have done to him; he might even have been capable of punching him in the eye.

In the house, people were running about; doors were being opened and closed noisily, shouts were heard and finally a shot was fired.

He made up his mind and jumped, in order to find out, because nobody was bothering about him now. In the public room a gendarme held the candle-manufacturer covered with his revolver, and the man, more terrified than ever, was weeping copiously and swearing that . . .

He was ready to swear whatever was required of him. The sight of the Little Doctor restored his hopes.

'The proof of my innocence is that Monsieur Dollent, whose help I sought to clear me from the charge . . .'

'Is going to get you jailed for as long as possible!' cut in Dollent.

'But . . .'

Another shot rang out behind them, in the direction of the garden. Then a sergeant came back with Germaine. She seemed quite unperturbed, in fact wore a slight smile.

'Hullo, so you're not drunk now . . . In that case, it's all been my fault . . . And yet I tickled you hard enough to . . .'

So she had done it deliberately! And it was only thanks to the Little Doctor's presence of mind . . .

'It's impossible to catch the other chap,' the second gendarme admitted. 'He's gone into the wood . . . We must ring up the station . . . He fired at me and only missed me by a hair's breadth . . . I even felt the wind whistle round my cap . . .'

A car drew up in front of the door; it brought the police Superintendent.

'What is happening? I met the taxi I had sent for you, which had broken down . . .'

'So much the better . . .'

'Why?'

'Because otherwise we should hardly have known anything . . . I should have told you the story, but I'd have had no proofs, I'd not have been sure I was right . . .'

The oddest part of the business was the way the Little Doctor eyed the bottle of calvados. He was feeling empty; a short while ago he had drunk some, indeed, but out of duty. Now he wanted to taste it.

'May I?'

Germaine was looking at him admiringly, and since he almost felt a certain admiration for her, he was pleased.

'You see, Superintendent, we are confronted here with an almost perfect crime . . . But for that tub of rancid fat, I think we should have had a perfect crime to deal with . . . Or rather we shouldn't have had to deal with it, since perfect crimes are never discovered. You would have learnt that a certain English lord had disappeared, but you would never have seen the connection between his disappearance and a certain incident on a train, during which a young woman pulled the communication cord so as to put an end to the attentions of a slimy character . . .'

Needless to say, the Superintendent understood not a word of all this. Jean Dollent, relaxed at last, was talking to satisfy himself and also, to some extent, to impress Germaine, who was listening to him with interest and who was quite capable of appreciating his story.

'Knowing what I do, I doubt whether you will lay hands on the murderer of the English lord . . . But you have another murderer before you . . . a murderer from motives of fear and cowardice . . . Monsieur Etienne Chaput, manufacturer of ecclesiastical candles and phony rapist when required . . .'

The gendarme had already telephoned headquarters. In less than an hour the whole neighbourhood would be surrounded to ensure the capture of Léon.

'You'll see that you won't catch him . . . A fellow who could bring off an almost perfect crime! But you've got the other, and that's almost better, for his sentence will be all the severer, as I hope . . .

'Come on, Superintendent. If you'd like to have dinner with me, at the station buffet at Laroche-Migennes, for instance, I'll tell you the whole story . . .'

Just as they were about to leave, he was seen to rush into a corner of the room. On the floor there lay a blacksmith's sledge-hammer. He picked it up, murmuring: 'May I take it away?'

'?'

'As a souvenir! This is what this gentleman was going to lay me out with during my sleep, and so you can see . . .'

It was the first item in his panoply, the start of a collection!

Arsenic Hall

I. In Which the Little Doctor Politely Asks Someone: Are You a Murderer? and is Received with Perfect Courtesy

After no more than a quarter of a second's hesitation he stood on tiptoe – he was not tall, and the bell was exaggeratedly high up. Immediately two distinct varieties of noise broke out, as though in rivalry: on the one hand the bell, which the Little Doctor had set ringing somewhere in the château, as loud as a whole carillon; on the other hand the barking of a multitude of dogs.

And this is no figure of speech; there really was a multitude, if one can so describe some forty horrible mongrels, dirty little ginger dogs of no particular breed, but all alike except that some were old and some young.

They, too, came from somewhere in the depths of the château, and rushed towards the garden gate, crossing what had at one time been a park but now consisted merely of a tangle of brambles around the feet of a few big trees.

The Little Doctor knew that he was being watched, not only from the château but from the village houses, where people must be wondering who, at such a moment, was bold enough to ring at that gate.

It was in the Orléans forest, a village in a clearing. But the clearing, like some old garment, had become too narrow for the big house and the handful of little ones. The forest spilled over, choking the hamlet, into which the sunlight could barely penetrate.

A few slate roofs: a general store, an inn, some low cottages. Then the château, too big, too old, dilapidated, looking like someone who has seen better days and whose clothes, though well cut, are now in rags.

Was the Little Doctor going to have to set that noisy bell ringing yet again, while all the little ginger dogs, baring their teeth, flung themselves in clusters against the gate?

A curtain twitched on the ground floor. A dim silhouette appeared for a moment behind the windows on the first floor. At last somebody came: a girl, or young woman, of twenty to twenty-five, an attractive maidservant, with comely face and figure, such as one would scarcely have expected to meet in such a place.

She drove away the dogs, picking them up by the scruff of the neck and flinging them off. 'What is it?' she asked.

'I should like to speak to Monsieur Mordaut . . .'

'Have you an appointment with him?'

'No.'

'Are you from the Department of Public Prosecution?'

'No. But if you'd be kind enough to hand him my card . . .'

She went off. The dogs' concert started up again. A little later she came back accompanied by another servant, a woman of about fifty with a wary look on her face.

'What d'you want with Monsieur Mordaut?'

Then the Little Doctor, feeling he would never get through this firmly guarded gate, decided to stake everything.

'It's about the poisonings,' he said with his most charming smile, as though offering a sweet.

The silhouette had reappeared behind the first floor window. It must surely be Monsieur Mordaut's.

'Come in, then . . . Is that your car? Bring it in too, because if you leave it outside the kids'll smash it up with stones . . .'

'Good morning, Monsieur. I apologize for practically forcing my way in, particularly as you have probably never heard my name?'

'Never,' the sad gentleman admitted, shaking his head.

'Just as others go in for graphology or water-divining, I have become passionately interested in the human problems, the puzzles, if you prefer, which criminal cases almost invariably present to begin with . . .'

The most difficult things still had to be done, or rather said. He was sitting there in a drawing-room. And that drawing-room represented a whole period, or rather the residue of a dozen periods, which had silted up there haphazardly over the years, indeed over the centuries.

Just like the outside of the château, everything inside was gloomy and dusty, faded, worn-out, shabby. And Monsieur Mordaut was like that himself; his jacket was so long that it recalled an old-fashioned frock coat, and his hollow cheeks were covered with a lichen growth of dingy grey beard.

'I'm ready to listen to you . . .'

Too late, now, to draw back!

'I was extremely interested, Monsieur, in the rumours which have been current lately about your château and about yourself. I understand that the legal authorities have ordered the exhumation of three bodies . . . I would rather tell you frankly that I have come in order to discover the truth, that's to say to learn whether you really poisoned your aunt Emilie Duplantet, then your wife, *née* Félicie Maloir, and finally your niece Solange Duplantet . . .'

It was certainly the first time he had ever spoken to anyone in such terms and he was all the more uneasy in that he was now at a considerable distance from the road and from the village, with many closed doors in between. Monsieur Mordaut, however, remained perfectly unmoved. He was swinging an old-fashioned pince-nez at the end of a long black cord, and the expression on his face could only be described, yet again, as supremely sad.

He exuded sadness! He was sadness personified! He was the embodiment of all the sadness in the world!

'You were quite right to speak to me frankly. Can I offer you any refreshment?'

Involuntarily the Little Doctor shuddered, for it is somewhat unnerving to be offered a drink by somebody one has just more or less crudely accused of poisoning three people.

'Don't be afraid . . . I shall drink first . . . I still have an old distilled wine which we used to make in the château before the days of phylloxera . . . Did you come through the village?'

'I stopped at the inn for a moment to make sure I could have a room.'

'That's unnecessary, Monsieur . . . I didn't catch your name?'

'Jean Dollent.'

'May I offer you hospitality, Monsieur Dollent?'

He was uncorking a dusty bottle of an unusual shape; and the Little Doctor drank, almost without apprehension, one of the best *vins cuits* he had ever tasted.

'You must stay here as long as you like . . . You can have your meals at my table. You can move freely about the château, and I will answer your questions with absolute frankness . . . Will you allow me?'

He pulled a woollen bell-rope and a shrill bell tinkled somewhere. Then the elderly woman who had opened the gate to Dollent appeared.

'Ernestine, will you lay an extra place? And will you prepare the green bedroom for Monsieur . . . He is to feel completely at home here, do you understand, and you are to answer any questions he may ask.'

Alone once more with Dollent, he heaved a sigh: 'You may perhaps be surprised by your reception here? You may even find it somewhat extraordinary? I tell you, Monsieur Dollent, that there comes a moment when one accepts any chance of salvation. If a fortune-teller, a fakir or a dervish, or a gipsy, or one of those water-diviners of whom you were speaking, had offered to help me, I should give them the same opportunities . . .'

He spoke slowly, wearily, staring at the worn carpet and automatically wiping with exaggerated care the pince-nez which he never put on his nose.

'I am a man who has been unlucky from birth. If there were a competition for bad luck I am sure I should win first prize. Whatever I do turns out badly. All my actions, all my words prove detrimental to me. I was born to accumulate misfortunes not only on my own head but on all around me.

'My grandparents were very rich. My grandfather Mordaut was the man who built most of the Haussmann district in Paris and he made millions. But on the day I was born he hanged himself on account of a scandal in which he was involved, together with a number of political men.

'My mother, overcome by the shock, succumbed in three days to puerperal fever.

'My father tried to rebuild the family fortunes . . . Of all my grandfather's wealth, only this château remained. I was five when we came here; while playing in the tower I set fire to a whole wing, which was destroyed together with all the valuable objects it contained . . .'

This was too much! The thing was grotesque.

'At ten years old I had a little friend of my own age whom I loved dearly, Gisèle, the innkeeper's daughter. In those days there was still water in the moat. One day when we were fishing for frogs with a scrap of red rag, she slipped and was drowned before my eyes . . .

'I could go on for a long time relating my misfortunes . . .'

'Forgive me,' the Little Doctor broke in, 'it seems to me, so far, that these misfortunes have afflicted others rather than yourself.'

'And don't you think that's the worst misfortune of all? Eight years ago my aunt Duplantet, having lost her husband, came to live with us here, and within six months she died of a heart attack.'

'It has been said that she had been slowly poisoned with arsenic . . . Hadn't she taken out a life insurance to your advantage, and didn't you benefit by a considerable sum?'

'A hundred thousand francs. Barely enough to prop up the south tower, which was collapsing . . . Three years later, my wife . . .'

'Died in her turn, again as a result of a heart attack. She, too, had taken out a life insurance, which brought you . . .'

'Which brought me two hundred thousand francs and the accusations which you know of . . .'

He sighed, putting on his well-polished pince-nez.

'Finally,' went on the Little Doctor, 'a fortnight ago your niece, Solange Duplantet, now orphaned, died in this house at the age of twenty-eight, of heart disease, leaving you the Duplantet fortune of about half a million . . .'

'In lands and property,' corrected his strange host.

'This time people began to gossip, anonymous letters reached the Public Prosecutor's office and an investigation was set on foot.'

'The officials of the Parquet have already been here three times and found nothing. On two other occasions I was sent for to Orléans to be questioned and confronted with "their" witnesses. I believe that if I ventured into the village I should be assaulted . . .'

'Because traces of arsenic were found in the bodies . . .'

'Apparently they always are . . .'

And that was why the Little Doctor was here! He had stopped in Paris on his way, and had seen his friend Superintendent Lucas. And Lucas had told him:

'I'm convinced they'll not discover anything. Poisoning cases are always the most mysterious. Are there many of them, or few? We cannot even answer that question with certainty, but it's undoubtedly in that field that there are the greatest number of unpunished crimes.

'You'll see that they will find arsenic in the viscera, or what is left of them. The experts will argue over this at great length, some declaring that there is always a certain amount of arsenic in corpses and others inclining to the poisoning theory.

'If the case comes up before the assizes, the jury, bewildered and discouraged by these learned arguments and by so many contradictory conclusions, will bring in a negative verdict.

'It's in this field that a man like yourself, with a little luck, might . . .'

He was on the spot. He was sniffing about, steeping himself in this desperately gloomy atmosphere.

'May I ask why you have so many dogs, all of the same breed, so to speak? . . .'

Monsieur Mordaut was quite surprised at the question.

'So many dogs?' he repeated. 'Oh yes . . . Tom and Mirza . . . I must explain that my father had two dogs of which he was very fond. These dogs, Tom and Mirza, had puppies, which grew up and had puppies in their turn. Since my little friend was drowned before my eyes, I have never been willing to have puppies or kittens drowned. The dogs you have seen are the progeny of Tom and Mirza. I don't know how many of them there are. Nobody bothers about them. They live in the park and run wild . . .'

An idea seemed to strike him, and he pondered.

'It's odd,' he murmured. 'They are the only creatures in my household who have flourished . . . I'd never thought about that . . .'

'You have a son?'

'Yes, Hector; you must have heard speak of him. As a result of an illness in childhood, although Hector grew physically his brain ceased to develop. He lives at home. At twenty-two his intelligence is roughly that of a child of nine . . . Yet he's not ill-natured . . .'

'The woman who showed me in, and whom you called Ernestine: has she been in your service a long time?'

'All her life. She was the daughter of my father's gardener. Her parents died and she stayed on.'

'She never married?'

'Never . . .'

'And the young woman?'

'Rose?' said Monsieur Mordaut with a slight smile. 'She's a niece of Ernestine's. She's been living at the château for about ten years, as housemaid. She was only sixteen when she came to us.'

'You have no other domestic staff?'

'Nobody. I can't afford to live in a grand style. I've had the same car for twenty years, and people turn round to stare at it when I drive past. I live among my books and my curios . . .'

'Do you often go to Paris?'

'Practically never. What should I do there? I'm not rich enough to treat myself to entertainments; I'm not poor enough to take a clerk's job . . . And I'm sure that if I were to speculate I'd lose everything. It would be just my luck!'

Listening to that muffled monotonous voice, Dollent had at times the impression of being stifled by a vast wet blanket! Were all the creatures in this house, including the comely Rose, equally withdrawn into themselves? Could one imagine a burst of genuine happy laughter ever sounding in these rooms and passages?

Then the Little Doctor had a shock. He had just heard a familiar noise, that of Tin Lizzie's engine being started.

He looked sternly at his host. 'Somebody's touching my car,' he said. And he was almost inclined to think that . . .

'Well, yes . . . You see! You've only just come, and we were having a quiet talk; you'll see that it was Hector who . . .'

He went to open a window, sighing. And as he had foretold, a huge youth was installed on the seat of Dollent's car, manipulating the gears with a horrible grating sound.

'Hector! Get down!'

Hector's only reply was to put out his tongue at his father.

'Hector! If you don't leave that gentleman's car alone . . .'

Monsieur Mordaut rushed outside. The Little Doctor followed him, and there witnessed a scene which was both painful and grotesque. The father was trying to drag his son off the seat. But Hector was the taller by a head, and particularly strongly built.

'I want to drive it,' he persisted.

'If you don't get down at once . . .'

'I'm not going to let you whip me again, I tell you that.'

In the kitchen doorway Ernestine was standing with her hands on her hips, impassively watching the struggle.

Another door opened, however. Rose, who had put on a white apron to wait at table and looked even more attractive in it, rushed up to the car.

'Leave him alone,' she said to Monsieur Mordaut. 'You know he's always stubborn with you. Come now, Monsieur Hector, you're not going to break the doctor's car?'

'Is he a doctor?' the young man asked mistrustfully. 'Who's he come to see?'

'Now you just get down. Be good . . .'

She could undoubtedly influence him; the mere sound of her voice seemed to quieten the half-witted youth who now, abandoning Tin Lizzie's gear levers, was studying Dollent.

'Who's he come to see? Is it about Ernestine's cancer again?'

'Yes, that's right. He's come about Ernestine's cancer.'

Tin Lizzie was safely stowed away in the garage which already housed the ancient car belonging to Monsieur Mordaut, who now led the Little Doctor into the garden.

'I must point out that Ernestine has not got cancer. But she's always talking about it . . . Since her sister, Rose's mother, died of cancer, she is convinced that she has it too. But she's not sure where it is. Sometimes it's in her back, sometimes in her chest, sometimes in her stomach . . . She spends her time consulting doctors, and she's annoyed because they can find nothing wrong with her. If she tells you about her cancer I'd advise you . . .'

But Ernestine now stood before them in a fury.

'Well, are you going to come and eat, yes or no? If you think that lunch can be kept waiting for ever . . .'

And so three women, apart from the two servants, had lived in this house, and all three of them, at various ages, had died, ostensibly of heart disease, which is generally the superficial diagnosis of arsenic poisoning, at any rate of those cases of slow poisoning in which the murderer distils death, day by day for months on end, into his victim . . .

At table there was a carafe of wine and one of water. The meal itself was commonplace, if not meagre: a few sardines, a few radishes, as in a second-class restaurant, then a mutton stew, a bit of dry cheese and a couple of biscuits per person.

The Little Doctor, thinking of these three women, must have betrayed a touch of unease, for Monsieur Mordaut said sadly:

'Don't worry, I shall taste all the food and drink before you do . . . It doesn't matter to me now . . . I must tell you, doctor, that I am suffering from heart trouble myself. For the past three months I've been feeling the same symptoms as my aunt, my wife and my niece did in the early stages of their illness . . .'

One would really have had to be very hungry to partake of this meal! Jean Dollent felt he would have been wiser to eat and sleep at the inn.

Hector, however, was eating greedily, like an ill-mannered child, and the sight of this great lout of twenty-two with the expression of a sly schoolboy was not calculated to raise one's spirits.

'What do you plan to do this afternoon, doctor? Is there anything more I can do to help you?'

'I'd just as soon go about on my own . . . I'll explore the ground. I may perhaps put a few questions to the servants.'

That was what he did first. He went into the kitchen, where he found Ernestine busy washing dishes.

'What's he been telling you?' she asked, with typical peasant mistrustfulness. 'Did he talk about my cancer?'

'Yes . . .'

'He told you it wasn't true, didn't he? . . . But he swore he had a heart complaint. Well, I'm convinced it's just the contrary. He's never had any heart trouble. When he complains, you can see he's not really in pain. For one thing, he doesn't sweat the way those poor ladies did . . .'

'They used to sweat?'

'In the evenings they did. And whenever they made the least effort. Towards the end, they complained of dizziness and there were never enough blankets on their beds to keep them warm . . . They would shiver even with two hot water bottles. Does *he* look as if he was shivering?'

She carried on her work as she talked, and she was obviously robust and healthy. She must once have been a fine-looking girl, as full-figured as her niece Rose now was. She was self-confident, looked one in the eye and spoke her mind.

'I wanted to ask you, doctor . . . Can one get cancer through being given arsenic or some other poison?'

He evaded answering yes or no, for he preferred not to allay the elderly servant's anxiety. Instead, he asked her: 'What are your symptoms?'

'Stabbing pains, particularly in the small of the back, and sometimes between my shoulder-blades.'

He was careful not to smile, for that would have been enough to antagonize her. But what put it into his head to reply: 'If you like, I'll examine you presently?'

If it had been Rose, this would have been understandable. But Ernestine, who was over fifty? Fancy wanting to view her stripped!

'As soon as I've finished my washing-up,' she said promptly. 'Look, just these three plates and the cutlery. It'll only take me five minutes . . .'

Could she . . . No, that he would not believe. Of course, he had met women patients of that age who had plenty of life in them still and for whom a doctor seemed to have a special attraction. There had been one at Marsilly who came to see him every week with a pain somewhere or other, and who invariably insisted on undressing.

But Ernestine? And in this gloomy mansion?

'Right, I've done . . . I'll feed the dogs when we come down again. It's on the second floor. Come this way . . . Shall you need your case of instruments?'

The staircase was up a tower. They reached the second floor, where seven or eight rooms gave on to a long passage. The floor was uncarpeted. Old prints and worthless pictures still hung askew on the wall, covered with dust.

Ernestine opened a door. And he was surprised to find himself in a neat and even rather attractive room.

It was the room of a prosperous, tidy-minded peasant. A big mahogany bed, covered with an immaculate counterpane. A round, well-polished table. A stove. An armchair upholstered in tapestry, a foot-stool and in one corner, an eighteenth-century lady's desk with a pretty lock of gilded bronze.

'You mustn't mind the untidiness.'

There was no untidiness at all, not even a speck of dust.

'When you live in somebody else's house you can't show as much taste as if you were in your own home . . . I tell you, if I had a little place in the country, instead of in this wretched forest . . . Turn away, doctor, while I get undressed . . .'

He felt a little ashamed. It was almost like a breach of trust. He knew for a fact that she had no cancer. So what was the point of this examination, which was beginning to look fishy?

'Right! . . . You can turn round.'

Her flesh was extraordinarily white, almost like a girl's, and although she had grown somewhat stouter with age her figure was still shapely.

'This is the place, doctor . . . You feel . . .'

There was a knock at the door.

'Who's there?' asked Ernestine aggressively.

'It's me,' said Rose's voice. 'What are you doing?'

'If anybody asks you, say you don't know.'

'Is the doctor with you?'

'That's none of your business . . .'

'I'm looking for him to show him his room.'

'You can show it him presently . . .'

And she muttered between her teeth: 'The little pest! If she could, she'd look through the keyhole . . . But I took care to put the key inside . . . See, she's listening . . . She's pretended to go away, and she's come back quietly . . . That's what life is like in this house! There's always someone spying on someone else . . . You think you're alone somewhere and you always find somebody there whom you hadn't heard coming. Even the master goes in for that sort of game, and his son would climb along the gutters if need be to frighten you! . . . Don't talk too loud. There's no need for her to hear . . . Feel there. Don't you notice a sort of swelling?'

'Do you suppose I haven't heard all you've been saying!' Rose's voice taunted her from the passage. 'Have a good time, both of you . . .'

And this time she really seemed to have gone away.

II. In Which Two More Patients Strip, and the Little Doctor Scents Arsenic

'Can't you find anything?'

The examination had been going on for a good quarter of an hour, and each time the Little Doctor tried to bring it to a close Ernestine called him to order.

'You haven't taken my blood pressure . . .'

To make sure she knew what she was talking about, he asked:

'What was it last time?'

'Minimum 9, maximum 14, on a *Pachot* . . .'

Now very few patients, particularly those who live in the country, know whether their blood pressure is being taken with a *Pachot* or some other apparatus.

'I say, my dear lady,' the Little Doctor teased her, 'I see you're well informed about medical matters!'

'Of course!' she retorted. 'Health isn't to be bought in the market place, and if I want to live to a hundred and two like my grandmother . . .'

'You've read medical books?'

'To be sure I have! I had one sent from Paris only last week. I wonder now whether I hadn't better send a sample of my blood to be analysed to see whether I have urea . . .'

He had met others like her, almost morbidly obsessed by concern for their health, but in this arsenic-haunted house the slightest eccentricity assumed significance. He had no desire to smile now. He watched her getting dressed, and reflected that she certainly seemed strong enough to live a good many years longer provided . . .

'Your books discuss poisons, of course?'

'Sure they do . . . And I won't conceal the fact that I've read all they say about them . . . When one's had three examples under one's eyes, one needs to be on one's guard! Particularly when one's in the same situation as the other three!'

'What do you mean?'

It had been no chance remark. This woman did nothing at random; her every action was carefully thought out.

'What do you think they discovered when Madame Duplantet died? That she had taken out a life insurance for the benefit of Monsieur, her nephew . . . And when his wife died? Another life insurance! Well, my life is insured too . . .'

'For the benefit of your niece, I suppose?'

'Not at all! For the benefit of Monsieur, and not for some trifling sum either, but for a hundred thousand francs . . .'

Jean Dollent was dumbfounded. 'Your employer insured you for a hundred thousand francs? How long ago was this?'

'Fifteen years at least . . . It was long before his aunt Duplantet's death . . . So that I had no suspicions . . .'

It was before his aunt Duplantet's death . . . This was promptly pigeon-holed in a corner of Dollent's memory.

'You can understand that in the circumstances I keep wondering if it isn't going to be my turn next . . .'

'On what pretext did he insure you?'

'On no pretext at all . . . He just told me an insurance agent had been to see him, that it was an interesting proposition, that it would cost me nothing and that if anything unfortunate should happen to me, at least someone would be the better off . . .'

'You were forty years old when this policy was signed?'

'Thirty-eight.'

'And you'd already lived here for some years?'

'Practically all my life . . .'

'When he was a young man, was your employer already as depressed and – how shall I put it? – lifeless?'

'I've never known him any different.'

'Has he always lived so withdrawn? Has he never, to your knowledge, had any love affairs?'

'Never . . .'

'You know his private life, don't you? Are you sure he has no mistress in the neighbourhood?'

'Quite sure! He never goes out. And if a woman came here we should see her . . .'

'There is one possibility, though. Your niece Rose is young and pretty. Do you think that . . .'

She looked him in the eyes as she replied:

'Rose wouldn't stand for that. In any case he's not that sort of man. Nothing interests him except money. He spends his time making lists of all his possessions in the château, and sometimes he'll be all day hunting for some worthless object, some jar or ashtray that's missing . . . *That's his passion!*'

She had dressed long since, and had resumed the harsh expression of a surly servant. She seemed relieved. The look in her eyes said plainly: 'Now you know as much as I do. It wouldn't have been right for me not to speak . . .'

A strange house indeed. Built to hold a score of people, with innumerable rooms, nooks and crannies, staircases in unexpected places, it now housed no more than four inhabitants, apart from the revolting pack of ginger dogs.

Now these four beings, instead of uniting – if only to give themselves a feeling of being alive – seemed bent on seeking the most unsociable isolation.

Ernestine's room was at the far end of the second floor passage, in the left wing. When the Little Doctor went in search of Rose's, he opened all the doors on that floor in vain. The rooms were unoccupied and gave out a sickly, musty odour.

He had to look on the first floor. He had no difficulty in finding Monsieur Mordaut's room; hearing sounds within, he knocked.

'Would you direct me to your servant Rose's room?' he asked.

'She's changed rooms two or three times. I think she now has the one above the old orangery. When you get to the end of the corridor, turn left; it's the second or third door . . .'

'And your son?'

'I keep him near me; he has the room that was his poor mother's, and I'm obliged to lock him in every night, by way of precaution. How is your inquiry going, doctor? Did old Ernestine give you any interesting information? She's an honest creature, I think; but like others of her kind who have been allowed to wield too much authority, she tends to take advantage of it . . .'

He uttered all these remarks in the same lugubrious tone.

'Well then! If you need me, you'll always find me available. Do you know what I'm doing at the present moment? Come in if you like . . . This is my bedroom. It's rather untidy . . . When you knocked I was busy arranging in an album the photographs of the three women who died in this house . . . Here is my aunt Emilie . . . This is my wife, a few days before our wedding . . . Here she is as a child . . . She was never very pretty, was she? But she was mild and gentle. She spent all day at her embroidery. She never went out except to go to church. She was never bored . . . When I married her she was thirty. She was the daughter of a rich landowner in the neighbourhood, but since she seldom went anywhere she had never been asked in marriage . . .

'I might have known I bring bad luck . . .'

Dollent could no longer endure his tête-à-tête with this gloomy, dejected man, and he went in search of Rose's room. He had just made a rapid calculation: Rose had been in the house about one year when Aunt Emilie Duplantet had died, either from arsenic or from a heart attack.

Could one imagine a sixteen-year-old poisoner?

He listened at the door, heard nothing, and gently turned the knob. Then he had a shock. He had expected to slip noiselessly into an empty room, and suddenly he beheld before him the girl herself, calmly watching him.

'Well, come in!' she exclaimed impatiently. 'What are you waiting for?'

She had guessed he would come, that was obvious. And she had set the scene! The room had just been tidied, and the Little Doctor noticed that papers had been burnt in the fireplace.

'So I suppose it's my turn, after my aunt's?' she mocked. 'Must I get undressed too?'

He frowned. She had put an idea into his head.

'Why, I should rather like to examine you. There's so much talk of arsenic in this house that it might be interesting to make sure you're not being given small doses of it . . .'

With contemptuous unconcern, she had already pulled her dress over her head and she revealed a proud bosom, with flesh as white but firmer than her aunt's.

'Carry on!' she flung at him. 'Do you want me to take off the rest? While you're about it, don't stand on ceremony!'

'Bend forward . . . Right . . . Breathe in . . . Cough . . . Lie down . . .'

'You know, I may as well tell you right away that I'm as healthy as a pike . . .'

Why a pike? He never understood why this creature, more than any other, represented perfect health in Rose's mind.

'You were quite right . . . You can get dressed again. Monsieur Mordaut authorized me to question everybody in the house . . . So, if I may . . .'

'I'm ready . . . I already know what you're going to ask me. Since you've just been seeing my aunt . . . Admit that she told you I'd been sleeping with the master . . .'

Full of life, she bustled about the room, which was one of the most cheerful in the house and which, unlike the rest, had brightly coloured window curtains.

'My poor aunt thinks of nothing else! Because she's never had a husband or a lover, she's obsessed by the idea . . . When she talks about the village people, she's always imagining them going to bed with one another . . . For instance, now, she must be convinced that I'm making advances to you, or you to me . . . She thinks that as soon as a man and woman are together . . .'

'I noticed that Hector, in any case, looks at you in a way that . . .'

'Poor fellow! It's quite true that he hangs round me a bit. To begin with I was scared, because he's rather violent. But I soon realized that he wouldn't so much as dare to kiss me.'

He looked at the ashes in the fireplace and asked, slowly and softly:

'Haven't you a lover or a fiancé?'

'I might well, at my age, don't you think?'

'May one know his name?'

'If you can find it! Search away, since that's what you're here for! . . . Now I must go downstairs, because it's the day for cleaning the brass . . . Are you going to stay here?'

Why not? Why not be as brazen as she was?

'Yes, I shall stay, if you have no objection . . .'

She was annoyed, but she went out and he heard her going down the stairs. She probably did not realize that it is possible to read the writing on carbonized paper; she had not taken the trouble to scatter the ashes sufficiently, and there was one envelope of thicker paper than the rest which had remained almost intact. On one side the word *restante* could still be made out, which implied that Rose received her mail at the *poste restante*. On the other side the sender had written his address, of which the words COLONIAL INFANTRY REGIMENT were still legible, and underneath them . . . IVORY COAST.

Almost certainly Rose had an admirer, a lover or a fiancé in the colonial army, garrisoned on the Ivory Coast.

'I must disturb you again, Monsieur Mordaut, when you're so busy with your photograph album. You told me this morning that you suffered from some discomfort. As a doctor, I should like to investigate this, and in particular to make sure that it's not a case of slow poisoning . . .'

Resignedly, his host gave a slight, bitter smile and began to strip, as his two servants had done.

'For a long time now,' he sighed, 'I've been expecting to undergo the same fate as my wife and my aunt . . . When I saw Solange Duplantet die too . . .'

He dropped his arms wearily. Contrary to what one might have imagined from seeing him dressed, he was sturdily built, and his chest was particularly broad, covered with long hair, and with the pallid skin of one who lives mainly indoors.

'Would you like me to lie down or remain standing? Have you examined my servants?'

'They're both quite healthy . . . But . . . Don't move . . . Breathe normally . . . Bend forward a little . . .'

This time the examination lasted almost an hour, and the Little Doctor became increasingly grave.

'I wouldn't like to assert anything before discussing the matter with colleagues who know more about it than I do . . . Yet the discomfort you feel might be the result of poisoning by arsenic . . .'

'I told you so!'

He displayed neither indignation nor fear.

'One question, Monsieur Mordaut. Why did you insure Ernestine's life?'

'Did she tell you about that? It's quite simple. One day an insurance agent came to see me. He was a clever fellow, ready with convincing arguments. He pointed out to me that there were several of us in the household, mostly middle-aged . . . I can still hear his words: "One of you will inevitably die first," he said. "It'll be sad, of course. But why should not that death enable you to restore your château? By insuring your whole family . . ."'

'Excuse me,' the Little Doctor interrupted. 'Is Hector insured too?'

'The company will not insure mental defectives . . . So I let myself be persuaded. And as an extra precaution I insured Ernestine too, in spite of her excellent health.'

'One further question: did you insure your own life?'

The idea seemed to strike Monsieur Mordaut for the first time.

'No,' he replied reflectively.

'Why?'

'Yes, why indeed? The truth is that I never thought of it. No doubt I'm nothing but a sordid egoist. I assumed I should be the one to survive.'

'And you have in fact survived!'

He lowered his head and ventured timidly: 'For how long?'

Was he to be pitied as a lamentable specimen of humanity? Or on the contrary, were all his attitudes to be considered as displaying extreme cunning?

Why had he unhesitatingly left the Little Doctor a clear field?

Why had he told him about the symptoms from which he suffered?

If a man was capable of poisoning three women, including his own wife, wasn't he also capable of protecting himself from the death penalty by swallowing a non-lethal quantity of poison?

Jean Dollent, on leaving the room, remembered what Superintendent Lucas had said to him.

'There are all sorts of murderers,' the man from the Police Judiciaire had said, 'young and old, gentle and violent, cheerful and gloomy . . . People kill for a variety of reasons: love, jealousy, anger, envy, cupidity, in short, any of the seven deadly sins. But poisoners are almost always of the same kind. If you study the list of famous poisoners, men and women, what do you notice? Not one of them is a cheerful person; not one of them has lived a normal life, in the years preceding his crime. There is always a basic passion violent enough to dominate all other feelings, to inspire that atrocious cruelty which consists in watching one's victim die by inches . . .

'A physical passion . . . which in this case must be described as a vice, since love doesn't come into it. Or else the most sordid avarice . . . A poisoner has been known to sleep for years on a wretched straw mattress in which a fortune was concealed . . .'

An hour went by. The Little Doctor, overcome by a sort of nausea which only his curiosity enabled him to endure, wandered about the mansion and the park, where the dogs now left him in peace.

He had got as far as the gate, and was wondering whether to go into the village, if only for a change of atmosphere, when he heard a great to-do in the direction of the house, and a loud scream from Ernestine.

He rushed back, skirting part of the house, to where, not far from the kitchen, there stood a sort of barn which still contained straw and farm implements. Here Hector was lying, dead, his eyes glazed, his features distorted. Without even bending down to look, the Little Doctor recognized the symptoms.

'A heavy dose of arsenic . . .'

Beside the body, which was lying in the straw, there was a brown bottle labelled *Jamaica Rum*.

Monsieur Mordaut turned slowly round, a strange light in his eyes. Ernestine was weeping. Rose stood a little apart, with her head lowered, as though awe-struck by the sight of death.

III. In Which it Seems as Though all the Inhabitants of the Château have had a Narrow Escape, and the Police Make an Arrest

Half an hour later, while they were still waiting for the gendarmes, who had been summoned by telephone, the Little Doctor, his brow in a cold sweat, was beginning to wonder if he could carry through this inquiry to the end.

For he had just been elucidating, at least in part, the story of the bottle of rum.

'Don't you remember the conversation I had with Monsieur at the end of lunch?' Ernestine had said. 'And yet you were there! He asked me what I was preparing for dinner. I said bean soup and a cauliflower.'

That was correct. The Little Doctor had vaguely heard something of the sort, but had paid no attention.

'Monsieur replied that it wasn't enough, since you were dining with us, and he asked me to make a rum omelette as well . . .'

That, again, was true!

'Excuse me!' exclaimed Dollent. 'When you happen to need rum, where do you take it from?'

'From the sideboard in the dining-room. That's where all the bottles of spirits and apéritifs are kept.'

'Have you the key to it?'

'I ask for it when I need it.'

'Did you ask for it to take the rum?'

'Soon after you left me in my room.'

'Had the bottle been opened?'

'Yes. But it was a long time since any of that rum had been drunk. Some of it may have been used last winter to make an occasional toddy . . .'

'What did you do next?'

'I gave Monsieur back the key. Then I went into the kitchen and prepared the vegetables for the soup.'

'Where was the rum?'

'On the mantelpiece . . . I wasn't going to need it until I started the omelette . . .'

'Did nobody come into the kitchen? You didn't see Monsieur Hector prowling around?'

'No . . .'

'And you didn't go out?'

'Only for a few minutes, to take the dogs their food . . .'

'When you came back, was the rum still there?'

'I didn't notice . . .'

'Was Hector in the habit of getting hold of drinks?'

'Sometimes. Not only drinks! He was very greedy. He would pinch anything he could lay hands on and take it into a corner to eat it like a puppy.'

What would have happened if Hector had not . . .

Ernestine would have prepared the omelette. Would an unusual taste have been noticed? Wouldn't the bitterness have been attributed to the rum?

Who would have avoided eating any of the omelette? The omelette prepared in the kitchen and served by Rose to Monsieur Mordaut, Hector and the Little Doctor in the dining-room?

No dinner was served in the château that evening. The *gendarmerie* were still on the spot, and two constables, at the gate, were being hard put to it to control the village people, who were uttering threatening cries. The Orléans police had arrived, and so had the D.P.P. Lights were on in every room in the château, for the first time in many years, and thus it regained a little of its former splendour.

The search was going on everywhere. Policemen pulled about furniture and opened drawers, savagely, for indignation was at its height.

In the faded drawing-room Monsieur Mordaut, livid and wild-eyed, was trying to understand the questions of his investigators, who were all speaking at once and barely concealed their desire to manhandle him.

When the door opened and he emerged, he was wearing handcuffs; he was led into a neighbouring room and shut up there with two guards.

The examining magistrate from Orléans had been irritated at finding the Little Doctor already on the spot and so to speak entrenched there.

'You're not content with investigating crimes!' he commented sarcastically. 'Now you anticipate them . . .'

'I even believe I was the cause of this one . . .'

'What?'

'More exactly, of the accident which occurred . . . For there's no doubt that it was an accident . . . Nobody could foretell that Hector, who acted purely on impulse, would pass through the kitchen in Ernestine's absence and remove the bottle of rum . . .'

The magistrate stared at him in surprise.

'But . . . In that case . . . You might have been a victim yourself?'

'It's unlikely . . .'

'Why?'

'I may be wrong, and if so I apologize . . . But I think, rather, that my argument is sound. Suppose the omelette had been served. Everyone would have taken some of it, except the murderer, surely? Unless you assume that he wanted to kill himself and the whole household, myself included, with him. But in general murderers of that sort are cowards . . .

'I'll go back to my idea. *Everybody would die except the murderer.*

'Doesn't it seem to you improbable that a person who has already successfully brought off three crimes in ten years should behave in such a foolish fashion? For it would identify that person as the criminal! It would amount to a confession!'

The magistrate was pondering, somewhat perplexed.

'So in your opinion this was an accident?'

'I know it's hard to explain, and yet I do believe, yes, I do believe that young Hector was not the intended victim *today* . . . I think that nobody was *meant* to die today . . . I think that, for the murderer, what has happened amounts to a real catastrophe . . . That is why I am so anxious to reconstruct, minute by minute, the course of events this afternoon . . .'

IV. In Which the Little Doctor Reaches his Conclusion by Means of Certain 'Solid Bases'

How often had he repeated: '*Starting from a single solid basis, provided one doesn't go off the rails or lose the thread, one will automatically reach the truth . . .*'

Had he belonged to the Police Judiciaire, his colleagues would probably have nicknamed him Monsieur Solid-Basis!

Or else Monsieur In-the-skin, because of his other favourite slogan: '*Put yourself in the skin of your characters . . .*'

This time he felt reluctant to put himself in the skin of the inhabitants of this château with its pack of ginger dogs, which having been shut up by order of the police were yelping unremittingly.

The solid basis . . . Let's see:

1. Monsieur Mordaut made no attempt to hinder the Little Doctor's investigation, and insisted on keeping him in the house;
2. Ernestine was robust and vigorous; she expected to live to a hundred and two like her grandmother; she did everything possible to that end and was obsessed by the thought of sickness;
3. Ernestine declared that her niece was not Monsieur Mordaut's mistress;
4. Rose, too, was 'as healthy as a pike'; she had an admirer or a lover in the colonial army;
5. Rose, too, declared that she was not the mistress of her employer;
6. Monsieur Mordaut was suffering from the early stages of arsenical poisoning;
7. Ernestine, like two of the three dead women, had had her life

insured in favour of her employer.

'Do you want me to tell you what I really think?'

This from Ernestine who, in the dimly-lit drawing-room, was replying to the investigators' questions.

'The doctor here will confirm that I don't like speaking ill of people. Only this afternoon he questioned me and I didn't want to be spiteful. Particularly as I've got no proof . . . All the same, there were only us four here who could have poisoned those poor ladies. Monsieur Hector is out of the picture, since he's dead. So there are just three of us . . . Well, my belief is that the master had practically gone out of his mind. When he realized he was going to be caught, he tried to bring things to an end . . . But since he's a perverted sort of man who never behaved like normal people, he was determined that none of his former household should survive him . . .

'If poor Monsieur Hector hadn't drunk that rum we should all be dead by now, including the doctor . . .'

Every time he thought about it, Dollent felt a cold shiver run down his back. To think that, next day, the house would have been full of nothing but corpses . . . And these would not have been discovered right away, since nowadays nobody came to ring at the garden gate . . .

And possibly the starving dogs . . .

'You have nothing to say?' the examining magistrate asked Rose, who was gazing fixedly at the floor.

'Nothing.'

'You noticed nothing out of the ordinary?'

She glanced at the Little Doctor hesitantly. What did that mean? What was she hesitating to admit?

'*If anyone was likely to notice something out of the ordinary, it would have been the doctor* . . .'

If anyone was likely to notice . . . If anyone . . .

Dollent flushed. What was she referring to? How could she know that he had noticed. . . ?

'Explain yourself clearly,' said the magistrate.

'I don't know anything . . . I simply said that the doctor, who knows what he's about, made a serious investigation. If he didn't notice anything, it must have been that . . .'

She did not complete her remark.

'It must have been that?'

'Nothing . . . I thought that when one took the trouble to examine everybody . . .'

Why yes, good heavens, she was right! Why hadn't he thought of it earlier?

'*Monsieur le juge,*' he blurted out, moving towards the door, 'I should like to speak to you in private for a moment . . .'

They went into the passage, which was as poorly lit as the rest of the house.

'I assume . . . I hope you have the authority to . . . It's still time . . . If a Superintendent goes by car . . .'

He had finished his job. Something had clicked, and as usual it had happened all at once.

Scattered elements . . . Little gleams of light amid the fog . . . Then, suddenly . . .

He knew now why he had taken so long about it! It was because in that poison-haunted house, he had scarcely dared drink anything to sharpen his wits.

V. A Meditative Duet over a Rabbit Stew with Mushrooms, accompanied by some Lively White Wine

The two men, the magistrate and the Little Doctor, had found no other way to escape from public curiosity than to commandeer the big dining-room on the first floor of the inn.

They had been served with an omelette not *au rhum* but *aux fines herbes*, followed by a rabbit stew with mushrooms which they were now enjoying, while each spoke in turn and each, more particularly the Little Doctor, raised his glass of white wine and drained it.

'Until we have the solicitor's answer, all that I can tell you, *monsieur le juge*, is purely hypothetical. Now the Law, which you represent, has a horror of hypotheses. Perhaps that's why it so often makes mistakes!'

'I must protest and . . .'

'Come on, drink up! . . . Well, what was the first thing that struck you during your interrogations? . . . Nothing! . . . Have some more mushrooms? . . . Pity, they're delicious . . . Well, what struck *me* was the fact that a man who insures everybody else's life is not insured himself. Suppose this man to be a murderer . . . Suppose he intends to take advantage of these insurances . . . What will he do to cover himself? First and foremost, he'll insure his own life so as to make his attitude seem plausible . . .'

'Murderers, as you have so often maintained, my dear doctor, are almost always idiots . . .'

'But complicated idiots! Idiots who take ten precautions where one would do! And as often as not it's these precautions that get them arrested . . .

'So then, Monsieur Mordaut has no life insurance. And for some time now he has had no relatives. For some time, too, he has been suffering the effects of arsenical poisoning, just like the previous victims. I put the question to you: at his death, who is going to inherit his fortune? That is why I asked you to send a Superintendent to the lawyer who . . .'

The innkeeper came to ask their verdict on the rabbit and to offer them an appetizing local cheese.

'Please follow me carefully, *monsieur le juge* . . . The person who is to be Monsieur Mordaut's heir is practically bound to be the murderer . . .

'Emilie Duplantet dies. Who, apparently, stands to gain by her death? Monsieur Mordaut. If there's an inquiry, he will be the suspect. But otherwise, who stands to gain, *except the person who is to be Monsieur Mordaut's heir?*

'His wife dies next. So she could not have committed the first murder. She was simply part of a series.

'And so the money accumulates; it's like what gamblers call a martingale . . . Only in this case the stakes are doubled in a gamble with death . . .

'Solange Duplantet comes to the château; her uncle is her heir; her death, too, will increase the fortune. She dies . . .'

'It's hard to believe!' sighed the magistrate, who was relishing his creamy cheese.

'All crimes are hard to believe for people who aren't criminals. . . . Where had we got to? Who is the heir, so far? Mordaut. After him, his son. And after his son?'

'Only the will can tell us that.'

'In the meantime, I've got to clear up one further point . . . The murderer must have had a considerable stock of arsenic in the house . . . I had just arrived; I was apparently carrying on my investigation . . .'

'I'm listening . . .'

'And I'm thinking . . . At midday, Mordaut happens to mention a rum omelette. What better way to cast suspicion on him than to put poison in the rum? Even if it meant saying subsequently that one had thought it smelt rather odd. For I'm sure that the rum would never have been poured over the omelette . . . I've spoken about that already . . . So by now the arsenic would be out of the hands of the person who'd had possession of it . . .

'If, into the bargain, Hector, whose morbid hunger impels him to prowl about the kitchen, could . . .

'Believe me, *monsieur le juge*. The person who committed all these murders . . .'

'Is who?'

'Wait a minute . . . Shall I tell you who, in my opinion, is Mordaut's heir? . . . The girl Rose . . .'

'So then?'

'Don't go so fast. And let me do some romancing, if I may use the term, until your Superintendent comes back with precise details. Remember what Rose pointed out just now: *I examined everybody in the house . . . Didn't I observe anything?*

'Yes! I made a medical observation: namely that Ernestine is by no means what one can describe as an old maid; everything about her suggests a complete woman, in every sense of the word . . . I'd take my oath that Mordaut, in his youth, made her his mistress. Like all those who have no social life, he became obsessed by sexual passion; he lived for nothing else . . .

'Years went by; he married, to set his affairs in order, and Ernestine raised no objection. Only, she killed his wife by slow degrees, in the same way that she had just killed the aunt whose death brought in money . . .

'She was *something more than Mordaut's wife; she was his heir* . . . She knew that all he possessed would some day revert to her . . .

'I could swear that it was she, rather than any insurance agent, who engineered the series of life-insurances.

'And she had the brilliant idea of having one taken out for herself, so that she could one day pose as a potential victim.

'Can you not understand this, *monsieur le juge*? That's because you don't live in the country as I do, and you're not familiar with that sort of long-term project.

'She wanted to live to a great age. It didn't matter if she had to waste twenty or thirty years with Mordaut . . . Afterwards she would be free, she would be rich, she would have the home of her dreams and live to be as old as her grandmother . . .

'That's why she is so afraid of illness. She doesn't want to have done all that work for nothing.

'First of all the pile has got to be substantial . . .

'Emilie Duplantet, Madame Mordaut, Solange Duplantet . . .

'She's running no risk; she will not be suspected, since to all appearances she gains nothing from these murders . . . Nobody knows that she has persuaded her lover to make a will naming her, in the absence of direct heirs, as residuary legatee . . .

'So *she can safely kill* . . .

'If there is any trouble, Mordaut is the one who will go to prison and be sentenced . . .

'She only begins to worry when she becomes aware of the growing influence of the niece whom she has involuntarily brought into the house . . . For Rose is younger and more attractive. And Mordaut . . .'

'It's disgusting!' cut in the magistrate.

'It's life, unfortunately! His passion for Ernestine is transferred to her niece. Rose has an admirer or a lover, but that doesn't matter; she's like her aunt in this respect, she can wait a few years, wait for the heritage that Mordaut has promised her. *She* doesn't need to kill anybody! She may suspect these murders, but she simply has to remain ignorant of them. She will gain by them eventually, because . . .'

'It was a long business, *monsieur le juge*,' sighed the Superintendent, who had had no dinner and was eyeing the remains of their meal longingly. 'Monsieur Mordaut's residuary legatee, apart from the share reserved for his son, is Mademoiselle Rose Saupiquet . . .'

The Little Doctor's eyes sparkled.

'Is there no other will?' asked the magistrate.

'There was an earlier one, in favour of Mademoiselle Ernestine Saupiquet . . . This will was altered nearly eight years ago.'

'Was Mademoiselle Ernestine aware of this?'

'No. The alteration was made secretly.'

The Little Doctor was laughing derisively. The fact was that he had drunk more than a bottle of a white wine so dry that it had a flinty taste.

'So now, *monsieur le juge*, do you get it? Ernestine knew nothing about the new will. She felt sure of profiting by her crimes sooner or later. But Mordaut himself would have to be killed only when he had amassed a sufficient fortune . . .'

'And Rose?'

'Legally, she's certainly not an accomplice . . . I wonder none the less whether she hadn't guessed her aunt's plans. What could be easier than to let Ernestine go ahead, since actually it would some day be to the advantage of herself and her lover in the Colonial Infantry? . . .

'Just think . . .' He assumed a familiar tone, as always when he had been drinking. 'Sordid interests . . . Bitches capable of anything to make sure of the big money . . . And he, the wretched infatuated idiot, who couldn't live without docile women about him, enslaved by the pair of them, torn between them, not knowing which way to turn . . .

'You must admit that there are certain people, like this man Mordaut, who seem to have been born to tempt criminals . . .'

A fresh bottle had been set on the table, ostensibly for the Superintendent. The Little Doctor was the first to help himself, and, smacking his lips, declared:

'Do you know what first aroused my suspicions? It was when Ernestine vouched for her niece's virtue. For to doubt that would have meant doubting Mordaut's virtue . . . And if I doubted that, I should inevitably have begun to suspect . . .

'In short, we interrupted her in the middle of her operations: Hector, whom she killed only by accident, in an attempt to get rid of the poison and also to ruin Mordaut, *who had ordered the rum omelette in my presence* . . .

'Rose would come next, then Mordaut . . . And then she would have the fine bright house in the country, with forty more years to live as she had dreamed of living . . .'

The Little Doctor helped himself again and concluded;

'For there are still people, *monsieur le juge*, particularly in the countryside, who nurse long-term dreams . . . That's why they are so keen to live to a ripe old age!'

Death in a Department Store

I. About a Gentleman with a Passion for Buying Slippers, and another who Frequents the Toy Department

He arrived at about a quarter past six as usual, a stoutish man with a perpetually damp forehead which he mopped with a coloured handkerchief as he made a preliminary tour of the department.

It was in one of the big stores near the Opéra. At this time of day a flood of human beings was streaming along the pavements, and the cars in the street were making slow, jerky progress, ten in a row.

Only this placid man, who looked like some humble pensioner, seemed immune to the general excitement, as though unaware that the establishment was going to close at half past six.

The slipper department was not far from door C. He sat down, and Gaby, the salesgirl, sighed resignedly.

'What can I get you today?' she asked, trying to retain at any rate the semblance of commercial good manners.

It was time to be making up one's face, not to be trying slippers on a crank!

'I should like something in soft brown leather.'

'Like the ones you bought yesterday?'

'No. The soles were too thick on the ones I bought yesterday.'

It had been going on for a whole week, and every day the same thing happened. The customer gazed meekly at Gaby, like a timid admirer. He took off his left shoe, while she fetched boxes.

'Do you like these?'

'The colour's a bit light. Haven't you anything darker?'

And Gaby knew, as did her friends, that this would go on until the last minute. He would try on ten, twenty pairs of slippers before choosing one, and when the closing bell rang at last he would make his way towards the cash desk with his parcel under his arm.

Gaby had thought of a dodge to discourage him. Her friend Antoinette, from the fancy-leather-goods department, was commissioned to come and tell her, in the customer's hearing; 'Your fiancé's just gone by.' And she had added an invention of her own: 'Is he still just as jealous?'

The man had not batted an eyelid. He was the picture of placidity, patience and gentleness. Another, more cruel trick had been equally ineffective: Gaby had tried, by means of shoe-horns, to force his feet into slippers a size too small, and he had merely pulled a wry face.

Was he going to keep on coming for weeks, months, years maybe, buying a pair of slippers every day, and invariably a few minutes before closing time?

And now Gaby's eyes were full of tears. She was looking at the chair in which her admirer usually sat, and explaining to the Little Doctor:

'It was the day before yesterday . . . I couldn't think what slippers to show him . . . I had a bad-tempered lady with a little boy . . . I bent down to take some boxes from under this counter . . . Without looking up, I took hold of my customer's foot. I had a blue slipper in my other hand . . .

'I don't know why, I had a funny feeling . . . I looked up . . . I thought he'd fallen asleep, for his chin was down on his chest . . .

'I shook him a little, and he nearly fell over on top of me . . .

'He collapsed limply, like a sandbag . . . I screamed . . . People came running up. The shop detective said: "Give him some air. It's probably a heart attack."

'Because we do sometimes see that sort of accident . . . But it wasn't that! When they took off his collar and tie there was blood on his shirt, and the policeman found that he'd been shot through the chest . . .

'Here, Monsieur, yes! Right here in the shop! Among all the crowds of people! And nobody had heard anything!

'He had been dead already when I tried to put on the slipper! It makes me quite ill, so that I've asked to be transferred to another department. Every time I catch sight of that chair . . .'

When the Little Doctor had arrived in Paris that morning, Superintendent Lucas had already completed a preliminary inquiry. He had taken Dollent to the second floor of the store and stopped in the toy department.

This was just beside the balustrade, and overlooked part of the ground floor, including the slipper department.

'The shot was fired from here. You can see the chair in which the victim was sitting. The murderer was just at this spot. I questioned all the assistants. They remember a youngish man prowling for some time about the department. One of the assistants asked him if he wanted anything and he replied: "I'm waiting for my wife."

'It was about a quarter past six. The stranger seemed to be taking an interest in the soldiers' outfits. He picked up several toy pistols of the Eureka brand.

'Do you understand, now, how the crime was worked? He must

have had in his pocket, or in a parcel, or perhaps in a briefcase, a compressed-air pistol or some other high-precision weapon, possibly fitted with a silencer.

'You could not kill anyone from this distance with a revolver, even a heavy bore revolver. A rifle would have been cumbersome. But there are pistols which can kill a man at fifty metres or more . . .

'The murderer was innocently handling toy guns, as was quite natural in that department; he pretended to take aim, and nobody was surprised. Then the bell rang to warn people that the store was closing. At that moment the din in the place was at its height. Nobody heard the slight noise made by a compressed-air weapon or a pistol with a silencer.

'The management are appalled. They want us to do everything possible to discover the criminal. That's why we have been asked to recommend a private detective capable of carrying on an investigation at the same time as that of the Police Judiciaire. I gave your address . . . You see, doctor, I'm not jealous of your successes . . .

'Good luck to you!'

The manager was a young man. He was nervously pacing up and down in his office, occasionally glancing somewhat dubiously at Jean Dollent, whose appearance was somewhat unimpressive. Why couldn't the Little Doctor bring himself, once and for all, in order to inspire confidence, to assume some eccentricity, to adopt a mannerism, a fad, to wear a monocle or to smoke peculiar cigarettes? This slight thirty-year-old, whose clothes always seemed a little skimpy, looked almost like a student.

'Listen to me carefully . . . The police seem to think the crime was committed by a professional killer. I hope this is so. Yet I cannot see why a professional should have attacked this poor man, who was an obvious crank. What I'm most afraid of, don't you see, is that it may have been a homicidal maniac. You probably know that large stores, like newspaper offices and certain public buildings, have an attraction for the mentally deranged . . . If this should be the case, if the shot from the toy department was fired by an insane person, it's almost certain that he will do the same thing again. Madmen tend to repeat their actions in a series.

'Now in spite of all the precautions we may take, it's hard for us to prevent the repetition of such an action.

'The report of the incident in some newspapers has already done us undoubted harm. Yesterday the takings at the slipper department and those nearby were practically nil; a few people went by out of curiosity, keeping at a distance . . .

'Make your investigation. I don't know your methods; they say you have no methods . . . Here's a card which will enable you to circulate freely throughout the store and to question members of the staff . . .

'Now I only have to put you in touch with Mademoiselle Alice from the jewellery department. She made a statement to me last night, which she shall repeat to you. I'm rather mistrustful of statements made by women; I know how readily their imagination works . . .'

He pressed a bell.

'Ask Mademoiselle Alice to come in.'

She was a tall, pale girl, one of those who, as the manager had said, readily let their fancy roam, and she was probably a great reader of novels or a film-star fan.

'Would you repeat to Monsieur . . .'

She was obviously upset, and she spoke volubly at some length.

'It was like this . . . When I saw the photo in the papers . . . For when the catastrophe happened it was my day off . . . Yesterday I saw the photo of the poor man in the papers and I recognized him immediately . . . Before he started paying attention to Gaby it was I . . . it was me . . .'

'What are you trying to say? Did he make advances to you?'

'No. . . But several days running . . . I could check the actual number of days . . . he came to my department . . .'

'At a quarter past six?'

'Between five and six o'clock . . . It often happens that customers come for the sake of us girls and we always realise it at once, because they only buy unimportant little things . . . You see what I mean? . . . He wanted a snap-hook. I showed him about a dozen and he eventually bought one. Next day he came back. The snap-hook wasn't on its chain. He told me he'd broken it and I didn't believe him, because these are solid articles . . . He dithered a long time, he couldn't make up his mind . . . and in the end he bought another . . .'

'And he came back again next day? Still at the same time?'

'Yes . . . For a fortnight he came each afternoon, and each time he bought another snap-hook . . .'

'Tell me, Mademoiselle Alice, didn't it occur to you that he might be a shop-lifter? One gathers there are a good many of them about.'

'I thought of that . . . So I watched him carefully . . . I even asked the shop detective to keep an eye on him while I was serving him.'

'And?'

'No!'

'Tell me something else. Where is your department?'

'Well, that's just it . . . It's on the first floor, just above the slipper department and just below the toy department. That's what struck me yesterday when I read the paper. I asked to speak to the manager . . .'

A few minutes later, when Mademoiselle Alice had left, the manager said to the Little Doctor:

'I have my doubts, as I told you. However, I passed on her report to the police and I asked them to make discreet inquiries about this particular assistant. The fact is that for the past few weeks valuable objects have been disappearing from her department . . .'

'To an unusual extent?'

'We expect a percentage of thefts, which remains more or less constant, except round Christmas time when, needless to say, professional thieves seize their opportunity. But the value and the number of articles stolen recently from the jewellery department is particularly high and . . .'

It was somewhat alarming, on leaving the manager's office at the top of the building, to look down into that huge hall, larger than any cathedral, from which rose the continuous murmur of the crowd. How on earth was one to set about it?

The Little Doctor shrugged his shoulders, took a lift and was soon down in the Rue de la Chaussée d'Antin. Calmly, as though he were swallowing an aspirin tablet, he downed two glasses of brandy.

Then he made for the Rue Notre-Dame-de-Lorette and looked for no. 67. He was about to knock on the concierge's door when, through the window, he saw Superintendent Lucas questioning the woman.

For the dead man had been identified. His name was Justin Galmet, aged forty-eight, no known occupation, who had lived for the past twenty years in the Rue Notre-Dame-de-Lorette.

II. Concerning the Peculiar Purchases made by the Late Justin Galmet and his No Less Peculiar Past History

'Do you want to question her yourself?' proposed Lucas, opening the door of the concierge's lodge. 'Otherwise, you can come upstairs with me to Galmet's apartment.'

It was the traditional home of the Parisian petty bourgeois, particularly the petty bourgeois of Montmartre. The house itself was old, with dark paintwork, smells of cooking seeping through under every door together with voices, children's cries and wafts of radio music.

Up on the fourth floor back, overlooking the courtyard, Galmet's apartment was a three-roomed dwelling furnished with solid old provincial stuff; at the window, between two geraniums in pots, there was a canary in a cage.

'Nobody will come and disturb us,' Lucas declared. 'The

concierge says Justin Galmet never had any visitors. He was a confirmed bachelor, and moreoever the tidiest of men. Once a week the concierge herself went up to do his housework, "thoroughly", so she declares, though I think she exaggerates a bit. The rest of the time Justin Galmet used to make his own bed, prepare his own breakfast and lunch, go out about two in the afternoon and come back about nine, almost always laden with parcels.

'He took his evening meal in a restaurant at the corner of the Rue Lepic, and I've rung the place already. They knew him well; he had a table kept for him by the window. He was rather greedy, and he used to order special delicacies . . . He would eat slowly, reading the evening papers meanwhile, then he would drink his coffee and a glass of spirits and make his way home peacefully . . .

'Now another, more surprising, piece of information . . .'

Lucas took his time, observing the Little Doctor's reactions.

'I found Justin Galmet's name in our archives. Not among the criminals, but among the policemen . . . Twenty-five years ago he joined the Force; he stayed in it for four years, as an inspector. Then he gave in his notice, saying that he'd received a small legacy and was going to live on his private income henceforward.

'I questioned some of our chaps who'd known him. Even then he was an unsociable, introverted type of fellow. He showed no zest for his work, but would spend hours sipping glasses of beer all by himself on some sunny terrace, and already at this period he liked to treat himself to little feasts . . . As you see, the typical specimen of a confirmed bachelor . . .

'Now shall we look round the place?'

It would be going too far to say the place was clean. But considering that its occupier looked after it practically single-handed, one might have expected a worse mess. Jean Dollent began by feeding the canary, and through the open window he looked out at the familiar scene of the roof-tops of Paris gleaming in the sunlight.

Meanwhile Lucas had opened a huge wardrobe; he summoned his companion.

'Look at this! Here are all his purchases, not even unwrapped . . . Will you help me cut the strings?'

They unpacked; it was a fantastic spectacle! They discovered not only the six pairs of slippers, but other far more unexpected articles: china plates, lengths of artificial silk, toothbrushes, combs, bottles of hair lotion; one parcel contained nothing but pipes, whereas the concierge had told them her tenant never smoked.

Most of the articles still bore their labels.

'What d'you think of this, doctor?'

'I think this is not just the result of petty larceny . . . For one thing, nothing is of sufficient value to have been worth stealing. For another, I notice that all these objects are carefully wrapped up, just as they came from the shops, and some of them even have the receipt tucked into the string . . .'

'Do you think, then, that our Justin was a crank with a passion for shop girls, who bought all these things as a way of approaching them? You'll agree it must have become expensive in the long run . . . The slippers alone represent some fifty to sixty francs a day. And yet our man didn't live on a grand scale. Would you like me to tell you what I really think?

'Don't get a swollen head about it . . . I know your methods now. I know what you can do better than we can, and what we can do better than you . . . Well, this is a case for you.

'This is something outside normal life. Justin Galmet has nothing in common with the victims we are accustomed to dealing with . . . As for his murderer, there's something terrifying about the calm audacity of his action, the self-assurance it betrays . . .'

Instead of thanking him for the compliment, the Little Doctor heaved a sigh.

'The job doesn't thrill you?'

He answered gloomily: 'Never before I've discovered my basic truth . . . Now I've been puzzling in vain . . .'

'If you need any help . . .'

'I'd just like you to check with the stores from which these articles came whether Justin Galmet invariably came back several days running, and whether he always dealt with the same assistant . . .'

It was fortunate that he did not mind making a fool of himself. It didn't worry him that the assistants at the neighbouring counters, who had probably been warned of his visit, watched him from a distance, neglecting their own customers, nudging one another and sometimes finding it hard to restrain a giggle.

The fact was that he had eaten an excellent lunch and since then, after a coffee and a chaser, he had treated himself to a few drinks preliminary to the next meal.

What had he been asked to do, after all? A man had died, a man about whom nothing was known. There couldn't be a more colourless and yet more mysterious figure than Justin Galmet.

He had no friends and no relations. He seemed to live in the most Olympian solitude.

And yet somebody had killed him. Therefore, it had been to somebody's advantage that he should be killed.

A single solid basis, as the Little Doctor liked to say. Regularly every day, at the same time, in different shops, Justin Galmet bought some object from the same salesgirl; subsequently, not knowing what to do with that object, he thrust it, still unwrapped, into his huge wardrobe and the various cupboards in his home.

At a quarter past six Dollent was sitting there, on the dead man's usual chair. He had taken off his left shoe; and he had said to Gaby, who was in such a state of nerves that her fingers were all thumbs:

'Now do just what you did with your customer.'

'Do you want to try on some slippers?'

'Bring me some slippers to try on, exactly as you did with him.'

'Am I to hurt you, too?' she ventured with a faint smile.

Now, what could he make out from where he sat? Looking up, he could see part of the jewellery display on the first floor. And Alice, who had recognized him, came at intervals to watch him over the balustrade.

Just above that was the toy department, where he noticed a fine military outfit with two pistols; these were not dangerous, however, since they only fired darts.

From where he was sitting he could not see beyond the gilt balustrade of the higher floors.

'Why, so you've got music,' the Little Doctor observed, meanwhile pulling a face because the slipper he was trying on was too tight. 'I say, do you always have music?'

'Don't talk to me about it! That's the hardest thing to get used to. The radio's on from morning till night. It's not so bad when the music's low; but just now, to encourage customers to hurry up, they play nothing but marches and quicksteps . . . Shall I carry on?'

He scanned the ground floor. There was a bargain counter in front of him; he was informed that the articles were changed every week. On the left, a cash desk surmounted by the number 89. Immediately behind that, a gilt door and beyond it, the pavement, black with people . . .

He started asking: 'Why is there a bigger crowd just there . . .' But he got the answer when he noticed the entrance to a métro station.

'I've already tried six pairs on you . . .'

'How many did you try on him?'

'Sometimes seven . . . Once, nine . . .'

'What did it depend on?'

'I couldn't say . . .'

It couldn't have depended on the slippers, because Justin Galmet never wore them, never even unwrapped them!

A thought made him smile . . . He had just glanced down . . . Could it be . . ? Oh no, surely not a motive for killing! And the victim would have to be extremely naïve . . . True, as she bent down to try on his slippers Gaby's cleavage slipped a little, disclosing the upper curve of her breasts.

But before he took to coming to the slipper department Justin had frequented the jewellery counter, and there, Alice had not needed to bend down . . . And elsewhere he had bought other articles . . .

'You'll have to make up your mind,' the salesgirl suddenly said. 'The bell's ringing.'

And in fact a mighty clangour rang out through the huge building. People rushed towards the exits, assistants bustled about, shopwalkers in tail coats rounded up the crowd like sheep-dogs, repeating: 'Hurry up, please, ladies and gentlemen . . .'

At cash desk no. 89 the last purchases were being paid for. The cashier laid down a big yellow envelope for a moment as she paid a few francs into the till.

'Are you taking this pair?'

'Any pair will do . . .'

He wanted to carry through his experiment to the end, – to '*put himself in the skin of . . .*'

That was the burning question. What had Justin Galmet – who was no longer there to answer – been looking at, the previous day?

Gaby helped him on with his left shoe. She told him: 'This way.'

He was about to ask why she was dragging him off in the opposite direction to the exit, but then he understood. The cashier of no. 89 was leaving her desk, with the yellow envelope in her hand. Above the cash desk there was now a notice saying. 'Closed.'

The Little Doctor was watching keenly as he followed his salesgirl, with some difficulty, through the crowd, against the stream.

'Thirty-eight francs ninety . . .'

He turned round, straining his eyes, and thought he could recognize the cashier from desk no. 89 making towards the lift, still clutching her yellow envelope.

A small parcel was thrust into his hand. Gaby gazed at him as though to ask whether he had discovered anything. He shrugged his shoulders, and had to search his pockets to find the odd ninety centimes.

'Are you coming back tomorrow?' Gaby asked excitedly.

'Maybe . . . Yes . . .'

Outside, he didn't know what to do with the slippers, so he took advantage of the crowd to bend down and leave the parcel on the edge of the pavement.

'Hello, that you, doctor? Lucas here . . . We've traced our man's bank account . . . It was at his local branch of the Crédit Lyonnais. Generally he paid in about five hundred francs a week . . . Except for payments of several thousand francs at long intervals. But there had only been about ten of these in the past twenty years . . . Hello, are you still there?'

'Go on . . .'

'For the past three months the sums paid in had been considerably higher . . . Twenty thousand francs last week . . . Twelve thousand the week before . . . seven or eight the week before that, I've not got the figures in front of me . . . The previous months, four or five thousand a week . . .'

'I say, that makes quite a tidy sum!'

'And notably a disproportionate one. Over the first twenty years, barely two hundred thousand francs, since there were withdrawals. On the other hand, almost a hundred and fifty thousand during the last three months . . .

'And that's not all. We have just had a visitor at Headquarters, an estate agent from the Faubourg Saint-Martin. Ten days ago, Justin Galmet called on him to inquire if he had a little house for sale somewhere in the country, on the banks of the Loire if possible . . . They were negotiating about a pretty little house worth two hundred thousand francs in the neighbourhood of Cléry. The contract was going to be signed next week . . .'

'Did Justin Galmet visit the house?'

'Yes, last Tuesday. He went over there in a taxi. That in itself must have cost a pretty penny . . . He had a girl with him, and she examined the place as though she was going to live there . . .'

'You're keeping the surprise for the end?'

'How did you guess?'

'Never mind . . . Go on . . . Was it Gaby?'

'You're getting warm . . . But it's even more unexpected. None the less I'm pretty sure . . . While you were making off with your parcel just now I was at the staff door with my estate agent. He spotted her unhesitatingly, particularly as he had already recognized her mustard yellow coat from a distance . . .'

'Tell me!'

'Mademoiselle Alice, from the jewellery department . . . Listen, doctor . . . I don't want to hurt your feelings or disappoint you. But I'm beginning to think that, contrary to what I told you this morning, this is a case for me rather than for you. Since this girl Alice was . . . Do you follow? You'll see that it'll prove to be a policeman turned thief . . . Hello? . . . Haven't you anything to say? Are you annoyed?'

'Me?'

'Say something, for heaven's sake! I'm still in my office. Will you come and have a drink with me before going to bed?'

'No!'

'You're angry?'

'No!'

Now it was Lucas who did not know what to say, and, being a good-natured fellow, was afraid of having mortified the Little Doctor.

'Come on! You'll make up for it another time . . . Would it amuse you to come round tomorrow morning at nine? I've got the girl Alice coming for an interview. I don't know whether we shall have to put pressure on her, but I fancy it may be interesting . . .'

'Goodnight to you . . .'

'You'll come?'

'Maybe . . . Goodnight, I'm sleepy . . .'

And this was true, for, as invariably happened when he first became involved in an investigation, the Little Doctor had drunk rather too much.

III. In Which the Story of Mademoiselle Alice and her Little Brothers Proves so Touching that Superintendent Lucas Pretends to Blow his Nose

Purely by chance, the Little Doctor got into the very métro carriage in which Mademoiselle Alice was already sitting. It was opening time for shops and banks; the carriage was crowded, and the girl did not notice the doctor, who was able to observe her at leisure.

'I'd like to know,' he reflected, 'what a girl like that can be thinking about, after having lied to the police and received a sudden summons to the Quai des Orfèvres . . .'

Nothing very cheerful, at all events! Unlike her lively colleague Gaby, Alice was a melancholy sort of girl, one of those who are not actually plain, indeed quite good-looking if you examine them in detail, but who take life so seriously that they become rather dreary.

That morning her eyes were red. A girl of her nature was quite capable of having wept all night. She had put on her powder patchily, and her hair was badly done.

She lived in a small apartment near the Rue Lamarck. She had probably not bothered to stop in a bar for a hasty cup of coffee and a croissant for breakfast.

'I'm surely not going to begin feeling sorry for her,' growled the Little Doctor, as he left the métro at the Pont-Neuf.

The weather was magnificent; it was the sort of morning you'd have liked to go on for ever, with the sunlight as sparkling as champagne and a slight mist rising from the Seine. Alice walked fast, without turning back. In front of the gloomy portals of Police Headquarters she hesitated for a moment, then went up to the policeman on duty and finally made her way up the dusty staircase.

Dollent saw her again in the glassed-in waiting-room, and he went into Lucas's office, where he was expected.

'Look here, Superintendent, you said something yesterday about putting pressure on her. Don't be too harsh with her, please. She seems so depressed already . . .'

'Send in the young lady who's waiting,' ordered Lucas in his gruffest voice.

He was in a good temper that morning. All the springtime in the world was coming in through his wide open windows and, exceptionally, he was wearing a fancy tie, blue with white polka dots. If he played the bogey man, there was none the less a merry twinkle in his eye.

'Sit down, Mademoiselle Alice. I won't conceal the fact that your case is extremely serious, and that your action may cost you dear . . .'

Already the girl's eyes were brimming with tears, and she dabbed at them with a screwed-up handkerchief.

'Yesterday, when you were questioned, you failed to tell the police the whole truth. Actually, you were guilty of perjury, which is an indictable offence under article . . . some article or other of the Code . . .'

'I . . . I thought . . .'

'What did you think?'

'That our . . . our relations would never be discovered . . . I was so upset by that terrible happening . . .'

'How long had you known Justin Galmet?'

'About three weeks . . .'

'And you'd already become his mistress?'

'Oh no, *monsieur le commissaire*! . . . I swear I hadn't, on the life of my little brothers . . .'

'On *whose* life?'

'My little brothers' . . . I must tell you that I'm an orphan with two little brothers . . . They're both still at school; the youngest is at nursery school . . .'

'I don't see the connection between your little brothers and Justin Galmet.'

'I'll explain . . . If it had only depended on me I'd never have listened to him . . . He was a much older man and he wasn't quite my sort of person . . .'

'Excuse me, let's begin at the beginning. Was it in the shop that you met Galmet?'

'Yes, at our counter . . . He came every day to buy a snap-hook for his watch-chain . . . He was very respectful . . . If he hadn't been so respectful I shouldn't even have listened to him . . . Now I really don't know what to think, but I'm sure he had serious intentions . . .

'On the third or fourth day he asked me straight out, in a timid voice: "Mademoiselle, are you engaged?"

'And I told him that I had my two little brothers, and that on their account I should probably never get married . . .'

The Little Doctor glanced at the Superintendent, who in spite of himself had assumed a kindly expression and found it hard to speak gruffly.

'In short, on the third or fourth day this man whom you didn't know from Adam made advances to you?'

'It's hard to explain. He wasn't like other men. He was very gentle. He confided to me that he was alone in the world, that he'd always been a lonely person . . .'

'While he was trying out snap-hooks?'

'No! He asked me to lunch with him in a little restaurant in the Chaussée d'Antin. And then he told me that his life was about to change because he expected to receive a legacy . . .'

Lucas and Jean Dollent exchanged a swift glance. Decidedly, Justin Galmet had an obsession with legacies! Wasn't that what he had announced formerly, when he left the Police Judiciaire?

'He wanted to settle in the country, on the banks of the Loire if possible. He asked me whether, if I liked the house, I'd be willing to marry him. And he immediately added that my little brothers would live with us, that he'd be happy to have a ready-made family, that he'd undertake to give them a good education . . .'

She was weeping, and you couldn't say whether it was from fear, from grief or from pity.

'That's the sort of man he was! I asked for a day's leave to visit the house at Cléry. On the way there he was as respectful as ever . . . "In a few days' time," he told me, "there'll be nothing to keep me in Paris . . . We'll have the banns published immediately . . ." '

'Tell me something, Mademoiselle Alice. Didn't it seem rather odd to you to see your admirer, or rather your fiancé, change his allegiance to the slipper department and pay his attention to your friend Gaby?'

'The first day it did, because he hadn't warned me . . .'

'And afterwards?'

'He gave me his word that he wasn't interested in Gaby, that he couldn't tell me anything, but that I must trust him. Besides, from where I was I could keep an eye on them . . .'

'So it seemed to you quite natural that . . .'

'He had never spoken to me about his profession, but to tell you the truth I thought that . . . that he was . . .'

'That he was what?'

'Something to do with the police . . . We have a lot of them in the store, because of shop-lifting . . . When I learned that he was dead I

. . . I immediately thought of my little brothers . . . I'd already told them we were going to live in the country . . .'

Was Lucas really obliged to blow his nose at this point? At all events, he did so.

'You're quite sure you've told me the whole truth this time?'

'I think so . . . I can't remember anything else . . .'

'Did your fiancé never say anything that might have thrown light on his personality?'

'He was very respectful, very gentle . . .'

That was her *leitmotiv*.

'In spite of the difference in our ages, I felt I should not be unhappy with him . . .'

And the Little Doctor thought: 'She's going to talk about her little brothers again . . .'

But before she could do so, Lucas interrupted: 'You can go now, Mademoiselle. If I need you again I shall send for you.'

'And I'm not going to be in any trouble?'

She could not believe that it was all over already, that she was free, that she could leave that awe-inspiring house, which she had entered in such fear and trembling!

'Thank you, *monsieur le commissaire* . . . I don't know how to thank you . . . If you only knew how . . . how . . .'

'All right! . . . Goodbye now.'

He ushered her out, and when he turned round again, after shutting the door, his face betrayed rather more emotion than he would have liked.

'I wasn't too fierce, was I?' he asked the Little Doctor, jokingly.

'I was just thinking how the same facts, the same events can assume a different aspect according to which side of the stage they are seen from . . . It's like at the theatre; on one side you have the spectators, who believe in the action taking place before their eyes; on the other, the stage hands, the actors putting on their wigs. Thus, what a lot of things the death of Justin Galmet means to this girl, whereas for you and me it's just an exciting little mystery, a problem to be solved . . . What do you think about the fellow?'

Lucas could only shrug his shoulders. It was all so unexpected! The day before, Justin Galmet had merely been one of those mysterious figures of whom one meets so many specimens in any large city.

And now he had come to evoke compassion, almost sympathy.

Was he really planning to marry this decent girl Alice, and take her to live in the country with her little brothers?

If he was, why had a bullet come to put an end to his plans just as they were about to be realised?

For he had said: '*in a few days' time, there'll be nothing to keep me in Paris any longer . . .*'

A few days . . . Not a few weeks, but a few days, whereas he had been living there for so many years . . .

Nothing to keep him in Paris, the Little Doctor repeated to himself in a low voice, as though trying to discover all the possible meanings of those simple words.

After all, it was quite simple! There were not ten questions to be answered, or three, or even two; there was just one, so ordinary as to be puerile: *What could still be keeping Justin Galmet in Paris for a few days longer?*

Once that was known, everything else would follow!

'Where are you off to?' asked Superintendent Lucas, lighting his pipe and sitting down at his desk.

'For a drink . . . D'you know, Superintendent, why drunkards exist?'

'Why, I don't know . . . I suppose that . . .'

'I'm sure you've got it all wrong. Drunkards exist solely because the only way to cure a hangover is to go on drinking . . . You see the vicious circle!'

It was impossible to say whether he was speaking seriously or joking. He went out, whistling to himself. Walking through the Paris streets, he looked like a man whose only concern is to breathe in life through every pore, and nobody would have guessed that one question was bothering him as relentlessly as a big fly on a thundery day.

'*What could be keeping him in Paris for a few days longer?*'

And suddenly he rushed off to the big store where Gaby and Alice were at their respective posts, one selling slippers and the other jewellery.

'Forgive me for bothering you again, Mademoiselle Alice. I'm a very gentle, respectful man myself, that's why I'm taking the liberty of inviting you to lunch with me in a little restaurant in the Chaussée d'Antin. At what time are you free?'

'At half past twelve . . .'

'All right, I'll wait for you then outside the métro station.'

IV. In Which the Little Doctor, After a Good Lunch, Suddenly Becomes Aware of the Date and Rushes Off to see the Superintendent

'Don't hesitate to choose a dish with extra charge, Mademoiselle. I give you my word that it's at the firm's expense.'

He had selected a small *prix fixe* restaurant, and the people round them were chiefly clerks and shop assistants from the nearby department stores.

Alice was not quite at her ease yet, but her companion's lively good humour, enhanced by the three apéritifs he had drunk while waiting for her, brought an occasional faint smile to her lips.

'Eat just what you fancy . . . What about some scalloped lobster? Don't you care for lobster?'

'It gives me urticaria,' she admitted ingenuously.

On the other hand, what she was obviously longing to order – a neighbour was eating some, and she was savouring the smell of it – was braised tripe *à la mode de Caen.*

'You like tripe? That's good, so do I! Waiter, two tripes . . .'

There are days when the sky seems to have been washed clean for ever, and then the air is light, Paris smiles like a girl, colours are dazzling, everything seems lovely, life is good.

Sitting in a spruce little restaurant, on a day like that, how could one believe that somebody had gone to the toy department of a shop, carrying a pistol which unfortunately was no toy, and had taken aim, pressed the trigger . . . And that a poor man who was trying on slippers . . .

'Listen to me, Mademoiselle Alice. You mustn't get excited, you must think things over calmly, you must remember certain details, even though they may seem to you unimportant . . .

'For instance, the last time Justin Galmet went to your department . . .'

The mention of Galmet's name saddened her, and he was vexed with himself for spoiling her enjoyment of tripe *à la mode de Caen.*

'It was a Saturday,' she murmured reflectively. 'I remember, because Saturday is such a busy day . . .'

'Do you have many more customers on a Saturday than on other days?'

'More than twice as many. By the evening we're done in . . .'

'So you're sure it was a Saturday . . . Was Justin Galmet sitting down?'

'In our department customers don't often sit down. Sometimes a lady who wants to look at a great many articles . . . *He* never sat down.'

'So from where he stood, he could look down . . .'

'He could see the slipper department, the counter with the week's bargains, cash desk no. 89 and the exit. Just what I look down at all day . . .'

'Don't be in a hurry to reply. That Saturday, did he give a start of surprise, as though he had recognized somebody in the crowd?'

She stayed motionless, her eyes wide open.

'I don't know,' she muttered at last. 'But there's one thing. He didn't buy a snap-hook that day.'

'He didn't buy a snap-hook? And you never mentioned it? In other words, he left you in a hurry?'

'Yes . . . He went downstairs . . .'

'Did anything else strike you that day?'

He seemed to be trying to hypnotize her, to force her to remember, and he actually achieved this result.

'I had a lot of customers . . . For at least a quarter of an hour I didn't think about him . . . Then, as I was showing a lady to the cash desk, I glanced down . . . I was surprised to notice that he hadn't left the shop . . .'

'Where was he?'

'Standing up, not far from Gaby . . .'

'Anything else?'

'As I said, I was very busy. Moreover, because of all those thefts in the shop I was keeping a close eye on my department. But I'm almost certain I saw him a second time, long after . . . I wouldn't like you to build on what I'm going to say. Besides, when you see people from up above, close together and elbowing one another, it's difficult to be sure . . . Yet I believe he was talking to a man . . .'

'Could you describe the man?'

'No . . . A man in a grey hat . . . Afterwards I didn't see him again except on the Monday, in Gaby's department . . . Next day at midday he was waiting for me at the exit. I didn't want to speak to him. That was when he asked me not to pay any attention to what he did. He promised to explain it all to me some day . . . Eventually I let myself be persuaded, and we came here for lunch. We sat just there, by the way! On the left of the door . . . Two days later he took me to see the house at Cléry. He was very happy . . . He was in a hurry to get there . . . What's the matter?'

The Little Doctor had grown so grave, with knitted brows and a fixed stare, that she wondered what he had discovered. Suddenly, he demanded:

'What day is it today?'

'Saturday . . .'

He gave a start, and then looked down at the plates as though longing for the meal to be over.

'Would you like dessert?' he asked.

She dared not say yes. He called the waiter.

'My bill, quick as you can!'

He did not trouble to escort his guest back to the door of the shop, but leapt into a taxi.

'Quai des Orfèvres . . . Yes, Police Headquarters . . . Why are you looking at me like that?'

V. In Which the Little Doctor Takes Himself Seriously as a Strategist, Thereby Disquietening Lucas

'You're back already?' was the surprised comment of Superintendent Lucas, who looked the very picture of impassivity beside the tempestuous Little Doctor.

'Back already, yes . . . One question first: can you tell me on what scale the thefts in department stores have been?'

'That's easily done, since these stores keep up-to-date statistics which are both precise and terrifying . . . Be prepared for a shock: a single one of these shops, on the left bank, reckons that on an average a million francs a year are lost through shop-lifting. The rest are more or less in the same situation, which explains why they employ whole armies of shop-walkers.'

'Are all these thefts committed by professionals?'

'Yes and no. There are the small fry, to begin with: women and girls who can't afford the things they want and pinch small articles, particularly lengths of material.

'Then the heavy brigade, so to speak. Women again, since it's easier for them to conceal their booty. They generally have a shopping basket, or some contraption concealed in their dress. One was arrested who pretended to be pregnant and had a sort of kangaroo's pouch under her coat, which she invariably filled . . .

'These thieves work mostly in pairs, so that one can distract the assistant while the other operates . . .

'We know nearly all of them. But they're so clever that it's very hard to catch them in the act. They know our detectives. As soon as they catch sight of them they slip into the crowd like eels and it would hardly be possible to arrest them without causing a sensation.

'And the rule is to avoid a sensation at all costs . . .'

'Isn't there any bigger game?'

Lucas looking embarrassed, admitted:

'Yes, to be sure. Some thefts are too daring and too intelligently planned to have been committed by common or garden shoplifters. Unfortunately we haven't as yet laid hands on those birds . . .'

'Organized gangs?'

'I don't know . . . I'd like to be able to say yes, but I've got no proof.'

'Have there been many thefts of that sort during recent months?'

'The usual number, I suppose; at least if we consider only the big department stores.'

He was playing absent-mindedly with his paper-knife, and the Little Doctor waited quietly. He was rewarded, for Lucas presently remarked with a sigh:

'However, there has been an increase in thefts of another sort, mainly in shops selling luxury goods, particularly jewellers'. A customer suddenly picks up a heap of jewels and rushes outside, where a waiting car takes him off at top speed. You've read about that in the papers. It seems almost impossible and yet it invariably succeeds.

'It's a matter of psychology. The robbers bank on the effect of surprise. The shopkeeper is engaged with other customers, who may even be accomplices, and it takes him a few moments to recover his presence of mind and sound the alarm.

'Outside, the same thing happens. The robbery takes place in a busy street. A car starts up . . . Seconds pass before shouts are heard, and the car's a long way off by then, so that while people are still jostling one another and getting in each other's way the thieves are out of reach . . . Why are you smiling?'

'Me?' asked the Little Doctor innocently. 'Am I smiling?'

'Something seems to be amusing you . . .'

'Why not? . . . By the way, how many men can you let me have tonight? . . . One minute! I don't want any detectives that are too well known. Do you see what I mean? . . . Men who could go through the crowd unnoticed . . .'

'That depends what you want to do . . .'

'Maybe nothing . . . Maybe quite a lot . . . It depends on one thing: does my argument hold together? If it does, if there's no flaw or weakness in it . . .'

'Well?'

'No! I'll tell you all about it afterwards . . . I don't want to make a fool of myself if it doesn't come off . . . Well then? How many men?'

'Would you like six?'

'Not enough . . .'

'What?'

'I'd like at least a dozen . . . And a fast car, without any distinguishing mark . . .'

'D'you know that for an operation on that scale I shall have to consult my superior officers?'

And Jean Dollent, imperturbable, merely muttered:

'Go on then, consult them!'

'It's only six o'clock, Superintendent . . . We've got plenty of time.'

'If something's going to happen, how do you know that . . .'

'If anything happens it will be at half past six precisely . . . Let's have another!'

They were drinking beer by now, sitting at a café terrace just opposite the big department store. In spite of regulations, one of the best cars of the Police Judiciaire had drawn up in front of one of the doors, close to the métro station.

Instructions had been given by the Little Doctor, not on the spot, where he might have been conspicuous, but in Lucas's office, with a sheet of paper which had soon come to look like an ordnance survey map.

Each detective had been allotted a specific role.

'You, the redhead . . . At exactly six-fifteen you must be in the shoe department and you must try on as many slippers as necessary to take you up to six-thirty . . . At six-thirty you must keep your eyes fixed on cash desk no. 89 . . .

'You, sir, yes, you . . . you must take the opportunity to treat yourself to a wallet . . . Don't worry, Lucas, the management will pay . . . You must still be in the leather-goods department when the bell rings. And at that point you must have your eyes fixed on . . .'

Meanwhile he was marking little crosses on the plan of that part of the store.

'Three men beside the door . . . But they must not go near it before half-past six. No point in warning people by creating the impression of a mouse-trap . . . Three others in the métro station . . .'

Although he had already brought off quite a number of successful investigations, this was the Little Doctor's first venture into police strategy, and Lucas was watching him quizzically.

'Will that be all?' he asked with a touch of irony.

'No! I'd like one man to be stationed in the toy department . . . I shouldn't like to suffer the same fate as Justin Galmet . . .'

And now, on the café terrace, watch in hand, the Little Doctor was waiting, provoking the Superintendent with scraps of enigmatic remarks.

'Do you believe that, if Galmet had been a professional shop-lifter, he could have been killed by one or more of his accomplices? Don't answer too quickly . . . Let's suppose that Galmet was a shop-lifter. We have to agree that he was not an important operator, for we know his bank balance.

'Only petty thieves, I imagine, would take such risks for the sake of five hundred francs a month.

'You may say that during the last few months . . . No, Superintendent!'

'But I said nothing!'

'I know what you're thinking . . . Three hundred thousand francs saved after twenty years of repeated thefts doesn't amount to much, and I can't believe that such an insignificant figure could have inspired a crime as intelligent as the one of which he was the victim.

'That's my basis! That's the crucial idea, such as I always look for at the outset. I had made a mistake when I took Galmet for my starting point . . . *I ought to have started with his murderer* . . . And a man capable of conceiving and carrying out that murder from the toy department was a real professional, you'll admit!

'I could swear that Justin Galmet, from the jewellery counter, suddenly caught sight of a man . . . He rushed down . . . Alice isn't sure whether they spoke to one another. If they did so, I'm convinced they could only have exchanged a few words . . . And from then on we find Justin Galmet every evening, at a quarter past six, at his post in the slipper department . . .

'Doesn't that suggest anything to you?'

Lucas merely growled: 'May I remind you that it's a quarter past six now?'

'One more beer and we'll go . . .'

He emptied a last glass, entered the store by another door, went up to the first floor and a few minutes later stood with Lucas at the jewellery counter. Alice, who was serving customers, glanced anxiously at the pair of them, but Dollent made a reassuring gesture.

'We can't count on your redhead to run,' commented the Little Doctor, looking down, 'because he's only got one shoe on . . . Just like Justin Galmet.

'I say, Superintendent . . . If you had to rob a bank clerk or a shop assistant, which day would you choose?'

He had never been quite so tiresome, but that might have been his way of allaying his own impatience.

'Which day? What do you mean?'

'Just what I said! Which day would you choose to rob a bank clerk? Would you do it, for instance, on January 16th?'

'I don't see why . . .'

'That's too bad! On January 16th, Superintendent, you'd find him out of pocket . . . It's the day after quarter day. Before that there was Christmas and the New Year . . . A bank clerk must be robbed on the first of the month – any month – when he's just been paid his salary . . . Don't you notice anything going on round you?'

Lucas was furious, and made no reply. The Little Doctor nevertheless went on soliloquizing:

'There are twice as many people as yesterday. And they're all buying things! And the money's piling in the tills!'

This time the Superintendent pricked up his ears. 'Could it be that . . .'

He did not finish his sentence. The bell was ringing loudly, filling the whole store with its clangour, while the loud speaker blared forth a military march to speed things up.

'You'll see . . . If something happens it'll happen quickly. Don't lean over too far; you'll only attract attention . . .'

He himself knew what to look out for. The cashier of no. 89 was sealing a large yellow envelope and leaving her desk. The crowd flowed by like a stream of lava between the counters. The cashier had to make her way against the stream to reach the lift, and suddenly she uttered a cry, at the precise moment when the Little Doctor caught sight of a light grey hat close beside her.

What took place next . . . who could have described it? The movements of a crowd are chaotic. Nobody knew what was happening. A woman screamed. A small boy had been knocked over and his mother screamed even louder. Some people, possibly remembering the death of Justin Galmet, took to their heels, while the red-headed detective leapt forward, minus his left shoe.

'It's not worth our going down,' declared the Little Doctor with ill-concealed exultation. 'We should be too late in any case. If your men do what's needed . . .'

The grey hat was nowhere to be seen. The crowd was gathering by the doorway and passing through to encounter another crowd out on the pavement.

The man in the grey hat was there in Lucas's office, his clothes somewhat rumpled, his collar torn off, his face scratched. He had been arrested, not without difficulty, as he was jumping into a taxi parked just in front of the police car. But the envelope was not in his possession; and he had not thrown it down at random either. Through how many hands had it passed before vanishing? How many accomplices were involved along the route between the cash desk and the car?

The operation had been skilfully carried out. The man himself, in fact, was unperturbed. He was staring with considerable surprise at the Little Doctor who, in return, examined him with interest.

'Unless I'm greatly mistaken, Superintendent, this is the leader of those daring thieves you were telling me about just now . . .'

'You'll never be able to prove that!' the fellow sneered. 'I defy the cashier to say it was I who took the envelope from her. In such a crowd, anyone could have grabbed it . . .'

That was true. The robbery had been carried out with consummate efficiency.

'Do you know what struck me, Superintendent?' went on the Little Doctor, still scrutinizing the fellow as though he were some rare object. 'It was that the place where Justin Galmet was sitting when he was killed was, so to speak, a strategic position, and that this corner of the store is unique in that, firstly, cash desk no. 89 is the only one standing close to an exit, and secondly, that this is the busiest exit of all, because it is near the métro station.

'Now it was on a Saturday that poor Galmet suddenly came down from the jewellery department . . .

'What had he seen? I'll tell you . . . He had seen this gentleman . . . And he knew that when you meet this gentleman somewhere there's dirty work afoot.'

The Little Doctor was thirsty, but there was nothing to drink. He lit a cigarette, nervously. He was feverishly excited; the tension had been going on too long.

'I bet that when he was in the Police Force, Galmet must have been responsible for watching department stores. In fact, in my opinion that's what must have decided him to resign from the Force.

'He did a little reckoning. He said to himself that if each thief paid him a fee of ten or twenty per cent . . .

'Do you see? He merely had to know the thieves, not so as to arrest them but so as to get something out of them . . .

'Not a very honourable profession, I admit . . . But we must also admit that it was quite ingenious.

'A quiet life, without risk or fatigue. He kept his eye on people. He made little purchases. He'd soon spotted the thief, man or woman, and subsequently knew how to claim his due . . .

'That explains his petty bourgeois way of life, the five hundred francs paid into his bank account each week, the savings typical of the "average Frenchman" . . .

'Until the day when he happened on bigger game . . .'

The man in the grey hat was now looking at the Little Doctor with an admiration that made Lucas feel a little melancholy, and he went so far as to challenge Dollent unceremoniously:

'Say, you! You're not going to tell me you're a dick?'

To which Dollent replied politely: 'Dr Jean Dollent, general practitioner at Marsilly, near La Rochelle, Charente-Maritime . . . As I was saying . . . Yes! By dint of hunting about on every side, our Justin Galmet happened, a few months ago, on this gentleman's gang, which works on a big scale . . . He demanded his quota, which they found it hard to refuse him. Payments into his bank account became substantial, and he contemplated retiring into the country . . .

'Then something else occurs . . . Galmet the confirmed bachelor, who ostensibly flirts with salesgirls because that's almost part of his job, is attracted by Alice's austere charm, her quiet resignation. He considers marrying her. He has been on the track of a thief and, lo and behold, he has found a wife . . .

'Why does he have to catch sight of this gentleman's familiar figure on a lower floor of the shop?

'He immediately suspects that there's a reason for the man's presence. He goes down. He tries to find out what's happening . . .

'For several days running he takes up his position in the same spot so as to witness the robbery and get his share.

'He guesses that the cashier will be involved . . . What is there likely to be in a till like that on a Saturday night? I made inquiries . . . Three or four hundred thousand francs in cash . . .

'The levy he'll get from the thieves will go a good way towards paying for his house and will save him from making too big a hole in his capital . . .

'That was why *he had to wait a few days longer in Paris* . . . Until this gentleman had made up his mind to do the job . . .

'After that there would be wedding bells, Alice's little brothers, the whole works . . Kitchen garden and flower garden . . . A nice quiet life . . .

'He had failed to anticipate one possibility: that our prisoner might get sick of being milked. Justin Galmet knew too much and had become too expensive; he must be got rid of.

'The set-up was in the murderer's favour; he fired his pistol and . . .'

The man in the grey hat was showing signs of agitation. But at that moment the door opened, on a signal from Lucas, and in came the salesman from the toy department.

'Yes, that's him,' he declared promptly. 'I didn't see him fire, but that day he was playing about with toy weapons and I'm convinced that . . .'

'Poor fellow!' sighed the Little Doctor, who was now at his fourth or fifth glass.

Lucas and he were at the station buffet; Dollent was catching the night train back to Marsilly.

'It was damned ingenious . . . He'd taken to robbing robbers! A respectable bourgeois robber who did his own housework . . . Do you know, Lucas, what I find most touching about him, and what makes me want to lay a wreath on his grave? It's Alice and her little brothers . . . I'm convinced that he'd have brought up the little boys and that they'd have lived as happy as kings in their little house on the banks of the Loire . . . It's a real disaster for Alice . . .'

'Why?'

'Because she's likely to remain an old maid, of course!'

And, turning to the waiter: 'Bill, please . . .'